PYRAMIDS

A Discworld Novel

PYRAMIDS

(THE BOOK OF GOING FORTH)

by

TERRY PRATCHETT

GUILD PUBLISHING LONDON

This edition published 1989 by
Guild Publishing
by arrangement with Victor Gollancz Ltd.

CN 6682

Typeset by Action Typesetting Ltd, Gloucester
Printed in Great Britain by
St Edmundsbury Press Ltd, Bury St Edmunds, Suffolk

BOOK I

The Book of Going Forth

Nothing but stars, scattered across the blackness as though the Creator had smashed the windscreen of his car and hadn't bothered to stop to sweep up the pieces.

This is the gulf between universes, the chill deeps of space that contain nothing but the occasional random molecule, a few lost comets and...

...but a circle of blackness shifts slightly, the eye reconsiders perspective, and what was apparently the awesome distance of interstellar wossname becomes a world under darkness, its stars the lights of what will charitably be called civilisation.

For, as the world tumbles lazily, it is revealed as the Discworld — flat, circular, and carried through space on the back of four elephants who stand on the back of Great A'tuin, the only turtle ever to feature on the Hertzsprung-Russell Diagram, a turtle ten thousand miles long, dusted with the frost of dead comets, meteor-pocked, albedo-eyed. No-one knows the reason for all this, but it is probably quantum.

Much that is weird could happen on a world on the back of a turtle like that.

It's happening already.

The stars below are campfires, out in the desert, and the lights of remote villages high in the forested mountains. Towns are smeared nebulae, cities are vast constellations; the great sprawling city of Ankh-Morpork, for example, glows like a couple of colliding galaxies.

But here, away from the great centres of population, where the Circle Sea meets the desert, there is a line of cold blue fire. Flames as chilly as the slopes of Hell roar towards the sky. Ghostly light flickers across the desert.

The pyramids in the ancient valley of the Djel are flaring their power into the night.

The energy streaming up from their paracosmic peaks may, in chapters to come, illuminate many mysteries: why tortoises hate philosophy, why too much religion is bad for goats, and what it is that handmaidens actually *do*.

It will certainly show what our ancestors would be thinking if they were alive today. People have often speculated about this. Would they approve of modern society, they ask, would they marvel at present-day achievements? And of course this misses a fundamental point. What our ancestors would really be thinking, if they were alive today, is: "Why is it so dark in here?"

In the cool of the river valley dawn the high priest Dios opened his eyes. He didn't sleep these days. He couldn't remember when he last slept. Sleep was too close to the other thing and, anyway, he didn't seem to need it. Just lying down was enough — at least, just lying down *here*. The fatigue poisons dwindled away, like everything else. For a while.

Long enough, anyway.

He swung his legs off the slab in the little chamber. With barely a conscious prompting from his brain his right hand grasped the snake-entwined staff of office. He paused to make another mark on the wall, pulled his robe around him and stepped smartly down the sloping passage and out into the sunlight, the words of the Invocation of the New Sun already lining up in his mind. The night was forgotten, the day was ahead. There was much careful advice and guidance to be given, and Dios existed only to serve.

Dios didn't have the oddest bedroom in the world. It was just the oddest bedroom anyone has ever walked out of.

And the sun toiled across the sky.

Many people have wondered why. Some people think a giant

dung beetle pushes it. As explanations go it lacks a certain technical edge, and has the added drawback that, as certain circumstances may reveal, it is possibly correct.

It reached sundown without anything particularly unpleasant happening to it*, and its dying rays chanced to shine in through a window in the city of Ankh-Morpork and gleam off a mirror.

It was a full-length mirror. All assassins had a full-length mirror in their rooms, because it would be a terrible insult to anyone to kill them when you were badly dressed.

Teppic examined himself critically. The outfit had cost him his last penny, and was heavy on the black silk. It whispered as he moved. It was pretty good.

At least the headache was going. It had nearly crippled him all day; he'd been in dread of having to start the run with purple spots in front of his eyes.

He sighed and opened the black box and took out his rings and slipped them on. Another box held a set of knives of Klatchian steel, their blades darkened with lamp black. Various cunning and intricate devices were taken from velvet bags and dropped into pockets. A couple of long-bladed throwing *tlingas* were slipped into their sheaths inside his boots. A thin silk line and folding grapnel were wound around his waist, over the chain-mail shirt. A blowpipe was attached to its leather thong and dropped down his back under his cloak; Teppic pocketed a slim tin container with an assortment of darts, their tips corked and their stems braille-coded for ease of selection in the dark.

He winced, checked the blade of his rapier and slung the baldric over his right shoulder, to balance the bag of lead slingshot ammunition. As an afterthought he opened his sock drawer and took a pistol crossbow, a flask of oil, a roll of lockpicks and, after some consideration, a punch dagger, a bag of assorted caltraps and a set of brass knuckles.

Teppic picked up his hat and checked its lining for the coil of cheesewire. He placed it on his head at a jaunty angle, took a last satisfied look at himself in the mirror, turned on his heel and, very slowly, fell over.

*

*Such as being buried in the sand and having eggs laid in it.

It was high summer in Ankh-Morpork. In fact it was more than high. It was stinking.

The great river was reduced to a lava-like ooze between Ankh, the city with the better address, and Morpork on the opposite bank. Morpork was not a good address. Morpork was twinned with a tar pit. There was not a lot that could be done to make Morpork a worse place. A direct hit by a meteorite, for example, would count as gentrification.

Most of the river bed was a honeycomb crust of cracked mud. Currently the sun appeared to be a big copper gong nailed to the sky. The heat that had dried up the river fried the city by day and baked it by night, curling ancient timbers, turning the traditional slurry of the streets into a drifting, choking ochre dust.

It wasn't Ankh-Morpork's proper weather. It was by inclination a city of mists and drips, of slithers and chills. It sat panting on the crisping plains like a toad on a firebrick. And even now, around midnight, the heat was stifling, wrapping the streets like scorched velvet, searing the air and squeezing all the breath out of it.

High in the north face of the Assassins' Guildhouse there was a click as a window was pushed open.

Teppic, who had with considerable reluctance divested himself of some of the heavier of his weapons, took a deep draught of the hot, dead air.

This was *it.*

This was the *night.*

They said you had one chance in two unless you drew old Mericet as examiner, in which case you might as well cut your throat right at the start.

Teppic had Mericet for Strategy and Poison Theory every Thursday afternoon, and didn't get along with him. The dormitories buzzed with rumours about Mericet, the number of kills, the astonishing technique. . . He'd broken all the records in his time. They said he'd even killed the Patrician of Ankh-Morpork. Not the present one, that is. One of the dead ones.

Maybe it would be Nivor, who was fat and jolly and liked his food and did Traps and Deadfalls on Tuesdays. Teppic was good at traps, and got on well with the master. Or it could be the

Kompt de Yoyo, who did Modern Languages and Music. Teppic was gifted at neither, but the Kompt was a keen edificeer and liked boys who shared his love of dangling by one hand high above the city streets.

He stuck one leg over the sill and unhitched his line and grapnel. He hooked the gutter two floors up and slipped out of the window.

No assassin ever used the stairs.

In order to establish continuity with later events, this may be the time to point out that the greatest mathematician in the history of the Discworld was lying down and peacefully eating his supper.

It is interesting to note that, owing to this mathematician's particular species, what he was eating for his supper was his lunch.

Gongs around the Ankh-Morpork sprawl were announcing midnight when Teppic crept along the ornate parapet four storeys above Filigree Street, his heart pounding.

There was a figure outlined against the afterglow of the sunset. Teppic paused alongside a particularly repulsive gargoyle to consider his options.

Fairly solid classroom rumour said that if he inhumed his examiner before the test, that was an automatic pass. He slipped a Number Three throwing knife from its thigh sheath and hefted it thoughtfully. Of course, any attempt, any overt move which missed would attract immediate failure and loss of privileges*.

The silhouette was absolutely still. Teppic's eyes swivelled to the maze of chimneys, gargoyles, ventilator shafts, bridges

*Breathing, for a start.

and ladders that made up the rooftop scenery of the city.

Right, he thought. That's some sort of dummy. I'm supposed to attack it and that means he's watching me from somewhere else.

Will I be able to spot him? No.

On the other hand, maybe I'm *meant* to think it's a dummy. Unless he's thought of that as well. . .

He found himself drumming his fingers on the gargoyle, and hastily pulled himself together. What is the sensible course of action at this point?

A party of revellers staggered through a pool of light in the street far below.

Teppic sheathed the knife and stood up.

"Sir," he said, "I am here."

A dry voice by his ear said, rather indistinctly, "Very well."

Teppic stared straight ahead. Mericet appeared in front of him, wiping grey dust off his bony face. He took a length of pipe out of his mouth and tossed it aside, then pulled a clipboard out of his coat. He was bundled up even in this heat. Mericet was the kind of person who could freeze in a volcano.

"Ah," he said, his voice broadcasting disapproval, "Mr Teppic. Well, well."

"A fine night, sir," said Teppic. The examiner gave him a chilly look, suggesting that observations about the weather acquired an automatic black mark, and made a note on his clipboard.

"We'll take a few questions first," he said.

"As you wish, sir."

"What is the maximum permitted length of a throwing knife?" snapped Mericet.

Teppic closed his eyes. He'd spent the last week reading nothing but *The Cordat*; he could see the page now, floating tantalisingly just inside his eyelids — they never ask you lengths and weights, students had said knowingly, they expect you to bone up on the weights and lengths and throwing distances but they never —

Naked terror hotwired his brain and kicked his memory into gear. The page sprang into focus.

"'Maximum length of a throwing knife may be ten finger

widths, or twelve in wet weather',", he recited. "'Throwing distance is — '"

"Name three poisons acknowledged for administration by ear."

A breeze sprang up, but it did nothing to cool the air; it just shifted the heat about.

"Sir, wasp agaric, Achorion purple and Mustick, sir," said Teppic promptly.

"Why not spime?" snapped Mericet, fast as a snake.

Teppic's jaw dropped open. He floundered for a while, trying to avoid the gimlet gaze a few feet away from him.

"S-sir, spime isn't a poison, sir," he managed. "It is an extremely rare antidote to certain snake venoms, and is obtained — " He settled down a bit, more certain of himself: all those hours idly looking through the old dictionaries had paid off — "is obtained from the liver of the inflatable mongoose, which — "

"What is the meaning of this sign?" said Mericet.

" — is found only in the . . ." Teppic's voice trailed off. He squinted down at the complex rune on the card in Mericet's hand, and then stared straight past the examiner's ear again.

"I haven't the faintest idea, sir," he said. Out of the corner of his ear he thought he heard the faintest intake of breath, the tiniest seed of a satisfied grunt.

"But if it were the other way up, sir," he went on, "it would be thiefsign for 'Noisy dogs in this house'."

There was absolute silence for a moment. Then, right by his shoulder, the old assassin's voice said, "Is the killing rope permitted to all categories?"

"Sir, the rules call for three questions, sir," Teppic protested.

"Ah. And that is your answer, is it?"

"Sir, no, sir. It was an observation, sir. Sir, the answer you are looking for is that all categories may bear the killing rope, but only assassins of the third grade may use it as one of the three options, sir."

"You are sure of that, are you?"

"Sir."

"You wouldn't like to reconsider?" You could have used the examiner's voice to grease a wagon.

"Sir, no, sir."

"Very well." Teppic relaxed. The back of his tunic was sticking to him, chilly with sweat.

"Now, I want you to proceed at your own pace towards the Street of Book-keepers," said Mericet evenly, "obeying all signs and so forth. I will meet you in the room under the gong tower at the junction with Audit Alley. And — take this, if you please."

He handed Teppic a small envelope.

Teppic handed over a receipt. Then Mericet stepped into the pool of shade beside a chimney pot, and disappeared.

So much for the ceremony.

Teppic took a few deep breaths and tipped the envelope's contents into his hand. It was a Guild bond for ten thousand Ankh-Morpork dollars, made out to 'Bearer'. It was an impressive document, surmounted with the Guild seal of the double-cross and the cloaked dagger.

Well, no going back now. He'd taken the money. Either he'd survive, in which case of course he'd traditionally donate the money to the Guild's widows and orphans fund, or it would be retrieved from his dead body. The bond looked a bit dog-eared, but he couldn't see any bloodstains on it.

He checked his knives, adjusted his swordbelt, glanced behind him, and set off at a gentle trot.

At least this was a bit of luck. The student lore said there were only half a dozen routes used during the test, and on summer nights they were alive with students tackling the roofs, towers, eaves and colls of the city. Edificing was a keen inter-house sport in its own right; it was one of the few things Teppic was sure he was good at — he'd been captain of the team that beat Scorpion House in the Wallgame finals. And this was one of the easiest courses.

He dropped lightly over the edge of the roof, landed on a ridge, ran easily across the sleeping building, jumped a narrow gap on to the tiled roof of the Young Men's Reformed-Cultists-of-the-Ichor-God-Bel-Shamharoth Association gym, jogged gently over the grey slope, swarmed up a twelve foot wall without slowing down, and vaulted on to the wide flat roof of the Temple of Blind Io.

A full, orange moon hung on the horizon. There was a real breeze up here, not much, but as refreshing as a cold shower after the stifling heat of the streets. He speeded up, enjoying the coolness on his face, and leapt accurately off the end of the roof on to the narrow plank bridge that led across Tinlid Alley.

And which someone, in defiance of all probability, had removed.

At times like this one's past life flashes before one's eyes...

His aunt had wept, rather theatrically, Teppic had thought, since the old lady was as tough as a hippo's instep. His father had looked stern and dignified, whenever he could remember to, and tried to keep his mind free of beguiling images of cliffs and fish. The servants had been lined up along the hall from the foot of the main stairway, handmaidens on one side, eunuchs and butlers on the other. The women bobbed a curtsey as he walked by, creating a rather nice sine wave effect which the greatest mathematician on the Disc, had he not at this moment been occupied by being hit with a stick and shouted at by a small man wearing what appeared to be a nightshirt, might well have appreciated.

"But," Teppic's aunt blew her nose, "it's *trade*, after all."

His father patted her hand. "Nonsense, flower of the desert," he said, "it is a profession, at the very least."

"What is the difference?" she sobbed.

The old man sighed. "The money, I understand. It will do him good to go out into the world and make friends and have a few corners knocked off, and it will keep him occupied and prevent him from getting into mischief."

"But... *assassination*... he's so young, and he's never shown the *least* inclination..." She dabbed at her eyes. "It's not from our side of the family," she added accusingly. "That brother-in-law of yours — "

"Uncle Vyrt," said his father.

"Going all over the world killing people!"

"I don't believe they use that word," said his father. "I think they prefer words like conclude, or annul. Or inhume, I understand."

"Inhume?"

"I think it's like exhume, O flooding of the waters, only it's *before* they bury you."

"I think it's terrible." She sniffed. "But I heard from Lady Nooni that only one boy in fifteen actually passes the final exam. Perhaps we'd just better let him get it out of his system."

King Teppicymon XXVII nodded gloomily, and went by himself to wave goodbye to his son. He was less certain than his sister about the unpleasantness of assassination; he'd been reluctantly in politics for a long time, and felt that while assassination was probably worse than debate it was certainly better than war, which some people tended to think of as the same thing only louder. And there was no doubt that young Vyrt always had plenty of money, and used to turn up at the palace with expensive gifts, exotic suntans and thrilling tales of the interesting people he'd met in foreign parts, in most cases quite briefly.

He wished Vyrt was around to advise. His majesty had also heard that only one student in fifteen actually became an assassin. He wasn't entirely certain what happened to the other fourteen, but he was pretty sure that if you were a poor student in a school for assassins they did a bit more than throw the chalk at you, and that the school dinners had an extra dimension of uncertainty.

But everyone agreed that the assassins' school offered the best all-round education in the world. A qualified assassin should be at home in any company, and able to play at least one musical instrument. Anyone inhumed by an alumnus of the Guild school could go to his rest satisfied that he had been annulled by someone of taste and discretion.

And, after all, what was there for him at home? A kingdom two miles wide and one hundred and fifty miles long, which was almost entirely underwater during the flood season, and threatened on either side by stronger neighbours who tolerated its existence only because they'd be constantly at war if it wasn't there.

Oh, Djelibeybi* had been great once, when upstarts like Tsort and Ephebe were just a bunch of nomads with their towels on their heads. All that remained of those great days was the ruinously-expensive palace, a few dusty ruins in the desert and — the pharaoh sighed — the pyramids. Always the pyramids.

His ancestors had been keen on pyramids. The pharaoh wasn't. Pyramids had bankrupted the country, drained it drier than ever the river did. The only curse they could afford to put on a tomb these days was 'Bugger Off'.

The only pyramids he felt comfortable about were the very small ones at the bottom of the garden, built every time one of the cats died.

He'd promised the boy's mother.

He missed Artela. There'd been a terrible row about taking a wife from outside the Kingdom, and some of her foreign ways had puzzled and fascinated even him. Maybe it was from her he'd got the strange dislike of pyramids; in Djelibeybi that was like disliking breathing. But he'd promised that Pteppic could go to school outside the kingdom. She'd been insistent about that. "People never learn anything in this place," she'd said. "They only remember things."

If only she'd remembered about not swimming in the river . . .

He watched two of the servants load Teppic's trunk on to the back of the coach, and for the first time either of them could remember laid a paternal hand on his son's shoulder.

In fact he was at a loss for something to say. We've never really had time to get to know one another, he thought. There's so much I could have given him. A few bloody good hidings wouldn't have come amiss.

"Um," he said. "Well, my boy."

"Yes, father?"

"This is, er, the first time you've been away from home by yourself — "

"No, father. I spent last summer with Lord Fhem-pta-hem, you remember."

"Oh, did you?" The pharaoh recalled the palace had seemed

*Lit. 'Child of the Djel'.

quieter at the time. He'd put it down to the new tapestries.

"Anyway," he said, "you're a young man, nearly thirteen — "

Twelve, father," said Teppic patiently.

"Are you sure?"

"It was my birthday last month, father. You bought me a warming pan."

"Did I? How singular. Did I say why?"

"No, father." Teppic looked up at his father's mild, puzzled features. "It was a very *good* warming pan," he added reassuringly. "I like it a lot."

"Oh. Good. Er." His majesty patted his son's shoulder again, in a vague way, like a man drumming his fingers on his desk while trying to think. An idea appeared to occur to him.

The servants had finished strapping the trunk on to the roof of the coach and the driver was patiently holding open the door.

"When a young man sets out in the world," said his majesty uncertainly, "there are, well, it's very important that he remembers...The point is, that it is a very big world after all, with all sorts...And of course, especially so in the city, where there are many additional...." He paused, waving one hand vaguely in the air.

Teppic took it gently.

"It's quite all right, father," he said. "Dios the high priest explained to me about taking regular baths, and not going blind."

His father blinked at him.

"You're not going blind?" he said.

"Apparently not, father."

"Oh. Well. Jolly good," said the king. "Jolly, jolly good. That *is* good news."

"I think I had better be going, father. Otherwise I shall miss the tide."

His majesty nodded, and patted his pockets.

"There was something..." he muttered, and then tracked it down, and slipped a small leather bag into Teppic's pocket. He tried the shoulder routine again.

"A little something," he murmured. "Don't tell your aunt. Oh, you can't, anyway. She's gone for a lie-down. It's all been rather too much for her."

All that remained then was for Teppic to go and sacrifice a chicken at the statue of Khuft, the founder of Djelibeybi, so that his ancestor's guiding hand would steer his footsteps in the world. It was only a small chicken, though, and when Khuft had finished with it the king had it for lunch.

Djelibeybi really was a small, self-centred kingdom. Even its plagues were half-hearted. All self-respecting river kingdoms have vast supernatural plagues, but the best the Old Kingdom had been able to achieve in the last hundred years was the Plague of Frog*.

That evening, when they were well outside the delta of the Djel and heading across the Circle Sea to Ankh-Morpork, Teppic remembered the bag and examined its contents. With love, but also with his normal approach to things, his father had presented him with a cork, half a tin of saddlesoap, a small bronze coin of uncertain denomination, and an extremely elderly sardine.

It is a well-known fact that when one is about to die the senses immediately become excruciatingly sharp, and it has always been believed that this is to enable their owner to detect any possible exit from his predicament other than the obvious one.

This is not true. The phenomenon is a classical example of displacement activity. The senses are desperately concentrating on anything apart from the immediate problem — which in Teppic's case consisted of a broad expanse of cobblestones some eighty feet away and closing — in the hope that it will go away.

The trouble is that it soon will.

Whatever the reason, Teppic was suddenly acutely aware of things around him. The way the moonlight glowed on the

---

*It was quite a big frog, however, and got into the air ducts and kept everyone awake for weeks.

rooftops. The smell of fresh bread wafting from a nearby bakery. The whirring of a cockchafer as it barrelled past his ear, upwards. The sound of a baby crying, in the distance, and the bark of a dog. The gentle rush of the air, with particular reference to its thinness and lack of handholds...

There had been more than seventy of them enrolling that year. The Assassins didn't have a very strenuous entrance examination; the school was easy to get into, easy to get out of (the trick was to get out *upright*). The courtyard in the centre of the Guild buildings was thronged with boys who all had two things in common — overlarge trunks, which they were sitting on, and clothes that had been selected for them to grow into, and which they were more or less sitting *in*. Some optimists had brought weapons with them, which were confiscated and sent home over the next few weeks.

Teppic watched them carefully. There were distinct advantages to being the only child of parents too preoccupied with their own affairs to worry much about him, or indeed register his existence for days at a time.

His mother, as far as he could remember, had been a pleasant woman and as self-centred as a gyroscope. She'd liked cats. She didn't just venerate them — everyone in the kingdom did *that* — but she actually liked them, too. Teppic knew that it was traditional in river kingdoms to approve of cats, but he suspected that usually the animals in question were graceful, stately creatures; his mother's cats were small, spitting, flat-headed, yellow-eyed maniacs.

His father spent a lot of time worrying about the kingdom and occasionally declaring that he was a seagull, although this was probably from general forgetfulness. Teppic had occasionally speculated about his own conception, since his parents were rarely in the same frame of reference, let alone the same state of mind.

But it had apparently happened and he was left to bring himself up on a trial and error basis, mildly hindered and occasionally enlivened by a succession of tutors. The ones hired by his father were best, especially on those days when he was flying as high as he could, and for one glorious winter Teppic had as his tutor an elderly ibis poacher who had in fact wandered into the royal gardens in search of a stray arrow.

That had been a time of wild chases with soldiers, moonlight rambles in the dead streets of the necropolis and, best of all, the introduction to the puntbow, a fearsomely complicated invention which at considerable risk to its operators could turn a slough full of innocent waterfowl into so much floating pâté.

He'd also had the run of the library, including the locked shelves — the poacher had several other skills to ensure gainful employment in inclement weather — which had given him many hours of quiet study; he was particularly attached to *The Shuttered Palace*, Translated from the Khalian by A Gentleman, with Hand-Coloured Plates for the Connoisseur in A Strictly Limited Edition. It was confusing but instructive and, when a rather fey young tutor engaged by the priests tried to introduce him to certain athletic techniques favoured by the classical Pseudopolitans, Teppic considered the suggestion for some time and then floored the youth with a hatstand.

Teppic hadn't been educated. Education had just settled on him, like dandruff.

It started to rain, in the world outside his head. Another new experience. He'd heard about it, of course, how water came down out of the sky in small bits. He just hadn't expected there to be so much of it. It never rained in Djelibeybi.

Masters moved among the boys like damp and slightly scruffy blackbirds, but he was eyeing a group of older students lolling near the pillared entrance to the school. They also wore black — different colours of black.

That was his first introduction to the tertiary colours, the colours on the far side of blackness, the colours that you get if you split blackness with an eight-sided prism. They are also almost impossible to describe in a non-magical environment, but if someone were to try they'd probably start by telling you to smoke something illegal and take a good look at a starling's wing.

The seniors were critically inspecting the new arrivals.

Teppic stared at them. Apart from the colours, their clothes were cut off the edge of the latest fashion, which was currently inclining towards wide hats, padded shoulders, narrow waists and pointed shoes and gave its followers the appearance of being very well-dressed nails.

I'm going to be like them, he told himself.

Although probably better dressed, he added.

He recalled Uncle Vyrt, sitting out on the steps overlooking the Djel on one of his brief, mysterious visits. "Satin and leather are no good. Or jewelry of any kind. You can't have anything that will shine or squeak or clink. Stick to rough silk or velvet. The important thing is not how many people you inhume, it's how many fail to inhume *you*."

He'd been moving at an unwise pace, which might assist now. As he arced over the emptiness of the alley he twisted in the air, thrust out his arms desperately, and felt his fingertips brush a ledge on the building opposite. It was enough to pivot him; he swung around, hit the crumbling brickwork with sufficient force to knock what remained of his breath out of him, and slid down the sheer wall . . .

"Boy!"

Teppic looked up. There was a senior assassin standing beside him, with a purple teaching sash over his robes. It was the first assassin he'd seen, apart from Vyrt. The man was pleasant enough. You could imagine him making sausages.

"Are you talking to me?" he said.

"You will stand up when you address a master," said the rosy face.

"I will?" Teppic was fascinated. He wondered how this could be achieved. Discipline had not hitherto been a major feature in his life. Most of his tutors had been sufficiently unnerved by the sight of the king occasionally perched on top of a door that they raced through such lessons as they had and then locked themselves in their rooms.

"I will *sir*," said the teacher. He consulted the list in his hand. "What is your name, boy?" he continued.

"Prince Pteppic of the Old Kingdom, the Kingdom of the Sun," said Teppic easily. "I appreciate you are ignorant of the etiquette, but you should not call me sir, and you should touch the ground with your forehead when you address me."

"Pateppic, is it?" said the master.

"No. *Pt*eppic."

"Ah. Teppic," said the master, and ticked off a name on his list. He gave Teppic a generous smile.

"Well, now, your majesty," he said, "I am Grunworth Nivor, your housemaster. You are in Viper House. To my certain knowledge there are at least eleven Kingdoms of the Sun on the Disc and, before the end of the week, you will present me with a short essay detailing their geographical location, political complexion, capital city or principal seat of government, and a suggested route into the bedchamber of the head of state of your choice. However, in all the world there is only one Viper House. Good morning to you, boy."

He turned away and homed in on another cowering pupil.

"He's not a bad sort," said a voice behind Teppic. "Anyway, all the stuff's in the library. I'll show you if you like. I'm Chidder."

Teppic turned. He was being addressed by a boy of about his own age and height, whose black suit — plain black, for First Years — looked as though it had been nailed on to him in bits. The youth was holding out a hand. Teppic gave it a polite glance.

"Yes?" he said.

"What's your name, kiddo?"

Teppic drew himself up. He was getting fed up with this treatment. "Kiddo? I'll have you know the blood of pharaohs runs in my veins!"

The other boy looked at him unabashed, with his head on one side and a faint smile on his face.

"Would you like it to stay there?" he said.

The bakery was just along the alley, and a handful of the staff had stepped out into the comparative cool of the pre-dawn air for a quick smoke and a break from the desert heat of the ovens. Their chattering spiralled up to Teppic, high in the shadows, gripping a fortuitous window sill while his feet scrabbled for a purchase among the bricks.

It's not that bad, he told himself. You've tackled worse. The hubward face of the Patrician's palace last winter, for example, when all the gutters had overflowed and the walls were solid ice. This isn't much more than a 3, maybe a 3.2. You and old Chiddy used to go up walls like this rather than stroll down the street, it's just a matter of perspective.

Perspective. He glanced down, at seventy feet of infinity. Splat City, man, get a grip on yourself. On the *wall*. His right foot found a worn section of mortar, into which his toes planted themselves with barely a conscious instruction from a brain now feeling too fragile to take more than a distant interest in the proceedings.

He took a breath, tensed, and then dropped one hand to his belt, seized a dagger, and thrust it between the bricks beside him before gravity worked out what was happening. He paused, panting, waiting for gravity to lose interest in him again, and then swung his body sideways and tried the same thing a second time.

Down below one of the bakers told a suggestive joke, and brushed a speck of mortar from his ear. As his colleagues laughed Teppic stood up in the moonlight, balancing on two slivers of Klatchian steel, and gently walked his palms up the wall to the window whose sill had been his brief salvation.

It was wedged shut. A good blow would surely open it, but only at about the same moment as it sent him reeling back into empty air. Teppic sighed and, moving with the delicacy of a watchmaker, drew his diamond compasses from their pouch and dragged a slow, gentle circle on the dusty glass...

"You carry it yourself," said Chidder. "That's the rule around here."

Teppic looked at the trunk. It was an intriguing notion.

"At home we've people who do that," he said. "Eunuchs and so on."

"You should of brought one with you."

"They don't travel well," said Teppic. In fact he'd adamantly refused all suggestions that a small retinue should accompany him, and Dios had sulked for days. That was not how a member of the royal blood should go forth into the world, he said. Teppic had remained firm. He was pretty certain that assassins weren't expected to go about their business accompanied by handmaidens and buglers. Now, however, the idea seemed to have some merit. He gave the trunk an experimental heave, and managed to get it across his shoulders.

"Your people are pretty rich, then?" said Chidder, ambling along beside him.

Teppic thought about this. "No, not really," he said. "They mainly grow melons and garlic and that kind of thing. And stand in the streets and shout 'hurrah'."

"This is your parents you're talking about?" said Chidder, puzzled.

"Oh, them? No, my father's a pharaoh. My mother was a concubine, I think."

"I thought that was some sort of vegetable."

"I don't think so. We've never really discussed it. Anyway, she died when I was young."

"How dreadful," said Chidder cheerfully.

"She went for a moonlight swim in what turned out to be a crocodile." Teppic tried politely not to be hurt at the boy's reaction.

"My father's in commerce," said Chidder, as they passed through the archway.

"That's fascinating," said Teppic dutifully. He felt quite broken by all these new experiences, and added, "I've never been to Commerce, but I understand they're very fine people."

Over the next hour or two Chidder, who ambled gently through life as though he'd already worked it all out, introduced Teppic to the various mysteries of the dormitories, the classrooms and the plumbing. He left the plumbing until last, for all sorts of reasons.

"Not *any*?" he said.

"There's buckets and things," said Teppic vaguely, "and lots of servants."

"Bit old fashioned, this kingdom of yours?"

Teppic nodded. "It's the pyramids," he said. "They take all the money."

"Expensive things, I should imagine."

"Not particularly. They're just made of stone." Teppic sighed. "We've got lots of stone," he said, "and sand. Stone and sand. We're really big on them. If you ever need any stone and sand, we're the people for you. It's fitting out the insides that is really expensive. We're still avoiding paying for grandfather's, and that wasn't very big. Just three chambers." Teppic turned and looked out of the window; they were back in the dormitory at this point.

"The whole kingdom's in debt," he said, quietly. "I mean even our *debts* are in debt. That's why I'm here, really. Someone in our house needs to earn some money. A royal prince can't hang around looking ornamental any more. He's got to get out and do something useful in the community."

Chidder leaned on the window sill.

"Couldn't you take some of the stuff out of the pyramids, then?" he said.

"Don't be silly."

"Sorry."

Teppic gloomily watched the figures below.

"There's a lot of people here," he said, to change the subject. "I didn't realise it would be so big." He shivered. "Or so cold," he added.

"People drop out all the time," said Chidder. "Can't stand the course. The important thing is to know what's what and who's who. See that fellow over there?"

Teppic followed his pointing finger to a group of older students, who were lounging against the pillars by the entrance.

"The big one? Face like the end of your boot?"

"That's Fliemoe. Watch out for him. If he invites you for toast in his study, *don't go.*"

"And who's the little kid with the curls?" said Teppic. He pointed to a small lad receiving the attentions of a washed-out looking lady. She was licking her handkerchief and dabbing apparent smudges off his face. When she stopped that, she straightened his tie.

Chidder craned to see. "Oh, just some new kid," he said. "Arthur someone. Still hanging on to his mummy, I see. He won't last long."

"Oh, I don't know," said Teppic. "We do, too, and we've lasted for thousands of years."

A disc of glass dropped into the silent building and tinkled on the floor. There was no other sound for several minutes. Then there was the faint clonk-clonk of an oil can. A shadow that had been lying naturally on the window sill, a morgue for blue-bottles, turned out to be an arm which was moving with vegetable slowness towards the window's catch.

There was a scrape of metal, and then the whole window swung out in tribological silence.

Teppic dropped over the sill and vanished into the shadow below it.

For a minute or two the dusty space was filled with the intense absence of noise caused by someone moving with extreme care. Once again there was the squirting of oil, and then a metallic whisper as the bolt of a trapdoor leading on to the roof moved gently aside.

Teppic waited for his breath to catch up with him, and in that moment heard the sound. It was down among the white noise at the edge of hearing, but there was no doubt about it. Someone was waiting just above the trapdoor, and they'd just put their hand on a piece of paper to stop it rattling in the breeze.

His own hand dropped from the bolt. He eased his way with exquisite care back across the greasy floor and felt his way along a rough wooden wall until he came to a door. This time he took no chances, but uncorked his oil can and let a silent drop fall on to the hinges.

A moment later he was through. A rat, idly patrolling the drafty passage beyond, had to stop itself from swallowing its own tongue as he floated past.

There was another doorway at the end, and a maze of musty storerooms until he found a stairway. He judged himself to be about thirty yards from the trapdoor. There hadn't been any flues that he could see. There ought to be a clear shot across the roof.

He hunkered down and pulled out his knife roll, its velvet blackness making a darker oblong in the shadows. He selected a Number Five, not everyone's throwing knife, but worthwhile if you had the trick of it.

Shortly afterwards his head rose very carefully over the edge of the roof, one arm bent behind it but ready to uncurl in a complex interplay of forces that would combine to send a few ounces of steel gliding across the night.

Mericet was sitting by the trapdoor, looking at his clipboard. Teppic's eyes swivelled to the oblong of the plank bridge, stored meticulously against the parapet a few feet away.

He was certain he had made no noise. He'd have to swear that the examiner heard the sound of his gaze falling on him.

The old man raised his bald head.

"Thank you, Mr Teppic," he said, "you may proceed."

Teppic felt the sweat of his body grow cold. He stared at the plank, and then at the examiner, and then at his knife.

"Yes, sir," he said. This didn't seem like enough, in the circumstances. He added, "Thank you, sir."

He'd always remember the first night in the dormitory. It was long enough to accommodate all eighteen boys in Viper House, and draughty enough to accommodate the great outdoors. Its designer may have had comfort in mind, but only so that he could avoid it wherever possible: he had contrived a room that could actually be colder than the weather outside.

"I thought we got rooms to ourselves," said Teppic.

Chidder, who had laid claim to the least exposed bed in the whole refrigerator, nodded at him.

"Later on," he said. He lay back, and winced. "Do they sharpen these springs, do you reckon?"

Teppic said nothing. The bed was in fact rather more

comfortable than the one he'd slept in at home. His parents, being high born, naturally tolerated conditions for their children which would have been rejected out of hand by destitute sandflies.

He stretched out on the thin mattress and analysed the day's events. He'd been enrolled as an assassin, all right, a student assassin, for more than seven hours and they hadn't even let him lay a hand on a knife yet. Of course, tomorrow was another day. . .

Chidder leaned over.

"Where's Arthur?" he said.

Teppic looked at the bed opposite him. There was a pathetically small sack of clothing positioned neatly in its centre, but no sign of its intended occupant.

"Do you think he's run away?" he said, staring around at the shadows.

"Could be," said Chidder. "It happens a lot, you know. Mummy's boys, away from home for the first time — "

The door at the end of the room swung open slowly and Arthur entered, backwards, tugging a large and very reluctant billy goat. It fought him every step of the way down the aisle between the bedsteads.

The boys watched in silence for several minutes as he tethered the animal to the end of his bed, upended the sack on the blankets, and took out several black candles, a sprig of herbs, a rope of skulls, and a piece of chalk. Taking the chalk, and adopting the shiny, pink-faced expression of someone who is going to do what they know to be right no matter what, Arthur drew a double circle around his bed and then, getting down on his chubby knees, filled the space between them with as unpleasant a collection of occult symbols as Teppic had ever seen. When they were completed to his satisfaction he placed the candles at strategic points and lit them; they spluttered and gave off a smell that suggested that you really wouldn't want to know what they were made of.

He drew a short, red-handled knife from the jumble on the bed and advanced towards the goat —

A pillow hit him on the back of the head.

"Garn! Pious little bastard!"

Arthur dropped the knife and burst into tears. Chidder sat up in bed.

"That was you, Cheesewright!" he said. "I saw you!"

Cheesewright, a skinny young man with red hair and a face that was one large freckle, glared at him.

"Well, it's too much," he said. "A fellow can't sleep with all this religion going on. I mean, only little kids say their prayers at bedtime these days, we're supposed to be learning to be *assassins* — "

"You can jolly well shut up, Cheesewright," shouted Chidder. "It'd be a better world if more people said their prayers, you know. I know I don't say mine as often as I should — "

A pillow cut him off in mid-sentence. He bounded out of bed and vaulted at the red-haired boy, fists flailing.

As the rest of the dormitory gathered around the scuffling pair Teppic slid out of bed and padded over to Arthur, who was sitting on the edge of his bed and sobbing.

He patted him uncertainly on the shoulder, on the basis that this sort of thing was supposed to reassure people.

"I shouldn't cry about it, youngster," he said, gruffly.

"But — but all the runes have been scuffed," said Arthur. "It's all too late now! And that means the Great Orm will come in the night and wind out my entrails on a stick!"

"Does it?"

"And suck out my eyes, my mother said!"

"Gosh!" said Teppic, fascinated. "Really?" He was quite glad his bed was opposite Arthur's, and would offer an unrivalled view. "What religion would this be?"

"We're Strict Authorised Ormits," said Arthur. He blew his nose. "I noticed you don't pray," he said. "Don't you have a god?"

"Oh yes," said Teppic hesitantly, "no doubt about that."

"You don't seem to want to talk to him."

Teppic shook his head. "I can't," he said, "not here. He wouldn't be able to hear, you see."

"*My* god can hear *me* anywhere," said Arthur fervently.

"Well, mine has difficulty if you're on the other side of the room," said Teppic. "It can be very embarrassing."

"You're not an Offlian, are you?" said Arthur. Offler was a Crocodile God, and lacked ears.

"No."

"What god *do* you worship, then?"

"Not exactly worship," said Teppic, discomforted. "I wouldn't say worship. I mean, he's all right. He's my father, if you must know."

Arthur's pink-rimmed eyes widened.

"You're the son of a *god*?" he whispered.

"It's all part of being a king, where I come from," said Teppic hurriedly. "He doesn't have to do very much. That is, the priests do the actual running of the country. He just makes sure that the river floods every year, d'you see, and services the Great Cow of the Arch of the Sky. Well, *used* to."

"The Great — "

"My mother," explained Teppic. "It's all very embarrassing."

"Does he smite people?"

"I don't think so. He's never said."

Arthur reached down to the end of the bed. The goat, in the confusion, had chewed through its rope and trotted out of the door, vowing to give up religion in future.

"I'm going to get into awful trouble," he said. "I suppose you couldn't ask your father to explain things to the Great Orm?"

"He might be able to," said Teppic doubtfully. "I was going to write home tomorrow anyway."

"The Great Orm is normally to be found in one of the Nether Hells," said Arthur, "where he watches everything we do. Everything I do, anyway. There's only me and mother left now, and she doesn't do much that needs watching."

"I'll be sure and tell him."

"Do you think the Great Orm will come tonight?"

"I shouldn't think so. I'll ask my father to be sure and tell him not to."

At the other end of the dormitory Chidder was kneeling on Cheesewright's back and knocking his head repeatedly against the wall.

"Say it again," he commanded. "Come on —'There's nothing wrong —'"

"'There's nothing wrong with a chap being man enough —' curse you, Chidder, you beastly — "

"I can't hear you, Cheesewright," said Chidder.

"'Man enough to say his prayers in front of other chaps', you rotter."

"Right. And don't you forget it."

.   After lights out Teppic lay in bed and thought about religion. It was certainly a very complicated subject.

The valley of the Djel had its own private gods, gods which had nothing to do with the world outside. It had always been very proud of the fact. The gods were wise and just and regulated the lives of men with skill and foresight, there was no question about that, but there were some puzzles.

For example, he knew his father made the sun come up and the river flood and so on. That was basic, it was what the pharaohs had done ever since the time of Khuft, you couldn't go around questioning things like that. The point was, though, did he just make the sun come up in the Valley or everywhere in the world? Making the sun come up in the Valley seemed a more reasonable proposition, after all, his father wasn't getting any younger, but it was rather difficult to imagine the sun coming up everywhere else and *not* the Valley, which led to the distressing thought that the sun would come up even if his father forgot about it, which was a very likely state of affairs. He'd never seen his father do anything much about making the sun rise, he had to admit. You'd expect at least a grunt of effort round about dawn. His father never got up until after breakfast. The sun came up just the same.

He took some time to get to sleep. The bed, whatever Chidder said, was too soft, the air was too cold and, worst of all, the sky outside the high windows was too dark. At home it would have been full of flarelight from the necropolis, its silent flames eerie but somehow familiar and comforting, as though the ancestors were watching over their valley. He didn't like the darkness...

The following night in the dormitory one of the boys from further along the coast shyly tried to put the boy in the next bed inside a wickerwork cage he made in Craft and set fire to him, and the night after that Snoxall, who had the bed by the door and came from a little country out in the forests somewhere, painted himself green and asked for volunteers to have their intestines wound around a tree. On Thursday a small war broke out between those who worshipped the Mother Goddess

in her aspect of the Moon and those who worshipped her in her
aspect of a huge fat woman with enormous buttocks. After that
the masters intervened and explained that religion, while a fine
thing, could be taken too far.

Teppic had a suspicion that unpunctuality was unforgivable.
But surely Mericet would have to be at the tower ahead of him?
And he was going by the direct route. The old man couldn't
possibly get there before him. Mind you, he couldn't possibly
have got to the bridge in the alley first. . . He must have taken
the bridge away before he met me and then he climbed up on the
roof while I was climbing up the wall, Teppic told himself,
without believing a word of it.

He ran along a roof ridge, senses alert for dislodged tiles or
tripwires. His imagination equipped every shadow with
watching figures.

The gong tower loomed ahead of him. He paused, and looked
at it. He had seen it a thousand times before, and scaled it many
times although it barely rated a 1.8, notwithstanding that the
brass dome on top was an interesting climb. It was just a
familiar landmark. That made it worse now; it bulked in front
of him, a stubby menacing shape against the greyness of the
sky.

He advanced more slowly now, approaching the tower
obliquely across the sloping roof. It came to him that his initials
were up there, on the dome, along with Chiddy's and those of
hundreds of other young assassins, and that they'd carry on
being up there even if he died tonight. It was sort of comforting.
Only not very.

He unslung his rope and made an easy throw on to the wide
parapet that ran around the tower, just under the dome. He
tested it, and heard the gentle clink as it caught.

Then he tugged it as hard as possible, bracing himself with
one foot on a chimney stack.

Abruptly, and with no sound, a section of parapet slid
outwards and dropped.

There was a crash as it hit the roof below and then slid down the tiles. Another pause was punctuated by a distant thump as it hit the silent street. A dog barked.

Stillness ruled the rooftops. Where Teppic had been the breeze stirred the burning air.

After several minutes he emerged from the deeper shadow of a chimney stack, smiling a strange and terrible smile.

Nothing the examiner could do could possibly be unfair. An assassin's clients were invariably rich enough to pay for extremely ingenious protection, up to and including hiring assassins of his own*. Mericet wasn't trying to kill him; he was merely trying to make him kill himself.

He sidled up to the base of the tower and found a drainpipe. It hadn't been coated with slipall, rather to his surprise, but his gently questing fingers did find the poisoned needles painted black and glued to the inner face of the pipe. He removed one with his tweezers and sniffed it.

Distilled *bloat*. Pretty expensive stuff, with an astonishing effect. He took a small glass phial from his belt and collected as many needles as he could find, and then put on his armoured gloves and, with the speed of a sloth, started to climb.

"Now it may well be that, as you travel across the city on your lawful occasions, you will find yourselves in opposition to fellow members, even one of the gentlemen with whom you are currently sharing a bench. And this is quite right and *what are you doing Mr Chidder no don't tell me I'm sure I wouldn't want to know see me afterwards* proper. It is open to everyone to defend themselves as best they may. There are, however, other enemies who will dog your steps and against whom you are all ill-prepared *who are they Mr Cheesewright?*"

Mericet spun round from his blackboard like a vulture who has just heard a death-rattle and pointed the chalk at Cheesewright, who gulped.

"Thieves' Guild, sir?" he managed.

---

*It was said that life was cheap in Ankh-Morpork. This was, of course, completely wrong. Life was often very expensive; you could get *death* for free.

"Step out here, boy."

There were whispered rumours in the dormitories about what Mericet had done to slovenly pupils in the past, which were always vague but horrifying. The class relaxed. Mericet usually concentrated on one victim at a time, so all they had to do now was look keen and enjoy the show. Crimson to his ears, Cheesewright got to his feet and trooped down the aisle between the desks.

The master inspected him thoughtfully.

"Well, now," he said, "and here we have Cheesewright, G., skulking across the quaking rooftops. See the determined ears. See the firm set of those knees."

The class tittered dutifully. Cheesewright gave them an idiotic grin and rolled his eyes.

"But what are these sinister figures that march in step with him, hey? *Since you find this so funny, Mr Teppic, perhaps you would be so good as to tell Mr Cheesewright?*"

Teppic froze in mid-laugh.

Mericet's gaze bored into him. He's just like Dios the high priest, Teppic thought. Even *father*'s frightened of Dios.

He knew what he ought to do, and he was damned if he was going to do it. He ought to be scared.

"Ill-preparedness," he said. "Carelessness. Lack of concentration. Poor maintenance of tools. Oh, and over-confidence, sir."

Mericet held his gaze for some time, but Teppic had practised on the palace cats.

Finally the teacher gave a brief smile that had absolutely nothing to do with humour, tossed the chalk in the air, caught it again, and said: "Mr Teppic is exactly right. Especially about the over-confidence."

There was a ledge leading to an invitingly open window. There was oil on the ledge, and Teppic invested several minutes in screwing small crampons into cracks in the stonework before advancing.

He hung easily by the window and proceeded to take a

number of small metal rods from his belt. They were threaded at the ends, and after a few seconds' brisk work he had a rod about three feet long on the end of which he affixed a small mirror.

That revealed nothing in the gloom beyond the opening. He pulled it back and tried again, this time attaching his hood into which he'd stuffed his gloves, to give the impression of a head cautiously revealing itself against the light. He was confident that it would pick up a bolt or a dart, but it remained resolutely unattacked.

He was chilly now, despite the heat of the night. Black velvet looked good, but that was about all you could say for it. The excitement and the exertion meant he was now wearing several pints of clammy water.

He advanced.

There was a thin black wire on the window sill, and a serrated blade screwed to the sash window above it. It was the work of a moment to wedge the sash with more rods and then cut the wire; the window dropped a fraction of an inch. He grinned in the darkness.

A sweep with a longer rod inside the room revealed that there was a floor, apparently free of obstructions. There was also a wire at about chest height. He drew the rod back, affixed a small hook on the end, sent it back, caught the wire, and tugged.

There came the dull smack of a crossbow bolt hitting old plaster.

A lump of clay on the end of the same rod, pushed gently across the floor, revealed several caltraps. Teppic hauled them back and inspected them with interest. They were copper. If he'd tried the magnet technique, which was the usual method, he wouldn't have found them.

He thought for a while. He had slip-on priests in his pouch. They were devilish things to prowl around a room in, but he shuffled into them anyway. (Priests were metal-reinforced overshoes. They saved your soles. This is an Assassin joke.) Mericet was a poisons man, after all. Bloat! If he tipped them with that Teppic would plate himself all over the walls. They wouldn't need to bury him, they'd just redecorate over the top.*

---

*Bloat is extracted from the deep sea blowfish, *Singularis minutia gigantica*, which protects itself from enemies by inflating itself to many times its normal size. If taken by humans the effect is to make every cell in the body instantaneously try to swell some 2,000 times. This is invariably fatal, and very loud.

The rules. Mericet would have to obey the rules. He couldn't simply kill him, with no warning. He'd have to let him, by carelessness or over-confidence, kill himself.

He dropped lightly on to the floor inside the room and let his eyes adjust to the darkness. A few exploratory swings with the rods detected no more wires; there was a faint crunch underfoot as a priest crushed a caltrap.

"In your own time, Mr Teppic."

Mericet was standing in a corner. Teppic heard the faint scratching of his pencil as he made a note. He tried to put the man out of his mind. He tried to think.

There was a figure lying on a bed. It was entirely covered by a blanket.

This was the last bit. This was the room where everything was decided. This was the bit the successful students never told you about. The unsuccessful ones weren't around to ask.

Teppic's mind filled up with options. At a time like this, he thought, some divine guidance would be necessary. Where are you, dad?

He envied his fellow students who believed in gods that were intangible and lived a long way away on top of some mountain. A fellow could really *believe* in gods like that. But it was extremely hard to believe in a god when you saw him at breakfast every day.

He unslung his crossbow and screwed its greased sections together. It wasn't a proper weapon, but he'd run out of knives and his lips were too dry for the blowpipe.

There was a clicking from the corner. Mericet was idly tapping his teeth with his pencil.

It could be a dummy under there. How would he know? No, it had to be a real person. You heard tales. Perhaps he could try the rods —

He shook his head, raised the crossbow, and took careful aim.

"Whenever you like, Mr Teppic."

This was it.

This was where they found out if you could kill.

This was what he had been trying to put out of his mind.

He knew he couldn't.

*

Octeday afternoons was Political Expediency with Lady T'malia, one of the few women to achieve high office in the Guild. In the lands around the Circle Sea it was generally agreed that one way to achieve a long life was not to have a meal with her Ladyship. The jewelry of one hand alone carried enough poison to inhume a small town. She was stunningly beautiful, but with the kind of calculated beauty that is achieved by a team of skilled artists, manicurists, plasterers, corsetiers and dressmakers and three hours' solid work every morning. When she walked there was the faint squeak of whalebone under incredible stress.

The boys were learning. As she talked they didn't watch her figure. They watched her fingers.

"And thus," she said, "let us consider the position before the founding of the Guild. In this city, and indeed in many places elsewhere, civilisation is nurtured and progresses by the dynamic interplay of interests among many large and powerful advantage cartels.

"In the days before the founding of the Guild the seeking of advancement among these consortia invariably resulted in regrettable disagreements which were terminated with extreme prejudice. These were extremely deleterious to the common interest of the city. Please understand that where disharmony rules, commerce flags.

"And yet, and yet." She clasped her hands to her bosom. There was a creak like a galleon beating against a gale.

"Clearly there was a need for an extreme yet responsible means of settling irreconcilable differences," she went on, "and thus was laid the groundwork for the Guild. What *bliss* — " the sudden peak in her voice guiltily jerked several dozen young men out of their private reveries — "it must have been to have been present in those early days, when men of stout moral purpose set out to forge the ultimate political *tool* short of warfare. How *fortunate* you are now, in training for a guild which demands so much in terms of manners, deportment, bearing and esoteric skills, and yet offers a power once the preserve only of the gods. Truly, the world is the mollusc of your choice . . ."

Chidder translated much of this behind the stables during the dinner break.

"I know what Terminate with Extreme Prejudice means," said Cheesewright loftily. "It means to inhume with an axe."

"It bloody well doesn't," said Chidder.

"How do you know, then?"

"My family have been in commerce for years," said Chidder.

"Huh," said Cheesewright. "*Commerce.*"

Chidder never went into details about what kind of commerce it was. It had something to with moving items around and supplying needs, but exactly what items and which needs was never made clear.

After hitting Cheesewright he explained carefully that Terminate with Extreme Prejudice did not simply require that the victim was inhumed, preferably in an extremely thorough way, but that his associates and employees were also intimately involved, along with the business premises, the building, and a large part of the surrounding neighbourhood, so that everyone involved would know that the man had been unwise enough to make the kind of enemies who could get very angry and indiscriminate.

"Gosh," said Arthur.

"Oh, that's nothing," said Chidder, "one Hogswatchnight my grandad and his accounts department went and had a high-level business conference with the Hubside people and fifteen bodies were never found. Very bad, that sort of thing. Upsets the business community."

"All the business community, or just that part of it floating face down in the river?" said Teppic.

"That's the point. Better it should be like this," said Chidder, shaking his head. "You know. *Clean.* That's why my father said I should join the Guild. I mean, you've got to get on with the business these days, you can't spend your whole time on public relations."

The end of the crossbow trembled.

He liked everything else about the school, the climbing, the music studies, the broad education. It was the fact that you ended up killing people that had been preying on his mind. He'd never killed anyone.

That's the whole point, he told himself. This is where everyone finds out if you can, including you.

If I get it wrong now, I'm dead.

In his corner, Mericet began to hum a discouraging little tune.

There was a price the Guild paid for its licence. It saw to it that there were no careless, half-hearted or, in a manner of speaking, murderously inefficient assassins. You never met *anyone* who'd failed the test.

People did fail. You just never met them. Maybe there was one under there, maybe it was Chidder, even, or Snoxall or any one of the lads. They were all doing the run this evening. Maybe if he failed he'd be bundled under there...

Teppic tried to sight on the recumbent figure.

"Ahem," coughed the examiner.

His throat was dry. Panic rose like a drunkard's supper.

His teeth wanted to chatter. His spine was freezing, his clothes a collection of damp rags. The world slowed down.

No. He wasn't going to. The sudden decision hit him like a brick in a dark alley, and was nearly as surprising. It wasn't that he hated the Guild, or even particularly disliked Mericet, but this wasn't the way to test anyone. It was just wrong.

He decided to fail. Exactly what could the old man do about it, here?

And he'd fail with flair.

He turned to face Mericet, looked peacefully into the examiner's eyes, extended his crossbow hand in some vague direction to his right, and pulled the trigger.

There was a metallic twang.

There was a click as the bolt ricocheted off a nail in the window sill. Mericet ducked as it whirred over his head. It hit a torch bracket on the wall, and went past Teppic's white face purring like a maddened cat.

There was a thud as it hit the blanket, and then silence.

"Thank you, Mr Teppic. If you could bear with me just one moment."

The old assassin pored over his clipboard, his lips moving.

He took the pencil, which dangled from it by a bit of frayed string, and made a few marks on a piece of pink paper.

"I will not ask you to take it from my hands," he said, "what with one thing and another. I shall leave it on the table by the door."

It wasn't a particularly pleasant smile: it was thin and dried-up, a smile with all the warmth long ago boiled out of it; people normally smiled like that when they had been dead for about two years under the broiling desert sun. But at least you felt he was making the effort.

Teppic hadn't moved. "I've passed?" he said.

"That would appear to be the case."

"But — "

"I am sure you know that we are not allowed to discuss the test with pupils. However, I can tell you that I personally do not approve of these modern flashy techniques. Good morning to you." And Mericet stalked out.

Teppic tottered over to the dusty table by the door and looked down, horrified, at the paper. Sheer habit made him extract a pair of tweezers from his pouch in order to pick it up.

It was genuine enough. There was the seal of the Guild on it, and the crabbed squiggle that was undoubtedly Mericet's signature; he'd seen it often enough, generally at the bottom of test papers alongside comments like *3/10. See me.*

He padded over to the figure on the bed and pulled back the blanket.

It was nearly one in the morning. Ankh-Morpork was just beginning to make a night of it.

It had been dark up above the rooftops, in the aerial world of thieves and assassins. But down below the life of the city flowed through the streets like a tide.

Teppic walked through the throng in a daze. Anyone else who tried that in the city was asking for a guided tour of the bottom of the river, but he was wearing assassin's black and the crowd just automatically opened in front of him and closed behind. Even the pickpockets kept away. You never knew what you might find. He wandered aimlessly through the gates of the Guild House and sat down on a black marble seat, with his chin on his knuckles.

The fact was that his life had come to an end. He hadn't thought about what was going to happen next. He hadn't dared to think that there was going to *be* a next.

Someone tapped him on the shoulder. As he turned, Chidder sat down beside him and wordlessly produced a slip of pink paper.

"Snap," he said.

"You passed too?" said Teppic.

Chidder grinned. "No problem," he said. "It was Nivor. No problem. He gave me a bit of trouble on the Emergency Drop, though. How about you?"

"Hmm? Oh. No." Teppic tried to get a grip on himself. "No trouble," he said.

"Heard from any of the others?"

"No."

Chidder leaned back. "Cheesewright will make it," he said loftily, "and young Arthur. I don't think some of the others will. We could give them twenty minutes, what do you say?"

Teppic turned an agonised face towards him.

"Chiddy, I — "

"What?"

"When it came to it, I — "

"What about it?"

Teppic looked at the cobbles. "Nothing," he said.

"You're lucky — you just had a good airy run over the rooftops. I had the sewers and then up the garderobe in the Haberdashers' Tower. I had to go in and change when I got here."

"You had a dummy, did you?" said Teppic.

"Good grief, didn't you?"

"But they let us think it was going to be real!" Teppic wailed.

"It felt real, didn't it?"

"Yes!"

"Well, then. And you passed. So no problem."

"But didn't you wonder who might be under the blanket, who it was, and why — "

"I was worried that I might not do it properly," Chidder admitted. "But then I thought, well, it's not up to me."

"But I — " Teppic stopped. What could he do? Go and explain?

Somehow that didn't seem a terribly good idea.

His friend slapped him on the back.

"Don't worry about it!" he said. "We've done it!"

And Chidder held up his thumb pressed against the first two fingers of his right hand, in the ancient salute of the assassins.

A thumb pressed against two fingers, and the lean figure of Dr Cruces, head tutor, looming over the startled boys.

"We do not *murder*," he said. It was a soft voice; the doctor never raised his voice, but he had a way of giving it the pitch and spin that could make it be heard through a hurricane.

"We do not *execute*. We do not *massacre*. We never, you may be very certain, we never *torture*. We have no truck with crimes of passion or hatred or pointless gain. We do not do it for a delight in inhumation, or to feed some secret inner need, or for petty advantage, or for some cause or belief; I tell you, gentlemen, that all these reasons are in the highest degree suspect. Look into the face of a man who will kill you for a belief and your nostrils will snuff up the scent of abomination. Hear a speech declaring a holy war and, I assure you, your ears should catch the clink of evil's scales and the dragging of its monstrous tail over the purity of the language.

"No, we do it for the money.

"And, because we above all must know the value of a human life, we do it for a great deal of money.

"There can be few cleaner motives, so shorn of all pretence.

"*Nil mortifi, sine lucre.* Remember. No killing without payment."

He paused for a moment.

"And always give a receipt," he added.

"So it's all okay," said Chidder. Teppic nodded gloomily. That was what was so likeable about Chidder. He had this enviable ability to avoid thinking seriously about anything he did.

A figure approached cautiously through the open gates.* The light from the torch in the porters' lodge glinted off blond curly hair.

"You two made it, then," said Arthur, nonchalantly flourishing the slip.

Arthur had changed quite a lot in seven years. The continuing failure of the Great Orm to wreak organic revenge for lack of piety had cured him of his tendency to run everywhere with his coat over his head. His small size gave him a natural advantage in those areas of the craft involving narrow spaces. His innate aptitude for channelled violence had been revealed on the day when Fliemoe and some cronies had decided it would be fun to toss the new boys in a blanket, and picked Arthur first; ten seconds later it had taken the combined efforts of every boy in the dormitory to hold Arthur back and prise the remains of the chair from his fingers. It had transpired that he was the son of the late Johan Ludorum, one of the greatest assassins in the history of the Guild. Sons of dead assassins always got a free scholarship. Yes, it could be a caring profession at times.

There hadn't been any doubt about Arthur passing. He'd been given extra tuition and was allowed to use really complicated poisons. He was probably going to stay on for post-graduate work.

They waited until the gongs of the city struck two. Clockwork was not a precise technology in Ankh-Morpork, and many of the city's various communities had their own ideas of what constituted an hour in any case, so the chimes went on bouncing around the rooftops for five minutes.

When it was obvious that the city's consensus was in favour of it being well past two the three of them stopped looking silently at their shoes.

"Well, that's it," said Chidder.

"Poor old Cheesewright," said Arthur. "It's tragic, when you think about it."

"Yes, he owed me fourpence," agreed Chidder. "Come on. I've arranged something for us."

*

*The gates of the Assassins' Guild were never shut. This was said to be because Death was open for business all the time, but it was really because the hinges had rusted centuries before and no-one had got around to doing anything about it.

King Teppicymon XXVII got out of bed and clapped his hands over his ears to shut out the roar of the sea. It was strong tonight.

It was always louder when he was feeling out of sorts. He needed something to distract himself. He could send for Ptraci, his favourite handmaiden. She was *special*. Her singing always cheered him up. Life seemed so much brighter when she stopped.

Or there was the sunrise. That was always comforting. It was pleasant to sit wrapped in a blanket on the topmost roof of the palace, watching the mists lift from the river as the golden flood poured over the land. You got that warm, contented feeling of another job well done. Even if you didn't actually know how you'd done it . . .

He got up, shuffled on his slippers, and padded out of his bedroom and down the wide corridor that led to the huge spiral stairs and the roof. A few rushlights illuminated the statues of the other local gods, painting the walls with shifting shadow pictures of things dog-headed, fish-bodied, spider-armed. He'd known them since childhood. His juvenile nightmares would have been quite formless without them.

The sea. He'd only seen it once, when he was a boy. He couldn't recall a lot about it, except the size. And the noise. And the seagulls.

They'd preyed on his mind. They seemed to have it far better worked out, seagulls. He wished he could come back as one, one day, but of course that wasn't an option if you were a pharaoh. You never came back. You didn't exactly go away, in fact.

"Well, what *is* it?" said Teppic.

"Try it," said Chidder, "just try it. You'll never have the chance again."

"Seems a shame to spoil it," said Arthur gallantly, looking down at the delicate pattern on his plate. "What are all the little red things?"

"They're just radishes," said Chidder dismissively. "They're not the important part. Go on."

Teppic reached over with the little wooden fork and skewered a paper-thin sliver of white fish. The *squishi* chef was scrutinising him with the air of one watching a toddler on his first birthday. So, he realised, was the rest of the restaurant.

He chewed it carefully. It was salty and faintly rubbery, with a hint of sewage outfall.

"Nice?" said Chidder anxiously. Several nearby diners started to clap.

"Different," Teppic conceded, chewing. "What is it?"

"Deep sea blowfish," said Chidder.

"It's all right," he said hastily as Teppic laid down his fork meaningfully, "it's perfectly safe provided every bit of stomach, liver and digestive tract is removed, that's why it cost so much, there's no such thing as a second-best blowfish chef, it's the most expensive food in the world, people write poems about it — "

"Could be a taste explosion," muttered Teppic, getting a grip on himself. Still, it must have been done properly, otherwise the place would now be wearing him as wallpaper. He poked carefully at the sliced roots which occupied the rest of the plate.

"What do these do to you?" he said.

"Well, unless they're prepared in exactly the right way over a six-week period they react catastrophically with your stomach acids," said Chidder. "Sorry. I thought we should celebrate with the most expensive meal we could afford."

"I see. Fish and chips *for Men*," said Teppic.

"Do they have any vinegar in this place?" said Arthur, his mouth full. "And some mushy peas would go down a treat."

But the wine was good. Not incredibly good, though. Not one of the great vintages. But it did explain why Teppic had gone through the whole of the day with a headache.

It had been the hangunder. His friend had bought four bottles of otherwise quite ordinary white wine. The reason it was so expensive was that the grapes it was made from hadn't actually been planted yet.*

---

*Counterwise wine is made from grapes belonging to that class of flora — reannuals — that grow only in excessively high magic fields. Normal plants grow after the seeds have been planted — with reannuals it's *the other way round*. Although reannual wine causes inebriation in the normal way, the action of the digestive system on its molecules causes an unusual reaction whose net effect is to thrust the ensuing hangover backwards in time, to a point some hours before the wine is drunk. Hence the saying: have a hair of the dog that's going to bite you.

Light moves slowly, lazily on the Disc. It's in no hurry to get anywhere. Why bother? At lightspeed, everywhere is the same place.

King Teppicymon XXVII watched the golden disc float over
the edge of the world. A flight of cranes took off from the mist-
covered river.

He'd been conscientious, he told himself. No-one had ever
explained to him *how* one made the sun come up and the river
flood and the corn grow. How could they? *He* was the god, after
all. He should know. But he didn't, so he'd just gone through life
hoping like hell that it would all work properly, and that seemed
to have done the trick. The trouble was, though, that if it didn't
work, he wouldn't know why not. A recurrent nightmare was of
Dios the high priest shaking him awake one morning, only it
wouldn't be a morning, of course, and of every light in the palace
burning and an angry crowd muttering in the star-lit darkness
outside and everyone looking expectantly at him . . .

And all he'd be able to say was, "Sorry".

It terrified him. How easy to imagine the ice forming on the
river, the eternal frost riming the palm trees and snapping off
the leaves (which would smash when they hit the frozen ground)
and the birds dropping lifeless from the sky . . .

Shadow swept over him. He looked up through eyes misted
with tears at a grey and empty horizon, his mouth dropping
open in horror.

He stood up, flinging aside the blanket, and raised both hands
in supplication. But the sun had gone. He was the god, this was
his job, it was the only thing he was here to do, and he had failed
the people.

Now he could hear in his mind's ear the anger of the crowd, a
booming roar that began to fill his ears until the rhythm became
insistent and familiar, until it reached the point where it pressed
in no longer but drew him out, into that salty blue desert where
the sun always shone and sleek shapes wheeled across the sky.

The pharaoh raised himself on his toes, threw back his head,
spread his wings. And leapt.

As he soared into the sky he was surprised to hear a thump
behind him. And the sun came out from behind the clouds.

Later on, the pharaoh felt awfully embarrassed about it.

*

The three new assassins staggered slowly along the street, constantly on the point of falling over but never quite reaching it, trying to sing "A Wizard's Staff Has A Knob On The End" in harmony or at least in the same key.

"Tis big an' i'ss round an' weighs three to the — " sang Chidder. "Blast, what've I stepped in?"

"Anyone know where we are?" said Arthur.

"We — we were headed for the Guildhouse," said Teppic, "only must of took the wrong way, that's the river up ahead. Can smell it."

Caution penetrated Arthur's armour of alcohol.

"Could be dangerous pep — plep — people around, this time o' night," he hazarded.

"Yep," said Chidder, with satisfaction, "us. Got ticket to prove it. Got test and everything. Like to see anyone try anything with us."

"Right," agreed Teppic, leaning against him for support of a sort. "We'll slit them from wossname to thingy."

"Right!"

They lurched uncertainly out on to the Brass Bridge.

In fact there *were* dangerous people around in the pre-dawn shadows, and currently these were some twenty paces behind them.

The complex system of criminal Guilds had not actually made Ankh-Morpork a safer place, it just rationalised its dangers and put them on a regular and reliable footing. The major Guilds policed the city with more thoroughness and certainly more success than the old Watch had ever managed, and it was true that any freelance and unlicensed thief caught by the Thieves' Guild would soon find himself remanded in custody for social inquiry reports plus having his knees nailed together*. However, there were always a few spirits who would venture a precarious living outside the lawless, and five men of this description were closing cautiously on the trio to introduce them to this week's special offer, a cut throat plus theft and burial in the river mud of your choice.

---

*When the Thieves' Guild declared a General Strike in the Year of the Engaging Sloth, the actual level of crime doubled.

People normally keep out of the way of assassins because of an instinctive feeling that killing people for very large sums of money is disapproved of by the gods (who generally prefer people to be killed for very small sums of money or for free) and could result in hubris, which is the judgement of the gods. The gods are great believers in justice, at least as far as it extends to humans, and have been known to dispense it so enthusiastically that people miles away are turned into a cruet.

However, assassin's black doesn't frighten everyone, and in certain sections of society there is a distinct cachet in killing an assassin. It's rather like smashing a sixer in conkers.

Broadly, therefore, the three even now lurching across the deserted planks of the Brass Bridge were dead drunk assassins and the men behind them were bent on inserting the significant comma.

Chidder wandered into one of the heraldic wooden hippopotami* that lined the seaward edge of the bridge, bounced off and flopped over the parapet.

"Feel sick," he announced.

"Feel free," said Arthur, "that's what the river's for."

Teppic sighed. He was attached to rivers, which he felt were designed to have water lilies on top and crocodiles underneath, and the Ankh always depressed him because if you put a water lily in it, it would dissolve. It drained the huge silty plains all the way to the Ramtop mountains, and by the time it had passed through Ankh-Morpork, pop. one million, it could only be called a liquid because it moved faster than the land around it; actually being sick in it would probably make it, on average, marginally cleaner.

---

*One of the two† legends about the founding of Ankh-Morpork relates that the two orphaned brothers who built the city were in fact found and suckled by a hippopotamus (lit. *orijeple*, although some historians hold that this is a mistranslation of *orejaple*, a type of glass-fronted drinks cabinet). Eight heraldic hippos line the bridge, facing out to sea. It is said that if danger ever threatens the city, they will run away.

†The other legend, not normally recounted by citizens, is that at an even earlier time a group of wise men survived a flood sent by the gods by building a huge boat, and on this boat they took two of every type of animal then existing on the Disc. After some weeks the combined manure was beginning to weigh the boat low in the water so — the story runs — they tipped it over the side, and called it Ankh-Morpork.

He stared down at the thin trickle that oozed between the central pillars, and then raised his gaze to the grey horizon.

"Sun's coming up," he announced.

"Don't remember eating that," muttered Chidder.

Teppic stepped back, and a knife ripped past his nose and buried itself in the buttocks of the hippo next to him.

Five figures stepped out of the mists. The three assassins instinctively drew together.

"You come near me, you'll really regret it," moaned Chidder, clutching his stomach. "The cleaning bill will be *horrible*."

"Well now, what have we here?" said the leading thief. This is the sort of thing that gets said in these circumstances.

"Thieves' Guild, are you?" said Arthur.

"No," said the leader, "we're the small and unrepresentative minority that gets the rest a bad name. Give us your valuables and weapons, please. This won't make any difference to the outcome, you understand. It's just that corpse robbing is unpleasant and degrading."

"We could rush them," said Teppic, uncertainly.

"Don't look at me," said Arthur, "I couldn't find my arse with an atlas."

"You'll really be sorry when I'm sick," said Chidder.

Teppic was aware of the throwing knives stuffed up either sleeve, and that the chances of him being able to get hold of one in time still to be alive to throw it were likely to be very small.

At times like this religious solace is very important. He turned and looked towards the sun, just as it withdrew from the cloudbanks of the dawn.

There was a tiny dot in the centre of it.

The late King Teppicymon XXVII opened his eyes.

"I was flying," he whispered, "I remember the feeling of wings. What am I doing here?"

He tried to stand up. There was a temporary feeling of heaviness, which suddenly dropped away so that he rose to his feet almost without any effort. He looked down to see what had caused it.

"Oh dear," he said.

The culture of the river kingdom had a lot to say about death and what happened afterwards. In fact it had very little to say about life, regarding it as a sort of inconvenient prelude to the main event and something to be hurried through as politely as possible, and therefore the pharaoh reached the conclusion that he was dead very quickly. The sight of his mangled body on the sand below him played a major part in this.

There was a greyness about everything. The landscape had a ghostly look, as though he could walk straight through it. Of course, he thought, I probably can.

He rubbed the analogue of his hands. Well, this is it. This is where it gets interesting; this is where I start to really *live*.

Behind him a voice said, GOOD MORNING.

The king turned.

"Hallo," he said. "You'd be — "

DEATH, said Death.

The king looked surprised.

"I understood that Death came as a three-headed giant scarab beetle," he said.

Death shrugged. WELL. NOW YOU KNOW.

"What's that thing in your hand?"

THIS? IT'S A SCYTHE.

"Strange-looking object, isn't it?" said the pharaoh. "I thought Death carried the Flail of Mercy and the Reaping Hook of Justice."

Death appeared to think about this.

WHAT IN? he said.

"Pardon?"

ARE WE STILL TALKING ABOUT A GIANT BEETLE?

"Ah. In his mandibles, I suppose. But I think he's got arms in one of the frescoes in the palace." The king hesitated. "Seems a bit silly, really, now I come to tell someone. I mean, a giant beetle with arms. And the head of an ibis, I seem to recall."

Death sighed. He was not a creature of Time, and therefore past and future were all one to him, but there had been a period when he'd made an effort to appear in whatever form the client expected. This foundered because it was usually impossible to know what the client was expecting until after they were dead.

And then he'd decided that, since no-one ever really expected to
die anyway, he might as well please himself and he'd hence-
forth stuck to the familiar black-cowled robe, which was neat
and very familiar and acceptable everywhere, like the best
credit cards.

"Anyway," said the pharaoh, "I expect we'd better be going."

WHERE TO?

"Don't *you* know?"

I AM HERE ONLY TO SEE THAT YOU DIE AT THE APPOINTED TIME.
WHAT HAPPENS NEXT IS UP TO YOU.

"Well..." The king automatically scratched his chin. "I
suppose I have to wait until they've done all the preparations
and so forth. Mummified me. And build a bloody pyramid. Um.
Do I have to hang around here to wait for all that?"

I ASSUME SO. Death clicked his fingers and a magnificent white
horse ceased its grazing on some of the garden greenery and
trotted towards him.

"Oh. Well, I think I shall look away. They take all the squishy
inside bits out first, you know." A look of faint worry crossed his
face. Things that had seemed perfectly sensible when he was
alive seemed a little suspect now that he was dead.

"It's to preserve the body so that it may begin life anew in the
Netherworld," he added, in a slightly perplexed voice. "And
then they wrap you in bandages. At least *that* seems logical."

He rubbed his nose. "But then they put all this food and drink
in the pyramid with you. Bit weird, really."

WHERE ARE ONE'S INTERNAL ORGANS AT THIS POINT?

"That's the funny thing, isn't it? They're in a jar in the next
room," said the king, his voice edged with doubt. "We even put
a damn great model cart in dad's pyramid."

His frown deepened. "Solid wood, it was," he said, half to
himself, "with gold leaf all over it. And four wooden bullocks to
pull it. Then we whacked a damn great stone over the door..."

He tried to think, and found that it was surprisingly easy.
New ideas were pouring into his mind in a cold, clear stream.
They had to do with the play of light on the rocks, the deep blue
of the sky, the manifold possibilities of the world that stretched
away on every side of him. Now that he didn't have a body to
importune him with its insistent demands the world seemed

full of astonishments, but unfortunately among the first of them was the fact that much of what you thought was true now seemed as solid and reliable as marsh gas. And also that, just as he was fully equipped to enjoy the world, he was going to be buried inside a pyramid.

When you die, the first thing you lose is your life. The next thing is your illusions.

I CAN SEE YOU HAVE GOT A LOT TO THINK ABOUT, said Death, mounting up. AND NOW, IF YOU'LL EXCUSE ME —

"Hang on a moment — "

YES?

"When I . . . fell, I could have sworn that I was flying."

THAT PART OF YOU THAT WAS DIVINE DID FLY, NATURALLY. YOU ARE NOW FULLY MORTAL.

"Mortal?"

TAKE IT FROM ME. I KNOW ABOUT THESE THINGS.

"Oh. Look, there's quite a few questions I'd like to ask — "

THERE ALWAYS ARE. I'M SORRY. Death clapped his heels to his horse's flanks, and vanished.

The king stood there as several servants came hurrying along the palace wall, slowed down as they approached his corpse, and advanced with caution.

"Are you all right, O jewelled master of the sun?" one of them ventured.

"No, I'm not," snapped the king, who was having some of his basic assumptions about the universe severely rattled, and that never puts anyone in a good mood. "I'm by way of being dead just at the moment. Amazing, isn't it," he added bitterly.

"Can you hear us, O divine bringer of the morning?" inquired the other servant, tiptoeing closer.

"I've just fallen off a hundred foot wall on to my head, what do you think?" shouted the king.

"I don't think he can hear us, Jahmet," said the other servant.

"Listen," said the king, whose urgency was equalled only by the servants' total inability to hear anything he was saying, "you must find my son and tell him to forget about the pyramid business, at least until I've thought about it a bit, there are one or two points which seem a little self-contradictory about the whole afterlife arrangements, and — "

"Shall I shout?" said Jahmet.

"I don't think you can shout loud enough. I think he's dead."

Jahmet looked down at the stiffening corpse.

"Bloody hell," he said eventually. "Well, that's tomorrow up the spout for a start."

The sun, unaware that it was making its farewell performance, continued to drift smoothly above the rim of the world. And out of it, moving faster than any bird should be able to fly, a seagull bore down on Ankh-Morpork, on the Brass Bridge and eight still figures, on one staring face . . .

Seagulls were common enough in Ankh. But as this one flew over the group it uttered one long, guttural scream that caused three of the thieves to drop their knives. Nothing with feathers ought to have been able to make a noise like that. It had claws in it.

The bird wheeled in a tight circle and fluttered to a perch on a convenient wooden hippo, where it glared at the group with mad red eyes.

The leading thief tore his fascinated gaze away from it just as he heard Arthur say, quite pleasantly, "This is a no.2 throwing knife. I got ninety-six per cent for throwing knives. Which eyeball don't you need?"

The leader stared at him. As far as the other young assassins were concerned, he noticed, one was still staring fixedly at the seagull while the other was busy being noisily sick over the parapet.

"There's only one of you," he said. "There's five of us."

"But soon there will only be four of you," said Arthur.

Moving slowly, like someone in a daze, Teppic reached out his hand to the seagull. With any normal seagull this would have resulted in the loss of a thumb, but the creature hopped on to it with the smug air of the master returning to the old plantation.

It seemed to make the thieves increasingly uneasy. Arthur's smile wasn't helping either.

"That's a nice bird," said the leader, in the inanely cheerful tones of the extremely worried. Teppic was dreamily stroking its bullet head.

"I think it would be a good idea if you went away," said Arthur, as the bird shuffled sideways on to Teppic's wrist. Gripping with webbed feet, thrusting out its wings to maintain its balance, it should have looked clownish but instead looked full of hidden power, as though it was an eagle's secret identity. When it opened its mouth, revealing a ridiculous purple bird tongue, there was a suggestion that this seagull could do a lot more than menace a seaside tomato sandwich.

"Is it magic?" said one of the thieves, and was quickly hushed.

"We'll be going, then," said the leader, "sorry about the misunderstanding — "

Teppic gave him a warm, unseeing smile.

Then they all heard the insistent little noise. Six pairs of eyes swivelled around and down; Chidder's were already in position.

Below them, pouring darkly across the dehydrated mud, the Ankh was rising.

Dios, First Minister and high priest among high priests, wasn't a naturally religious man. It wasn't a desirable quality in a high priest, it affected your judgement, made you *unsound*. Start believing in things and the whole business became a farce.

Not that he had anything against belief. People needed to believe in gods, if only because it was so hard to believe in people. The gods were necessary. He just required that they stayed out of the way and let him get on with things.

Mind you, it was a blessing that he had the looks for it. If your genes saw fit to give you a tall frame, a bald head and a nose you could plough rocks with, they probably had a definite aim in mind.

He instinctively distrusted people to whom religion came easily. The naturally religious, he felt, were unstable and given to wandering in the desert and having revelations — as if the gods would lower themselves to that sort of thing. And they never got anything done. They started thinking that rituals weren't important. They started thinking that you could talk to the gods direct. Dios knew, with the kind of rigid and unbending certainty you could pivot the world on, that the gods of Djelibeybi liked ritual as much as anyone else. After all, a god who was against ritual would be like a fish who was against water.

He sat on the steps of the throne with his staff across his knees, and passed on the king's orders. The fact that they were not currently being issued by any king was not a problem. Dios had been high priest now for, well, more years than he cared to remember, he knew quite clearly what orders a sensible king would be giving, and he gave them.

Anyway, the Face of the Sun was on the throne, and that was what mattered. It was a solid gold, head-enveloping mask, to be worn by the current ruler on all public occasions; its expression, to the sacrilegious, was one of good-natured constipation. For thousands of years it had symbolised kingship in Djelibeybi. It had also made it very difficult to tell kings apart.

This was extremely symbolic as well, although no-one could remember what of.

There was a lot of that sort of thing in the Old Kingdom. The staff across his knees, for example, with its very symbolic snakes entwined symbolically around an allegorical camel prod. The people believed this gave the high priests power over the gods and the dead, but this was probably a metaphor, i.e., a lie.

Dios shifted position.

"Has the king been ushered to the Room of Going Forth?" he said.

The circle of lesser high priests nodded.

"Dil the embalmer is attending upon him at this instant, O Dios."

"Very well. And the builder of pyramids has been instructed?"

Hoot Koomi, high priest of Khefin, the Two-Faced God of Gateways, stepped forward.

"I took the liberty of attending to that myself, O Dios," he purred.

Dios tapped his fingers on his staff. "Yes," he said, "I have no doubt that you did."

It was widely expected by the priesthood that Koomi would be the one to succeed Dios in the event of Dios ever actually dying, although hanging around waiting for Dios to die had never seemed to be a rewarding occupation. The only dissenting opinion was that of Dios himself who, if he had any friends, would probably have confided in them certain conditions that would need to apply first, viz., blue moons, aerial pigs and he, Dios, being seen in Hell. He would probably have added that the only difference between Koomi and a sacred crocodile was the crocodile's basic honesty of purpose.

"Very well," he said.

"If I may remind your lordship?" said Koomi. The faces of the other priests went a nice safe blank as Dios glared.

"Yes, Koomi?"

"The prince, O Dios. Has he been summoned?"

"No," said Dios.

"Then how will he know?" said Koomi.

"He will know," said Dios firmly.

"How will this be?"

"He will *know*. And now you are all dismissed. Go away. See to your gods!"

They scurried out, leaving Dios alone on the steps. It had been his accustomed position for so long that he'd polished a groove in the stonework, into which he fitted exactly.

Of course the prince would know. It was part of the neatness of things. But in the grooves of his mind, ground deep by the years of ritual and due observance, Dios detected a certain uneasiness. It was not at home in there. Uneasiness was something that happened to other people. He hadn't got where he was today by allowing room for doubt. Yet there was a tiny thought back there, a tiny *certainty*, that there was going to be trouble with this new king.

Well. The boy would soon learn. They all learned.

He shifted position, and winced. The aches and pains were back, and he couldn't allow that. They got in the way of his duty, and his duty was a sacred trust.

He'd have to visit the necropolis again. Tonight.

*

"He's not himself, you can see that."

"Who is he, then?" said Chidder.

They splashed unsteadily down the street, not drunkenly this time, but with the awkward gait of two people trying to do the steering for three. Teppic was walking, but not in a way that gave them any confidence that his mind was having any part of it.

Around them doors were being thrown open, curses were being cursed, there was the sound of furniture being dragged up to first-floor rooms.

"Must have been a hell of a storm up in the mountains," said Arthur. "It doesn't usually flood like this even in the spring."

"Maybe we should burn some feathers under his nose," suggested Chidder.

"That bloody seagull would be favourite," Arthur growled.

"What seagull?"

"You saw it."

"Well, what about it?"

"You *did* see it, didn't you?" Uncertainty flickered its dark flame in Arthur's eyes. The seagull had disappeared in all the excitement.

"My attention was a bit occupied," said Chidder diffidently. "It must have been those mint wafers they served with the coffee. I thought they were a bit off."

"Definitely a touch eldritch, that bird," said Arthur. "Look, let's put him down somewhere while I empty the water out of my boots, can we?"

There was a bakery nearby, its doors thrown open so that the trays of new loaves could cool in the early morning. They propped Teppic against the wall.

"He looks as though someone hit him on the head," said Chidder. "No-one did, did they?"

Arthur shook his head. Teppic's face was locked in a gentle grin. Whatever his eyes were focused on wasn't occupying the usual set of dimensions.

"We ought to get him back to the Guild and into the san — "

He stopped. There was a peculiar rustling sound behind him. The loaves of bread were bouncing gently on their trays. One or two of them vibrated on to the floor, where they spun around like overturned beetles.

Then, their crusts cracking open like eggshells, they sprouted hundreds of green shoots.

Within a few seconds the trays were waving stands of young corn, their heads already beginning to fill out and bend over. Through them marched Chidder and Arthur, poker-faced, doing the 100-metre nonchalant walk with Teppic held rigidly between them.

"Is it him doing all this?"

"I've got a feeling that — " Arthur looked behind them, just in case any angry bakers had come out and spotted such aggressively wholemeal produce, and stopped so suddenly that the other two swung around him, like a rudder.

They looked thoughtfully at the street.

"Not something you see every day, that," said Chidder at last.

"You mean the way there's grass and stuff growing up everywhere he puts his feet?"

"Yes."

Their eyes met. As one, they looked down at Teppic's shoes. He was already ankle-deep in greenery, which was cracking the centuries-old cobbles in its urgency.

Without speaking a word, they gripped his elbows and lifted him into the air.

"The san," said Arthur.

"The san," agreed Chidder.

But they both knew, even then, that this was going to involve more than a hot poultice.

The doctor sat back.

"Fairly straightforward," he said, thinking quickly. "A case of *mortis portalis tackulatum* with complications."

"What's that mean?" said Chidder.

"In layman's terms," the doctor sniffed, "he's as dead as a doornail."

"What are the complications?"

The doctor looked shifty. "He's still breathing," he said. "Look, his pulse is nearly humming and he's got a temperature you could fry eggs on." He hesitated, aware that this was

probably too straightforward and easily understood; medicine
was a new art on the Disc, and wasn't going to get anywhere if
people could understand it.

"*Pyrocerebrum ouerf culinaire*," he said, after working it out
in his head.

"Well, what can you do about it?" said Arthur.

"Nothing. He's dead. All the medical tests prove it. So, er . . .
bury him, keep him nice and cool, and tell him to come and see
me next week. In daylight, for preference."

"But he's still breathing!"

"These are just reflex actions that might easily confuse the
layman," said the doctor airily.

Chidder sighed. He suspected that the Guild, who after all
had an unrivalled experience of sharp knives and complex
organic compounds, were much better at elementary
diagnostics than were the doctors. The Guild might kill people,
but at least it didn't expect them to be grateful for it.

Teppic opened his eyes.

"I must go home," he said.

"Dead, is he?" said Chidder.

The doctor was a credit to his profession. "It's not unusual for
a corpse to make distressing noises after death," he said
valiantly, "which can upset relatives and — "

Teppic sat bolt upright.

"Also, muscular spasms in the stiffening body can in certain
circumstances — " the doctor began, but his heart wasn't in it
any more. Then an idea occurred to him.

"It's a rare and mysterious ailment," he said, "which is going
around a lot at the moment. It's caused by a — a — by something
so small it can't be detected in any way whatsoever," he
finished, with a self-congratulatory smile on his face. It was a
good one, he had to admit. He'd have to remember it.

"Thank you very much," said Chidder, opening the door and
ushering him through. "Next time we're feeling really well,
we'll definitely call you in."

"It's probably a walrus," said the doctor, as he was gently but
firmly propelled out of the room. "He's caught a walrus, there's
a lot of it going — "

The door slammed shut.

Teppic swung his legs off the bed and clutched at his head.

"I've got to go home," he repeated.

"Why?" said Arthur.

"Don't know. The kingdom wants me."

"You seemed to be taken pretty bad there — " Arthur began. Teppic waved his hands dismissively.

"Look," he said, "please, I don't want anyone sensibly pointing out things. I don't want anyone telling me I should rest. None of it matters. I will be back in the kingdom as soon as possible. It's not a case of *must*, you understand. I *will*. And you can help me, Chiddy."

"How?"

"Your father has an extremely fast vessel he uses for smuggling," said Teppic flatly. "He will lend it to me, in exchange for favourable consideration of future trading opportunities. If we leave inside the hour, it will do the journey in plenty of time."

"My father is an honest trader!"

"On the contrary. Seventy per cent of his income last year was from undeclared trading in the following commodities — " Teppic's eyes stared into nothingness — "From illegal transport of gullanes and leuchars, nine per cent. From nightrunning of untaxed — "

"Well, thirty per cent honest," Chidder admitted, "which is a lot more honest than most. You'd better tell me how you know. Extremely quickly."

"I — don't know," said Teppic. "When I was...asleep, it seemed I knew everything. Everything about everything. I think my father is dead."

"Oh," said Chidder. "Gosh. I'm sorry."

"Oh, no. It's not like that. It's what he would have wanted. I think he was rather looking forward to it. In our family, death is when you really start to, you know, enjoy life. I expect he's rather enjoying it."

In fact the pharaoh was sitting on a spare slab in the ceremonial preparation room watching his own soft bits being carefully removed from his body and put into the special canopic jars.

This is not a sight often seen by people — at least, not by people in a position to take a thoughtful interest.

He was rather upset. Although he was no longer officially inhabiting his body he was still attached to it by some sort of occult bond, and it is hard to be very happy at seeing two artisans up to the elbows in bits of you.

The jokes aren't funny, either. Not when you are, as it were, the butt.

"Look, master Dil," said Gern, a plump, red-faced young man who the king had learned was the new apprentice, "Look ... right ... watch this, watch this ... look ... your name in lights. Get it? Your name in lights, see?"

"Just put them in the jar, boy," said Dil wearily. "And while we're on the subject I didn't think much of the Gottle of Geer routine, either."

"Sorry, master."

"And pass me over a number three brain hook while you're up that end, will you?"

"Coming right up, master," said Gern.

"And don't jog me. This is a fiddly bit."

"Sure thing."

The king craned nearer.

Gern rummaged around at his end of the job and then gave a long, low whistle.

"Will you look at the colour of this!" he said. "You wouldn't think so, would you? Is it something they eat, master?"

Dil sighed. "Just put it in the pot, Gern."

"Right you are, master. Master?"

"Yes, lad?"

"Which bit's got the god in it, master?"

Dil squinted up the king's nostril, trying to concentrate.

"That gets sorted out before he comes down here," he said patiently.

"I wondered," said Gern, "because there's not a jar for it, see."

"No. There wouldn't be. It'd have to be a rather strange jar, Gern."

Gern looked a bit disappointed. "Oh," he said, "so he's just ordinary, then, is he?"

"In a strictly organic sense," said Dil, his voice slightly muffled.

"Our mum said he was all right as a king," said Gern. "What do you think?"

Dil paused with a jar in his hand, and seemed to give the conversation some thought for the first time.

"Never think about it until they come down here," he said. "I suppose he was better than most. Nice pair of lungs. Clean kidneys. Good big sinuses, which is what I always look for in a king." He looked down, and delivered his professional judgement. "Pleasure to work with, really."

"Our mum said his heart was in the right place," said Gern. The king, hovering dismally in the corner, gave a gloomy nod. Yes, he thought. Jar three, top shelf.

Dil wiped his hands on a rag, and sighed. Possibly thirty-five years in the funeral business, which had given him a steady hand, a philosophic manner and a keen interest in vegetarianism, had also granted him powers of hearing beyond the ordinary. Because he was almost persuaded that, right beside his ear, someone else sighed too.

The king wandered sadly over to the other side of the room, and stared at the dull liquid of the preparation vat.

Funny, that. When he was alive it had all seemed so sensible, so *obvious*. Now he was dead it looked a huge waste of effort.

It was beginning to annoy him. He watched Dil and his apprentice tidy up, burn some ceremonial resins, lift him — it— up, carry it respectfully across the room and slide it gently into the oily embrace of the preservative.

Teppicymon XXVII gazed into the murky depths at his own body lying sadly on the bottom, like the last pickled gherkin in the jar.

He raised his eyes to the sacks in the corner. They were full of straw. He didn't need telling what was going to be done with it.

The boat didn't glide. It *insinuated* itself through the water, dancing across the waves on the tips of the twelve oars, spreading like an oil slick, gliding like a bird. It was matt black and shaped like a shark.

There was no drummer to beat the rhythm. The boat didn't want the weight. Anyway, he'd have needed the full kit, including snares.

Teppic sat between the lines of silent rowers, in the narrow gully that was the cargo hold. Better not to speculate what cargoes. The boat looked designed to move very small quantities of things very quickly and without anyone noticing, and he doubted whether even the Smugglers' Guild was aware of its existence. Commerce was more interesting than he thought.

They found the delta with suspicious ease — how many times had this whispering shadow slipped up the river, he wondered — and above the exotic smells from the mysterious former cargo he could detect the scents of home. Crocodile dung. Reed pollen. Waterlily blossoms. Lack of plumbing. The rank of lions and reek of hippos.

The leading oarsman tapped him gently on the shoulder and motioned him up, steadied him as he stepped overboard into a few feet of water. By the time he'd waded ashore the boat had turned and was a mere suspicion of a shadow downstream.

Because he was naturally curious, Teppic wondered where it would lie up during the day, since it had the look about it of a boat designed to travel only under cover of darkness, and decided that it'd probably lurk somewhere in the high reed marshes on the delta.

And because he was now a king, he made a mental note to have the marshes patrolled periodically from now on. A king should know things.

He stopped, ankle deep in river ooze. He had known *everything*.

Arthur had rambled on vaguely about seagulls and rivers and loaves of bread sprouting, which suggested he'd drunk too much. All Teppic could remember was waking up with a terrible sense of loss, as his memory failed to hold and leaked away its new treasures. It was like the tremendous insights that come in dreams and vanish on waking. He'd known everything, but as soon as he tried to remember what it was it poured out of his head, as from a leaky bucket.

But it had left him with a new sensation. Before, his life had been ambling along, bent by circumstance. Now it was clicking along on bright rails. Perhaps he hadn't got it in him to be an assassin, but he knew he could be a king.

His feet found solid ground. The boat had dropped him off a little way downstream of the palace and, blue in the moonlight, the pyramid flares on the far bank were filling the night with their familiar glow.

The abodes of the happy dead came in all sizes although not, of course, in all shapes. They clustered thickly nearer the city, as though the dead like company.

And even the oldest ones were all complete. No-one had borrowed any of the stones to build houses or make roads. Teppic felt obscurely proud of that. No-one had unsealed the doors and wandered around inside to see if the dead had any old treasures they weren't using any more. And every day, without fail, food was left in the little antechambers; the commissaries of the dead occupied a large part of the palace.

Sometimes the food went, sometimes it didn't. The priests, however, were very clear on this point. Regardless of whether the food was consumed or not, *it had been eaten by the dead.* Presumably they enjoyed it; they never complained, or came back for seconds.

Look after the dead, said the priests, and the dead would look after you. After all, they were in the majority.

Teppic pushed aside the reeds. He straightened his clothing, brushed some mud off his sleeve and set off for the palace.

Ahead of him, dark against the flarelight, stood the great statue of Khuft. Seven thousand years ago Khuft had led his people out of — Teppic couldn't remember, but somewhere where they hadn't liked being, probably, and for thoroughly good reasons; it was at times like this he wished he knew more history — and had prayed in the desert and the gods of the place had shown him the Old Kingdom. And he had entered, yea, and taken possession thereof, that it should ever be the dwelling place of his seed. Something like that, anyway. There were probably more yeas and a few verilys, with added milk and honey. But the sight of that great patriarchal face, that outstretched arm, that chin you could crack stones on, bold in the flarelight, told him what he already knew.

He was home, and he was never going to leave again.
The sun began to rise.

The greatest mathematician alive on the Disc, and in fact the last one in the Old Kingdom, stretched out in his stall and counted the pieces of straw in his bedding. Then he estimated the number of nails in the wall. Then he spent a few minutes proving that an automorphic resonance field has a semi-infinite number of irresolute prime ideals. After that, in order to pass the time, he ate his breakfast again.

BOOK II

The Book of the Dead

Two weeks went past. Ritual and ceremony in their due times kept the world under the sky and the stars in their courses. It was astonishing what ritual and ceremony could do.

The new king examined himself in the mirror, and frowned.

"What's it made of?" he said. "It's rather foggy."

"Bronze, sire. Polished bronze," said Dios, handing him the Flail of Mercy.

"In Ankh-Morpork we had glass mirrors with silver on the back. They were very good."

"Yes, sire. Here we have bronze, sire."

"Do I really have to wear this gold mask?"

"The Face of the Sun, sire. Handed down through all the ages. Yes, sire. On all public occasions, sire."

Teppic peered out through the eye slots. It was certainly a handsome face. It smiled faintly. He remembered his father visiting the nursery one day and forgetting to take it off; Teppic had screamed the place down.

"It's rather heavy."

"It is weighted with the centuries," said Dios, and passed over the obsidian Reaping Hook of Justice.

"Have you been a priest long, Dios?"

"Many years, sire, man and eunuch. Now — "

"Father said you were high priest even in grandad's time. You must be very old."

"Well-preserved, sir. The gods have been kind to me," said Dios, in the face of the evidence. "And now, sire, if we could just hold this as well . . ."

"What is it?"

"The Honeycomb of Increase, sire. Very important."

Teppic juggled it into position.

"I expect you've seen a lot of changes," he said politely.

A look of pain passed over the old priest's face, but quickly, as if it was in a hurry to get away. "No, sire," he said smoothly, "I have been very fortunate."

"Oh. What's this?"

"The Sheaf of Plenty, sire. Extremely significant, very symbolic."

"If you could just tuck it under my arm, then . . . Have you ever heard of plumbing, Dios?"

The priest snapped his fingers at one of the attendants. "No, sire," he said, and leaned forward. "This is the Asp of Wisdom. I'll just tuck it in here, shall I?"

"It's like buckets, but not as, um, smelly."

"Sounds dreadful, sire. The smell keeps bad influences away, I have always understood. This, sire, is the Gourd of the Waters of the Heavens. If we could just raise our chin . . ."

"This is all necessary, is it?" said Teppic indistinctly.

"It is traditional, sire. If we could just rearrange things a little, sire . . . here is the Three-Pronged Spear of the Waters of the Earth; I think we will be able to get *this* finger around it. We shall have to see about our marriage, sire."

"I'm not sure we would be compatible, Dios."

The high priest smiled with his mouth. "Sire is pleased to jest, sire," he said urbanely. "However, it is essential that you marry."

"I am afraid all the girls I know are in Ankh-Morpork," said Teppic airily, knowing in his heart that this broad statement referred to Mrs Collar, who had been his bedder in the sixth form, and one of the serving wenches who'd taken a shine to him and always gave him extra gravy. (But . . . and his blood pounded at the memory . . . there had been the annual Assassin's Ball and, because the young assassins were trained to move freely in society and were expected to dance well, and because well-cut black silk and long legs attracted a certain type of older woman, they'd whirled the night away through baubons, galliards and slow-stepping pavonines, until the air thickened with musk and hunger. Chidder, whose simple open face and easygoing manner were a winner every time, came

back to bed very late for days afterwards and tended to fall
asleep during lessons...)

"Quite unsuitable, sire. We would require a consort well-
versed in the observances. Of course, our aunt is available,
sire."

There was a clatter. Dios sighed, and motioned the attendants
to pick things up.

"If we could just begin again, sire? This is the Cabbage of
Vegetative Increase — "

"Sorry," said Teppic, "I didn't hear you say I should marry my
aunt, did I?"

"You did, sire. Interfamilial marriage is a proud tradition of
our lineage," said Dios.

"But my aunt is my *aunt*!"

Dios rolled his eyes. He'd advised the late king repeatedly
about the education of his son, but the man was stubborn,
stubborn. Now he'd have to do it on the fly. The gods were
testing him, he decided. It took decades to make a monarch, and
he had weeks to do it in.

"Yes, sire," he said patiently. "Of course. And she is also your
uncle, your cousin and your father."

"Hold on. My father — "

The priest raised his hand soothingly. "A technicality," he
said. "Your great-great-grandmother once declared she is king
as a matter of political expediency and I don't believe the edict
is ever rescinded."

"But she *was* a woman, though?"

Dios looked shocked. "Oh no, sire. She is a man. She herself
declared this."

"But look, a chap's aunt — "

"Quite so, sire. I quite understand."

"Well, thank you," said Teppic.

"It is a great shame that we have no sisters."

"Sisters!"

"It does not do to water the divine blood, sire. The sun might
not like it. Now *this*, sire, is the Scapula of Hygiene. Where
would you like it put?"

*

King Teppicymon XXVII was watching himself being stuffed. It was just as well he didn't feel hunger these days. Certainly he would never want to eat chicken again.

"Very nice stitching there, master."

"Just keep your finger still, Gern."

"My mother does stitching like that. She's got a pinny with stitching like that, has our mum," said Gern conversationally.

"Keep it still, I said."

"It's got all ducks and hens on it," Gern supplied helpfully.

Dil concentrated on the job in hand. It was good workmanship, he was prepared to admit. The Guild of Embalmers and Allied Trades had awarded him medals for it.

"It must make you feel really proud," said Gern.

"What?"

"Well, our mam says the king goes on living, sort of thing, after all this stuffing and stitching. Sort of in the Netherworld. With your stitching in him."

And several sacks of straw and a couple of buckets of pitch, thought the shade of the king sadly. And the wrapping off Gern's lunch, although he didn't blame the lad, who'd just forgotten where he'd put it. All eternity with someone's lunch wrapping as part of your vital organs. There had been half a sausage left, too.

He'd become quite attached to Dil, and even to Gern. He seemed still to be attached to his body, too — at least, he felt uncomfortable if he wandered more than a few hundred yards away from it — and so in the course of the last couple of days he'd learned quite a lot about them.

Funny, really. He'd spent the whole of his life in the kingdom talking to a few priests and so forth. He knew objectively there had been other people around — servants and gardeners and so forth — but they figured in his life as blobs. He was at the top, and then his family, and then the priests and the nobles of course, and then there were the blobs. Damn fine blobs, of course, some of the finest blobs in the world, as loyal a collection of blobs as a king might hope to rule. But blobs, none the less.

But now he was absolutely engrossed in the daily details of Dil's shy hopes for advancement within the Guild, and the unfolding story of Gern's clumsy overtures to Glwenda, the

garlic farmer's daughter who lived nearby. He listened in
fascinated astonishment to the elaboration of a world as full of
subtle distinctions of grade and station as the one he had so
recently left; it was terrible to think that he might never know
if Gern overcame her father's objections and won his intended,
or if Dil's work on this job — on *him* — would allow him to aspire
to the rank of Exalted Grand Ninety-Degree Variance of the
Natron Lodge of the Guild of Embalmers and Allied Trades.

It was as if death was some astonishing optical device which
turned even a drop of water into a complex hive of life.

He found an overpowering urge to counsel Dil on elementary
politics, or apprise Gern of the benefits of washing and looking
respectable. He tried it several times. They could sense him, there
was no doubt about that. But they just put it down to draughts.

Now he watched Dil pad over to the big table of bandages, and
come back with a thick swatch which he held reflectively against
what even the king was now prepared to think of as his corpse.

"I think the linen," he said at last. "It's definitely his colour."

Gern put his head on one side.

"He'd look good in the hessian," he said. "Or maybe the
calico."

"Not the calico. Definitely not the calico. On him it's too big."

"He could moulder into it. With wear, you know."

Dil snorted. "Wear? Wear? You shouldn't talk to me about
calico and wear. What happens if someone robs the tomb in a
thousand years' time and him in calico, I'd like to know. He'd
lurch halfway down the corridor, maybe throttle one of them,
I'll grant you, but then he's coming undone, right? The elbows'll
be out in no time, I'll never live it down."

"But you'll be dead, master!"

"Dead? What's that got to do with it?" Dil riffled through the
samples. "No, it'll be the hessian. Got plenty of give in it,
hessian. Good traction, too. He'll really be able to lurch up speed
in the passages, if he ever needs to."

The king sighed. He'd have preferred something lightweight
in taffeta.

"And go and shut the door," Dil added. "It's getting breezy in
here."

*

"And now it's time," said the high priest, "for us to see our late father." He allowed himself a quiet smile. "I am sure he is looking forward to it," he added.

Teppic considered this. It wasn't something *he* was looking forward to, but at least it would get everyone's mind off him marrying relatives. He reached down in what he hoped was a kingly fashion to stroke one of the palace cats. This also was not a good move. The creature sniffed it, went cross-eyed with the effort of thought, and then bit his fingers.

"Cats are sacred," said Dios, shocked at the words Teppic uttered.

"Long-legged cats with silver fur and disdainful expressions are, maybe," said Teppic, nursing his hand, "I don't know about this sort. I'm sure sacred cats don't leave dead ibises under the bed. And I'm certain that sacred cats that live surrounded by endless sand don't come indoors and do it in the king's sandals, Dios."

"All cats are cats," said Dios, vaguely, and added, "If we would be so gracious as to follow us." He motioned Teppic towards a distant arch.

Teppic followed slowly. He'd been back home for what seemed like ages, and it still didn't feel right. The air was too dry. The clothes felt wrong. It was too hot. Even the buildings seemed wrong. The pillars, for one thing. Back ho — back at the Guild, pillars were graceful fluted things with little bunches of stone grapes and things around the top. Here they were massive pear-shaped lumps, where all the stone had run to the bottom.

Half a dozen servants trailed behind him, carrying the various items of regalia.

He tried to imitate Dios's walk, and found the movements coming back to him. You turned your torso *this* way, then you turned your head *this* way, and extended your arms at forty-five degrees to your body with the palms down, and then you attempted to move.

The high priest's staff raised echoes as it touched the flagstones. A blind man could have walked barefoot through the palace by tracing the time-worn dimples it had created over the years.

"I am afraid that we will find that our father has changed

somewhat since we last saw him," said Dios conversationally, as they undulated by the fresco of Queen Khaphut accepting Tribute from the Kingdoms of the World.

"Well, yes," said Teppic, bewildered by the tone. "He's dead, isn't he?"

"There's that, too," said Dios, and Teppic realised that he hadn't been referring to something as trivial as the king's current physical condition.

He was lost in a horrified admiration. It wasn't that Dios was particularly cruel or uncaring, it was simply that death was a mere irritating transition in the eternal business of existence. The fact that people died was just an inconvenience, like them being out when you called.

It's a strange world, he thought. It's all busy shadows, and it never changes. And I'm part of it.

"Who's he?" he said, pointing to a particularly big fresco showing a tall man with a hat like a chimney and a beard like a rope riding a chariot over a lot of other, much smaller, people.

"His name *is* in the cartouche below," said Dios primly.

"What?"

"The small oval, sire," said Dios.

Teppic peered closely at the dense hieroglyphics.

"'Thin eagle, eye, wiggly line, man with a stick, bird sitting down, wiggly line'," he read. Dios winced.

"I believe we must apply ourselves more to the study of modern languages," he said, recovering a bit. "His name is Pta-ka-ba. He is king when the Djel Empire extends from the Circle Sea to the Rim Ocean, when almost half the continent pays tribute to us."

Teppic realised what it was about the man's speech that was strange. Dios would bend any sentence to breaking point if it meant avoiding a past tense. He pointed to another fresco.

"And her?" he said.

"She is Queen Khat-leon-ra-pta," said Dios. "She wins the kingdom of Howandaland by stealth. This is the time of the Second Empire."

"But she is dead?" said Teppic.

"I understand so," said the high priest, after the slightest of pauses. Yes. The past tense definitely bothered Dios.

"I have learned seven languages," said Teppic, secure in the knowledge that the actual marks he had achieved in three of them would remain concealed in the ledgers of the Guild.

"Indeed, sire?"

"Oh, yes. Morporkian, Vanglemesht, Ephebe, Laotation and — several others . . ." said Teppic.

"Ah." Dios nodded, smiled, and continued to proceed down the corridor, limping slightly but still measuring his pace like the ticking of centuries. "The barbarian lands."

Teppic looked at his father. The embalmers had done a good job. They were waiting for him to tell them so.

Part of him, which still lived in Ankh-Morpork, said: this is a dead body, wrapped up in bandages, surely they can't think that this will help him *get better*? In Ankh, you die and they bury you or burn you or throw you to the ravens. Here, it just means you slow down a bit and get given all the best food. It's ridiculous, how can you run a kingdom like this? They seem to think that being dead is like being deaf, you just have to speak up a bit.

But a second, older voice said: We've run a kingdom like this for seven thousand years. The humblest melon farmer has a lineage that makes kings elsewhere look like mayflies. We used to own the continent, before we sold it again to pay for pyramids. We don't even *think* about other countries less than three thousand years old. It all seems to work.

"Hallo, father," he said.

The shade of Teppicymon XXVII, which had been watching him closely, hurried across the room.

"You're looking well!" he said. *"Good to see you! Look, this is urgent. Please pay attention, it's about death — "*

"He says he is pleased to see you," said Dios.

"You can hear him?" said Teppic. "I didn't hear anything."

"The dead, naturally, speak through the priests," said the priest. "That is the custom, sire."

"But he can hear me, can he?"

"Of course."

"I've been thinking about this whole pyramid business and, look, I'm not certain about it."

Teppic leaned closer. "Auntie sends her love," he said loudly. He thought about this. "That's my aunt, not yours." I hope, he added.

"I say? I say? Can you hear me?"

"He bids you greetings from the world beyond the veil," said Dios.

"Well, yes, I suppose I do, but LOOK, I don't want you to go to a lot of trouble and build — "

"We're going to build you a marvellous pyramid, father. You'll really like it there. There'll be people to look after you and everything." Teppic glanced at Dios for reassurance. "He'll like that, won't he?"

"I don't WANT one!" screamed the king. *"There's a whole interesting eternity I haven't seen yet. I forbid you to put me in a pyramid!"*

"He says that is very proper, and you are a dutiful son," said Dios.

"Can you see me? How many fingers am I holding up? Think it's fun, do you, spending the rest of your death under a million tons of rock, watching yourself crumble to bits? Is that your idea of a good epoch?"

"It's rather draughty in here, sire," said Dios. "Perhaps we should get on."

"Anyway, you can't possibly afford it!"

"And we'll put your favourite frescoes and statues in with you. You'll like that, won't you," said Teppic desperately. "All your bits and pieces around you."

"He will like it, won't he?" he asked Dios, as they walked back to the throne room. "Only, I don't know, I somehow got a feeling he isn't too happy about it."

"I assure you, sire," said Dios, "he can have no other desire."

Back in the embalming room King Teppicymon XXVII tried to tap Gern on the shoulder, which had no effect. He gave up and sat down beside himself.

"Don't do it, lad," he said bitterly. *"Never have descendants."*

*

And then there was the Great Pyramid itself.

Teppic's footsteps echoed on the marble tiles as he walked around the model. He wasn't sure what one was supposed to do here. But kings, he suspected, were often put in that position; there was always the good old fallback, which was known as taking an interest.

"Well, well," he said. "How long have you been designing pyramids?"

Ptaclusp, architect and jobbing pyramid builder to the nobility, bowed deeply.

"All my life, O light of noonday."

"It must be fascinating," said Teppic. Ptaclusp looked sidelong at the high priest, who nodded.

"It has its points, O fount of waters," he ventured. He wasn't used to kings talking to him as though he was a human being. He felt obscurely that it wasn't right.

Teppic waved a hand at the model on its podium.

"Yes," he said uncertainly. "Well. Good. Four walls and a pointy tip. Jolly good. First class. Says it all, really." There still seemed to be too much silence around. He plunged on.

"Good show," he said. "I mean, there's no doubt about it. This is . . . a . . . pyramid. And what a pyramid it is! Indeed."

This still didn't seem enough. He sought for something else. "People will look at it in centuries to come and they'll say, they'll say . . . that *is* a pyramid. Um."

He coughed. "The walls slope nicely," he croaked.

"But," he said.

Two pairs of eyes swivelled towards his.

"Um," he said.

Dios raised an eyebrow.

"Sire?"

"I seem to remember once, my father said that, you know, when he died, he'd quite like to, sort of thing, be buried at sea."

There wasn't the choke of outrage he had expected. "He meant the delta. It's very soft ground by the delta," said Ptaclusp. "It'd take months to get decent footings in. Then there's your risk of sinking. And the damp. Not good, damp, inside a pyramid."

"No," said Teppic, sweating under Dios's gaze, "I think what he meant was, you know, *in* the sea."

Ptaclusp's brow furrowed. "Tricky, that," he said thoughtfully. "Interesting idea. I suppose one *could* build a small one, a million tonner, and float it out on pontoons or something..."

"No," said Teppic, trying not to laugh, "I think what he meant was, buried *without* — "

"Teppicymon XXVII means that he would want to be buried without delay," said Dios, his voice like greased silk. "And there is no doubt that he would require to honour the very best you can build, architect."

"No, I'm sure you've got it wrong," said Teppic.

Dios's face froze. Ptaclusp's slid into the waxen expression of someone with whom it is, suddenly, nothing to do. He started to stare at the floor as if his very survival depended on his memorising it in extreme detail.

"Wrong?" said Dios.

"No offence. I'm sure you mean well," said Teppic. "It's just that, well, he seemed very clear about it at the time and — "

"I mean well?" said Dios, tasting each word as though it was a sour grape. Ptaclusp coughed. He had finished with the floor. Now he started on the ceiling.

Dios took a deep breath. "*Sire*," he said, "we have always been pyramid builders. All our kings are buried in pyramids. It is how we do things, sire. It is how things are done."

"Yes, but — "

"It does not admit of dispute," said Dios. "Who could wish for anything else? Sealed with all artifice against the desecrations of Time — " now the oiled silk of his voice became armour, hard as steel, scornful as spears — "Shielded for all Time against the insults of Change."

Teppic glanced down at the high priest's knuckles. They were white, the bone pressing through the flesh as though in a rage to escape.

His gaze slid up the grey-clad arm to Dios's face. Ye gods, he thought, it's really true, he *does* look like they got tired of waiting for him to die and pickled him anyway. Then his eyes met those of the priest, more or less with a clang.

He felt as though his flesh was being very slowly blown off his bones. He felt that he was no more significant than a mayfly. A necessary mayfly, certainly, a mayfly that would be accorded all due respect, but still an insect with all the rights thereof. And as much free will, in the fury of that gaze, as a scrap of papyrus in a hurricane.

"The king's will is that he be interred in a pyramid," said Dios, in the tone of voice the Creator must have used to sketch out the moon and stars.

"Er," said Teppic.

"The finest of pyramids for the king," said Dios.

Teppic gave up.

"Oh," he said. "Good. Fine. Yes. The very best, of course."

Ptaclusp beamed with relief, produced his wax tablet with a flourish, and took a stylus from the recesses of his wig. The important thing, he knew, was to clinch the deal as soon as possible. Let things slip in a situation like this and a man could find himself with 1,500,000 tons of bespoke limestone on his hands.

"Then that will be the standard model, shall we say, O water in the desert?"

Teppic looked at Dios, who was standing and glaring at nothing now, staring the bulldogs of Entropy into submission by willpower alone.

"I think something larger," he ventured hopelessly.

"That's the Executive," said Ptaclusp. "Very exclusive, O base of the eternal column. Last you a perpetuality. Also our special offer this aeon is various measurements of paracosmic significance built into the very fabric at no extra cost."

He gave Teppic an expectant look.

"Yes. Yes. That will be fine," said Teppic.

Dios took a deep breath. "The king requires far more than that," he said.

"I do?" said Teppic, doubtfully.

"Indeed, sire. It is your express wish that the greatest of monuments is erected for your father," said Dios smoothly. This was a contest, Teppic knew, and he didn't know the rules or how to play and he was going to *lose.*

"It is? Oh. Yes. Yes. I suppose it is, really. Yes."

"A pyramid unequalled along the Djel," said Dios. "That is the command of the king. It is only right and proper."

"Yes, yes, something like that. Er. Twice the normal size," said Teppic desperately, and had the brief satisfaction of seeing Dios look momentarily disconcerted.

"Sire?" he said.

"It is only right and proper," said Teppic.

Dios opened his mouth to protest, saw Teppic's expression, and shut it again.

Ptaclusp scribbled busily, his adam's apple bobbing. Something like this only happened once in a business career.

"Can do you a very nice black marble facing on the outside," he said, without looking up. "We may have *just* enough in the quarry. O king of the celestial orbs," he added hurriedly.

"Very good," said Teppic.

Ptaclusp picked up a fresh tablet. "Shall we say the capstone picked out in electrum? It's cheaper to have built in right from the start, you don't want to use just silver and then say later, I wish I'd had a — "

"Electrum, yes."

"And the usual offices?"

"What?"

"The burial chamber, that is, and the outer chamber. I'd recommend the Memphis, very select, that comes with a matching extra large treasure room, so handy for all those little things one cannot bear to leave behind." Ptaclusp turned the tablet over and started on the other side. "And of course a similar suite for the Queen, I take it? O King who shall live forever."

"Eh? Oh, yes. Yes. I suppose so," said Teppic, glancing at Dios. "Everything. You know."

"Then there's mazes," said Ptaclusp, trying to keep his voice steady. "Very popular this era. Very important, your maze, it's no good deciding you ought to have put a maze in after the robbers have been. Maybe I'm old-fashioned, but I'd go for the Labrys every time. Like we say, they may get in all right, but they'll never get out. It costs that little bit extra, but what's money at a time like this? O master of the waters."

Something we don't have, said a warning voice in the back of Teppic's head. He ignored it. He was in the grip of destiny.

"Yes," he said, straightening up. "The Labrys. Two of them."

Ptaclusp's stylus went through his tablet.

"His 'n hers, O stone of stones," he croaked. "Very handy, very convenient. With selection of traps from stock? We can offer deadfalls, pitfalls, sliders, rolling balls, dropping spears, arrows — "

"Yes, yes," said Teppic. "We'll have them. We'll have them all. All of them."

The architect took a deep breath.

"And of course you'll require all the usual steles, avenues, ceremonial sphinxes — " he began.

"Lots," said Teppic. "We leave it entirely up to you."

Ptaclusp mopped his brow.

"Fine," he said. "Marvellous." He blew his nose. "Your father, if I may make so bold, O sower of the seed, is extremely fortunate in having such a dutiful son. I may add — "

"You may *go*," said Dios. "And we will expect work to start imminently."

"Without delay, I assure you," said Ptaclusp. "Er."

He seemed to be wrestling with some huge philosophical problem.

"Yes?" said Dios coldly.

"It's uh. There's the matter of uh. Which is not to say uh. Of course, oldest client, valued customer, but the fact is that uh. Absolutely no doubt about credit worthiness uh. Would not wish to suggest in any way whatsoever that uh."

Dios gave him a stare that would have caused a sphinx to blink and look away.

"You wish to say something?" he said. "His majesty's time is extremely limited."

Ptaclusp worked his jaw silently, but the result was a foregone conclusion. Even gods had been reduced to sheepish mumbling in the face of Dios's face. And the carved snakes on his staff seemed to be watching him too.

"Uh. No, no. Sorry. I was just, uh, thinking aloud. I'll depart, then, shall I? Such a lot of work to be done. Uh." He bowed low.

He was halfway to the archway before Dios added:

"Completion in three months. In time for Inundation."*

"*What?*"

"You are talking to the 1,398th monarch," said Dios icily.

Ptaclusp swallowed. "I'm sorry," he whispered, "I mean, *what?*, O great king. I mean, block haulage alone will take. Uh." The architect's lips trembled as he tried out various comments and, in his imagination, ran them full tilt into Dios's stare. "Tsort wasn't built in a day," he mumbled.

"We do not believe we laid the specifications for that job," said Dios. He gave Ptaclusp a smile. In some ways it was worse than everything else. "We will, of course," he said, "pay extra."

"But you never pa — " Ptaclusp began, and then sagged.

"The penalties for not completing on time will, of course, be terrible," said Dios. "The usual clause."

Ptaclusp hadn't the nerve left to argue. "Of course," he said, utterly defeated. "It is an honour. Will your eminences excuse me? There are still some hours of daylight left."

Teppic nodded.

"Thank you," said the architect. "May your loins be truly fruitful. Saving your presence, Lord Dios."

They heard him running down the steps outside.

"It will be magnificent. Too big, but — magnificent," said Dios. He looked out between the pillars at the necropolic panorama on the far bank of the Djel.

"Magnificent," he repeated. He winced once more at the stab of pain in his leg. Ah. He'd have to cross the river again tonight, no doubt of it. He'd been foolish, putting it off for days. But it would be unthinkable not to be in a position to serve the kingdom properly...

"Something wrong, Dios?" said Teppic.

"Sire?"

"You looked a bit pale, I thought."

---

*Like many river valley cultures the Kingdom has no truck with such trivia as summer, springtime and winter, and bases its calendar squarely on the great heartbeat of the Djel; hence the three seasons, Seedtime, Inundation and Sog. This is logical, straightforward and practical, and only disapproved of by barbershop quartets.†

†Because you feel an idiot singing "In the Good Old Inundation", that's why.

A look of panic flickered over Dios's wrinkled features. He pulled himself upright.

"I assure, you, sire, I am in the best of health. The best of health, sire!"

"You don't think you've been overdoing it, do you?"

This time there was no mistaking the expression of terror.

"Overdoing what, sire?"

"You're always bustling, Dios. First one up, last one to bed. You should take it easy."

"I exist only to serve, sire, " said Dios, firmly. "I exist only to serve."

Teppic joined him on the balcony. The early evening sun glowed on a man-made mountain range. This was only the central massif; the pyramids stretched from the delta all the way up to the second cataract, where the Djel disappeared into the mountains. And the pyramids occupied the best land, near the river. Even the farmers would have considered it sacrilegious to suggest anything different.

Some of the pyramids were small, and made of rough-hewn blocks that contrived to look far older than the mountains that fenced the valley from the high desert. After all, mountains had always been there. Words like 'young' and 'old' didn't apply to them. But those first pyramids had been built by human beings, little bags of thinking water held up briefly by fragile accumulations of calcium, who had cut rocks into pieces and then painfully put them back together again in a better shape. They were *old*.

Over the millennia the fashions had fluctuated. Later pyramids were smooth and sharp, or flattened and tiled with mica. Even the steepest of them, Teppic mused, wouldn't rate more than 1.0 on any edificeer's scale, although some of the stelae and temples, which flocked around the base of the pyramids like tugboats around the dreadnoughts of eternity, could be worthy of attention.

Dreadnoughts of eternity, he thought, sailing ponderously through the mists of Time with every passenger travelling first class. . .

A few stars had been let out early. Teppic looked up at them. Perhaps, he thought, there is life somewhere else. On the stars, maybe. If it's true that there are billions of universes stacked alongside one another, the thickness of a thought apart, then there must be people elsewhere.

But wherever they are, no matter how mightily they try, no matter how magnificent the effort, they surely can't manage to be as godawfully stupid as us. I mean, we work at it. We were given a spark of it to start with, but over hundreds of thousands of years we've really improved on it.

He turned to Dios, feeling that he ought to repair a little bit of the damage.

"You can feel the age radiating off them, can't you," he said conversationally.

"Pardon, sire?"

"The pyramids, Dios. They're so old."

Dios glanced vaguely across the river. "Are they?" he said. "Yes, I suppose they are."

"Will you get one?" said Teppic.

"A pyramid?" said Dios. "Sire, I have one already. It pleased one of your forebears to make provision for me."

"That must have been a great honour," said Teppic. Dios nodded graciously. The staterooms of forever were usually reserved for royalty.

"It is, of course, very small. Very plain. But it will suffice for my simple needs."

"Will it?" said Teppic, yawning. "That's nice. And now, if you don't mind, I think I'll turn in. It's been a long day."

Dios bowed as though he was hinged in the middle. Teppic had noticed that Dios had at least fifty finely-tuned ways of bowing, each one conveying subtle shades of meaning. This one looked like No.3, I Am Your Humble Servant.

"And a very good day it was too, if I may say so, sire."

Teppic was lost for words. "You thought so?" he said.

"The cloud effects at dawn were particularly effective."

"They were? Oh. Do I have to do anything about the sunset?"

"Your majesty is pleased to joke," said Dios. "Sunsets happen by themselves, sire. Haha."

"Haha," echoed Teppic.

Dios cracked his knuckles. "The trick is in the sunrise," he said.

The crumbling scrolls of Knot said that the great orange sun
was eaten every evening by the sky goddess What, who saved
one pip in time to grow a fresh sun for next morning. And Dios
knew that this was so.

The *Book of Staying in The Pit* said that the sun was the Eye
of Yay, toiling across the sky each day in His endless search for
his toenails.* And Dios knew that this was so.

The secret rituals of the Smoking Mirror held that the sun
was in fact a round hole in the spinning blue soap bubble of the
goddess Nesh, opening into the fiery real world beyond, and the
stars were the holes that the rain comes through. And Dios
knew that this, also, was so.

Folk myth said the sun was a ball of fire which circled the
world every day, and that the world itself was carried through
the everlasting void on the back of an enormous turtle. And
Dios also knew that this was so, although it gave him a bit of
trouble.

And Dios knew that Net was the Supreme God, and that Fon
was the Supreme God, and so were Hast, Set, Bin, Sot, Io, Dhek,
and Ptooie; that Herpetine Triskeles alone ruled the world of
the dead, and so did Syncope, and Silur the Catfish-Headed God,
and Orexis-Nupt.

Dios was maximum high priest to a national religion that had
fermented and accreted and bubbled for more than seven
thousand years and never threw a god away in case it turned
out to be useful. He knew that a great many mutually-
contradictory things were all true. If they were not, then ritual
and belief were as nothing, and if they were nothing, then the
world did not exist. As a result of this sort of thinking, the
priests of the Djel could give mindroom to a collection of ideas
that would make even a quantum mechanic give in and hand
back his toolbox.

Dios's staff knocked echoes from the stones as he limped alone
in the darkness down little-frequented passages until he
emerged on a small jetty. Untying the boat there, the high
priest climbed in with difficulty, unshipped the oars and pushed

---

*Lit. 'Dhar-ret-kar-mon', or 'clipping of the foot'. But some scholars say that it
should be 'Dar-rhet-kare-mhun', lit. 'hot-air paint stripper'.

himself out into the turbid waters of the dark Djel.

His hands and feet felt too cold. Foolish, foolish. He should have done this before.

The boat jerked slowly into midstream as full night rolled over the valley. On the far bank, in response to the ancient laws, the pyramids started to light the sky.

Lights also burned late in the house of Ptaclusp Associates, Necropolitan Builders to the Dynasties. The father and his twin sons were hunched over the huge wax designing tray, arguing.

"It's not as if they ever *pay*," said Ptaclusp IIa. "I mean it's not just a case of not being able to, they don't seem to have grasped the *idea*. At least dynasties like Tsort pay up within a hundred years or so. Why didn't you — "

"We've built pyramids along the Djel for the last three thousand years," said his father stiffly, "and we haven't lost by it, have we? No, we haven't. Because the other kingdoms look to the Djel, they say there's a family that really knows its pyramids, connysewers, they say we'll have what they're having, if you please, with knobs on. Anyway, they're real royalty," he added, "not like some of the ones you get these days — here today, gone next millennium. They're half gods, too. You don't expect real royalty to pay its way. That's one of the signs of real royalty, not having any money."

"You don't get more royal than them, then. You'd need a new word," said IIa. "*We're* nearly royal in that case."

"You don't understand business, my son. You think it's all book-keeping. Well, it isn't."

"*It's a question of mass. And the power to weight ratio.*"

They both glared at Ptaclusp IIb, who was sitting staring at the sketches. He was turning his stylus over and over in his hands, which were trembling with barely-suppressed excitement.

"We'll have to use granite for the lower slopes," he said, talking to himself, "the limestone wouldn't take it. Not with all the power flows. Which will be, whooeee, they'll be big. I mean we're not talking razor blades here. This thing could put an edge on a rolling pin."

Ptaclusp rolled his eyes. He was only one generation into a dynasty and already it was trouble. One son a born accountant, the other in love with this new-fangled cosmic engineering. There hadn't been any such thing when he was a lad, there was just architecture. You drew the plans, and then got in ten thousand lads on time-and-a-half and double bubble at weekends. They just had to pile the stuff up. You didn't have to be *cosmic* about it.

Descendants! The gods had seen fit to give him one son who charged you for the amount of breath expended in saying "Good morning", and another one who worshipped geometry and stayed up all night designing aqueducts. You scrimped and saved to send them to the best schools, and then they went and paid you back by getting educated.

"What are you talking about?" he snapped.

"The discharge alone. . . " IIb pulled his abacus towards him and rattled the pottery beads along the wires. "Let's say we're talking twice the height of the Executive model, which gives us a mass of . . . plus additional coded dimensions of occult significance as per spec. . . we couldn't do this sort of thing even a hundred years ago, you realise, not with the primitive techniques we had then. . . " His finger became a blur.

IIa gave a snort and grabbed his own abacus.

"Limestone at two talents the ton. . . " he said. "Wear and tear on tools. . . masonry charges. . . demurrage. . . breakages . . .oh dear, oh dear. . . on-cost. . . black marble at replacement prices. . . "

Ptaclusp sighed. Two abaci rattling in tandem the whole day long, one changing the shape of the world and the other one deploring the cost. Whatever happened to the two bits of wood and a plumbline?

The last beads clicked against the stops.

"It'd be a whole quantum leap in pyramidology," said IIb, sitting back with a messianic grin on his face.

"It'd be a whole kwa — " IIa began.

"Quantum," said IIb, savouring the word.

"It'd be a whole *quantum* leap in bankruptcy," said IIa. "They'd have to invent a new word for that too."

"It'd be worth it as a loss leader," said IIb.

"Sure enough. When it comes to making a loss, we'll be in the lead," said IIa sourly.

"It'd practically glow! In millennia to come people will look at it and say 'That Ptaclusp, he knew his pyramids all right'."

"They'll call it Ptaclusp's Folly, you mean!"

By now the brothers were both standing up, their noses a few inches apart.

"The trouble with you, sibling, is that you know the cost of everything and the value of nothing!"

"The trouble with *you* is — is — is that you don't!"

"Mankind must strive ever upwards!"

"Yes, on a sound financial footing, by Khuft!"

"The search for knowledge — "

"The search for probity — "

Ptaclusp left them to it and stood staring out at the yard, where, under the glow of torches, the staff were doing a feverish stocktaking.

It'd been a small business when father passed it on to him — just a yard full of blocks and various sphinxes, needles, steles and other stock items, and a thick stack of unpaid bills, most of them addressed to the palace and respectfully pointing out that our esteemed account presented nine hundred years ago appeared to have been overlooked and prompt settlement would oblige. But it had been fun in those days. There was just him, five thousand labourers, and Mrs Ptaclusp doing the books.

You had to do pyramids, dad said. All the profit was in mastabas, small family tombs, memorial needles and general jobbing necropoli, but if you didn't do pyramids, you didn't do anything. The meanest garlic farmer, looking for something neat and long lasting with maybe some green marble chippings but within a budget, wouldn't go to a man without a pyramid to his name.

So he'd done pyramids, and they'd been good ones, not like some you saw these days, with the wrong number of sides and walls you could put your foot through. And yes, somehow they'd gone from strength to strength.

To build the biggest pyramid ever. . .

In three months. . .

With terrible penalties if it wasn't done on time. Dios hadn't specified how terrible, but Ptaclusp knew his man and they probably involved crocodiles. They'd be pretty terrible, all right...

He stared at the flickering light on the long avenues of statues, including the one of bloody Hat the Vulture-Headed God of Unexpected Guests, bought on the offchance years ago and turned down by the client owing to not being up to snuff in the beak department and unshiftable ever since even at a discount.

The biggest pyramid ever...

And after you'd knocked your pipes out seeing to it that the nobility had their tickets to eternity, were you allowed to turn your expertise homeward, i.e., a bijou pyramidette for self and Mrs Ptaclusp, to ensure safe delivery into the Netherworld? Of course not. Even dad had only been allowed to have a mastaba, although it was one of the best on the river, he had to admit, that red-veined marble had been ordered all the way from Howonderland, a lot of people had asked for the same, it had been good for business, that's how dad would have liked it...

The biggest pyramid ever...

And they'd never remember who was under it.

It didn't matter if they called it Ptaclusp's Folly or Ptaclusp's Glory. They'd call it *Ptaclusp's*.

He surfaced from this pool of thought to hear his sons still arguing.

If this was his posterity, he'd take his chances with 600-ton limestone blocks. At least they were quiet.

"Shut up, the pair of you," he said.

They stopped, and sat down, grumbling.

"I've made up my mind," he said.

IIb doodled fitfully with his stylus. IIa strummed his abacus.

"We're going to do it," said Ptaclusp, and strode out of the room. "And any son who doesn't like it will be cast into the outer darkness where there is a wailing and a crashing of teeth," he called over his shoulder.

The two brothers, left to themselves, glowered at each other.

At last IIa said, "What does 'quantum' mean, anyway?"

IIb shrugged. "It means add another nought," he said.

"Oh," said IIa, "is that all?"

*

All along the river valley of the Djel the pyramids were flaring silently into the night, discharging the accumulated power of the day.

Great soundless flames erupted from their capstones and danced upwards, jagged as lightning, cold as ice.

For hundreds of miles the desert glittered with the constellations of the dead, the aurora of antiquity. But along the valley of the Djel the lights ran together in one solid ribbon of fire.

It was on the floor and it had a pillow at one end. It had to be a bed.

Teppic found he was doubting it as he tossed and turned, trying to find some part of the mattress that was prepared to meet him halfway. This is stupid, he thought, I grew up on beds like this. And pillows carved out of rock. I was born in this palace, this is my heritage, I must be prepared to accept it . . .

I must order a proper bed and a feather pillow from Ankh, first thing in the morning. I, the king, have said this shall be done.

He turned over, his head hitting the pillow with a thud.

And plumbing. What a great idea that was. It was amazing what you could do with a hole in the ground.

Yes, plumbing. And bloody doors. Teppic definitely wasn't used to having several attendants waiting on his will all the time, so performing his ablutions before bed had been extremely embarrassing. And the people, too. He was definitely going to get to know the people. It was wrong, all this skulking in palaces.

And how was a fellow supposed to sleep with the sky over the river glowing like a firework?

Eventually sheer exhaustion wrestled his body into some zone between sleeping and waking, and mad images stalked across his eyeballs.

There was the shame of his ancestors when future archaeologists translated the as-yet unpainted frescoes of his reign: " 'Squiggle, constipated eagle, wiggly line, hippo's bottom, squiggle': And in the year of the Cycle of Cephnet the Sun God Teppic had Plumbing Installed and Scorned the Pillows of his Forebears."

He dreamed of Khuft — huge, bearded, speaking in thunder and lightning, calling down the wrath of the heavens on this descendant who was betraying the noble past.

Dios floated past his vision, explaining that as a result of an edict passed several thousand years ago it was essential that he marry a cat.

Various-headed gods vied for his attention, explaining details of godhood, while in the background a distant voice tried to attract his attention and screamed something about not wanting to be buried under a load of stone. But he had no time to concentrate on this, because he saw seven fat cows and seven thin cows, one of them playing a trombone.

But that was an old dream, he dreamt that one nearly every night...

And then there was a man firing arrows at a tortoise...

And then he was walking over the desert and found a tiny pyramid, only a few inches high. A wind sprang up and blew away the sand, only now it wasn't a wind, it was the pyramid rising, sand tumbling down its gleaming sides...

And it grew bigger and bigger, bigger than the world, so that at last the pyramid was so big that the whole world was a speck in the centre.

And in the centre of the pyramid, something very strange happened.

And the pyramid grew smaller, taking the world with it, and vanished...

Of course, when you're a pharaoh, you get a very high class of obscure dream.

Another day dawned, courtesy of the king, who was curled up on the bed and using his rolled-up clothes as a pillow. Around the stone maze of the palace the servants of the kingdom began to wake up.

Dios's boat slid gently through the water and bumped into the jetty. Dios climbed out and hurried into the palace, bounding up the steps three at a time and rubbing his hands together at the thought of a fresh day laid out before him, every hour and ritual ticking neatly into place. So much to organise, so much to be needed for . . .

The chief sculptor and maker of mummy cases folded up his measure.

"You done a good job there, Master Dil," he said.

Dil nodded. There was no false modesty between craftsmen.

The sculptor gave him a nudge. "What a team, eh?" he said. "You pickle 'em, I crate 'em."

Dil nodded, but rather more slowly. The sculptor looked down at the wax oval in his hands.

"Can't say I think much of the death mask, mind," he said.

Gern, who was working hard on the corner slab on one of the Queen's late cats, which he been allowed to do all by himself, looked up in horror.

"I done it very careful," he said sulkily.

"That's the whole point," said the sculptor.

"I know," said Dil sadly, "it's the nose, isn't it."

"It was more the chin."

"And the chin."

"Yes."

"Yes."

They looked in gloomy silence at the waxen visage of the pharaoh. So did the pharaoh.

"Nothing wrong with my chin."

"You could put a beard on it," said Dil eventually. "It'd cover a lot of it, would a beard."

"There's still the nose."

"You could take half an inch off that. And do something with the cheekbones."

"Yes."

"Yes."

Gern was horrified. "That's the face of our late king you're talking about," he said. "You can't do that sort of thing!

Anyway, people would notice." He hesitated. "Wouldn't they?"

The two craftsmen eyed one another.

"Gern," said Dil patiently, "certainly they'll notice. But they won't say anything. They expect us to, er, *improve* matters."

"After all," said the chief sculptor cheerfully, "you don't think they're going to step up and say 'It's all wrong, he really had a face like a short-sighted chicken', do you?"

"Thank you very much. Thank you very much indeed, I must say." The pharaoh went and sat by the cat. It seemed that people only had respect for the dead when they thought the dead were listening.

"I suppose," said the apprentice, with some uncertainty, "he did look a bit ugly compared to the frescoes."

"That's the point, isn't it," said Dil meaningfully.

Gern's big honest spotty face changed slowly, like a cratered landscape with clouds passing across it. It was dawning on him that this came under the heading of initiation into ancient craft secrets.

"You mean even the *painters* change the — " he began.

Dil frowned at him.

"We don't talk about it," he said.

Gern tried to force his features into an expression of worthy seriousness.

"Oh," he said. "Yes. I see, master."

The sculptor clapped him on the back.

"You're a bright lad, Gern," he said. "You catch on. After all, it's bad enough being ugly when you're alive. Think how terrible it would be to be ugly in the netherworld."

King Teppicymon XXVII shook his head. We all have to look alike when we're alive, he thought, and now they make sure we're identical when we're dead. What a kingdom. He looked down and saw the soul of the late cat, which was washing itself. When he was alive he'd hated the things, but just now it seemed positively companionable. He patted it gingerly on its flat head. It purred for a moment, and then attempted to strip the flesh from his hand. It was on a definite hiding to nothing there.

He was aware with growing horror that the trio was now discussing a pyramid. *His* pyramid. It was going to be the biggest one ever. It was going to go on a highly fertile piece of sloping ground on a prime site in the necropolis. It was going to make even the biggest existing pyramid look like something a child might construct in a sand tray. It was going to be surrounded by marble gardens and granite obelisks. It was going to be the greatest memorial ever built by a son for his father.

The king groaned.

Ptaclusp groaned.

It had been *better* in his father's day. You just needed a bloody great heap of log rollers and twenty years, which was useful because it kept everyone out of trouble during Inundation, when all the fields were flooded. Now you just needed a bright lad with a piece of chalk and the right incantations.

Mind you, it was impressive, if you liked that kind of thing.

Ptaclusp IIb walked around the great stone block, tidying an equation here, highlighting a hermetic inscription there. He glanced up and gave his father a brief nod.

Ptaclusp hurried back to the king, who was standing with his retinue on the cliff overlooking the quarry, the sun gleaming off the mask. A royal visit, on top of everything else . . .

"We're ready, if it please you, O arc of the sky," he said, breaking into a sweat, hoping against hope that . . .

Oh gods. The king was going to Put Him at his Ease again.

He looked imploringly at the high priest, who with the merest twitch of his features indicated that there was nothing he proposed to do about it. This was too much, he wasn't the only one to object to this, Dil the master embalmer had been subjected to half an hour of having to Talk about his Family only yesterday, it was wrong, people expected the king to stay in the palace, it was too . . .

The king ambled towards him in a nonchalant way designed to make the master builder feel he was among friends. Oh no, Ptaclusp thought, he's going to Remember my Name.

"I must say you've done a tremendous amount in nine weeks, it's a very good start. Er. It's Ptaclusp, isn't it?" said the king.

Ptaclusp swallowed. There was no help for it now.

"Yes, O hand upon the waters," he said, "O fount of — "

"I think 'your majesty' or 'sire' will do," said Teppic.

Ptaclusp panicked and glanced fearfully at Dios, who winced but nodded again.

"The king wishes you to address him — " a look of pain crossed his face — "informally. In the fashion of the barba — of foreign lands."

"You must consider yourself a very fortunate man to have such talented and hard-working sons," said Teppic, staring down at the busy panorama of the quarry.

"I . . . will, O . . . sire," mumbled Ptaclusp, interpreting this as an order. Why couldn't kings order people around like in the old days? You knew where you were then, they didn't go round being charming and treating you as some sort of equal, as if *you* could make the sun rise too.

"It must be a fascinating trade," Teppic went on.

"As your sire wishes, sire," said Ptaclusp. "If your majesty would just give the word — "

"And how exactly does all this *work*?"

"Your sire?" said Ptaclusp, horrified.

"You make the blocks fly, do you?"

"Yes, O sire."

"That is very interesting. How do you do it?"

Ptaclusp nearly bit through his lip. Betray Craft secrets? He was horrified. Against all expectation, Dios came to his aid.

"By means of certain secret signs and sigils, sire," he said, "into the origin of which it is not wise to inquire. It is the wisdom of — " he paused — "the moderns."

"So much quicker than all that heaving stuff around, I expect," said Teppic.

"It had a certain glory, sire," said Dios. "Now, if I may suggest. . . ?"

"Oh. Yes. Press on, by all means."

Ptaclusp wiped his forehead, and ran to the edge of the quarry.

He waved a cloth.

*

All things are defined by names. Change the name, and you change the thing. Of course there is a lot more to it than that, but paracosmically that is what it boils down to. . .

Ptaclusp IIb tapped the stone lightly with his staff.

The air above it wavered in the heat and then, shedding a little dust, the block rose gently until it bobbed a few feet off the ground, held in check by mooring ropes.

That was all there was to it. Teppic had expected some thunder, or at least a gout of flame. But already the workers were clustering around another block, and a couple of men were towing the first block down towards the site.

"Very impressive," he said sadly.

"Indeed, sire," said Dios. "And now, we must go back to the palace. It will soon be time for the Ceremony of the Third Hour."

"Yes, yes, all right," snapped Teppic. "Very well done, Ptaclusp. Keep up the good work."

Ptaclusp bowed like a seesaw in flustered excitement and confusion.

"Very good, your sire," he said, and decided to go for the big one. "May I show your sire the latest plans?"

"The king has approved the plans already," said Dios. "And, excuse me if I am mistaken, but it seems that the pyramid is well under construction."

"Yes, yes, but," said Ptaclusp, "it occurred to us, this avenue here, you see, overlooking the entrance, what a place, we thought, for a statue of for instance Hat the Vulture-Headed God of Unexpected Guests at practically cost — "

Dios glanced at the sketches.

"Are those supposed to be wings?" he said.

"Not even cost, not even cost, tell you what I'll do — " said Ptaclusp desperately.

"Is that a nose?" said Dios.

"More a beak, more a beak," said Ptaclusp. "Look, O priest, how about — "

"I think not," said Dios. "No. I really think not." He scanned the quarry for Teppic, groaned, thrust the sketches into the builder's hands and started to run.

Teppic had strolled down the path to the waiting chariots,

looking wistfully at the bustle around him, and paused to watch
a group of workers who were dressing a corner piece. They froze
when they felt his gaze on them, and stood sheepishly watching
him.

"Well, well," said Teppic, inspecting the stone, although all
he knew about stonemasonry could have been chiselled on a
sand grain. "What a splendid piece of rock."

He turned to the nearest man, whose mouth fell open.

"You're a stonemason, are you?" he said. "That must be a
very interesting job."

The man's eyes bulged. He dropped his chisel. "Erk," he said.

A hundred yards away Dios's robes flapped around his legs as
he pounded down the path. He grasped the hem and galloped
along, sandals flapping.

"What's your name?" said Teppic. "Aaaargle," said the man,
terrified.

"Well, jolly good," said Teppic, and took his unresisting hand
and shook it.

"Sire!" Dios bellowed. "No!"

And the mason spun away, holding his right hand by the
wrist, fighting it, screaming . . .

Teppic gripped the arms of the throne and glared at the high
priest.

"But it's a gesture of fellowship, nothing more. Where I come
from — "

"*Where you come from, sire, is here!*" thundered Dios.

"But, good grief, cutting it off? It's too cruel!"

Dios stepped forward. Now his voice was back to its normal
oil-smooth tones.

"Cruel, sire? But it will be done with precision and care, with
drugs to take away the pain. He will certainly live."

"But *why?*"

"I did explain, sire. He cannot use the hand again without
defiling it. He is a devout man and knows this very well. You
see, sire, you are a *god*, sire."

"But *you* can touch me. So can the servants!"

"I am a priest, sire," said Dios gently. "And the servants have special dispensation."

Teppic bit his lip.

"This is barbaric," he said.

Dios's features did not move.

"It will not be done," Teppic said. "I am the king. I forbid it to be done, do you understand?"

Dios bowed. Teppic recognised No.49, Horrified Disdain.

"Your wish will certainly be done, O fountain of all wisdom. Although, of course, the man himself may take matters into, if you will excuse me, his own hands."

"What do you mean?" snapped Teppic.

"Sire, if his colleagues had not stopped him he would have done it himself. With a chisel, I understand."

Teppic stared at him and thought, I am a stranger in a familiar land.

"I see," he said eventually.

He thought a little further.

"Then the — operation is to be done with all care, and the man is to be given a pension afterwards, d'you see?"

"As you wish, sire."

"A proper one, too."

"Indeed, sire. A golden handshake, sire," said Dios impassively.

"And perhaps we can find him some light job around the palace?"

"As a one-handed stonemason, sire?" Dios's left eyebrow arched a fraction.

"As whatever, Dios."

"Certainly, sire. As you wish. I will undertake to see if we are currently short-handed in any department."

Teppic glared at him. "I *am* the king, you know," he said sharply.

"The fact attends me with every waking hour, sire."

"Dios?" said Teppic, as the high priest was leaving.

"Sire?"

"I ordered a feather bed from Ankh-Morpork some weeks ago. I suppose you would not know what became of it?"

Dios waved his hands in an expressive gesture.

"I gather, sire, that there is considerable pirate activity off the Khalian coast," he said.

"Doubtless the pirates are also responsible for the non-appearance of the expert from the Guild of Plumbers and Dunnikindivers?" Teppic said sourly*.

"Yes, sire. Or possibly bandits, sire."

"Or perhaps a giant two-headed bird swooped down and carried him off," said Teppic.

"All things are possible, sire," said the high priest, his face radiating politeness.

"You may go, Dios."

"Sire. May I remind you, sire, that the emissaries from Tsort and Ephebe will be attending you at the fifth hour."

"Yes. You may go."

Teppic was left alone, or at least as alone as he ever was, which meant that he was all by himself except for two fan wavers, a butler, two enormous Howonder guards by the door, and a couple of handmaidens.

Oh, yes. Handmaidens. He hadn't quite come to terms with the handmaidens yet. Presumably Dios chose them, as he seemed to oversee everything in the palace, and he had shown surprisingly good taste in the matter of, for example, olive skins, bosoms and legs. The clothing these two wore would between them have covered a small saucer. And this was odd, because the net effect was to turn them into two attractive and mobile pieces of furniture, as sexless as pillars. Teppic sighed with the recollection of women in Ankh-Morpork who could be clothed from neck to ankle in brocade and still cause a classroom full of boys to blush to the roots of their hair.

He reached down for the fruit bowl. One of the girls immediately grasped his hand, moved it gently aside, and took a grape.

"Please don't peel it," said Teppic. "The peel's the best part. Full of nourishing vitamins and minerals. Only I don't suppose you've heard about them, have you, they've only been invented

---

*Dunnikindiver: a builder and cleaner of cesspits. A particularly busy profession in Ankh-Morpork, where the water table is generally at ground level, and one which attracts considerable respect. At least, everyone passes by on the other side of the street when a dunnikindiver walks by.

recently," he added, mainly to himself. "I mean, within the last
seven thousand years," he finished sourly.

So much for time flowing past, he thought glumly. It might do
that everywhere else, but not here. Here it just piles up, like
snow. It's as though the pyramids slow us down, like those
things they used on the boat, whatd'youcallem, sea anchors.
Tomorrow here is just like yesterday, warmed over.

She peeled the grape anyway, while the snowflake seconds
drifted down.

At the site of the Great Pyramid the huge blocks of stone floated
into place like an explosion in reverse. They were *flowing*
between the quarry and the site, drifting silently across the
landscape above deep rectangular shadows.

"I've got to hand it to you," said Ptaclusp to his son, as they
stood side by side in the observation tower. "It's astonishing.
One day people will wonder how we did it."

"All that business with the log rollers and the whips is old
hat," said IIb. "You can throw them away." The young architect
smiled, but there was a manic hint to the rictus.

It *was* astonishing. It was more astonishing than it ought to
be. He kept getting the feeling that the pyramid was. . .

He shook himself mentally. He should be ashamed of that sort
of thinking. You could get superstitious if you weren't careful,
in this job.

It was natural for things to form a pyramid — well, a cone, anyway. He'd experimented this morning. Grain, salt, sand. . . not
water, though, that'd been a mistake. But a pyramid was only a
neat cone, wasn't it, a cone which had decided to be a bit tidier.

Perhaps he'd overdone it just a gnat on the paracosmic
measurements?

His father slapped him on the back.

"Very well done," he repeated. "You know, it almost looks as
though it's building itself!"

IIb yelped and bit his wrist, a childish trait that he always
resorted to when he was nervous. Ptaclusp didn't notice,
because at that moment one of the foremen was running to the
foot of the tower, waving his ceremonial measuring rod.

Ptaclusp leaned over.

"What?" he demanded.

"I said, please to come at once, O master!"

On the pyramid itself, on the working surface about halfway up, where some of the detailed work on the inner chambers was in progress, the word 'impressive' was no longer appropriate. The word 'terrifying' seemed to fit the bill.

Blocks were stacking up in the sky overhead in a giant, slow dance, passing and re-passing, their mahouts yelling at one another and at the luckless controllers down on the pyramid top, who were trying to shout instructions above the noise.

Ptaclusp waded into the cluster of workers around the centre. Here, at least, there was silence. Dead silence.

"All right, all right," he said. "What's going. . . oh."

Ptaclusp IIb peered over his father's shoulder, and stuck his wrist in his mouth.

The thing was wrinkled. It was ancient. It clearly had once been a living thing. It lay on the slab like a very obscene prune.

"It was my lunch," said the chief plasterer. "It was my bloody lunch. I was really looking forward to that apple."

"But it can't start yet," whispered IIb. "It can't form temporal nodes yet, I mean, how does it *know* it's going to be a pyramid?"

"I put my hand down for it, and it felt just like. . . it felt pretty unpleasant," the plasterer complained.

"And it's a negative node, too," added IIb. "We shouldn't be getting them at *all*."

"Is it still there?" said Ptaclusp, and added. "Tell me yes."

"If more blocks have been set into position it won't be," said his son, looking around wildly. "As the centre of mass changes, you see, the nodes will be pulled around."

Ptaclusp pulled the young man to one side.

"What are you telling me now?" he demanded, in a camel whisper.*

"We ought to put a cap on it," mumbled IIb. "Flare off the trapped time. Wouldn't be any problems then. . ."

"How can we cap it? It isn't damn well finished," said Ptaclusp. "What have you been and gone and done? Pyramids

---

*Hoarse whispers are not suitable for a desert environment.

don't start accumulating until they're finished. Until they're *pyramids*, see? Pyramid energy, see? Named after pyramids. That's why it's called pyramid energy."

"It must be something to do with the mass, or something," the architect hazarded, "and the speed of construction. The time is getting trapped in the fabric. I mean, in theory you could get small nodes during construction, but they'd be so weak you wouldn't notice; if you went and stood in one maybe you'd become a few hours older or younger or — " he began to gabble.

"I recall when we did Kheneth XIV's tomb the fresco painter said it took him two hours to do the painting in the Queen's Room, and we said it was three days and fined him," said Ptaclusp, slowly. "There was a lot of Guild fuss, I remember."

"You just said that," said IIb.

"Said what?"

"About the fresco painter. Just a moment ago."

"No, I didn't. You couldn't have been listening," said Ptaclusp.

"Could have sworn you did. Anyway, this is worse than that business," said his son. "And it's probably going to happen again."

"We can expect more like it?"

"Yes," said IIb. "We shouldn't get negative nodes, but it looks as though we will. We can expect fast flows and reverse flows and probably even short loops. I'm afraid we can expect all kinds of temporal anomalies. We'd better get the men off."

"I suppose you couldn't work out a way we could get them to work in fast time and pay them for slow time?" said Ptaclusp. "It's just a thought. Your brother's bound to suggest it."

"No! Keep everyone off! We'll get the blocks in and cap it first!"

"All right, all right. I was just thinking out loud. As if we didn't have enough problems . . ."

Ptaclusp waded into the cluster of workers around the centre. Here, at least, there was silence. Dead silence.

"All right, all right," he said. "What's going. . . .oh."

Ptaclusp IIb peered over his father's shoulder, and stuck his wrist in his mouth.

The thing was wrinkled. It was ancient. It clearly had once been a living thing. It lay on the slab like a very obscene prune.

"It was my lunch," said the chief plasterer. "It was my bloody lunch. I was really looking forward to that apple."

Ptaclusp hesitated. This all seemed very familiar. He'd had this feeling before. An overwhelming sensation of *reja vu**.

He met the horrified gaze of his son. Together, dreading what they might see, they turned around slowly.

They saw themselves standing behind themselves, bickering over something IIb was swearing that he had already heard.

He has, too, Ptaclusp realised in dread. That's me over there. I look a lot different from the outside. And it's me over *here*, too. As well. Also.

It's a loop. Just like in the river, a tiny whirlpool, only it's in the flow of time. And I've just gone round it twice.

The other Ptaclusp looked up at him.

There was a long, agonising moment of temporal strain, a noise like a mouse blowing bubblegum, and the loop broke, and the figure faded.

"I know what's causing it," muttered IIb indistinctly, because of his wrist. "I know the pyramid isn't complete, but it *will* be, so the effects are sort of echoing backwards, dad, we ought to stop right now, it's too *big*, I was wrong — "

"Shut up. Can you work out where the nodes will form?" said Ptaclusp. "And come away over here, all the lads are staring. Pull yourself together, son."

IIb instinctively put his hand to his belt abacus.

"Well, yes, probably," he said. "It's just a function of mass distribution and — "

"Right," said the builder firmly. "Start doing it. And then get all the foremen to come and see me."

There was a glint like mica in Ptaclusp's eye. His jaw was squared like a block of granite. Maybe it's the pyramid that's got me thinking like this, he said, I'm thinking fast, I know it.

"And get your brother up here, too," he added.

It *is* the pyramid effect. I'm remembering an idea I'm going to have.

Best not to think too hard about that. Be practical.

He stared around at the half-completed site. The gods knew

---

*Lit: "I am going to be here again."

we couldn't do it in time, he said. Now we don't have to. We can take as long as we like!

"Are you all right?" said IIb. "Dad, are you all right?"

"Was that one of your time loops?" said Ptaclusp dreamily. What an idea! No-one would ever beat them on a contract ever again, they'd win bonuses for completion and it didn't matter how long it took!

"No! Dad, we ought — "

"But you're sure you can work out where these loops will occur, are you?"

"Yes, I expect so, but — "

"Good." Ptaclusp was trembling with excitement. Maybe they'd have to pay the men more, but it would be worth it, and IIa would be bound to think up some sort of scheme, finance was nearly as good as magic. The lads would have to accept it. After all, they'd complained about working with free men, they'd complained about working with Howondanians, they'd complained about working with everyone except proper paid-up Guild members. So they could hardly complain about working with themselves.

IIb stepped back, and gripped the abacus for reassurance.

"Dad," he said cautiously, "what are you thinking about?"

Ptaclusp beamed at him. "*Doppelgangs*," he said.

Politics was more interesting. Teppic felt that here, at least, he could make a contribution.

Djelibeybi was old. It was respected. But it was also small and in the sword-edged sense, which was what seemed to matter these days, had no power. It wasn't always thus, as Dios told it. Once it had ruled the world by sheer force of nobility, hardly needing the standing army of twenty-five thousand men it had in those high days.

Now it wielded a more subtle power as a narrow state between the huge and thrusting empires of Tsort and Ephebe, each one both a threat and a shield. For more than a thousand years the kings along the Djel had, with extreme diplomacy, exquisite manners and the footwork of a centipede on adrenaline, kept the

peace along the whole widdershins side of the continent. Merely
having existed for seven thousand years can be a formidable
weapon, if you use it properly.

"You mean we're neutral ground?" said Teppic.

"Tsort is a desert culture like us," said Dios, steepling his
hands. "We have helped to shape it over the years. As for
Ephebe — " He sniffed. "They have some very strange beliefs."

"How do you mean?"

"They believe the world is run by geometry, sire. All lines and
angles and numbers. That sort of thing, sire — " Dios frowned —
"can lead to some very unsound ideas."

"Ah," said Teppic, resolving to learn more about unsound ideas
as soon as possible. "So we're secretly on the side of Tsort, yes?"

"No. It is important that Ephebe remains strong."

"But we've more in common with Tsort?"

"So we allow them to believe, sire."

"But they *are* a desert culture?"

Dios smiled. "I am afraid they don't take pyramids seriously,
sire."

Teppic considered all this.

"So whose side are we really on?"

"Our own, sire. There is always a way. Always remember,
sire, that your family was on its third dynasty before our
neighbours had worked out, sire, how babies are made."

The Tsort delegation did indeed appear to have studied Djeli
culture assiduously, almost frantically. It was also clear that
they hadn't begun to understand it; they'd merely borrowed as
many bits as seemed useful and then put them together in
subtly wrong ways. For example, to a man they employed the
Three-Turning-Walk, as portrayed on friezes, and only used by
the Djeli court on certain occasions. Occasional grimaces
crossed their faces as their vertebrae protested.

They were also wearing the Khruspids of Morning and the
bangles of Going Forth, as well as the kilt of Yet with, and no
wonder even the maidens on fan duty were hiding their smiles,
matching greaves!*

---

*Some translation is needed here. If a foreign ambassador to the Court of St
James wore (out of a genuine desire to flatter) a bowler hat, a claymore, a Civil
War breastplate, Saxon trousers and a Jacobean haircut, he'd create pretty
much the same impression.

Even Teppic had to cough hurriedly. But then, he thought, they don't know any better. They're like children.

And this thought was followed by another one which added, These children could wipe us off the map in one hour.

Hot on the synapses of the other two came a third thought, which said: It's only clothes, for goodness sake, you're beginning to take it all seriously.

The group from Ephebe were more sensibly dressed in white togas. They had a certain sameness about them, as if somewhere in the country there was a little press that stamped out small bald men with curly white beards.

The two parties halted before the throne, and bowed.

"Hallo," said Teppic.

"His Greatness the King Teppicymon XXVIII, Lord of the Heavens, Charioteer of the Wagon of the Sun, Steersman of the Barque of the Sun, Guardian of the Secret Knowledge, Lord of the Horizon, Keeper of the Way, the Flail of Mercy, the High-Born One, the Never-Dying King, bids you welcome and commands you to take wine with him," said Dios, clapping his hands for a butler.

"Oh yes," said Teppic. "Do sit down, won't you?"

"His Greatness the King Teppicymon XXVIII, Lord of the Heavens, Charioteer of the Wagon of the Sun, Steersman of the Barque of the Sun, Guardian of the Secret Knowledge, Lord of the Horizon, Keeper of the Way, the Flail of Mercy, the High-Born One, the Never-Dying King, commands you to be seated," said Dios.

Teppic racked his brains for a suitable speech. He'd heard plenty in Ankh-Morpork. They were probably the same the whole world over.

"I'm sure we shall get on — "

"His Greatness the King Teppicymon XXVIII, Lord of the Heavens, Charioteer of the Wagon of the Sun, Steersman of the Barque of the Sun, Guardian of the Secret Knowledge, Lord of the Horizon, Keeper of the Way, the Flail of Mercy, the High-Born One, the Never-Dying King, bids you harken!" Dios boomed.

" — long history of friendship — "

"Harken to the wisdom of His Greatness the King

Teppicymon XXVIII, Lord of the Heavens, Charioteer of the
Wagon of the Sun, Steersman of the Barque of the Sun
Guardian of the Secret Knowledge, Lord of the Horizon, Keeper
of the Way, the Flail of Mercy, the High-Born One, the Never-
Dying King!"

The echoes died away.

"Could I have a word with you a moment, Dios?"

The high priest leaned down.

"Is all this necessary?" hissed Teppic.

Dios's aquiline features took on the wooden expression of one
who is wrestling with an unfamiliar concept.

"Of course, sire. It is traditional," he said, at last.

"I thought I was supposed to talk to these people. You know,
about boundaries and trade and so on. I've been doing a lot of
thinking about it and I've got several ideas. I mean, it's going to
be a little difficult if you're going to keep shouting."

Dios gave him a polite smile.

"Oh no, sire. That has all been sorted out, sire. I met with
them this morning."

"What am I supposed to do, then?"

Dios made a slight circling motion with one hand.

"Just as you wish, sire. It is normal to smile a little, and put
them at their ease."

"Is that *all*?"

"Sire could ask them whether they enjoy being diplomats,
sire," said Dios. He met Teppic's glare with eyes as expression-
less as mirrors.

"I am the *king*," Teppic hissed.

"Certainly, sire. It would not do to sully the office with mere
matters of leaden state, sire. Tomorrow, sire, you will be
holding supreme court. A very fit office for a monarch, sire."

"Ah. Yes."

It was quite complicated. Teppic listened carefully to the case,
which was alleged cattle theft compounded by Djeli's onion-
layered land laws. This is what it should all be about, he

thought. No-one else can work out who owns the bloody ox, this is the sort of thing kings have to do. Now, let's see, five years ago, *he* sold the ox to *him*, but as it turned out —

He looked from the face of one worried farmer to the other. They were both clutching their ragged straw hats close to their chests, and both of them wore the paralysed wooden expressions of simple men who, in pursuit of their parochial disagreement, now found themselves on a marble floor in a great room with their god enthroned before their very eyes. Teppic didn't doubt that either one would cheerfully give up all rights to the wretched creature in exchange for being ten miles away.

It's a fairly mature ox, he thought, time it was slaughtered, even if it's *his* it's been fattening on his neighbour's land all these years, half each would be about right, they're really going to remember this judgement...

He raised the Sickle of Justice.

"His Greatness the King Teppicymon XXVIII, Lord of the Heavens, Charioteer of the Wagon of the Sun, Steersman of the Barque of the Sun, Guardian of the Secret Knowledge, Lord of the Horizon, Keeper of the Way, the Flail of Mercy, the High-Born One, the Never-Dying King, will give judgement! Cower to the justice of His Greatness the King Tep — "

Teppic cut Dios off in mid-intone.

"Having listened to both sides of the case," he said firmly, the mask giving it a slight boom, "and, being impressed by the argument and counter-argument, it seems to us only just that the beast in question should be slaughtered without delay and shared with all fairness between both plaintiff and defendant."

He sat back. They'll call me Teppic the Wise, he thought. The common people go for this sort of thing.

The farmers gave him a long blank stare. Then, as if they were both mounted on turntables, they turned and looked to where Dios was sitting in his place on the steps in a group of lesser priests.

Dios stood up, smoothed his plain robe, and extended the staff.

"Harken to the interpreted wisdom of His Greatness the King Teppicymon XXVIII, Lord of the Heavens, Charioteer of the Wagon of the Sun, Steersman of the Barque of the Sun, Guardian of the Secret Knowledge, Lord of the Horizon, Keeper of the Way, the Flail of Mercy, the High-Born One, the Never-Dying King," he said. "It is our divine judgement that the beast in dispute is the property of Rhumusphut. It is our divine judgement that the beast be sacrificed upon the altar of the Concourse of Gods in thanks for the attention of Our Divine Self. It is our further judgement that both Rhumusphut and Ktoffle work a further three days in the fields of the King in payment for this judgement."

Dios raised his head until he was looking along his fearsome nose right into Teppic's mask. He raised both hands.

"Mighty is the wisdom of His Greatness the King Teppicymon XXVIII, Lord of the Heavens, Charioteer of the Wagon of the Sun, Steersman of the Barque of the Sun, Guardian of the Secret Knowledge, Lord of the Horizon, Keeper of the Way, the Flail of Mercy, the High-Born One, the Never-Dying King!"

The farmers bobbed in terrified gratitude and backed out of the presence, framed between the guards.

"Dios," said Teppic, levelly.

"Sire?"

"Just attend upon me a moment, please?"

"Sire?" repeated Dios, materialising by the throne.

"I could not help noticing, Dios, excuse me if I am wrong, a certain flourish in the translation there."

The priest looked surprised.

"Indeed no, sire. I was most precise in relaying your decision, saving only to refine the detail in accordance with precedent and tradition."

"How was that? The damn creature really belonged to both of them!"

"But Rhumusphut is known to be punctilious in his devotions, sire, seeking every opportunity to laud and magnify the gods, whereas Ktoffle has been known to harbour foolish thoughts."

"What's that got to do with justice?"

"Everything, sire," said Dios smoothly.

"But now neither of them has the ox!"

"Quite so, sire. But Ktoffle does not have it because he does not deserve it, while Rhumusphut, by his sacrifice, has ensured himself greater stature in the netherworld."

"And you'll eat beef tonight, I suppose," said Teppic.

It was like a blow; Teppic might as well have picked up the
throne and hit the priest with it. Dios took a step backward,
aghast, his eyes two brief pools of pain. When he spoke, there
was a raw edge to his voice.

"I do not eat meat, sire," he said. "It dilutes and tarnishes the
soul. May I summon the next case, sire?"

Teppic nodded. "Very well."

The next case was a dispute over the rent of a hundred square
yards of riverside land. Teppic listened carefully. Good growing
land was at a premium in Djeli, since the pyramids took up so
much of it. It was a serious matter.

It was especially serious because the land's tenant was by all
accounts hard-working and conscientious, while its actual owner
was clearly rich and objectionable*. Unfortunately, however one
chose to stack the facts, he was also in the right.

Teppic thought deeply, and then squinted at Dios. The priest
nodded at him.

"It seems to me — " said Teppic, as fast as possible but not fast
enough.

"Harken to the judgement of His Greatness the King
Teppicymon XXVIII, Lord of the Heavens, Charioteer of the
Wagon of the Sun, Steersman of the Barque of the Sun, Guardian
of the Secret Knowledge, Lord of the Horizon, Keeper of the Way,
the Flail of Mercy, the High-Born One, the Never-Dying King!"

"It seems to me — to us," Teppic repeated, "that, taking all
matters in consideration beyond those of mere mortal artifice,
the true and just outcome in this matter — " He paused. This, he
thought, isn't how a god king speaks.

"The landlord has been weighed in the balance and found
wanting," he boomed through the mask's mouth slit. "We find
for the tenant."

As one man the court turned to Dios, who held a whispered
consultation with the other priests and then stood up.

"Hear now the interpreted word of His Greatness the King
Teppicymon XXVIII, Lord of the Heavens, Charioteer of the

---

*Younger assassins, who are usually very poor, have very clear ideas about the
morality of wealth until they become older assassins, who are usually very rich,
when they begin to take the view that injustice has its good points.

Wagon of the Sun, Steersman of the Barque of the Sun, Guardian of the Secret Knowledge, Lord of the Horizon, Keeper of the Way, the Flail of Mercy, the High-Born One, the Never-Dying King! Ptorne the farmer will at once pay 18 *toons* in back rent to Prince Imtebos! Prince Imtebos will at once pay 12 *toons* into the temple offerings of the gods of the river! Long live the king! Bring on the next case!"

Teppic beckoned to Dios again.

"Is there any point in me being here?" he demanded in an overheated whisper.

"Please be calm, sire. If you were not here, how would the people know that justice had been done?"

"But you twist everything I say!"

"No, sire. Sire, you give the judgement of the man. I interpret the judgement of the king."

"I see," said Teppic grimly. "Well, from now on — "

There was a commotion outside the hall. Clearly there was a prisoner outside who was less than confident in the king's justice, and the king didn't blame him. He wasn't at all happy about it, either.

It turned out to be a dark-haired girl, struggling in the arms of two guards and giving them the kind of blows with fist and heel that a man would blush to give. She wasn't wearing the right kind of costume for the job, either. It would be barely adequate for lying around peeling grapes in.

She saw Teppic and, to his secret delight, flashed him a glance of pure hatred. After an afternoon of being treated like a mentally-deficient statue it was a pleasure to find someone prepared to take an interest in him.

He didn't know what she had done, but judging by the thumps she was landing on the guards it was a pretty good bet that she had done it to the very limits of her ability.

Dios bent down to the level of the mask's ear holes.

"Her name is Ptraci," he said. "A handmaiden of your father. She has refused to take the potion."

"What potion?" said Teppic.

"It is customary for a dead king to take servants with him into the netherworld, sire."

Teppic nodded gloomily. It was a jealously-guarded privilege, the only way a penniless servant could ensure immortality. He remembered grandfather's funeral, and the discreet clamour of the old man's personal servants. It had made father depressed for days.

"Yes, but it's not compulsory," he said.

"Yes, sire. It is not compulsory."

"Father had plenty of servants."

"I gather she was his favourite, sire."

"What exactly has she done wrong, then?"

Dios sighed, as one might if one were explaining things to an extremely backward child.

"She has refused to take the potion, sire."

"Sorry. I thought you said it wasn't compulsory, Dios."

"Yes, sire. It is not, sire. It is entirely voluntary. It is an act of free will. And she has refused it, sire."

"Ah. One of *those* situations," said Teppic. Djelibeybi was built on those sort of situations. Trying to understand them could drive you mad. If one of his ancestors had decreed that night was day, people would go around groping in the light.

He leaned forward.

"Step forward, young lady," he said.

She looked at Dios.

"His Greatness the King Teppicymon XXVIII — "

"Do we have to go all through that every time?"

"Yes, sire — Lord of the Heavens, Charioteer of the Wagon of the Sun, Steersman of the Barque of the Sun, Guardian of the Secret Knowledge, Lord of the Horizon, Keeper of the Way, the Flail of Mercy, the High-Born One, the Never-Dying King, bids you declare your guilt!"

The girl shook herself out of the guards' grip and faced Teppic, trembling with terror.

"*He* told me he didn't want to be buried in a pyramid," she said. "He said the idea of those millions of tons of rock on top of him gave him nightmares. I don't want to die yet!"

"You refuse to gladly take the poison?" said Dios.

"Yes!"

"But, child," said Dios, "then the king will have you put to death anyway. Surely it is better to go honourably, to a worthy life in the netherworld?"

"I don't want to be a servant in the netherworld!"

There was a groan of horror from the assembled priests. Dios nodded.

"Then the Eater of Souls will take you," he said. "Sire, we look to your judgement."

Teppic realised he was staring at the girl. There was something hauntingly familiar about her which he couldn't quite put his finger on. "Let her go," he said.

"His Greatness the King Teppicymon XXVIII, Lord of the Heavens, Charioteer of the Wagon of the Sun, Steersman of the Barque of the Sun, Guardian of the Secret Knowledge, Lord of the Horizon, Keeper of the Way, the Flail of Mercy, the High-Born One, the Never-Dying King, has spoken! Tomorrow at dawn you will be cast to the crocodiles of the river. Great is the wisdom of the king!"

Ptraci turned and glared at Teppic. He said nothing. He did not dare, for fear of what it might become.

She went away quietly, which was worse than sobbing or shouting.

"That is the last case, sire," said Dios.

"I will retire to my quarters," said Teppic coldly. "I have much to think about."

"Therefore I will have dinner sent in," said the priest. "It will be roast chicken."

"I hate chicken."

Dios smiled. "No, sire. On Wednesdays the king always enjoys chicken, sire."

The pyramids flared. The light they cast on the landscape was curiously subdued, grainy, almost grey, but over the capstone of each tomb a zigzag flame crackled towards the sky.

A faint clink of metal and stone sprang Ptraci from a fitful doze into extreme wakefulness. She stood up very carefully and crept towards the window.

Unlike proper cell windows, which should be large and airy and requiring only the removal of a few inconvenient iron bars to ensure the escape of any captives, this window was a slit six inches wide. Seven thousand years had taught the kings along the Djel that cells should be designed to keep prisoners *in*. The only way they could get out through this slit was in bits.

But there was a shadow against the pyramid light, and a voice said, "Psst."

She flattened herself against the wall and tried to reach up to the slit.

"Who are you?"

"I'm here to help you. Oh damn. Do they call this a window? Look, I'm lowering a rope."

A thick silken cord, knotted at intervals, dropped past her shoulder. She stared at it for a second or two, and then kicked off her curly-toed shoes and climbed up it.

The face on the other side of the slit was half-concealed by a black hood, but she could just make out a worried expression.

"Don't despair," it said.

"I wasn't despairing. I was trying to get some sleep."

"Oh. Pardon me, I'm sure. I'll just go away and leave you, shall I?"

"But in the morning I shall wake up and *then* I'll despair. What are you standing on, demon?"

"Do you know what a crampon is?"

"No."

"Well, it's two of them."

They stared at each other in silence.

"Okay," said the face at last. "I'll have to go around and come in through the door. Don't go away." And with that it vanished upwards.

Ptraci let herself slide back down to the chilly stones of the floor. Come in through the door! She wondered how it could manage that. Humans would need to open it first.

She crouched in the furthest corner of the cell, staring at the small rectangle of wood.

Long minutes went past. At one point she thought she heard a tiny noise, like a gasp.

A little later there was subtle clink of metal, so slight as to be almost beyond the range of hearing.

More time wound on to the spool of eternity and then the silence beyond the cell, which had been the silence caused by absence of sound, very slowly became the silence caused by someone making no noise.

She thought: it's right outside the door.

There was a pause in which Teppic oiled all the bolts and hinges so that, when he made the final assault, the door swished open in heart-gripping noiselessness.

"I say?" said a voice in the darkness.

Ptraci pressed herself still further into the corner.

"Look, I've come to rescue you."

Now she could make out a blacker shadow in the flarelight. It stepped forward with rather more uncertainty than she would have expected from a demon.

"Are you coming or not?" it said. "I've only knocked out the guards, it's not their fault, but we haven't got a lot of time."

"I'm to be thrown to the crocodiles in the morning," whispered Ptraci. "The king himself decreed it."

"He probably made a mistake."

Ptraci's eyes widened in horrified disbelief.

"The Soul Eater will take me!" she said.

"Do you want it to?"

Ptraci hesitated.

"Well, then," said the figure, and took her unresisting hand. He led her out of the cell, where she nearly tripped over the prone body of a guard.

"Who is in the other cells?" he said, pointing to the line of doors along the passage.

"I don't know," said Ptraci.

"Let's find out, shall we?"

The figure touched a can to the bolts and hinges of the next door and pushed it open. The flare from the narrow window illuminated a middle-aged man, seated cross-legged on the floor.

"I'm here to rescue you," said the demon.

The man peered up at him.

"Rescue?" he said.

"Yes. Why are you here?"

The man hung his head. "I spoke blasphemy against the king."

"How did you do that?"

"I dropped a rock on my foot. Now my tongue is to be torn out."

The dark figure nodded sympathetically.

"A priest heard you, did he?" he said.

"No. I told a priest. Such words should not go unpunished," said the man virtuously.

We're really good at it, Teppic thought. Mere animals couldn't possibly manage to act like this. You need to be a human being to be really stupid. "I think we ought to talk about this outside," he said. "Why not come with me?"

The man pulled back and glared at him.

"You want me to *run away*?" he said.

"Seems a good idea, wouldn't you say?"

The man stared into his eyes, his lips moving silently. Then he appeared to reach a decision.

"Guards!" he screamed.

The shout echoed through the sleeping palace. His would-be rescuer stared at him in disbelief.

"Mad," Teppic said. "You're all mad."

He stepped out of the room, grabbed Ptraci's hand, and hurried along the shadowy passages. Behind them the prisoner made the most of his tongue while he still had it and used it to scream a stream of imprecations.

"Where are you taking me?" said Ptraci, as they marched smartly around a corner and into a pillar-barred courtyard.

Teppic hesitated. He hadn't thought much beyond this point.

"Why do they bother to bolt the doors?" he demanded, eyeing the pillars. "That's what I want to know. I'm surprised you didn't wander back to your cell while I was in there."

"I — I don't want to die," she said quietly.

"Don't blame you."

"You mustn't say that! It's wrong not to want to die!"

Teppic glanced up at the roof around the courtyard and unslung his grapnel.

"I think I *ought* to go back to my cell," said Ptraci, without actually making any move in that direction. "It's wrong even to think of disobeying the king."

"Oh? What happens to you, then?"

"Something bad," she said vaguely.

"You mean, worse than being thrown to the crocodiles or

having your soul taken by the Soul Eater?" said Teppic, and
caught the grapnel firmly on some hidden ledge on the flat roof.

"That's an interesting point," said Ptraci, winning the Teppic
Award for clear thinking.

"Worth considering, isn't it?" Teppic tested his weight on the
cord.

"What you're saying is, if the worst is going to happen to you
anyway, you might as well not bother any more," said Ptraci. "If
the Soul Eater is going to get you whatever you do, you might
as well avoid the crocodiles, is that it?"

"You go up first," said Teppic, "I think someone's coming."

"Who *are* you?"

Teppic fished in his pouch. He'd come back to Djeli an aeon
ago with just the clothes he stood up in, but they were the
clothes he'd stood up in throughout his exam. He balanced a
Number Two throwing knife in his hand, the steel glinting in
the flarelight. It was possibly the only steel in the country; it
wasn't that Djelibeybi hadn't heard about iron, it was just that
if copper was good enough for your great-great-great-great-
grandfather, it was good enough for you.

No, the guards didn't deserve knives. They hadn't done
anything wrong.

His hand closed over the little mesh bag of caltraps. These
were a small model, a mere one inch per spike. Caltraps didn't
kill anyone, they just slowed them down a bit. One or two of
them in the sole of the foot induced extreme slowness and
caution in all except the terminally enthusiastic.

He scattered a few across the mouth of the passage and ran
back to the rope, hauling himself up in a few quick swings. He
reached the roof just as the leading guards ran under the lintel.
He waited until he heard the first curse, and then coiled up the
rope and hurried after the girl.

"They'll catch us," she said.

"I don't think so."

"And then the king will have us thrown to the crocodiles."

"Oh no, I don't think — " Teppic paused. It was an intriguing
idea.

"He might," he ventured. "It's very hard to be sure about
anything."

"So what shall we do now?"

Teppic stared across the river, where the pyramids were ablaze. The Great Pyramid was still under construction, by flarelight; a swarm of blocks, dwarfed by distance, hovered near its tip. The amount of labour Ptaclusp was putting on the job was amazing.

What a flare that will give, he thought. It'll be seen all the way to Ankh.

"Horrible things, aren't they," said Ptraci, behind him.

"Do you think so?"

"They're creepy. The old king hated them, you know. He said they nailed the Kingdom to the past."

"Did he say why?"

"No. He just hated them. He was a nice old boy. Very kind. Not like this new one." She blew her nose and replaced her handkerchief in its scarcely adequate space in her sequined bra.

"Er, what exactly did you have to do? As a handmaiden, I mean?" said Teppic, scanning the rooftop panorama to hide his embarrassment.

She giggled. "You're not from around here, are you?"

"No. Not really."

"Talk to him, mainly. Or just listen. He could really talk, but he always said no-one ever really listened to what he said."

"Yes," said Teppic, with feeling. "And that was all, was it?"

She stared at him, and then giggled again. "Oh, that? No, he was very kind. I wouldn't of minded, you understand, I had all the proper training. Bit of a disappointment, really. The women of my family have served under the kings for centuries, you know."

"Oh yes?" he managed.

"I don't know whether you've ever seen a book, it's called *The Shuttered* — "

" — *Palace*," said Teppic automatically.

"I thought a gentleman like you'd know about it," said Ptraci, nudging him. "It's a sort of textbook. Well, my great-great-grandmother posed for a lot of the pictures. Not recently," she added, in case he hadn't fully understood, "I mean, that would be a bit off-putting, she's been dead for twenty-five years. When she was younger. I look a lot like her, everyone says."

"Urk," agreed Teppic.

"She was famous. She could put her feet behind her head, you know. So can I. I've got my Grade Three."

"Urk?"

"The old king told me once that the gods gave people a sense of humour to make up for giving them sex. I think he was a bit upset at the time."

"Urk." Only the whites of Teppic's eyes were showing.

"You don't say much, do you?"

The breeze of the night was blowing her perfume towards him. Ptraci used scent like a battering ram.

"We've got to find somewhere to hide you," he said, concentrating on each word. "Haven't you got any parents or anything?" He tried to ignore the fact that in the shadowless flarelight she appeared to glow, and didn't have much success.

"Well, my mother still works in the palace somewhere," said Ptraci. "But I don't think she'd be very sympathetic."

"We've got to get you away from here," said Teppic fervently. "If you can hide somewhere today, I can steal some horses or a boat or something. Then you could go to Tsort or Ephebe or somewhere."

"Foreign, you mean? I don't think I'd like that," said Ptraci.

"Compared to the netherworld?"

"Well. Put like that, of course . . . " She took his arm. "Why did you rescue me?"

"Er? Because being alive is better than being dead, I think."

"I've read up to number 46, Congress of the Five Auspicious Ants," said Ptraci. "If you've got some yoghurt, we could — "

"No! I mean, no. Not here. Not now. There must be people looking for us, it's nearly dawn."

"There's no need to yelp like that! I was just trying to be kind."

"Yes. Good. Thank you." Teppic broke away and peered desperately over a parapet into one of the palace's numerous light wells.

"This leads to the embalmers' workshops," he said. "There must be plenty of places to hide down here." He unwound the cord again.

Various rooms led off the well. Teppic found one lined with

benches and floored with wood shavings; a doorway led through
to another room stacked with mummy cases, each one
surmounted by the same golden dolly face he'd come to know
and loathe. He tapped on a few, and raised the lid of the nearest.

"No-one at home," he said. "You can have a nice rest in here.
I can leave the lid open a bit so you can get some air."

"You can't think I'd risk that? Supposing you didn't come
back!"

"I'll be back tonight," said Teppic. "And — and I'll see if I can
drop some food and water in some time today."

She stood on tiptoe, her ankle bangles jingling all the way
down Teppic's libido. He glanced down involuntarily and saw
that every toenail was painted. He remembered Cheesewright
telling them behind the stables one lunch-hour that girls who
painted their toenails were . . . well, he couldn't quite remember
now, but it had seemed pretty unbelievable at the time.

"It looks very hard," she said.

"What?"

"If I've got to lie in it, it'll need some cushions."

"I'll put some wood shavings in, look!" said Teppic. "But
hurry up! Please!"

"All right. But you will be back, won't you? Promise?"

"Yes, yes! I promise!"

He wedged a splinter of wood on the case to allow an airhole,
heaved the lid back on and ran for it.

The ghost of the king watched him go.

The sun rose. As the golden light spilled down the fertile valley
of the Djel the pyramid flares paled and became ghost dancers
against the lightening sky. They were now accompanied by a
noise. It had been there all the time, far too high-pitched for
mortal ears, a sound now dropping down from the far
ultrasonic . . .

KKKkkkkkkhhheeee . . .

It screamed out of the sky, a thin rind of sound like a violin
bow dragged across the raw surface of the brain.

kkkhheeeeeee . . .

Or a wet fingernail dragged over an exposed nerve, some said.
You could set your watch by it, they would have said, if anyone
knew what one was.

... *keeee*...

It went deeper and deeper as the sunlight washed over the
stones, passing through cat scream to dog growl.

... *ee*... *ee*... *ee*...

The flares collapsed.

... *ops.*

"A fine morning, sire. I trust you slept well?"

Teppic waved a hand at Dios, but said nothing. The barber
was working through the Ceremony of Going Forth Shaven.

The barber was trembling. Until recently he had been a one-
handed, unemployed stonemason. Then the terrible high priest
had summoned him and ordered him to be the king's barber, but
it meant you had to touch the king but it was all right because
it was all sorted out by the priests and nothing more had to be
chopped off. On the whole, it was better than he had thought,
and a great honour to be single-handedly responsible for the
king's beard, such as it was.

"You were not disturbed in any way?" said the high priest.
His eyes scanned the room on a raster of suspicion; it was
surprising that little lines of molten rock didn't drip off the
walls.

"Verrr — "

"If you would but hold still, O never-dying one," said the
barber, in the pleading tone of voice employed by one who is
assured of a guided tour of a crocodile's alimentary tract if he
nicks an ear.

"You heard no strange noises, sire?" said Dios. He stepped
back suddenly so that he could see behind the gilded peacock
screen at the other end of the room.

"Norr."

"Your majesty looks a little peaky this morning, sire," said
Dios. He sat down on the bench with the carved cheetahs on
either end. Sitting down in the presence of the king, except on

ceremonial occasions, was not something that was allowed. It did, however, mean that he could squint under Teppic's low bed.

Dios was rattled. Despite the aches and the lack of sleep, Teppic felt oddly elated. He wiped his chin.

"It's the bed," he said. "I think I have mentioned it. Mattresses, you know. They have feathers in them. If the concept is unfamiliar, ask the pirates of Khali. Half of them must be sleeping on goosefeather mattresses by now."

"His majesty is pleased to joke," said Dios.

Teppic knew he shouldn't push it any further, but he did so anyway.

"Something wrong, Dios?" he said.

"A miscreant broke into the palace last night. The girl Ptraci is missing."

"That is very disturbing."

"Yes, sire."

"Probably a suitor or a swain or something."

Dios's face was like stone. "Possibly, sire."

"The sacred crocodiles will be going hungry, then." But not for long, Teppic thought. Walk to the end of any of the little jetties down by the bank, let your shadow fall on the river, and the mud-yellow water would become, by magic, mud-yellow bodies. They looked like large, sodden logs, the main difference being that logs don't open at one end and bite your legs off. The sacred crocodiles of the Djel were the kingdom's garbage disposal, river patrol and occasional morgue.

They couldn't simply be called big. If one of the huge bulls ever drifted sideways on to the current, he'd dam the river.

The barber tiptoed out. A couple of body servants tiptoed in.

"I anticipated your majesty's natural reaction, sire," Dios continued, like the drip of water in deep limestone caverns.

"Jolly good," said Teppic, inspecting the clothes for the day. "What was it, exactly?"

"A detailed search of the palace, room by room."

"Absolutely. Carry on, Dios."

My face is perfectly open, he told himself. I haven't twitched a muscle out of place. I *know* I haven't. He can read me like a stele. I can outstare him.

"Thank you, sire."

"I imagine they'll be miles away by now," said Teppic. "Whoever they were. She was only a handmaiden, wasn't she?"

"It is unthinkable that anyone could disobey your judgements! There is no-one in the kingdom that would dare to! Their souls would be forfeit! They will be hunted down, sire! Hunted down and destroyed!"

The servants cowered behind Teppic. This wasn't mere anger. This was wrath. Real, old-time, vintage wrath. And waxing? It waxed like a hatful of moons.

"Are you feeling all right, Dios?"

Dios had turned to look out across the river. The Great Pyramid was almost complete. The sight of it seemed to calm him down or, at least, stabilise him on some new mental plateau.

"Yes, sire," he said. "Thank you." He breathed deeply. "Tomorrow, sire, you are pleased to witness the capping of the pyramid. A momentous occasion. Of course, it will be some time before the interior chambers are completed."

"Fine. Fine. And this morning, I think, I should like to visit my father."

"I am sure the late king will be pleased to see you, sire. It is your wish that I should accompany you."

"Oh."

It's a fact as immutable as the Third Law of Sod that there is no such thing as a good Grand Vizier. A predilection to cackle and plot is apparently part of the job spec.

High priests tend to get put in the same category. They have to face the implied assumption that no sooner do they get the funny hat than they're issuing strange orders, e.g., princesses tied to rocks for itinerant sea monsters and throwing little babies in the sea.

This is a gross slander. Throughout the history of the Disc most high priests have been serious, pious and conscientious men who have done their best to interpret the wishes of the gods, sometimes disembowelling or flaying alive hundreds of

people in a day in order to make sure they're getting it
absolutely right.

King Teppicymon XXVII's casket lay in state. Crafted it was of
foryphy, smaradgine, skelsa and delphinet, inlaid it was with
pink jade and shode, perfumed and fumed it was with many rare
resins and perfumes . . .

It looked very impressive but, the king considered, it wasn't
worth dying for. He gave up and wandered across the courtyard.

A new player had entered the drama of his death.

Grinjer, the maker of models.

He'd always wondered about the models. Even a humble
farmer expected to be buried with a selection of crafted
livestock, which would somehow become real in the netherworld. Many a man made do with one cow like a toast rack in
this world in order to afford a pedigree herd in the next. Nobles
and kings got the complete set, including model carts, houses,
boats and anything else too big or inconvenient to fit in the
tomb. Once on the other side, they'd somehow become the
genuine article.

The king frowned. When he was alive he'd known that it was
true. Not doubted it for a moment . . .

Grinjer stuck his tongue out of the corner of his mouth as,
with great care, he tweezered a tiny oar to a perfect $\frac{1}{80}$th scale
river trireme. Every flat surface in his corner of the workshop
was stacked with midget animals and artifacts; some of his
more impressive ones hung from wires on the ceiling.

The king had already ascertained from overheard conversation that Grinjer was twenty-six, couldn't find anything to
stop the inexorable advance of his acne, and lived at home with
his mother. Where, in the evenings, he made models. Deep in
the duffel coat of his mind he hoped one day to find a nice girl
who would understand the absolute importance of getting every
detail right on a ceremonial six-wheeled ox cart, and who would
hold his glue-pot, and always be ready with a willing thumb
whenever anything needed firm pressure until the paste dried.

He was aware of trumpets and general excitement behind

him. He ignored it. There always seemed to be a lot of fuss these days. In his experience it was always about trivial things. People just didn't have their priorities right. He'd been waiting two months for a few ounces of gum varneti, and it didn't seem to bother anyone. He screwed his eyeglass into a more comfortable position and slotted a minute steering oar into place.

Someone was standing next to him. Well, they could make themselves useful . . .

"Could you just put your finger here," he said, without glancing around. "Just for a minute, until the glue sets."

There seemed to be a sudden drop in temperature. He looked up into a smiling golden mask. Over its shoulder Dios's face was shading, in Grinjer's expert opinion, from No.13 (Pale Flesh) to No.37 (Sunset Purple, Gloss).

"Oh," he said.

"It's very good," said Teppic. "What is it?"

Grinjer blinked at him. Then he blinked at the boat.

"It's an eighty-foot Khali-fashion river trireme with fishtail spear deck and ramming prow," he said automatically.

He got the impression that more was expected of him. He cast around for something suitable.

"It's got more than five hundred bits," he added. "Every plank on the deck is individually cut, look."

"Fascinating," said Teppic. "Well, I won't hold you up. Carry on the good work."

"The sail really unfurls," said Grinjer. "See, if you pull this thread, the — "

The mask had moved. Dios was there instead. He gave Grinjer a short glare which indicated that more would be heard about this later on, and hurried after the king. So did the ghost of Teppicymon XXVII.

Teppic's eyes swivelled behind the mask. There was the open doorway into the room of caskets. He could just make out the one containing Ptraci; the wedge of wood was still under the lid.

"Our father, however, is over here. Sire," said Dios. He could move as silently as a ghost.

"Oh. Yes." Teppic hesitated and then crossed to the big case on its trestles. He stared down at it for some time. The gilded face on the lid looked like every other mask.

"A very good likeness, sire," prompted Dios.

"Ye-ess," said Teppic. "I suppose so. He definitely looks happier. I suppose."

"Hallo, my boy," said the king. He knew that no-one could hear him, but he felt happier talking to them all the same. It was better than talking to himself. He was going to have more than enough time for that.

"I think it brings out the best in him, O commander of the heavens," said the head sculptor.

"Makes me look like a constipated wax dolly."

Teppic cocked his head on one side.

"Yes," he said, uncertainly. "Yes. Er. Well done."

He half-turned to look through the doorway again.

Dios nodded to the guards on either side of the passageway.

"If you will excuse me, sire," he said urbanely.

"Hmm?"

"The guards will continue their search."

"Right. Oh — "

Dios bore down on Ptraci's casket, flanked by guards. He gripped the lid, thrust it backwards, and said. "Behold! What do we find?"

Dil and Gern joined him. They looked inside.

"Wood shavings," said Dil.

Gern sniffed. "They smell nice, though," he said.

Dios's fingers drummed on the lid. Teppic had never seen him at a loss before. The man actually started tapping the sides of the case, apparently seeking any hidden panels.

He closed the lid carefully and looked blankly at Teppic, who for the first time was very glad that the mask didn't reveal his expression.

"She's not in there," said the old king. *"She got out for a call of nature when the men went to have their breakfast."*

She must have climbed out, Teppic told himself. So where is she now?

Dios scanned the room carefully and then, after swinging slowly backwards and forwards like a compass needle, his eyes fixed on the king's mummy case. It was big. It was roomy. There was a certain inevitability about it.

He crossed the room in a couple of strides and heaved it open.

"Don't bother to knock," the king grumbled. *"It's not as if I'm going anywhere."*

Teppic risked a look. The mummy of the king was quite alone.

"Are you sure you're feeling all right, Dios?" he said.

"Yes, sire. We cannot be too careful, sire. Clearly they are not here, sire."

"You look as if you could do with a breath of fresh air," said Teppic, upbraiding himself for doing this but doing it, nevertheless. Dios at a loss was an awe-inspiring sight, and slightly disconcerting; it made one instinctively fear for the stability of things.

"Yes, sire. Thank you, sire."

"Have a sit down and someone will bring you a glass of water. And then we will go and inspect the pyramid."

Dios sat down.

There was a terrible little splintering noise.

"He's sat on the boat," said the king. *"First humorous thing I've ever seen him do."*

The pyramid gave a new meaning to the word 'massive'. It bent the landscape around it. It seemed to Teppic that its very weight was deforming the shape of things, stretching the kingdom like a lead ball on a rubber sheet.

He knew that was a ridiculous idea. Big though the pyramid was, it was tiny compared to, say, a mountain.

But big, very big, compared to anything else. Anyway, mountains were *meant* to be big, the fabric of the universe was used to the idea. The pyramid was a made thing, and much bigger than a made thing ought to be.

It was also very cold. The black marble of its sides was shining white with frost in the roasting afternoon sun. He was foolish enough to touch it and left a layer of skin on the surface.

"It's freezing!"

"It's storing already, O breath of the river," said Ptaclusp, who was sweating. "It's the wossname, the boundary effect."

"I note that you have ceased work on the burial chambers," said Dios.

"The men...the temperature...boundary effects...a bit too much to risk..." muttered Ptaclusp. "Er."

Teppic looked from one to the other.

"What's the matter?" he said. "Are there problems?"

"Er," said Ptaclusp.

"You're way ahead of schedule. Marvellous work," said Teppic. "You've put a tremendous amount of labour on the job."

"Er. Yes. Only."

There was silence except for the distant sounds of men at work, and the faint noise of the air sizzling where it touched the pyramid.

"It's bound to be all right when we get the capstone on," the pyramid builder managed eventually. "Once it's flaring properly, no problem. Er."

He indicated the electrum capstone. It was surprisingly small, only a foot or so across, and rested on a couple of trestles.

"We should be able to put it on tomorrow," said Ptaclusp. "Would your sire still be honouring us with the capping-out ceremony?" In his nervousness he gripped the hem of his robe and began to twist it. "There's drinks," he stuttered. "And a silver trowel that you can take away with you. Everyone shouts hurrah and throws their hats in the air."

"Certainly," said Dios. "It will be an honour."

"And for us too, your sire," said Ptaclusp loyally.

"I *meant* for you," said the high priest. He turned to the wide courtyard between the base of the pyramid and the river, which was lined with statues and stelae commemorating King Teppicymon's mighty deeds,* and pointed.

"And you can get rid of that," he added.

Ptaclusp gave him a look of unhappy innocence.

"That statue," said Dios, "is what I am referring to."

"Oh. Ah. Well, we thought once you saw it in place, you see,

---

*The carvers had to use quite a lot of imagination. The late king had had many fine attributes, but doing mighty deeds wasn't among them. The score was: Number of enemies ground as dust under his chariot wheels = 0. Number of thrones crushed beneath his sandalled feet = 0. Number of times world bestrode like colossus = 0. On the other hand: Reigns of terror = 0. Number of times own throne crushed beneath enemy sandals = 0. Faces of poor ground = 0. Expensive crusades embarked upon = 0. His life had, basically, been a no-score win.

in the right light, and what with Hat the Vulture-Headed God
being very — "

"It goes," said Dios.

"Right you are, your reverence," said Ptaclusp miserably. It
was, right now, the least of his problems, but on top of
everything else he was beginning to think that the statue was
following him around.

Dios leaned closer.

"You haven't seen a young woman anywhere on the site, have
you?" he demanded.

"No women on the site, my lord," said Ptaclusp. "Very bad
luck."

"This one was provocatively dressed," the high priest said.

"No, no women."

"The palace is not far, you see. There must be many places to
hide over here," Dios continued, insistently.

Ptaclusp swallowed. He knew that, all right. Whatever had
possessed him . . .

"I assure you, your reverence," he said.

Dios gave him a scowl, and then turned to where Teppic, as it
turned out, had been.

"Please ask him not to shake hands with anybody," said the
builder, as Dios hurried after the distant glint of sunlight on
gold. The king still didn't seem to be able to get alongside the
idea that the last thing the people wanted was a man of the
people. Those workers who couldn't get out of the way in time
were thrusting their hands behind their back.

Alone now, Ptaclusp fanned himself and staggered into the
shade of his tent.

Where, waiting to see him, were Ptaclusp IIa, Ptaclusp IIa,
Ptaclusp IIa and Ptaclusp IIa. Ptaclusp always felt uneasy in
the presence of accountants, and four of them together was very
bad, especially when they were all the same person. Three
Ptaclusp IIbs were there as well; the other two, unless it was
three by now, were out on the site.

He waved his hands in a conciliatory way.

"All right, all right," he said. "What are today's problems?"

One of the IIas pulled a stack of wax tablets towards him.

"Have you any idea, father," he began, employing that thin,

razor-edged voice that accountants use to preface something unexpected and very expensive, "what calculus is?"

"You tell me," said Ptaclusp, sagging on to a stool.

"It's what I've had to invent to deal with the wages bill, father," said another IIa.

"I thought that was algebra?" said Ptaclusp.

"We passed algebra last week," said a third IIa. "It's calculus now. I've had to loop myself another four times to work on it, and there's three of me working on — " he glanced at his brothers — "quantum accountancy."

"What's that for?" said his father wearily.

"Next week." The leading accountant glared at the top slab. "For example," he said. "You know Rthur the fresco painter?"

"What about him?"

"He — that is, *they* — have put in a bill for two years' work."

"Oh."

"They said they did it on Tuesday. On account of how time is fractal in nature, they said."

"They said that?" said Ptaclusp.

"It's amazing what they pick up," said one of the accountants, glaring at the paracosmic architects.

Ptaclusp hesitated. "How many of them are there?"

"How should we know? We *know* there were fifty-three. Then he went critical. We've certainly seen him around a lot." Two of the IIas sat back and steepled their fingers, always a bad sign in anyone having anything to do with money. "The problem is," one of them continued, "that after the initial enthusiasm a lot of the workers looped themselves unofficially so that they could stay at home and send themselves out to work."

"But that's ridiculous," Ptaclusp protested weakly. "They're not different people, they're just doing it to themselves."

"That's never stopped anyone, father," said IIa. "How many men have stopped drinking themselves stupid at the age of twenty to save a stranger dying of liver failure at forty?"

There was silence while they tried to work this one out.

"A stranger — ?" said Ptaclusp uncertainly.

"I mean himself, when older," snapped IIa. "That was philosophy," he added.

"One of the masons beat himself up yesterday," said one of the

IIbs gloomily. "He was fighting with himself over his wife. Now he's going mad because he doesn't know whether it's an earlier version of him or someone he hasn't been yet. He's afraid he's going to creep up on him. There's worse than that, too. Dad, we're paying forty thousand people, and we're only *employing* two thousand."

"It's going to bankrupt us, that's what you're going to say," said Ptaclusp. "I know. It's all my fault. I just wanted something to hand on to you, you know. I didn't expect all this. It seemed too easy to start with."

One of the IIas cleared his throat.

"It's. . .uh. . .not *quite* as bad as all that," he said quietly.

"What do you mean?"

The accountant laid a dozen copper coins on the table.

"Well, er," he said. "You see, eh, it occurred to me, since there's all this movement in time, that it's not just *people* who can be looped, and, er, look, you see these coins?"

One coin vanished.

"They're all the same coin, aren't they," said one of his brothers.

"Well, yes," said the IIa, very embarrassed, because interfering with the divine flow of money was alien to his personal religion. "The same coin at five minute intervals."

"And you're using this trick to pay the men?" said Ptaclusp dully.

"It's not a trick! I give them the money," said IIa primly. "What happens to it afterwards isn't my responsibility, is it?"

"I don't like any of this," said his father.

"Don't worry. It all evens out in the end," said one of the IIas. "Everyone gets what's coming to them."

"Yes. That's what I'm afraid of," said Ptaclusp.

"It's just a way of letting your money work for you," said another son. "It's probably quantum."

"Oh, good," said Ptaclusp weakly.

"We'll get the block on tonight, don't worry," said one of the IIbs. "After it's flared the power off we can all settle down."

"I told the king we'd do it tomorrow."

The Ptaclusp IIbs went pale in unison. Despite the heat, it suddenly seemed a lot colder in the tent.

"Tonight, father," said one of them. "Surely you mean tonight?"

"Tomorrow," said Ptaclusp, firmly. "I've arranged an awning and people throwing lotus blossom. There's going to be a band. Tocsins and trumpets and tinkling cymbals. And speeches and a meat tea afterwards. That's the way we've always done it. Attracts new customers. They like to have a look round."

"Father, you've seen the way it soaks up...you've seen the frost..."

"Let it soak. We Ptaclusps don't go around capping off pyramids as though we were finishing off a garden wall. We don't knock off like a wossname in the night. People expect a ceremony."

"But — "

"I'm not listening. I've listened to too much of this new-fangled stuff. Tomorrow. I've had the bronze plaque made, and the velvet curtains and everything."

One of the IIas shrugged. "It's no good arguing with him," he said. "I'm from three hours ahead. I remember this meeting. We couldn't change his mind."

"I'm from two hours ahead," said one of his clones. "I remember you saying that, too."

Beyond the walls of the tent, the pyramid sizzled with accumulated time.

There is nothing mystical about the power of pyramids.

Pyramids are dams in the stream of time. Correctly shaped and orientated, with the proper paracosmic measurements correctly plumbed in, the temporal potential of the great mass of stone can be diverted to accelerate or reverse time over a very small area, in the same way that a hydraulic ram can be induced to pump water *against the flow*.

The original builders, who were of course ancients and therefore wise, knew this very well and the whole point of a correctly-built pyramid was to achieve absolute null time in the central chamber so that a dying king, tucked up there, would indeed live forever — or at least, never actually die. The time that should have passed in the chamber was stored in the bulk of the pyramid and allowed to flare off once every twenty-four hours.

After a few aeons people forgot this and thought you could achieve the same effect by a) ritual b) pickling people and c) storing their soft inner bits in jars.

This seldom works.

And so the art of pyramid tuning was lost, and all the knowledge became a handful of misunderstood rules and hazy recollections. The ancients were far too wise to build very big pyramids. They could cause very strange things, things that would make mere fluctuations in time look tiny by comparison.

By the way, contrary to popular opinion pyramids don't sharpen razor blades. They just take them back to when they weren't blunt. It's probably because of quantum.

Teppic lay on the strata of his bed, listening intently.

There were two guards outside the door, and another two on the balcony outside, and — he was impressed at Dios's forethought — one on the roof. He could hear them trying to make no noise.

He'd hardly been able to protest. If black-clad miscreants were getting into the palace, then the person of the king had to be protected. It was undeniable.

He slipped off the solid mattress and glided through the twilight to the statue of Bast the Cat-Headed God in the corner, twisted off the head, and pulled out his assassin's costume. He dressed quickly, cursing the lack of mirrors, and then padded across and lurked behind a pillar.

The only problem, as far as he could see, was not laughing. Being a soldier in Djelibeybi was not a high risk job. There was never a hint of internal rebellion and, since either neighbour could crush the kingdom instantly by force of arms, there was no real point in selecting keen and belligerent warriors. In fact, the last thing the priesthood wanted was enthusiastic soldiers. Enthusiastic soldiers with no fighting to do soon get bored and start thinking dangerous thoughts, like how much better they could run the country.

Instead the job attracted big, solid men, the kind of men who could stand stock still for hours at a time without getting bored, men with the build of an ox and the mental processes to match. Excellent bladder control was also desirable.

He stepped out on to the balcony.

Teppic had learned how not to move stealthily. Millions of years of being eaten by creatures that know how to move stealthily has made humanity very good at spotting stealthy movement. Nor was it enough to make no noise, because little moving patches of silence always aroused suspicion. The trick was to glide through the night with a quiet reassurance, just like the air did.

There was a guard standing just outside the room. Teppic drifted past him and climbed carefully up the wall. It had been decorated with a complex bas relief of the triumphs of past monarchs, so Teppic used his family to give him a leg up.

The breeze was blowing off the desert as he swung his legs over the parapet and walked silently across the roof, which was still hot underfoot. The air had a recently-cooked smell, tinted with spice.

It was a strange feeling, to be creeping across the roof of your own palace, trying to avoid your own guards, engaged on a mission in direct contravention of your own decree and knowing that if you were caught you would have yourself thrown to the sacred crocodiles. After all, he'd apparently already instructed that he was to be shown no mercy if he was captured.

Somehow it added an extra thrill.

There was freedom of a sort up here on the rooftops, the only kind of freedom available to a king of the valley. It occurred to Teppic that the landless peasants down on the delta had more freedom than he did, although the seditious and non-kingly side of him said, yes, freedom to catch any diseases of their choice, starve as much as they wanted, and die of whatever dreadful ague took their fancy. But freedom, of a sort.

A faint noise in the huge silence of the night drew him to the riverward edge of the roof. The Djel sprawled in the moonlight, broad and oily.

There was a boat in midstream, heading back from the far bank and the necropolis. There was no mistaking the figure at the oars. The flarelight gleamed off his bald head.

One day, Teppic thought, I'll follow him. I'll find out what it is he does over there.

If he goes over in daylight, of course.

In daylight the necropolis was merely gloomy, as though the whole universe had shut down for early-closing. He'd even explored it, wandering through streets and alleys that contrived to be still and dusty no matter what the weather was on the other, the *living* side of the water. There was always a breathless feel about it, which was probably not to be wondered at. Assassins liked the night on general principles, but the night of the necropolis was something else. Or rather, it was the same thing, but a lot more of it. Besides, it was the only city anywhere on the Disc where an assassin couldn't find employment.

He reached the light well that opened on the embalmers' courtyard and peered down. A moment later he landed lightly on the floor and slipped into the room of cases.

"Hallo, lad."

Teppic opened the lid of the case. It was still empty.

"She's in one of the ones at the back," said the king. *"Never had much of a sense of direction."*

It was a great big palace. Teppic could barely find his way around it by daylight. He considered his chances of carrying out a search in pitch darkness.

"It's a family trait, you know. Your grandad had to have Left and Right painted on his sandals, it was that bad. It's lucky for you that you take after your mother in that respect."

It was strange. She didn't talk, she chattered. She didn't seem to be able to hold a simple thought in her head for more than about ten seconds. Her brain appeared to be wired directly to her mouth, so that as soon as a thought entered her head she spoke it out loud. Compared to the ladies he had met at soirees in Ankh, who delighted in entertaining young assassins and fed them expensive delicacies and talked to them of high and delicate matters while their eyes sparkled like carborundum drills and their lips began to glisten . . . compared to them, she was as empty as a, as a, well, as an empty thing. Nevertheless, he found he desperately wanted to find her. The sheer un-

demandingness of her was like a drug. The memory of her
bosom was quite beside the point.

"I'm glad you've come back for her," said the king vaguely.
*"She's your sister, you know. Half sister, that is. Sometimes I
wish I'd married her mother, but you see she wasn't royal. Very
bright woman, her mother."*

Teppic listened hard. There it was again: a faint breathing
noise, only heard at all because of the deep silence of the night.
He worked his way to the back of the room, listened again, and
lifted the lid of a case.

Ptraci was curled up on the bottom, fast asleep with her head
on her arm.

He leaned the lid carefully against the wall and touched her
hair. She muttered something in her sleep, and settled into a
more comfortable position.

"Er, I think you'd better wake up," he whispered.

She changed position again and muttered something like:
"Wstflgl."

Teppic hesitated. Neither his tutors nor Dios had prepared
him for this. He knew at least seventy different ways of killing
a sleeping person, but none to wake them up first.

He prodded her in what looked like the least embarrassing
area of her skin. She opened her eyes.

"Oh," she said. "It's you." And she yawned.

"I've come to take you away," said Teppic. "You've been
asleep all day."

"I heard someone talking," she said, stretching in a
fashion that made Teppic look away hurriedly. "It was that
priest, the one with the face like a bald eagle. He's really
horrible."

"He is, isn't he?" agreed Teppic, intensely relieved to hear it
said.

"So I just kept quiet. And there was the king. The *new* king."

"Oh. He was down here, was he?" said Teppic weakly. The
bitterness in her voice was like a Number Four stabbing knife
in his heart.

"All the girls say he's really *weird*," she added, as he helped
her out of the case. "You *can* touch me, you know. I'm not made
of china."

He steadied her arm, feeling in sore need of a cold bath and a quick run around the rooftops.

"You're an assassin, aren't you," she went on. "I remembered that after you'd gone. An assassin from foreign parts. All that black. Have you come to kill the king?"

"I wish I could," said Teppic. "He's really beginning to get on my nerves. Look, could you take your bangles off?"

"Why?"

"They make such a noise when you walk." Even Ptraci's earrings appeared to chime the hours when she moved her head.

"I don't want to," she said. "I'd feel naked without them."

"You're nearly naked *with* them," hissed Teppic. "Please!"

"She can play the dulcimer," said the ghost of Teppicymon XXVII, apropos of nothing much. *"Not very well, mind you. She's up to page five of 'Little Pieces for Tiny Fingers'."*

Teppic crept to the passage leading out of the embalming room and listened hard. Silence ruled in the palace, broken only by heavy breathing and the occasional clink behind him as Ptraci stripped herself of her jewelry. He crept back.

"Please hurry up," he said, "we haven't got a lot of — "

Ptraci was crying.

"Er," said Teppic. "Er."

"Some of these were presents from my granny," sniffed Ptraci. "The old king gave me some, too. These earrings have been in my family for ever such a long time. How would you like it if you had to do it?"

"You see, jewelry isn't just something she wears," said the ghost of Teppicymon XXVII. *"It's part of who she is."* My word, he added to himself, that's probably an Insight. Why is it so much easier to think when you're dead?

"I don't wear any," said Teppic.

"You've got all those daggers and things."

"Well, I need them to do my job."

"Well then."

"Look, you don't have to leave them here, you can put them in my pouch," he said. "But we must be going. Please!"

"Goodbye," said the ghost sadly, watching them sneak out to the courtyard. He floated back to his corpse, who wasn't the best of company.

*

The breeze was stronger when they reached the roof. It was hotter, too, and dry.

Across the river one or two of the older pyramids were already sending up their flares, but they were weak and looked wrong.

"I feel itchy," said Ptraci. "What's wrong?"

"It feels like we're in for a thunderstorm," said Teppic, staring across the river at the Great Pyramid. Its blackness had intensified, so that it was a triangle of deeper darkness in the night. Figures were running around its base like lunatics watching their asylum burn.

"What's a thunderstorm?"

"Very hard to describe," he said, in a preoccupied voice. "Can you see what they're doing over there?"

Ptraci squinted across the river.

"They're very busy," she said.

"Looks more like panic to me."

A few more pyramids flared, but instead of roaring straight up the flames flickered and lashed backwards and forwards, driven by intangible winds.

Teppic shook himself. "Come on," he said. "Let's get you away from here."

"I said we should have capped it this evening," shouted Ptaclusp IIb above the screaming of the pyramid. "I can't float it up now, the turbulence up there must be terrific!"

The ice of day was boiling off the black marble, which was already warm to the touch. He stared distractedly at the capstone on its cradle and then at his brother, who was still in his nightshirt.

"Where's father?" he said.

"I sent one of us to go and wake him up," said IIa.

"Who?"

"One of you, actually."

"Oh." IIb stared again at the capstone. "It's not that heavy," he said. "Two of us could manhandle it up there." He gave his brother an enquiring look.

"You must be mad. Send some of the men to do it."

"They've all run away — "

Down river another pyramid tried to flare, spluttered, and then ejected a screaming, ragged flame that arched across the sky and grounded near the top of the Great Pyramid itself.

"It's interfering with the others now!" shouted IIb. "Come on. We've got to flare it off, it's the only way!"

About a third of the way up the pyramid's flanks a crackling blue zigzag arced out and struck itself on a stone sphinx. The air above it boiled.

The two brothers slung the stone between them and staggered to the scaffolding, while the dust around them whirled into strange shapes.

"Can you hear something?" said IIb, as they stumbled on to the first platform.

"What, you mean the fabric of time and space being put through the wringer?" said IIa.

The architect gave his brother a look of faint admiration. It was an unusual remark for an accountant. Then his face returned to its previous look of faint terror.

"No, not that," he said.

"Well, the sound of the very air itself being subjected to horrible tortures?"

"Not that, either," said IIb, vaguely annoyed. "I mean the creaking noise."

Three more pyramids struck their discharges, which fizzled through the roiling clouds overhead and poured into the black marble above them.

"Can't hear anything like that," said IIa.

"I think it's coming from the pyramid."

"Well, you can put your ear against it if you like, but *I'm* not going to."

The scaffolding swayed in the storm as they eased their way up another ladder, the heavy capstone rocking between them.

"I said we shouldn't do it," muttered the accountant, as the stone slid gently on to his toes. "We shouldn't have built this."

"Just shut up and lift your end, will you?"

And so, one rocking ladder after another, the brothers Ptaclusp eased their bickering way up the flanks of the Great Pyramid, while the lesser tombs along the Djel fired one after another, and the sky streamed with lines of sizzling time.

It was around about this point that the greatest mathematician in the world, lying in cosy flatulence in his stall below the palace, stopped chewing the cud and realised that something very wrong was happening to numbers. All the numbers.

The camel looked along its nose at Teppic. Its expression made it clear that of all the riders in all the world it would least like to ride it, he was right at the top of the list. However, camels look like that at everyone. Camels have a very democratic approach to the human race. They hate every member of it, without making any distinctions for rank or creed.

This one appeared to be chewing soap.

Teppic looked distractedly down the shadowy length of the royal stables, which had once contained a hundred camels. He'd have given the world for a horse, and a moderately-sized continent for a pony. But the stables now held only a handful of rotting war chariots, relics of past glories, an elderly elephant whose presence was a bit of a mystery, and this camel. It looked an extremely inefficient animal. It was going threadbare at the knees.

"Well, this is it," he said to Ptraci. "I don't dare try the river during the night. I could try and get you over the border."

"Is that saddle on right?" said Ptraci. "It looks awfully funny."

"It's on an awfully odd creature," said Teppic. "How do we climb on to it?"

"I've seen the camel drivers at work," she replied. "I think they just hit them very hard with a big stick."

The camel knelt down and gave her a smug look.

Teppic shrugged, pulled open the doors to the outside world, and stared into the faces of five guards.

He backed away. They advanced. Three of them were holding the heavy Djel bows, which could propel an arrow through a door or turn a charging hippo into three tons of mobile kebab. The guards had never had to fire them at a fellow human, but looked as though they were prepared to entertain the idea.

The guard captain tapped one of the men on the shoulder, and said, "Go and inform the high priest."

He glared at Teppic.

"Throw down all your weapons," he said.

"What, *all* of them?"

"Yes. All of them."

"It might take some time," said Teppic cautiously.

"And keep your hands where I can see them," the captain added.

"We could be up against a real impasse here," Teppic ventured. He looked from one guard to another. He knew a variety of methods of unarmed combat, but they all rather relied on the opponent not being about to fire an arrow straight through you as soon as you moved. But he could probably dive sideways, and once he had the cover of the camel stalls he could bide his time. . .

And that would leave Ptraci exposed. Besides, he could hardly go around fighting his own guards. That wasn't acceptable behaviour, even for a king.

There was a movement behind the guards and Dios drifted into view, as silent and inevitable as an eclipse of the moon. He was holding a lighted torch, which reflected wild highlights on his bald head.

"Ah," he said. "The miscreants are captured. Well done." He nodded to the captain. "Throw them to the crocodiles."

"Dios?" said Teppic, as two of the guards lowered their bows and bore down on him.

"Did you speak?"

"You know who I am, man. Don't be silly."

The high priest raised the torch.

"You have the advantage of me, boy," he said. "Metaphorically speaking."

"This is not funny," said Teppic. "I order you to tell them who I am."

"As you wish. This *assassin*," said Dios, and the voice had the cut and sear of a thermic lance, "has killed the king."

"I *am* the king, damn it," said Teppic. "How could I kill myself?"

"We are not stupid," said Dios. "These men know the king does not skulk the palace at night, or consort with condemned criminals. All that remains for us to find out is how you disposed of the body."

His eyes fixed on Teppic's face, and Teppic realised that the high priest was, indeed, truly mad. It was the rare kind of madness caused by being yourself for so long that habits of sanity have etched themselves into the brain. I wonder how old he *really* is? he thought.

"These assassins are cunning creatures," said Dios. "Have a care of him."

There was a crash beside the priest. Ptraci had tried to throw a camel prod, and missed.

When everyone looked back Teppic had vanished. The guards beside him were busy collapsing slowly to the floor, groaning.

Dios smiled.

"Take the woman," he snapped, and the captain darted forward and grabbed Ptraci, who hadn't made any attempt to run away. Dios bent down and picked up the prod.

"There are more guards outside," he said. "I'm sure you will realise that. It will be in your interests to step forward."

"Why?" said Teppic, from the shadows. He fumbled in his boot for his blowpipe.

"You will then be thrown to the sacred crocodiles, by order of the king," said Dios.

"Something to look forward to, eh?" said Teppic, feverishly screwing bits together.

"It would certainly be preferable to many alternatives," said Dios.

In the darkness Teppic ran his fingers over the little coded knobs on the darts. Most of the really spectacular poisons would have evaporated or dissolved into harmlessness by now, but there were a number of lesser potions designed to give their clients nothing more than a good night's sleep. An assassin might have to work his way to a inhumee past a number of alert bodyguards. It was considered impolite to inhume them as well.

"You could let us go," said Teppic. "I suspect that's what you want, isn't it? For me to go away and never come back? That suits me fine."

Dios hesitated.

"You're supposed to say 'And let the girl go'," he said.

"Oh, yes. And that, too," said Teppic.

"No. I would be failing in my duty to the king," said Dios.

"For goodness sake, Dios, you *know* I am the king!"

"No. I have a very clear picture of the king. You are not the king," said the priest.

Teppic peered over the edge of the camel stall. The camel peered over his shoulder.

And then the *world* went mad.

All right, madder.

All the pyramids were blazing now, filling the sky with their sooty light as the brothers Ptaclusp struggled to the main working platform.

IIa collapsed on the planking, wheezing like an elderly bellows. A few feet away the sloping side was hot to the touch, and there was no doubt in his mind now that the pyramid *was* creaking, like a sailing ship in a gale. He had never paid much attention to the actual mechanics as opposed to the cost of pyramid construction, but he was pretty certain that the noise was as wrong as II and II making V.

His brother reached out to touch the stone, but drew his hand back as small sparks flashed around his fingers.

"You can feel the warmth," he said. "It's astonishing!"

"Why?"

"Heating up a mass like this. I mean, the sheer tonnage . . . "

"I don't like it, Two-bee," IIa quavered. "Let's just leave the stone here, shall we? I'm sure it'll be all right, and in the morning we can send a gang up here, they'll know exactly what — "

His words were drowned out as another flare crackled across the sky and hit the column of dancing air fifty feet above them. He grabbed part of the scaffolding.

"Sod take this," he said. "I'm off."

"Hang on a minute," said IIb. "I mean, what *is* creaking? Stone can't creak."

"The whole bloody scaffolding is moving, don't be daft!" He

stared goggle-eyed at his brother. "Tell me it's the scaffolding," he pleaded.

"No, I'm certain this time. It's coming from inside."

They stared at one another, and then at the rickety ladder leading up to the tip, or to where the tip should be.

"Come on!" said IIb. "It can't flare off, it's trying to find ways of discharging — "

There was a sound as loud as the groaning of continents.

Teppic felt it. He felt that his skin was several sizes too small. He felt that someone was holding his ears and trying to twist his head off.

He saw the guard captain sag to his knees, fighting to get his helmet off, and he leapt the stall.

Tried to leap the stall. Everything was wrong, and he landed heavily on a floor that seemed undecided about becoming a wall. He managed to get to his feet and was pulled sideways, dancing awkwardly across the stable to keep his balance.

The stables stretched and shrank like a picture in a distorting mirror. He'd gone to see some once in Ankh, the three of them hazarding a half-coin each to visit the transient marvels of Dr Mooner's Travelling Take Your Breath Away Emporium. But you knew then that it was only twisted glass that was giving you a head like a sausage and legs like footballs. Teppic wished he could be so certain that what was happening around him would allow of such a harmless explanation. You'd probably *need* a wobbly glass mirror to make it look normal.

He ran on taffy legs towards Ptraci and the high priest as the world was expanded and squeezed around him, and was momentarily gratified to see the girl squirm in Dios's grip and fetch him a tidy thump on the ear.

He moved as though in a dream, with the distances changing as though reality was an elastic thing. Another step sent him cannoning into the pair of them. He grabbed Ptraci's arm and staggered back to the camel stall, where the creature was still cudding and watching the scene with the nearest thing a camel will ever get to mild interest, and snatched its halter.

No-one seemed to be interested in stopping them as they helped each other through the doorway and out into the mad night.

"It helps if you shut your eyes," said Ptraci.

Teppic tried it. It worked. A stretch of courtyard that his eyes told him was a quivering rectangle whose sides twanged like bowstrings became, well, just a courtyard under his feet.

"Gosh, that was clever," he said. "How did you think of that?"

"I always shut my eyes when I'm frightened," said Ptraci.

"Good plan."

"What's *happening*?"

"I don't know. I don't want to find out. I think going away from here could be an amazingly sensible idea. How do you make a camel kneel, did you say? I've got any amount of sharp things."

The camel, who had a very adequate grasp of human language as it applied to threats, knelt down graciously. They scrambled aboard and the landscape lurched again as the beast jacked itself back on to its feet.

The camel knew perfectly well what was happening. Three stomachs and a digestive system like an industrial distillation plant give you a lot of time for sitting and thinking.

It's not for nothing that advanced mathematics tends to be invented in hot countries. It's because of the morphic resonance of all the camels, who have that disdainful expression and famous curled lip as a natural result of an ability to do quadratic equations.

It's not generally realised that camels have a natural aptitude for advanced mathematics, particularly where they involve ballistics. This evolved as a survival trait, in the same way as a human's hand and eye co-ordination, a chameleon's camouflage, and a dolphin's renowned ability to save drowning swimmers if there's any chance that biting them in half might be observed and commented upon adversely by other humans.

The fact is that camels are far more intelligent than dolphins*. They are so much brighter that they soon realised that the most prudent thing any intelligent animal can do, if it

* Never trust a species that grins all the time. It's up to something.

would prefer its descendants not to spend a lot of time on a slab with electrodes clamped to their brains or sticking mines on the bottom of ships or being patronised rigid by zoologists, is to make bloody certain humans don't find out about it. So they long ago plumped for a lifestyle that, in return for a certain amount of porterage and being prodded with sticks, allowed them adequate food and grooming and the chance to spit in a human's eye and get away with it.

And this particular camel, the result of millions of years of selective evolution to produce a creature that could count the grains of sand it was walking over, and close its nostrils at will, and survive under the broiling sun for many days without water, was called You Bastard.

And he was, in fact, the greatest mathematician in the world.

You Bastard was thinking: there seems to be some growing dimensional instability here, swinging from zero to nearly forty-five degrees by the look of it. How interesting. I wonder what's causing it? Let V equal 3. Let Tau equal Chi/4. *cudcudcud* Let Kappa/y be an Evil-Smelling-Bugger* differential tensor domain with four imaginary spin co-efficients...

Ptraci hit him across the head with her sandal. "Come on, get a move on!" she yelled. You Bastard thought: Therefore H to the enabling power equals V/s. *cudcudcud* Thus in hypersyllogic notation...

Teppic looked behind them. The strange distortions in the landscape seemed to be settling down, and Dios was...

Dios was striding out of the palace, and had actually managed to find several guards whose fear of disobedience overcame the terror of the mysteriously distorted world.

You Bastard stood stoically chewing ... *cudcudcud* which gives us an interesting shortening oscillation. What would be the period of this? Let period = x. *cudcudcud* Let t = time. Let initial period...

Ptraci bounced up and down on his neck and kicked hard with her heels, an action which would have caused any anthropoid

---

*Renowned as the greatest camel mathematician of all time, who invented a math of eight-dimensional space while lying down with his nostrils closed in a violent sandstorm.

male to howl and bang his head against the wall.

"It won't move! Can't you hit it?"

Teppic brought his hand down as hard as he could on You Bastard's hide, raising a cloud of dust and deadening every nerve in his fingers. It was like hitting a large sack full of coathangers.

"Come *on*," he muttered.

Dios raised a hand.

"Halt, in the name of the king!" he shouted.

An arrow thudded into You Bastard's hump.

. . .equals 6.3 recurring. Reduce. That gives us. . .*ouch*. . . 314 seconds. . .

You Bastard turned his long neck around. His great hairy eyebrows made accusing curves as his yellow eyes narrowed and took a fix on the high priest, and he put aside the interesting problem for a moment and dredged up the familiar ancient maths that his race had perfected long ago:

Let range equal forty-one feet. Let windspeed equal 2. Vector one-eight. *cud* Let glutinosity equal 7. . .

Teppic drew a throwing knife.

Dios took a deep breath. He's going to order them to fire on us, Teppic thought. In my own name, in my own kingdom, I'm going to be shot.

. . .Angle two-five. *cud Fire.*

It was a magnificent volley. The gob of cud had commendable lift and spin and hit with a sound like, a sound like half a pound of semi-digested grass hitting someone in the face. There was nothing else it could sound like.

The silence that followed was by way of being a standing ovation.

The landscape began to distort again. This was clearly not a place to linger. You Bastard looked down at his front legs.

Let legs equal four. . .

He lumbered into a run. Camels apparently have more knees than any other creature and You Bastard ran like a steam engine, with lots of extraneous movement at right angles to the direction of motion accompanied by a thunderous barrage of digestive noises.

"Bloody stupid animal," muttered Ptraci, as they jolted away from the palace, "but it looks like it finally got the idea."

...gauge-invariant repetition rate of 3.5/z. What's she talking about, Bloody Stupid lives over in Tsort...

Though they swung through the air as though jointed with bad elastic You Bastard's legs covered a lot of ground, and already they were bouncing through the sleeping packed-earth streets of the city.

"It's starting again, isn't it?" said Ptraci. "I'm going to shut my eyes."

Teppic nodded. The firebrick-hot houses around them were doing their slow motion mirror dance again, and the road was rising and falling in a way that solid land had no right to adopt.

"It's like the sea," he said.

"I can't see anything," said Ptraci firmly.

"I mean the sea. The ocean. You know. Waves."

"I've heard about it. Is anyone chasing us?"

Teppic turned in the saddle. "Not that I can make out," he said. "It looks as — "

From here he could see past the long, low bulk of the palace and across the river to the Great Pyramid itself. It was almost hidden in dark clouds, but what he could see of it was definitely wrong. He knew it had four sides, and he could see all eight of them.

It seemed to be moving in and out of focus, which he felt instinctively was a dangerous thing for several million tons of rock to do. He felt a pressing urge to be a long way away from it. Even a dumb creature like the camel seemed to have the same idea.

You Bastard was thinking: ... Delta squared. Thus, dimensional pressure k will result in a ninety-degree transformation in $Chi(16/x/pu)t$ for a K-bundle of any three invariables. Or four minutes, plus or minus ten seconds...

The camel looked down at the great pads of his feet.

Let speed equal *gallop*.

"How did you make it do that?" said Teppic.

"I didn't! It's doing it by itself! Hang on!"

This wasn't easy. Teppic had saddled the camel but neglected the harness. Ptraci had handfuls of camel hair to hang on to. All he had was handfuls of Ptraci. No matter where he tried to put his hands, they encountered warm, yielding flesh. Nothing in his long education had prepared him for this, whereas everything in Ptraci's obviously had. Her long hair whipped his face and smelled beguilingly of rare perfume.*

"Are you all right?" he shouted above the wind.

"I'm hanging on with my knees!"

"That must be very hard!"

"You get special training!"

Camels gallop by throwing their feet as far away from them as possible and then running to keep up. Knee joints clicking like chilly castanets, You Bastard thrashed up the sloping road out of the valley and windmilled along the narrow gorge that led, under towering limestone cliffs, to the high desert beyond.

And behind them, tormented beyond measure by the inexorable tide of geometry, unable to discharge its burden of Time, the Great Pyramid screamed, lifted itself off its base and, its bulk swishing through the air as unstoppably as something completely unstoppable, ground around precisely ninety degrees and did something perverted to the fabric of time and space.

You Bastard sped along the gorge, his neck stretched out to its full extent, his mighty nostrils flaring like jet intakes.

"It's terrified!" Ptraci yelled. "Animals always know about this sort of thing!"

"What sort of thing!"

"Forest fires and things!"

"We haven't got any trees!"

"Well, floods and — and things! They've got some strange natural instinct!"

...*Phi** 1700[u/v]. Lateral e/v. Equals a tranche of seven to twelve...

The sound hit them. It was as silent as a dandelion clock striking midnight, but it had *pressure*. It rolled over them, suffocating as velvet, nauseating as a battered saveloy.

And was gone.

You Bastard slowed to a walk, a complicated procedure that involved precise instructions to each leg in turn.

There was a feeling of release, a sense of stress withdrawn.

---

*An effect achieved by distilling the testicles of a small tree-dwelling species of bear with the vomit of a whale, and adding a handful of rose petals. Teppic probably would have felt no better for knowing this.

You Bastard stopped. In the pre-dawn glow he'd spotted a
clump of thorned syphacia bushes growing in the rocks by the
track.

. . . angle left. x equals 37. y equals 19. z equals 43. *Bite*. . .

Peace descended. There was no sound except for the
eructations of the camel's digestive tract and the distant
warbling of a desert owl.

Ptraci slid off her perch and landed awkwardly.

"My bottom," she announced, to the desert in general, "is one
huge blister."

Teppic jumped down and half-ran, half-staggered up the scree
by the roadside, then jogged across the cracked limestone
plateau until he could get a good look at the valley.

It wasn't there any more.

It was still dark when Dil the master embalmer woke up, his
body twanging with the sensation that something was wrong.
He slipped out of bed, dressed hurriedly, and pulled aside the
curtain that did duty as a door.

The night was soft and velvety. Behind the chirrup of the
insects there was another sound, a frying noise, a faint sizzling
on the edge of hearing.

Perhaps that was what had woken him up.

The air was warm and damp. Curls of mist rose from the river,
and —

The pyramids weren't flaring.

He'd grown up in this house: it had been in the family of the
master embalmers for thousands of years, and he'd seen the
pyramids flare so often that he didn't notice them, any more
than he noticed his own breathing. But now they were dark and
silent, and the silence cried out and the darkness glared.

But that wasn't the worst part. As his horrified eyes stared up
at the empty sky over the necropolis they saw the stars, and
what the stars were stuck to.

Dil was terrified. And then, when he had time to think about
it, he was ashamed of himself. After all, he thought, it's what
I've always been told is there. It stands to reason. I'm just

seeing it properly for the first time.

There. Does that make me feel any better?

No.

He turned and ran down the street, sandals flapping, until he reached the house that held Gern and his numerous family. He dragged the protesting apprentice from the communal sleeping mat and pulled him into the street, turned his face to the sky and hissed. "Tell me what you can see!"

Gern squinted.

"I can see the stars, master," he said.

"What are they on, boy?"

Gern relaxed slightly. "That's easy, master. Everyone knows the stars are on the body of the goddess Nept who arches herself from . . . oh, bloody hell."

"You can see her, too?"

"Oh, mummy," whispered Gern, and slid to his knees.

Dil nodded. He was a religious man. It was a great comfort knowing that the gods were there. It was knowing they were *here* that was the terrible part.

Because the body of a woman arched over the heavens, faintly blue, faintly shadowy in the light of the watery stars.

She was enormous, her statistics interstellar. The shadow between her galactic breasts was a dark nebula, the curve of her stomach a vast wash of glowing gas, her navel the seething, dark incandescence in which new stars were being born. She wasn't supporting the sky. She *was* the sky.

Her huge sad face, upside down on the turnwise horizon, stared directly at Dil. And Dil was realising that there are few things that so shake belief as seeing, clearly and precisely, the object of that belief. Seeing, contrary to popular wisdom, isn't believing. It's where belief stops, because it isn't needed any more.

"Oh, Sod," moaned Gern.

Dil struck him across the arm.

"Stop that," he said. "And come with me."

"Oh, master, whatever shall we do?"

Dil looked around at the sleeping city. He hadn't the faintest idea.

"We'll go to the palace," he said firmly. "It's probably a trick of the, of the, of the dark. Anyway, the sun will be up presently."

He strode off, wishing he could change places with Gern and show just a hint of gibbering terror. The apprentice followed him at a sort of galloping creep.

"I can see shadows against the stars, master! Can you see them, master? Around the edge of the world, master!"

"Just mists, boy," said Dil, resolutely keeping his eyes fixed in front of him and maintaining a dignified posture as appropriate to the Keeper of the Left Hand Door of the Natron Lodge and holder of several medals for needlework.

"There," he said. "See, Gern, the sun is coming up!"

They stood and watched it.

Then Gern whimpered, very quietly.

Rising up the sky, very slowly, was a great flaming ball. And it was being pushed by a dung beetle bigger than worlds.

BOOK III

The Book of the New Son

The sun rose and, because this wasn't the Old Kingdom out here, it was a mere ball of flaming gas. The purple night of the high desert evaporated under its blowlamp glare. Lizards scuttled into cracks in the rocks. You Bastard settled himself down in the sparse shadow of what was left of the syphacia bushes, peered haughtily at the landscape, and began to chew cud and calculate square roots in base seven.

Teppic and Ptraci eventually found the shade of a limestone overhang, and sat glumly staring out at the waves of heat wobbling off the rocks.

"I don't understand," said Ptraci. "Have you looked everywhere?"

"It's a country! It can't just bloody well fall through a hole in the ground!"

"Where is it, then?" said Ptraci evenly.

Teppic growled. The heat struck like a hammer, but he strode out over the rocks as though three hundred square miles could perhaps have been hiding under a pebble or behind a bush.

The fact was that the track dipped between the cliffs, but almost immediately rose again and continued across the dunes into what was quite clearly Tsort. He'd recognised a wind-eroded sphinx that had been set up as a boundary marker; legend said it prowled the borders in times of dire national need, although legend wasn't sure why.

He knew they had galloped into Ephebe. He should be looking across the fertile, pyramid-speckled valley of the Djel that lay between the two countries.

He'd spent an hour looking for it.

It was inexplicable. It was uncanny. It was also extremely embarrassing.

He shaded his eyes and stared around for the thousandth time at the silent, baking landscape. And moved his head. And saw Djelibeybi.

It flashed across his vision in an instant. He jerked his eyes back and saw it again, a brief flash of misty colour that vanished as soon as he concentrated on it.

Some minutes later Ptraci peered out of the shade and saw him get down on his hands and knees. When he started turning over rocks she decided it was time he should come back in out of the sun.

He shook her hand off his shoulder, and gestured impatiently.

"I've found it!" He pulled a knife from his boot and started poking at the stones.

"Where?"

"Here!"

She laid a ringed hand on his forehead.

"Oh yes," she said. "I see. Yes. Good. Now I think you'd better come into the shade."

"No, I mean it! Here! Look!"

She hunkered down and stared at the rock, to humour him.

"There's a crack," she said, doubtfully.

"Look at it, will you? You have to turn your head and sort of look out of the corner of your eye." Teppic's dagger smacked into the crack, which was no more than a faint line on the rock.

"Well, it goes on a long way," said Ptraci, staring along the burning pavement.

"All the way from the Second Cataract to the Delta," said Teppic. "Covering your eye with one hand helps. Please give it a try. Please!"

She put one hesitant hand over her eye and squinted obediently at the rock.

Eventually she said. "It's no good, I can't — *seeee* — "

She stayed motionless for a moment and then flung herself sideways on to the rocks. Teppic stopped trying to hammer the knife into the crack and crawled over to her.

"I was right on the edge!" she wailed.

"You saw it?" he said hopefully.

She nodded and, with great care, got to her feet and backed away.

"Did your eyes feel as though they were being turned inside out?" said Teppic.

"Yes," said Ptraci coldly. "Can I have my bangles, please?"

"What?"

"My bangles. You put them in your pocket. I want them, please."

Teppic shrugged, and fished in his pouch. The bangles were mostly copper, with a few bits of chipped enamel. Here and there the craftsman had tried, without much success, to do something interesting with twisted bits of wire and lumps of coloured glass. She took them and slipped them on.

"Do they have some occult significance?" he said.

"What's occult mean?" she said vaguely.

"Oh. What do you need them for, then?"

"I told you. I don't feel properly dressed without them on."

Teppic shrugged, and went back to rocking his knife in the crack.

"Why are you doing that?" she said. He stopped and thought about it.

"I don't know," he said. "But you did see the valley, didn't you?"

"Yes."

"Well, then?"

"Well what?"

Teppic rolled his eyes. "Didn't you think it was a bit, well, odd? A whole country just more or less vanishing? It's something you don't bloody well see every day, for gods' sake!"

"How should I know? I've never been out of the valley before. I don't know what it's supposed to look like from outside. And don't swear."

Teppic shook his head. "I think I *will* go and lie down in the shade," he said. "What's left of it," he added, for the brass light of the sun was burning away the shadows. He staggered over to the rocks and stared at her.

"The whole valley has just closed up," he managed at last. "All those people . . . "

"I saw cooking fires," said Ptraci, slumping down beside him.

"It's something to do with the pyramid," he said. "It looked very strange just before we left. It's magic, or geometry, or one of those things. How do you think we can get back?"

"I don't want to go back. Why should I want to go back? It's the crocodiles for me. I'm not going back, not just for crocodiles."

"Um. Perhaps I could pardon you, or something," said Teppic.

"Oh yes," said Ptraci, looking at her nails. "You said you were the king, didn't you."

"I *am* the king! That's my kingdom over — " Teppic hesitated, not knowing in which direction to point his finger — "somewhere. I'm king of it."

"You don't look like the king," said Ptraci.

"Why not?"

"He had a golden mask on."

"That was me!"

"So you ordered me thrown to the crocodiles?"

"Yes! I mean, no." Teppic hesitated. "I mean, the king did. I didn't. In a way. Anyway, I was the one who rescued you," he added gallantly.

"There you are, then. Anyway, if you were the king, you'd be a god, too. You aren't acting very god-like at the moment."

"Yes? Well. Er." Teppic hesitated again. Ptraci's literal-mindedness meant that innocent sentences had to be carefully examined before being sent out into the world.

"I'm basically good at making the sun rise," he said. "I don't know how, though. And rivers. You want any rivers flooding, I'm your man. God, I mean."

He lapsed into silence as a thought struck him.

"I wonder what's happening in there without me?" he said.

Ptraci stood up and set off down to the gorge.

"Where are you going?"

She turned. "Well, Mr King or God or assassin, or whatever, can you make water?"

"What, here?"

"I mean to drink. There may be a river hidden in that crack or there may not, but we can't get at it, can we? So we have to go somewhere where we can. It's so simple I should think even kings could understand it."

He hurried after her, down the scree to where You Bastard

was lying with his head and neck flat on the ground, flicking his ears in the heat and idly applying You Vicious Brute's Theory of Transient Integrals to a succession of promising cissoid numbers. Ptraci kicked him irritably.

"Do you know where there is water, then?" said Teppic.

. . .e/27. Eleven miles. . .

Ptraci glared at him from kohl-ringed eyes. "You mean *you* don't know? You were going to take me into the desert and you don't know where the water is?"

"Well, I rather expected I was going to be able to take some with me!"

"You didn't even think about it!"

"Listen, you can't talk to me like that! I'm a king!" Teppic stopped.

"You're absolutely right," he said. "I never thought about it. Where I come from it rains nearly every day. I'm sorry."

Ptraci's brows furrowed. "Who reigns nearly every day?" she said.

"No, I mean rain. You know. Very thin water coming out of the sky?"

"What a silly idea. Where *do* you come from?"

Teppic looked miserable. "Where I come from is Ankh-Morpork. Where I started from is here." He stared down the track. From here, if you knew what you were looking for, you could just see a faint crack running across the rocks. It climbed the cliffs on either side, a new vertical fault the thickness of a line that just happened to contain a complete river kingdom and 7,000 years of history.

He'd hated every minute of his time there. And now it had shut him out. And now, because he couldn't, he wanted to go back.

He wandered down to it and put his hand over one eye. If you jerked your head just right. . .

It flashed past his vision briefly, and was gone. He tried a few times more, and couldn't see it again.

If I hacked the rocks away? No, he thought, that's silly. It's a line. You can't get into a line. A line has no thickness. Well known fact of geometry.

He heard Ptraci come up behind him, and the next moment

her hands were on his neck. For a second he wondered how she knew the Catharti Death Grip, and then her fingers were gently massaging his muscles, stresses melting under their expert caress like fat under a hot knife. He shivered as the tension relaxed.

"That's nice," he said.

"We're trained for it. Your tendons are knotted up like ping-pong balls on a string," said Ptraci.

Teppic gratefully subsided on to one of the boulders that littered the base of the cliff and let the rhythm of her fingers unwind the problems of the night.

"I don't know what to do," he murmured. "That feels *good*."

"It's not all peeling grapes, being a handmaiden," said Ptraci. "The first lesson we learn is, when the master has had a long hard day it is not the best time to suggest the Congress of the Fox and the Persimmon. Who says you have to do anything?"

"I feel responsible." Teppic shifted position like a cat.

"If you know where there is a dulcimer I could play you something soothing," said Ptraci. "I've got as far as 'Goblins Picnic' in Book I."

"I mean, a king shouldn't let his kingdom just vanish like that."

"All the other girls can do chords and everything," said Ptraci wistfully, massaging his shoulders. "But the old king always said he'd rather hear me. He said it used to cheer him up."

"I mean, it'll be called the Lost Kingdom," said Teppic drowsily. "How will I feel then, I ask you?"

"He said he liked my singing, too. Everyone else said it sounded like a flock of vultures who've just found a dead donkey."

"I mean, king of a Lost Kingdom. It'd be dreadful. I've got to get it back."

You Bastard slowly turned his massive head to follow the flight of an errant blowfly; deep in his brain little columns of red numbers flickered, detailing vectors and speed and elevation. The conversation of human beings seldom interested him, but it crossed his mind that the males and females always got along best when neither actually listened fully to what the other one was saying. It was much simpler with camels.

Teppic stared at the line in the rock. Geometry. That was it.

"We'll go to Ephebe," he said. "They know all about geometry and they have some very unsound ideas. Unsound ideas are what I could do with right now."

"Why do you carry all these knives and things? I mean, *really*?"

"Hmm? Sorry?"

"All these knives. Why?"

Teppic thought about it. "I suppose I don't feel properly dressed without them," he said.

"Oh."

Ptraci dutifully cast around for a new topic of conversation. Introducing Topics of Amusing Discourse was also part of a handmaiden's duties. She'd never been particularly good at it. The other girls had come up with an astonishing assortment: everything from the mating habits of crocodiles to speculation about life in the netherworld. She'd found it heavy going after talking about the weather.

"So," she said. "You've killed a lot of people, I expect?"

"Mm?"

"As an assassin, I mean. You get paid to kill people. Have you killed lots? Do you know you tense your back muscles a lot?"

"I don't think I ought to talk about it," he said.

"I ought to know. If we've got to cross the desert together and everything. More than a hundred?"

"Good heavens, no."

"Well, less than fifty?"

Teppic rolled over.

"Look, even the most famous assassins never killed more than thirty people in all their lives," he said.

"Less than twenty, then?"

"Yes."

"Less than ten?"

"I think," said Teppic, "it would be best to say a number between zero and ten."

"Just so long as I know. These things are important."

They strolled back to You Bastard. But now it was Teppic who seemed to have something on his mind.

"All this senate . . ." he said.

"Congress," corrected Ptraci.

"You. . . er . . . more than fifty people?"

"There's a *different* name for that sort of woman," said Ptraci, but without much rancour.

"Sorry. Less than ten?"

"Let's say," said Ptraci, "a number between zero and ten."

You Bastard spat. Twenty feet away the blowfly was picked cleanly out of the air and glued to the rock behind it.

"Amazing how they do it, isn't it," said Teppic. "Animal instinct, I suppose."

You Bastard gave him a haughty glare from under his sweep-the-desert eyelashes and thought:

. . . Let $z=ei0$. *cudcudcud* Then $dz=ie[i0]d0=izd0$ or $d0=dz/iz$ . . .

Ptaclusp, still in his nightshirt, wandered aimlessly among the wreckage at the foot of the pyramid.

It was humming like a turbine. Ptaclusp didn't know why, knew nothing about the vast expenditure of power that had twisted the dimensions by ninety degrees and was holding them there against terrible pressures, but at least the disturbing temporal changes seemed to have stopped. There were fewer sons around than there used to be; in truth, he could have done with finding one or two.

First he found the capstone, which had shattered, its electrum sheathing peeling away. In its descent from the pyramid it had hit the statue of Hat the Vulture-Headed God, bending it double and giving it an expression of mild surprise.

A faint groan sent him tugging at the wreckage of a tent. He tore at the heavy canvas and unearthed IIb, who blinked at him in the grey light.

"It didn't work, dad!" he moaned. "We'd almost got it up there, and then the whole thing just sort of *twisted*!"

The builder lifted a spar off his son's legs.

"Anything broken?" he said quietly.

"Just bruised, I think." The young architect sat up, wincing, and craned to see around.

"Where's Two-ay?" he said. "He was higher up than me, nearly on the top — "

"I've found him," said Ptaclusp.

Architects are not known for their attention to subtle shades of meaning, but IIb heard the lead in his father's voice.

"He's not dead, is he?" he whispered.

"I don't think so. I'm not sure. He's alive. But. He's moving — he's moving. . .well, you better come and see. I think something quantum has happened to him."

You Bastard plodded onwards at about 1.247 metres per second, working out complex conjugate co-ordinates to stave off boredom while his huge, plate-like feet crunched on the sand.

Lack of fingers was another big spur to the development of camel intellect. Human mathematical development had always been held back by everyone's instinctive tendency, when faced with something really complex in the way of triform polynomials or parametric differentials, to count fingers. Camels started from the word go by counting *numbers*.

Deserts were a great help, too. There aren't many distractions. As far as camels were concerned, the way to mighty intellectual development was to have nothing much to do and nothing to do it with.

He reached the crest of the dune, gazed with approval over the rolling sands ahead of him, and began to think in logarithms.

"What's Ephebe like?" said Ptraci.

"I've never been there. Apparently it's ruled by a Tyrant."

"I hope we don't meet him, then."

Teppic shook his head. "It's not like that," he said. "They have a new Tyrant every five years and they do something to him first." He hesitated. "I think they *ee-lect* him."

"Is that something like they do to tomcats and bulls and things?"

"Er."

"You know. To make them stop fighting and be more peaceful."

Teppic winced. "To be honest, I'm not sure," he said. "But I don't think so. They've got something they do it with, I think it's called a mocracy, and it means everyone in the whole country can say who the new Tyrant is. One man, one — " He paused. The political history lesson seemed a very long while ago, and had introduced concepts never heard of in Djelibeybi or in Ankh-Morpork, for that matter. He had a stab at it, anyway "One man, one vet."

"That's for the eelecting, then?"

He shrugged. It might be, for all he knew. "The point is. though, that everyone can do it. They're very proud of it. Everyone has — " he hesitated again, certain now that things were amiss — "the vet. Except for women, of course. And children. And criminals. And slaves. And stupid people. And people of foreign extraction. And people disapproved of for, er, various reasons. And lots of other people. But everyone apart from them. It's a very enlightened civilisation."

Ptraci gave this some consideration.

"And that's a mocracy, is it?"

"They invented it in Ephebe, you know," said Teppic, feeling obscurely that he ought to defend it.

"I bet they had trouble exporting it," said Ptraci firmly.

The sun wasn't just a ball of flaming dung pushed across the sky by a giant beetle. It was also a boat. It depended on how you looked at it.

The light was wrong. It had a flat quality, like water left in a glass for weeks. There was no joy to it. It illuminated, but without life; like bright moonlight rather than the light of day.

But Ptaclusp was more worried about his son.

"Do you know what's wrong with him?" he said.

His other son bit his stylus miserably. His hand was hurting. He'd tried to touch his brother, and the crackling shock had taken the skin off his fingers.

"I might," he ventured.

"Can you cure it?"

"I don't think so."

"What *is* it, then?"

"Well, dad. When we were up on the pyramid . . . well, when it couldn't flare . . . you see, I'm sure it twisted around . . . time, you see, is just another dimension . . . um."

Ptaclusp rolled his eyes. "None of that architect's talk, boy," he said. "What's wrong with him?"

"I think he's dimensionally maladjusted, dad. Time and space has got a bit mixed up for him. That's why he's moving sideways all the time."

Ptaclusp IIb gave his father a brave little smile.

"He *always* used to move sideways," said Ptaclusp.

His son sighed. "Yes, dad," he said. "But that was just normal. All accountants move like that. Now he's moving sideways because that's like, well, it's like Time to him."

Ptaclusp frowned. Drifting gently sideways wasn't IIa's only problem. He was also flat. Not flat like a card, with a front, back and edge — but flat from any direction.

"Puts me exactly in mind of them people in the frescoes," he said. "Where's his depth, or whatever you call it?"

"I think that's in Time," said IIb, helplessly. "Ours, not his."

Ptaclusp walked around his son, noting how the flatness followed him. He scratched his chin.

"So he can walk in Time, can he?" he said slowly.

"That may be possible, yes."

"Do you think we could persuade him to stroll back a few months and tell us not to build that bloody pyramid?"

"He can't communicate, dad."

"Not much change *there*, then." Ptaclusp sat down on the rubble, his head in his hands. It had come to this. One son normal and stupid, one flat as a shadow. And what sort of life could the poor flat kid have? He'd go through life being used to open locks, clean the ice off windscreens, and sleeping cheaply in trouser-presses in hotel bedrooms*. Being able to get under doors and read books without opening them would not be much of a compensation.

---

*This is of course a loose translation, since Ptaclusp did not know the words for 'ice', 'windscreens' or 'hotel bedrooms'; interestingly, however, *Squiggle Eagle Eagle Vase Wavyline Duck* translates directly as 'a press for barbarian leg coverings'.

IIa drifted sideways, a flat cut-out on the landscape.

"Can't we do *anything*?" he said. "Roll him up neatly, or something?"

IIb shrugged. "We could put something in the way. That might be a good idea. It would stop anything worse happening to him because it, er, wouldn't have time to happen in. I think."

They pushed the bent statue of Hat the Vulture-Headed God into the flat one's path. After a minute or two his gentle sideways drift brought him up against it. There was a fat blue spark that melted part of the statue, but the movement stopped.

"Why the sparks?" said Ptaclusp.

"It's a bit like flarelight, I think."

Ptaclusp hadn't got where he was today — no, he'd have to correct himself — hadn't got to where he had been last night without eventually seeing the advantages in the unlikeliest situations.

"He'll save on clothing," he said slowly. "I mean, he can just paint it on."

"I don't think you've quite got the idea, dad," said IIb wearily. He sat down beside his father and stared across the river to the palace.

"Something going on over there," said Ptaclusp. "Do you think they've noticed the pyramid?"

"I shouldn't be surprised. It's moved around ninety degrees, after all."

Ptaclusp looked over his shoulder, and nodded slowly.

"Funny, that," he said. "Bit of structural instability there."

"Dad, it's a pyramid! We should have flared it! I *told* you! The forces involved, well, it's just too — "

A shadow fell across them. They looked around. They looked up. They looked up a bit more.

"Oh, my," said Ptaclusp. "It's Hat, the Vulture-Headed God . . ."

Ephebe lay beyond them, a classical poem of white marble lazing around its rock on a bay of brilliant blue —

"What's that?" said Ptraci, after studying it critically for some time.

"It's the sea," said Teppic. "I told you, remember. Waves and things."

"You said it was all green and rough."

"Sometimes it is."

"Hmm." The tone of voice suggested that she disapproved of the sea but, before she could explain why, they heard the sound of voices raised in anger. They were coming from behind a nearby sand dune.

There was a notice on the dune.

It said, in several languages: AXIOM TESTING STATION.

Below it, in slightly smaller writing, it added: CAUTION — UNRESOLVED POSTULATES.

As they read it, or at least as Teppic read it and Ptraci didn't, there was a twang from behind the dune, followed by a click, followed by an arrow zipping overhead. You Bastard glanced up at it briefly and then turned his head and stared fixedly at a very small area of sand.

A second later the arrow thudded into it.

Then he tested the weight on his feet and did a small calculation which revealed that two people had been subtracted from his back. Further summation indicated that they had been added to the dune.

"What did you do that for?" said Ptraci, spitting out sand.

"Someone fired at us!"

"I shouldn't think so. I mean, they didn't know we were here, did they? You needn't have pulled me off like that."

Teppic conceded this, rather reluctantly, and eased himself cautiously up the sliding surface of the dune. The voices were arguing again:

"Give in?"

"We simply haven't got all the parameters right."

"I know what we haven't got all right."

"What is that, pray?"

"We haven't got any more bloody tortoises. That's what we haven't got."

Teppic carefully poked his head over the top of the dune.

He saw a large cleared area, surrounded by complicated ranks of markers and flags. There were one or two buildings in it, mostly consisting of cages, and several other intricate constructions he could not recognise. In the middle of it all were two men — one small, fat and florid, the other tall and willowy and with an indefinable air of authority. They were wearing sheets. Clustered around them, and not wearing very much at all, were a group of slaves. One of them was holding a bow.

Several of them were holding tortoises on sticks. They looked a bit pathetic, like tortoise lollies.

"Anyway, it's cruel," said the tall man. "Poor little things. They look so sad with their little legs waggling."

"It's logically impossible for the arrow to hit them!" The fat man threw up his hands. "It shouldn't do it! You must be giving me the wrong type of tortoise," he added accusingly. " We ought to try again with faster tortoises."

"Or slower arrows?"

"Possibly, possibly."

Teppic was aware of a faint scuffling by his chin. There was a small tortoise scurrying past him. It had several ricochet marks on its shell.

"We'll have one last try," said the fat man. He turned to the slaves. "You lot — go and find that tortoise."

The little reptile gave Teppic a look of mingled pleading and hope. He stared at it, and then lifted it up carefully and tucked it behind a rock.

He slid back down the dune to Ptraci.

"There's something really weird going on over there," he said. "They're shooting tortoises."

"Why?"

"Search me. They seem to think the tortoise ought to be able to run away."

"What, from an arrow?"

"Like I said. Really weird. You stay here. I'll whistle if it's safe to follow me."

"What will you do if it *isn't* safe?"

"Scream."

He climbed the dune again and, after brushing as much sand as possible off his clothing, stood up and waved his cap at the little crowd. An arrow took it out of his hands.

"Oops!" said the fat man. "Sorry!"

He scurried across the trampled sand to where Teppic was

standing and staring at his stinging fingers.

"Just had it in my hand," he panted. "Many apologies, didn't realise it was loaded. Whatever will you think of me?"

Teppic took a deep breath.

"Xeno's the name," gasped the fat man, before he could speak. "Are you hurt? We did put up warning signs, I'm sure. Did you come in over the desert? You must be thirsty. Would you like a drink? Who are you? You haven't seen a tortoise up there, have you? Damned fast things, go like greased thunderbolts, there's no stopping the little buggers."

Teppic deflated again.

"Tortoises?" he said. "Are we talking about those, you know, stones on legs?"

"That's right, that's right," said Xeno. "Take your eyes off them for a second, and *vazoom!*"

"Vazoom?" said Teppic. He knew about tortoises. There were tortoises in the Old Kingdom. They could be called a lot of things — vegetarians, patient, thoughtful, even extremely diligent and persistent sex-maniacs — but never, up until now, fast. Fast was a word particularly associated with tortoises because they were not it.

"Are you sure?" he said.

"Fastest animal on the face of the disc, your common tortoise," said Xeno, but he had the grace to look shifty. "Logically, that is," he added*.

*To everyone without such a logical frame of reference the fastest animal† on the Disc is the extremely neurotic Ambiguous Puzuma, which moves so fast that it can actually achieve near-lightspeed in the Disc's magical field. This means that if you can see a puzuma, it isn't there. Most male puzumas die young of acute ankle failure caused by running very fast after females which aren't there and, of course, achieving suicidal mass in accordance with relativistic theory. The rest of them die of Heisenberg's Uncertainty Principle, since it is impossible for them to know who they are and where they are *at the same time*, and the see-sawing loss of concentration this engenders means that the puzuma only achieves a sense of identity when it is at rest — usually about fifty feet into the rubble of what remains of the mountain it just ran into at near light-speed. The puzuma is rumoured to be about the size of a leopard with a rather unique black and white check coat, although those specimens discovered by the Disc's sages and philosophers have inclined them to declare that in its natural state the puzuma is flat, very thin, and dead.

†The fastest *insect* is the .303 bookworm. It evolved in magical libraries, where it is necessary to eat extremely quickly to avoid being affected by the thaumic radiations. An adult .303 bookworm can eat through a shelf of books so fast that it ricochets off the wall.

The tall man gave Teppic a nod.

"Take no notice of him, boy," he said. "He's just covering himself because of the accident last week."

"The tortoise *did* beat the hare," said Xeno sulkily.

"The hare was *dead*, Xeno," said the tall man patiently. "Because you shot it."

"I was aiming at the tortoise. You know, trying to combine two experiments, cut down on expensive research time, make full use of available — " Xeno gestured with the bow, which now had another arrow in it.

"Excuse me," said Teppic. "Could you put it down a minute? Me and my friend have come a long way and it would be nice not to be shot at again."

These two seem harmless, he thought, and almost believed it.

He whistled. On cue, Ptraci came around the dune, leading You Bastard. Teppic doubted the capability of her costume to hold any pockets whatsoever, but she seemed to have been able to repair her makeup, re-kohl her eyes and put up her hair. She undulated towards the group like a snake in a skid, determined to hit the strangers with the full force of her personality. She was also holding something in her other hand.

"She's found the tortoise!" said Xeno. "Well done!"

The reptile shot back into its shell. Ptraci glared. She didn't have much in the world except herself, and didn't like to be hailed as a mere holder of testudinoids.

The tall man sighed. "You know, Xeno," he said, "I can't help thinking you've got the wrong end of the stick with this whole tortoise-and-arrow business."

The little man glared at him.

"The trouble with you, Ibid," he said, "is that you think you're the biggest bloody authority on everything."

The Gods of the Old Kingdom were awakening.

Belief is a force. It's a weak force, by comparison with gravity; when it comes to moving mountains, gravity wins every time. But it still exists, and now that the Old Kingdom was enclosed upon itself, floating free of the rest of the universe, drifting

away from the general consensus that is dignified by the name
of reality, the power of belief was making itself felt.

For seven thousand years the people of Djelibeybi had
believed in their gods.

Now their gods existed. They had, as it were, the complete Set.

And the people of the Old Kingdom were learning that, for
example, Vut the Dog-Headed God of the Evening looks a lot
better painted on a pot than he does when all seventy feet of
him, growling and stinking, is lurching down the street outside.

Dios sat in the throne room, the gold mask of the King on his
knees, staring out across the sombre air. The cluster of lesser
priests around the door finally plucked up the courage to
approach him, in the same general frame of mind as you would
approach a growling lion. No-one is more worried by the actual
physical manifestation of a god than his priests; it's like having
the auditors in unexpectedly.

Only Koomi stood a little aside from the others. He was
thinking hard. Strange and original thoughts were crowding
along rarely-trodden neural pathways, heading in unthinkable
directions. He wanted to see where they led.

"O Dios," murmured the high priest of Ket, the Ibis-Headed
God of Justice. "What is the king's command? The gods are
striding the land, and they are fighting and breaking houses, O
Dios. Where is the king? What would he have us do?"

"Yea," said the high priest of Scrab, the Pusher of the Ball of
the Sun. He felt something more was expected of him. "And
verily," he added. "Your lordship will have noticed that the sun
is wobbling, because all the Gods of the Sun are fighting for it
and —" he shuffled his feet — "the blessed Scrab made a
strategic withdrawal and has, er, made an unscheduled landing
on the town of Hort. A number of buildings broke his fall."

"And rightly so," said the high priest of Thrrp, the Charioteer
of the Sun. "For, as all know, my master is the true god of the —"
His words tailed off.

Dios was trembling, his body rocking slowly back and forth.
His eyes stared at nothing. His hands gripped the mask almost
hard enough to leave fingerprints in the gold, and his lips
soundlessly shaped the words of the Ritual of the Second Hour,
which had been said at this time for thousands of years.

"I think it's the shock," said one of the priests. "You know, he's always been so set in his ways."

The others hastened to show that there was at least *something* they could advise on.

"Fetch him a glass of water."

"Put a paper bag over his head."

"Sacrifice a chicken under his nose."

There was a high-pitched whistling noise, the distant crump of an explosion, and a long hissing. A few tendrils of steam curled into the room.

The priests rushed to the balcony, leaving Dios in his unnerving pool of trauma, and found that the crowds around the palace were staring at the sky.

"It would appear," said the high priest of Cephut, God of Cutlery, who felt that he could take a more relaxed view of the immediate situation, "that Thrrp has fumbled it and has fallen to a surprise tackle from Jeht, Boatman of the Solar Orb."

There was a distant buzzing, as of several billion bluebottles taking off in a panic, and a huge dark shape passed over the palace.

"But," said the priest of Cephut, "here comes Scrab again. . .yes, he's gaining height. . .Jeht hasn't seen him yet, he's progressing confidently towards the meridian. . .and here comes Sessifet, Goddess of the Afternoon! This is a surprise! What a surprise this is! A young goddess, yet to make her mark, but my word, what a lot of promise there, this is an astonishing bid, eunuchs and gentlemen, and. . .yes. . .Scrab has fumbled it! He's fumbled it!. . ."

The shadows danced and spun on the stones of the balcony.

". . .and. . .what's this? The elder gods are, there's no other word for it, they're co-operating against these brash newcomers! But plucky young Sessifet is hanging in there, she's exploiting the weakness. . .she's in!. . .and pulling away now, pulling away, Gil and Scrab appear to be fighting, she's got a clear sky and, yes, yes. . .yes!. . .it's noon! It's noon! It's *noon!*"

Silence. The priest was aware that everyone was staring at him.

Then someone said, "Why are you shouting into that bulrush?"

"Sorry. Don't know what came over me there."

The priestess of Sarduk, Goddess of Caves, snorted at him.

"Suppose one of them had dropped it?" she snapped.

"But...but..." He swallowed. "It's not possible, is it? Not really? We all must have eaten something, or been out in the sun too long, or something. Because, I mean, everyone *knows* that the gods aren't...I mean, the sun is a big flaming ball of gas, isn't it, that goes around the whole world every day, and, and, and the gods...well, you know, there's a very real need in people to *believe*, don't get me wrong here — "

Koomi, even with his head buzzing with thoughts of perfidy, was quicker on the uptake than his colleagues.

"Get him, lads!" he shouted.

Four priests grabbed the luckless cutlery worshipper by his arms and legs and gave him a high-speed run across the stones to the edge of the balcony, over the parapet and into the mud-coloured waters of the Djel.

He surfaced, spluttering.

"What did you go and do that for?" he demanded. "You all *know* I'm right. None of you really — "

The waters of the Djel opened a lazy jaw, and he vanished, just as the huge winged shape of Scrab buzzed threateningly over the palace and whirred off towards the mountains.

Koomi mopped his forehead.

"Bit of a close shave there," he said. His colleagues nodded, staring at the fading ripples. Suddenly, Djelibeybi was no place for honest doubt. Honest doubt could get you seriously picked up and your arms and legs torn off.

"Er," said one of them. "Cephut's going to be a bit upset, though, isn't he?"

"All hail Cephut," they chorused. Just in case.

"Don't see why," grumbled an elderly priest at the back of the crowd. "Bloody knife and fork artist."

They grabbed him, still protesting, and hurled him into the river.

"All hail — " They paused. "Who was he high priest of, anyway?"

"Bunu, the Goat-headed God of Goats? Wasn't he?"

"All hail Bunu, probably," they chorused, as the sacred

crocodiles homed in like submarines.

Koomi raised his hands, imploring. It is said that the hour brings forth the man. He was the kind of man that is brought forth by devious and unpleasant hours, and underneath his bald head certain conclusions were beginning to unfold, like things imprisoned for years inside stones. He wasn't yet sure what they were, but they were broadly on the subject of gods, the new age, the need for a firm hand on the helm, and possibly the inserting of Dios into the nearest crocodile. The mere thought filled him with forbidden delight.

"Brethren!" he cried.

"Excuse *me*," said the priestess of Sarduk.

"And sistren — "

"Thank *you*."

" — let us rejoice!" The assembled priests stood in total silence. This was a radical approach which had not hitherto occurred to them. And Koomi looked at their upturned faces and felt a thrill the like of which he had never experienced before. They were frightened out of their wits, and they were expecting him — *him* — to tell them what to do.

"Yea!" he said. "And, indeed, verily, the hour of the gods — "

" — *and* goddesses — "

" — yes, and goddesses, is at hand. Er."

What next? What, when you got right down to it, *was* he going to tell them to do? And then he thought: it doesn't matter. Provided I sound confident enough. Old Dios always drove them, he never tried to lead them. Without him they're wandering around like sheep.

"And, brethren — and sistren, of course — we must ask ourselves, we must ask ourselves, we, er, yes." His voice waxed again with new confidence. "Yes, we must ask ourselves *why* the gods are at hand. And without doubt it is because we have not been assiduous enough in our worship, we have, er, we have lusted after graven idols."

The priests exchanged glances. Had they? How did you do it, actually?

"And, yes, and what about sacrifices? Time was when a sacrifice was a sacrifice, not some messing around with a chicken and flowers."

This caused some coughing in the audience.

"Are we talking maidens here?" said one of the priests uncertainly.

"*Ahem.*"

"And inexperienced young men too, certainly," he said quickly. Sarduk was one of the older goddesses, whose female worshippers got up to no good in sacred groves; the thought of her wandering around the landscape somewhere, bloody to the elbows, made the eyes water.

Koomi's heart thumped. "Well, why not?" he said. "Things were better then, weren't they?"

"But, er, I thought we stopped all that sort of thing. Population decline and so forth."

There was a monstrous splash out in the river. Tzut, the Snake-Headed God of the Upper Djel, surfaced and regarded the assembled priesthood solemnly. Then Fhez, the Crocodile-Headed God of the Lower Djel, erupted beside him and made a spirited attempt at biting his head off. The two submerged in a column of spray and a minor tidal wave which slopped over the balcony.

"Ah, but maybe the population declined because we *stopped* sacrificing virgins — of both sexes, of course," said Koomi, hurriedly. "Have you ever thought of it like that?"

They thought of it. Then they thought of it again.

"I don't think the king would approve — " said one of the priests cautiously.

"The king?" shouted Koomi. "Where is the king? Show me the king! Ask Dios where the king is!"

There was a thud by his feet. He looked down in horror as the gold mask bounced, and rolled towards the priests. They scattered hurriedly, like skittles.

Dios strode out into the light of the disputed sun, his face grey with fury.

"The king is dead," he said.

Koomi swayed under the sheer pressure of anger, but rallied magnificently.

"Then his successor — " he began.

"There is *no* successor," said Dios. He stared up at the sky. Few people can look directly at the sun, but under the venom of Dios's gaze the sun itself might have flinched and looked away.

Dios's eyes sighted down that fearsome nose like twin range finders.

To the air in general he said: "Coming here as if they own the place. *How dare they?*"

Koomi's mouth dropped open. He started to protest, and a kilowatt stare silenced him.

Koomi sought support from the crowd of priests, who were busily inspecting their nails or staring intently into the middle distance. The message was clear. He was on his own. Although, if by some chance he won the battle of wills, he'd be surrounded by people assuring him that they had been behind him all along.

"Anyway, they do own the place," he mumbled.

"*What?*"

"They, er, they *do* own the place, Dios," Koomi repeated. His temper gave out. "They're the sodding *gods*, Dios!"

"They're *our* gods," Dios hissed. "We're not their people. They're *my* gods and they will learn to do as they are instructed!"

Koomi gave up the frontal assault. You couldn't outstare that sapphire stare, you couldn't stand the war-axe nose and, most of all, no man could be expected to dent the surface of Dios's terrifying righteousness.

"But — " he managed.

Dios waved him into silence with a trembling hand.

"They've no right!" he said. "I did not give any orders! *They have no right!*"

"Then what are you going to *do*?" said Koomi.

Dios's hands opened and closed fitfully. He felt like a royalist might feel — a good royalist, a royalist who cut out pictures of all the Royals and stuck them in a scrapbook, a royalist who wouldn't hear a word said about them, they did such a good job and they can't answer back — if suddenly all the Royals turned up in his living room and started rearranging the furniture. He longed for the necropolis, and the cool silence among his old friends, and a quick sleep after which he'd be able to think so much more clearly . . .

Koomi's heart leapt. Dios's discomfort was a crack which, with due care and attention, could take a wedge. But you couldn't use a hammer. Head on, Dios could outfight the world.

The old man was shaking again. "I do not presume to tell them how to run affairs in the Hereunder," he said. "They shall not presume to instruct me in how to run my kingdom."

Koomi salted this treasonable statement away for further study and patted him gently on the back.

"You're right, of course," he said. Dios's eyes swivelled.

"I am?" he said, suspiciously.

"I'm sure that, as the king's minister, you will find a way. You have our full support, O Dios." Koomi waved an uplifted hand at the priests, who chorused wholehearted agreement. If you couldn't depend on kings and gods, you could always rely on old Dios. There wasn't one of them that wouldn't prefer the uncertain wrath of the gods to a rebuke from Dios. Dios terrified them in a very positive, human way that no supernatural entity ever could. Dios would sort it out.

"And we take no heed to these mad rumours about the king's disappearance. They are undoubtedly wild exaggerations, with no foundation," said Koomi.

The priests nodded while, in each mind, a tiny rumour uncurled the length of its tail.

"What rumours?" said Dios out of the corner of his mouth.

"So enlighten us, master, as to the path we must now take," said Koomi.

Dios wavered.

He did not know what to do. For him, this was a new experience. This was Change.

All he could think of, all that was pressing forward in his mind, were the words of the Ritual of the Third Hour, which he had said at this time for — how long? Too long, too long! — And he should have gone to his rest long before, but the time had never been right, there was never anyone capable, they would have been lost without him, the kingdom would founder, he would be *letting everyone down*, and so he'd crossed the river . . . he swore every time that it was the last, but it never was, not when the chill fetched his limbs, and the decades had become — longer. And now, when his kingdom needed him, the words of a Ritual had scored themselves into the pathways of his brain and bewildered all attempts at thought.

"Er," he said.

You Bastard chewed happily. Teppic had tethered him too near a olive tree, which was getting a terminal pruning. Sometimes the camel would stop, gaze up briefly at the seagulls that circled everywhere above Ephebe city, and subject them to a short, deadly burst of olive stones.

He was turning over in his mind an interesting new concept in Thau-dimensional physics which unified time, space, magnetism, gravity and, for some reason, broccoli. Periodically he would make noises like distant quarry blasting, but which merely indicated that all stomachs were functioning perfectly.

Ptraci sat under the tree, feeding the tortoise on vine leaves.

Heat crackled off the white walls of the tavern but, Teppic thought, how different it was from the Old Kingdom. There even the heat was old; the air was musty and lifeless, it pressed like a vice, you felt it was made of boiled centuries. Here it was leavened by the breeze from the sea. It was edged with salt crystals. It carried exciting hints of wine; more than a hint in fact, because Xeno was already on his second amphora. This was the kind of place where things rolled up their sleeves and started.

"But I still don't understand about the tortoise," he said, with some difficulty. He'd just taken his first mouthful of Ephebian wine, and it had apparently varnished the back of his throat.

"'S quite simple," said Xeno. "Look, let's say this olive stone is the arrow and this, and this — " he cast around aimlessly — "and this stunned seagull is the tortoise, right? Now, when you fire the arrow it goes from here to the seag — the tortoise, am I right?"

"I suppose so, but — "

"*But*, by this time, the seagu — the tortoise has moved on a bit, hasn't he? Am I right?"

"I suppose so," said Teppic, helplessly. Xeno gave him a look of triumph.

"*So* the arrow has to go a bit further, doesn't it, to where the tortoise is now. Meanwhile the tortoise has flow — moved on, not much, I'll grant you, but it doesn't have to be much. Am I right? So the arrow has a bit further to go, but the point is that by the time it gets to where the tortoise is *now* the tortoise isn't there. So, if the tortoise keeps moving, the arrow will never hit it. It'll keep getting closer and closer but never hit it. QED."

"Are you right?" said Teppic automatically.

"No." said Ibid coldly. "There's a dozen tortoise kebabs to prove him wrong. The trouble with my friend here is that he doesn't know the difference between a postulate and a metaphor of human existence. Or a hole in the ground."

"It didn't hit it yesterday," snapped Xeno.

"Yes, I was watching. You hardly pulled the string back. I saw you," said Ibid.

They started to argue again.

Teppic stared into his wine mug. These men are philosophers, he thought. They had told him so. So their brains must be so big that they have room for ideas that no-one else would consider for five seconds. On the way to the tavern Xeno had explained to him, for example, why it was logically impossible to fall out of a tree.

Teppic had described the vanishing of the kingdom, but he hadn't revealed his position in it. He hadn't a lot of experience of these matters, but he had a very clear feeling that kings who hadn't got a kingdom any more were not likely to be very popular in neighbouring countries. There had been one or two like that in Ankh-Morpork — deposed royalty, who had fled their suddenly-dangerous kingdoms for Ankh's hospitable bosom carrying nothing but the clothes they stood up in and a few wagonloads of jewels. The city, of course, welcomed anyone — regardless of race, colour, class or creed — who had spending money in incredible amounts, but nevertheless the inhumation of surplus monarchs was a regular source of work for the Assassins' Guild. There was always someone back home who wanted to be certain that deposed monarchs stayed that way. It was usually a case of heir today, gone tomorrow.

"I think it got caught up in geometry," he said, hopefully. "I heard you were very good at geometry here," he added, "and perhaps you could tell me how to get back."

"Geometry is not my forte," said Ibid. "As you probably know."

"Sorry?"

"Haven't you read my *Principles of Ideal Government*?"

"I'm afraid not."

"Or my *Discourse on Historical Inevitability*?"

"No."

Ibid looked crestfallen. "Oh," he said.

"Ibid is a well-known authority on everything," said Xeno. "Except for geometry. And interior decorating. And elementary logic." Ibid glared at him.

"What about you, then?" said Teppic.

Xeno drained his mug. "I'm more into the destruct testing of axioms," he said. "The chap you need is Pthagonal. A very acute man with an angle."

He was interrupted by the clatter of hooves. Several horsemen galloped with reckless speed past the tavern and on up the winding, cobbled streets of the city. They seemed very excited about something.

Ibid picked a stunned seagull out of his wine cup and laid it on the table. He was looking thoughtful.

"If the Old Kingdom has really disappeared — " he said.

"It has," said Teppic firmly. "It's not something you can be mistaken about, really."

"Then that means our border is concurrent with that of Tsort," said Ibid ponderously.

"Pardon?" said Teppic.

"There's nothing between us," explained the philosopher. "Oh, dear. That means we shall be forced to make war."

"Why?"

Ibid opened his mouth, stopped, and turned to Xeno.

"Why does it mean we'll be forced to make war?" he said.

"Historical imperative," said Xeno.

"Ah, yes. I knew it was something like that. I am afraid it is inevitable. It's a shame, but there you are."

There was another clatter as another party of horsemen rounded the corner, heading downhill this time. They wore the high plumed helmets of Ephebian soldiery, and were shouting enthusiastically.

Ibid settled himself more comfortably on the bench and folded his hands.

"That'll be the Tyrant's men," he said, as the troop galloped through the city gates and out on to the desert. "He's sending them to check, you may depend upon it."

Teppic knew about the enmity between Ephebe and Tsort, of course. The Old Kingdom had profited mightily by it, by seeing that the merchants of both sides had somewhere discreet in which to trade with one another. He drummed his fingers on the table.

"You haven't fought each other for thousands of years," he said. "You were tiny countries in those days. It was just a scrap. Now you're huge. People could get hurt. Doesn't that worry you?"

"It's a matter of pride," said Ibid, but his voice was tinged with uncertainty. "I don't think there's much choice."

"It was that bloody wooden cow or whatever," said Xeno. "They've never forgiven us for it."

"If we don't attack them, they'll attack us first," said Ibid.

" 'S'right," said Xeno. "So we'd better retaliate before they have a chance to strike."

The two philosophers stared uncomfortably at one another.

"On the other hand," said Ibid, "war makes it very difficult to think straight."

"There is that," Xeno agreed. "Especially for dead people."

There was an embarrassed silence, broken only by Ptraci's voice singing to the tortoise and the occasional squeak of stricken seagulls.

"What day is it?" said Ibid.

"Tuesday," said Teppic.

"I think," said Ibid, "that it might be a good idea if you came to the symposium. We have one every Tuesday," he added. "All the greatest minds in Ephebe will be there. All this needs thinking about."

He glanced at Ptraci.

"However," he said, "your young woman cannot attend, naturally. Females are absolutely forbidden. Their brains overheat."

*

King Teppicymon XXVII opened his eyes. It's bloody dark in here, he thought.

And he realised that he could hear his own heart beating, but muffled, and some way off.

And then he remembered.

He was alive. He was alive *again*. And, this time, he was in bits.

Somehow, he'd assumed that you got assembled again once you got to the netherworld, like one of Grinjer's kits.

Get a grip on yourself, man, he thought.

It's up to you to pull yourself together.

Right, he thought. There were at least six jars. So my eyes are in one of them. Getting the lid off would be favourite, so we can see what we're at.

That's going to involve arms and legs and fingers.

This is going to be really tricky.

He reached out, tentatively, with stiff joints, and located something heavy. It felt as though it might give, so he moved his other arm into position, with a great deal of awkwardness, and pushed.

There was a distant thump, and a definite feeling of openness above him. He sat up, creaking all the way.

The sides of the ceremonial casket still hemmed him in, but his surprise he found that one slow arm movement brushed them out of the way like paper. Must be all the pickle and stuffing, he thought. Gives you a bit of weight.

He felt his way to the edge of the slab, lowered his heavy legs to the ground and, after a pause out of habit to wheeze a bit, took the first tottering lurch of the newly undead.

It is astonishingly difficult to walk with legs full of straw when the brain doing the directing is in a pot ten feet away, but he made it as far as the wall and felt his way along it until a crash indicated that he'd reached the shelf of jars. He fumbled the lids of the first one and dipped his hand gently inside.

It must be brains, he thought manically, because semolina doesn't squidge like that. I've collected my own thoughts, haha.

He tried one or two more jars until an explosion of daylight told him he'd found the one with his eyes in. He watched his own bandaged hand reach down, growing gigantic, and scoop them up carefully.

That seems to be the important bits, he thought. The rest can wait until later. Maybe when I need to eat something, and so forth.

He turned around, and realised that he was not alone. Dil and Gern were watching him. To squeeze any further into the far corner of the room, they would have needed triangular backbones.

"Ah. Ho there, good people," said the king, aware that his voice was a little hollow. "I know so much about you, I'd like to shake you by the hand." He looked down. "Only they're rather full at the moment," he added.

"Gkkk," said Gern.

"You couldn't do a bit of reassembly, could you?" said the king, turning to Dil. "Your stitches seem to be holding up nicely, by the way. Well done, that man."

Professional pride broke through the barrier of Dil's terror.

"You're alive?" he said.

"That was the general idea, wasn't it?" said the king.

Dil nodded. Certainly it was. He'd always believed it to be true. He'd just never expected it ever actually to happen. But it had, and the first words, well, nearly the first words that had been said were in praise of his needlework. His chest swelled. No-one else in the Guild had ever been congratulated on their work by a recipient.

"There," he said to Gern, whose shoulderblades were making a spirited attempt to dig their way through the wall. "Hear what has been said to your master."

The king paused. It was beginning to dawn on him that things weren't quite right here. Of *course* the netherworld was like this world, only better, and no doubt there were plenty of servants and so forth. But it seemed altogether far too much like this world. He was pretty sure that Dil and Gern shouldn't be in it yet. Anyway, he'd always understood that the common people had their own netherworld, where they would be more at ease and could mingle with their own kind and wouldn't feel awkward and socially out of place.

"I say," he said. "I may have missed a bit here. You're not dead, are you?"

Dil didn't answer immediately. Some of the things he'd seen

so far today had made him a bit uncertain on the subject. In the end, though, he was forced to admit that he probably was alive.

"Then what's happening?" said the king.

"We don't know, O king," said Dil. "Really we don't. It's all come true, O fount of waters!"

"What has?"

"Everything!"

"Everything?"

"The sun, O lord. And the gods! Oh, the gods! They're everywhere, O master of heaven!"

"We come in through the back way," said Gern, who had dropped to his knees. "Forgive us, O lord of justice, who has come back to deliver his mighty wisdom and that. I am sorry about me and Glwenda, it was a moment of wossname, mad passion, we couldn't control ourselves. Also, it was me — "

Dil waved him into a devout silence.

"Excuse me," he said to the king's mummy. "But could we have a word away from the lad? Man to — "

"Corpse?" said the king, trying to make it easy for him. "Certainly."

They wandered over to the other side of the room.

"The fact is, O gracious king of — " Dil began, in a conspiratorial whisper.

"I think we can dispense with all that," said the king briskly. "The dead don't stand on ceremony. 'King' will be quite sufficient."

"The fact *is*, then — king," said Dil, experiencing a slight thrill at this equitable treatment, "young Gern thinks it's all his fault. I've told him over and over again that the gods wouldn't go to all this trouble just because of one growing lad with urges, if you catch my drift." He paused, and added carefully, "They wouldn't, would they?"

"Shouldn't think so for one minute," said the king briskly. "We'd never see the back of them, otherwise."

"That's what I told him," said Dil, immensely relieved. "He's a good boy, sir, it's just that his mum is a bit funny about religion. We'd never see the back of them, those were my very words. I'd be very grateful if you could have a word with him, sir, you know, set his mind at rest — "

"Be happy to," said the king graciously.

Dil sidled closer.

"The fact is, sir, these gods, sir, they aren't right. We've been watching, sir. At least, I have. I climbed on the roof. Gern didn't, he hid under the bench. They're not right, sir!"

"What's wrong with them!"

"Well, they're here, sir! That's not right, is it? I mean, not to be really here. And they're just striding around and fighting amongst themselves and shouting at people." He looked both ways before continuing. "Between you and me, sir," he said, "they don't seem too bright."

The king nodded. "What are the priests doing about this?" he said.

"I saw them throwing one another in the river, sir."

The king nodded again. "That sounds about right," he said. "They've come to their senses at last."

"You know what I think, sir?" said Dil earnestly. "Everything we believe is coming true. And I heard something else, sir. This morning, if it was this morning, you understand, because the sun's all over the place, sir, and it's not the right sort of sun, but this morning some of the soldiers tried to get out along the Ephebe road, sir, and do you know what they found?"

"What did they find?"

"The road out, sir, leads in!" Dil took a step backwards the better to illustrate the seriousness of the revelations. "They got up into the rocks and then suddenly they were walking down the Tsort road. It all sort of curves back on itself. We're shut in, sir. Shut in with our gods."

And I'm shut in my body, thought the king. Everything we believe is true? And what we believe isn't what we think we believe.

I mean, we *think* we believe that the gods are wise and just and powerful, but what we really believe is that they are like our father after a long day. And we think we believe the netherworld is a sort of paradise, but we really believe it's right here and you go to it in your body and I'm *in* it and I'm never going to get away. Never, ever.

"What's my son got to say about all this?" he said.

Dil coughed. It was the ominous cough. The Spanish use an

upside-down question mark to tell you what you're about to hear is a question; this was the kind of cough that tells you what you're about to hear is a dirge.

"Don't know how to tell you this, sir," he said.

"Out with it, man."

"Sir, they say he's dead, sir. They say he killed himself and ran away."

"Killed himself?"

"Sorry, sir."

"And ran away afterwards?"

"On a camel, they say."

"We lead an active afterlife in our family, don't we?" observed the king drily.

"Beg pardon, sir?"

"I mean, the two statements could be held to be mutually exclusive."

Dil's face became a well-meaning blank.

"That is to say, they can't both be true," supplied the king, helpfully.

"Ahem," said Dil.

"Yes, but I'm a special case," said the king testily. "In this kingdom we believe you live after death only if you've been mumm — "

He stopped.

It was too horrible to think about. He thought about it, nevertheless, for some time.

Then he said, "We must do something about it."

Dil said, "Your son, sir?"

"Never mind about my son, he's not dead, I'd know about it," snapped the king. "He can look after himself, he's my *son*. It's my ancestors I'm worried about."

"But they're *dead* — " Dil began.

It has already been remarked that Dil had a very poor imagination. In a job like his a poor imagination was essential. But his mind's eye opened on a panorama of pyramids, stretching along the river, and his mind's ear swooped and curved through solid doors that no thief could penetrate.

And it heard the scrabbling.

And it heard the hammering.

And it heard the muffled shouting.

The king put a bandaged arm over his trembling shoulders.

"I know you're a good man with a needle, Dil," he said. "Tell me — how are you with a sledgehammer?"

Copolymer, the greatest storyteller in the history of the world, sat back and beamed at the greatest minds in the world, assembled at the dining table.

Teppic had added another iota to his store of new knowledge. 'Symposium' meant a knife-and-fork tea.

"Well," said Copolymer, and launched into the story of the Tsortean Wars.

"You see, what happened was, *he'd* taken *her* back home, and her father — this wasn't the old king, this was the one before, the one with the wossname, he married some girl from over Elharib way, she had a squint, what was her name now, began with a P. Or an L. One of them letters, anyway. Her father owned an island out on the bay there, Papylos I think it was. No, I tell a lie, it was Crinix. *Anyway* the king, the other king, he raised an army and they . . . . Elenor, that was her name. She had a squint, you know. But quite attractive, they say. When I say married, I trust I do not have to spell it out for you. I mean, it was a bit unofficial. Er. Anyway, there was this wooden horse and after they'd got in. . . Did I tell you about this horse? It was a horse. I'm pretty sure it was a horse. Or maybe it was a chicken. Forget my own name next! It was wossname's idea, the one with the limp. Yes. The limp in his leg, I mean. Did I mention him? There'd been this fight. No, that was the other one, I think. Yes. Anyway, this wooden pig, damn clever idea, they made it out of thing. Tip of my tongue. Wood. But that was later, you know. The fight! Nearly forgot the fight. Yes. Damn good fight. Everyone banging on their shields and yelling. Wossname's armour shone like shining armour. Fight and a half, that fight. Between thingy, not the one with the limp, the other one, wossname, had red hair. *You* know. Tall fellow, talked with a lisp. Hold on, just remembered, he was from some other island. Not him. The other one, with the limp. Didn't want to go, he said he was mad. Of course, he *was* bloody mad, definitely. I mean, a wooden cow! Like wossname said, the king, no, not that king, the other one, he saw the goat, he said, 'I fear the Ephebians, especially when they're mad enough to leave bloody great wooden livestock on the doorstep, talk about nerve, they must think we was born yesterday, set fire to it,' and, of course, wossname had nipped in round the back and put everyone to the sword, talk about laugh. Did I say she had a squint? They said she was pretty, but it takes all sorts. Yes. Anyway, that's now it happened. *Now*, of course, wossname — I think he was called Melycanus, had a limp — he wanted to go home, well, you would, they'd been there for *years*, he wasn't getting any younger. That's why he dreamt up the thing about the wooden wossname. Yes. I tell a lie, Lavaelous was the one with the knee. Pretty good fight, that fight, take it from me."

He lapsed into self-satisfied silence.

"Pretty good fight," he mumbled and, smiling faintly, dropped off to sleep.

Teppic was aware that his own mouth was hanging open. He shut it. Along the table several of the diners were wiping their eyes.

"Magic," said Xeno. "Sheer magic. Every word a tassel on the canopy of Time."

"It's the way he remembers every tiny detail. Pin-sharp," murmured Ibid.

Teppic looked down the length of the table, and then nudged Xeno beside him. "Who is everyone?" he said.

"Well, Ibid you already know. And Copolymer. Over there, that's Iesope, the greatest teller of fables in the world. And that's Antiphon, the greatest writer of comic plays in the world."

"Where is Pthagonal?" said Teppic. Xeno pointed to the far end of the table, where a glum-looking, heavy-drinking man was trying to determine the angle between two bread rolls. "I'll introduce you to him afterwards," he said.

Teppic looked around at the bald heads and long white beards, which seemed to be a badge of office. If you had a bald head and a long white beard, they seemed to indicate, whatever lay between them must be bursting with wisdom. The only exception was Antiphon, who looked as though he was built of pork.

They are great minds, he told himself. These are men who are trying to work out how the world fits together, not by magic, not by religion, but just by inserting their brains in whatever crack they can find and trying to lever it apart.

Ibid rapped on the table for silence.

"The Tyrant has called for war on Tsort," he said. "Now, let us consider the place of war in the ideal republic," he said. "We would require — "

"Excuse me, could you just pass me the celery?" said Iesope. "Thank you."

" — the ideal republic, as I was saying, based on the fundamental laws that govern — "

"And the salt. It's just by your elbow."

" — the fundamental laws, that is, which govern all men. Now, it is without doubt true that war . . . could you stop that, please?"

"It's celery," said Iesope, crunching cheerfully. "You can't help it with celery."

Xeno peered suspiciously at what was on his fork.

"Here, this is squid," he said. "I didn't ask for squid. Who ordered squid?"

" — without doubt," repeated Ibid, raising his voice, "without doubt, I put it to you — "

"I think this is the lamb couscous," said Antiphon.

"Was yours the squid?"

"I asked for marida and dolmades."

"*I* ordered the lamb. Just pass it along, will you?"

"I don't remember anyone asking for all this garlic bread," said Xeno.

"Look, *some* of us are trying to float a philosophical concept here," said Ibid sarcastically. "Don't let us interrupt you, will you?"

Someone threw a breadstick at him.

Teppic looked at what was on *his* fork. Seafood was unknown in the kingdom, and what was on his fork had too many valves and suckers to be reassuring. He lifted a boiled vine leaf with extreme care, and was sure he saw something scuttle behind an olive.

Ah. Something else to remember, then. The Ephebians made wine out of anything they could put in a bucket, and ate anything that couldn't climb out of one.

He pushed the food around on his plate. Some of it pushed back.

And philosophers didn't listen to one another. And they don't stick to the point. This probably is mocracy at work.

A bread roll bounced past him. Oh, and they get over-excited.

He noticed a skinny little man sitting opposite him, chewing primly on some anonymous tentacle. Apart from Pthagonal the geometrician, who was now gloomily calculating the radius of his plate, he was the only person not speaking his mind at the top of his voice. Sometimes he'd make little notes on a piece of parchment and slip it into his toga.

Teppic leaned across. Further down the table Iesope, encouraged by occasional olive stones and bread rolls, started a long fable about a fox, a turkey, a goose and a wolf, who had a wager to see who could stay longest underwater with heavy weights tied to their feet.

"Excuse me," said Teppic, raising his voice above the din. "Who are you?"

The little man gave him a shy look. He had extremely large ears. In a certain light, he could have been mistaken for a very thin jug.

"I'm Endos," he said.

"Why aren't you philosophising?"

Endos sliced a strange mollusc.

"I'm not a philosopher, actually," he said.

"Or a humorous playwright or something?" said Teppic.

"I'm afraid not. I'm a Listener. Endos the Listener, I'm known as."

"That's fascinating," said Teppic automatically. "What does that involve?"

"Listening."

"Just listening?"

"That's what they pay me for," said Endos. "Sometimes I nod. Or smile. Or nod and smile at the same time. Encouragingly, you know. They like that."

Teppic felt he was called upon to comment at this point. "Gosh," he said.

Endos gave him an encouraging nod, and a smile that suggested that of all the things Endos could be doing in the world right at this minute there was nothing so basically riveting as listening to Teppic. It was something about his ears. They appeared to be a vast aural black hole, begging to be filled up with words. Teppic felt an overpowering urge to tell him all about his life and hopes and dreams. . .

"I bet," he said, "that they pay you an awful lot of money."

Endos gave him a heartening smile.

"Have you listened to Copolymer tell his story lots of times?"

Endos nodded and smiled, although there was a faint trace of pain right behind his eyes.

"I expect," said Teppic, "that your ears develop protective rough surfaces after a while?"

Endos nodded. "Do go on," he urged.

Teppic glanced across at Pthagonal, who was moodily drawing right angles in his taramasalata.

"I'd love to stay and listen to you listening to me all day," he said. "But there's a man over there I'd like to see."

"That's amazing," said Endos, making a short note and turning his attention to a conversation further along the table. A philosopher had averred that although truth was beauty, beauty was not necessarily truth, and a fight was breaking out. Endos listened carefully*.

Teppic wandered along the table to where Pthagonal was sitting in unrelieved misery, and currently peering suspiciously under the crust of a pie.

Teppic looked over his shoulder.

"I think I saw something moving in there," he said.

"Ah," said the geometrician, taking the cork out of an amphora with his teeth. "The mysterious young man in black from the lost kingdom."

"I was hoping you could help me find it again?" said Teppic. "I

---

*The role of listeners has never been fully appreciated. However, it is well known that most people don't listen. They use the time when someone else is speaking to think of what they're going to say next. True Listeners have always been revered among oral cultures, and prized for their rarity value; bards and poets are ten a cow, but a good Listener is hard to find, or at least hard to find twice.

heard that you have some very unusual ideas in Ephebe."

"It had to happen," said Pthagonal. He pulled a pair of dividers from the folds of his robe and measured the pie thoughtfully. "Is it a constant, do you think? It's a depressing concept."

"Sorry?" said Teppic.

"The diameter divides into the circumference, you know. It ought to be three times. You'd think so, wouldn't you? But does it? No. Three point one four one and lots of other figures. There's no end to the buggers. Do you know how pissed off that makes me?"

"I expect it makes you extremely pissed off," said Teppic politely.

"Right. It tells me that the Creator used the wrong kind of circles. It's not even a proper number! I mean, three point five, you could respect. Or three point three. That'd look *right*." He stared morosely at the pie.

"Excuse me, you said something about it had to happen?"

"What?" said Pthagonal, from the depths of his gloom. "Pie!" he added.

"What had to happen?" Teppic prompted.

"You can't mess with geometry, friend. Pyramids? Dangerous things. Asking for trouble. I mean," Pthagonal reached unsteadily for his wine cup, "how long did they think they could go on building bigger and bigger pyramids for? I mean, where did they think power comes from? I mean," he hiccuped, "you've been in that place, haven't you? Ever noticed how slow it all seems to be?"

"Oh, yes," said Teppic flatly.

"That's because the time is sucked up, see? Pyramids. So they have to flare it off. Flarelight, they call it. They think it looks pretty! It's their *time* they're burning off!"

"All I know is the air feels as though it's been boiled in a sock," said Teppic. "And nothing actually changes, even if it doesn't stay the same."

"Right," said Pthagonal. "The reason being, it's past time. They use up past time, over and over again. The pyramids take all the new time. And if you don't let the pyramids flare, the power build up'll — " he paused. "I suppose," he went on, "that it'd escape along a wossname, a fracture. In space."

"I was there before the kingdom, er, went," said Teppic. "I thought I saw the big pyramid move."

"There you are then. It's probably moved the dimensions around by ninety degrees," said Pthagonal, with the assurance of the truly drunk.

"You mean, so length is height and height is width?"

Pthagonal shook an unsteady finger.

"Nonono," he said. "So that length is height and height is breadth and breadth is width and width is — " he burped — "time. S'nother dimessnon, see? Four of the bastards. Time's one of them. Ninety thingys to the other three. Degrees is what I mean. Only, only, it can't exist in *this* world like that, so the place had to sort of pop outside for a bit, see? Otherwise you'd have people getting older by walking sideways." He looked sadly into the depths of his cup. "And every birthday you'd age another mile," he added.

Teppic looked at him aghast.

"That's time and space for you," Pthagonal went on. "You can twist them all over the place if you're not careful. Three point one four one. What sort of a number d'you call that?"

"It sounds horrible," said Teppic.

"Damn right. Somewhere," Pthagonal was beginning to sway on his bench, "somewhere someone built a universe with a decent, respectable value of, of," he peered blearily at the table, "of pie. Not some damn number that never comes to an end, what kind of — "

"I meant, people getting older just by walking along!"

"I dunno, though. You could have a stroll back to where you were eighteen. Or wander up and see what you were going to look like when you're seventy. Travelling in width, though, that'd be the *real* trick."

Pthagonal smiled vacantly and then, very slowly, keeled over into his dinner, some of which moved out of the way*.

---

*He was wrong. Nature abhors dimensional abnormalities, and seals them neatly away so that they don't upset people. Nature, in fact, abhors a lot of things, including vacuums, ships called the *Marie Celeste*, and the chuck keys for electric drills.

Teppic became aware that the philosophic din around him had subsided a bit. He stared along the line until he spotted Ibid.

"It won't work," said Ibid. "The Tyrant won't listen to us. Nor will the people. Anyway — " he glanced at Antiphon — "we're not all of one mind on the subject."

"Damn Tsorteans need teaching a lesson," said Antiphon sternly. "Not room for two major powers on this continent. Damn bad sports, anyway, just because we stole their queen. Youthful high spirits, love will have its way — "

Copolymer woke up.

"You've got it wrong," he said mildly. "The great war, that was because they stole *our* queen. What was her name now, face that launched a thousand camels, began with an A or a T or — "

"Did they?" shouted Antiphon. "The bastards!"

"I'm reasonably certain," said Copolymer.

Teppic sagged, and turned to Endos the Listener. He was still eating his dinner, with the air of one who is determined to preserve his digestion.

"Endos?"

The Listener laid his knife and fork carefully on either side of his plate.

"Yes?"

"They're really all mad, aren't they?" said Teppic wearily.

"That's extremely interesting," said Endos. "Do go on." He reached shyly into his toga and brought forth a scrap of parchment, which he pushed gently towards Teppic.

"What's this?"

"My bill," said Endos. "Five minutes Attentive Listening. Most of my gentlemen have monthly accounts, but I understand you'll be leaving in the morning?"

Teppic gave up. He wandered away from the table and into the cold garden surrounding the citadel of Ephebe. White marble statues of ancient Ephebians doing heroic things with no clothes on protruded through the greenery and, here and there, there were statues of Ephebian gods. It was hard to tell the difference. Teppic knew that Dios had hard words to say about the Ephebians for having gods that looked just like people. If the gods looked just like everyone else, he used to say, how would people know how to treat them?

Teppic had rather liked the idea. According to legend the Ephebians' gods *were* just like humans, except that they used their godhood to get up to things humans didn't have the nerve to do. A favourite trick of Ephebian gods, he recalled, was turning into some animal in order to gain the favours of highly-placed Ephebian women. And one of them had reputedly turned himself into a golden shower in pursuit of his intended. All this raised interesting questions about everyday night life in sophisticated Ephebe.

He found Ptraci sitting on the grass under a poplar tree, feeding the tortoise. He gave it a suspicious look, in case it was a god trying it on. It did not look like a god. If it was a god, it was putting on an incredibly good act.

She was feeding it a lettuce leaf.

"Dear little ptortoise," she said, and then looked up. "Oh, it's you," she said flatly.

"You didn't miss much," said Teppic, sagging on to the grass. "They're a bunch of maniacs. When I left they were smashing the plates."

"That's ptraditional at the end of an Ephebian meal," said Ptraci.

Teppic thought about this. "Why not before?" he said.

"And then they probably dance to the sound of the bourzuki," Ptraci added. "I think it's a sort of dog."

Teppic sat with his head in his hands.

"I must say you speak Ephebian well," he said.

"Pthank you."

"Just a trace of an accent, though."

"Languages is part of the ptraining," she said. "And my grandmother told me that a ptrace of foreign accent is more fascinating."

"We learned the same thing," said Teppic. "An assassin should always be slightly foreign, no matter where he is. I'm *good* at that part," he added bitterly.

She began to massage his neck.

"I went down to the harbour," she said. "There's those things like big rafts, you know, camels of the sea — "

"Ships," said Teppic.

"And they go everywhere. We could go anywhere we want. The world is our pthing with pearls in it, if we like."

Teppic told her about Pthagonal's theory. She didn't seem surprised.

"Like an old pond where no new water comes in," she observed. "So everyone goes round and round in the same old puddle. All the ptime you live has been lived already. It must be like other people's bathwater."

"I'm going to go back."

Her fingers stopped their skilled kneading of his muscles.

"We could go anywhere," she repeated. "We've got ptrades, we could sell that camel. You could show me that Ankh-Morpork place. It sounds interesting."

Teppic wondered what effect Ankh-Morpork would have on the girl. Then he wondered what effect she would have on the city. She was definitely — flowering. Back in the Old Kingdom she'd never apparently had any original thoughts beyond the choice of the next grape to peel, but since she was outside she seemed to have changed. Her jaw hadn't changed, it was still quite small and, he had to admit, very pretty. But somehow it was more noticeable. She used to look at the ground when she spoke to him. She still didn't always look at him when she spoke to him, but now it was because she was thinking about something else.

He found he kept wanting to say, politely, without stressing it in any way, just as a very gentle reminder, that he was king. But he had a feeling that she'd say she hadn't heard, and would he please repeat it, and if she looked at him he'd never be able to say it twice.

"You could go," he said. "You'd get on well. I could give you a few names and addresses."

"And what would you do?"

"I dread to think what's going on back home," said Teppic. "I ought to do something."

"You can't. Why ptry? Even if you didn't want to be an assassin there's lots of pthings you could do. And you said the man said it's not a place people could get into any more. I hate pyramids."

"Surely there's people there you care about?"

Ptraci shrugged. "If they're dead there's nothing I can do about it," she said. "And if they're alive, there's nothing I can do about it. So I shan't."

Teppic stared at her in a species of horrified admiration. It was a beautiful summary of things as they were. He just couldn't bring himself to think that way. His body had been away for seven years but his blood had been in the kingdom for a thousand times longer. Certainly he'd wanted to *leave* it behind, but that was the whole point. It would have been there. Even if he'd avoided it for the rest of his life, it would have still been a sort of anchor.

"I feel so wretched about it," he repeated. "I'm sorry. That's all there is to it. Even to go back for five minutes, just to say, well, that I'm not coming back. That'd be enough. It's probably all my fault."

"But there isn't a way back! You'll just hang around sadly, like those deposed kings you ptold me about. You know, with pthreadbare cloaks and always begging for their food in a high-class way. There's nothing more useless than a king without a kingdom, you said. Just think about it."

They wandered through the sunset streets of the city, and towards the harbour. All streets in the city led towards the harbour.

Someone was just putting a torch to the lighthouse, which was one of the More Than Seven Wonders of the World and had been built to a design by Pthagonal using the Golden Rule and the Five Aesthetic Principles. Unfortunately it had then been built in the wrong place because putting it in the right place would have spoiled the look of the harbour, but it was generally agreed by mariners to be a very beautiful lighthouse and something to look at while they were waiting to be towed off the rocks.

The harbour below it was thronged with ships. Teppic and Ptraci picked their way past crates and bundles until they reached the long curved guard wall, harbour calm on one side, choppy with waves on the other. Above them the lighthouse flared and sparked.

Those boats would be going to places he'd only ever heard of, he knew. The Ephebians were great traders. He could go back to Ankh and get his diploma, and then the world would indeed be

the mollusc of his choice and he had any amount of knives to
open it with.

Ptraci put her hand in his.

And there'd be none of this marrying relatives business. The
months in Djelibeybi already seemed like a dream, one of those
circular dreams that you never quite seem able to shake off and
which make insomnia an attractive prospect. Whereas here was
a future, unrolling in front of him like a carpet.

What a chap needed at a time like this was a sign, some sort
of book of instructions. The trouble with life was that you didn't
get a chance to practise before doing it for real. You only —

"Good grief? It's Teppic, isn't it?"

The voice was addressing him from ankle height. A head
appeared over the stone of the jetty, quickly followed by its
body. An extremely richly dressed body, one on which no
expense had been spared in the way of gems, furs, silks and
laces, provided that all of them, every single one, was black.

It was Chidder.

"What's it doing now?" said Ptaclusp.

His son poked his head cautiously over the ruins of a pillar
and watched Hat, the Vulture-Headed God.

"It's sniffing around," he said. "I think it likes the statue.
Honestly, dad, why did you have to go and buy a thing like
that?"

"It was in a job lot," said Ptaclusp. "Anyway, I thought it
would be a popular line."

"With who?"

"Well, *he* likes it."

Ptaclusp IIb risked another squint at the angular monstrosity
that was still hopping around the ruins.

"Tell him he can have it if he goes away," he suggested. "Tell
him he can have it at cost."

Ptaclusp winced. "At a *discount*," he said. "A special cut rate
for our supernatural customers."

He stared up at the sky. From their hiding place in the ruins
of the construction camp, with the Great Pyramid still

humming like a powerhouse behind them, they'd had an excellent view of the arrival of the gods. At first he'd viewed them with a certain amount of equanimity. Gods would be good customers, they always wanted temples and statues, he could deal directly, cut out the middle man.

And then it had occurred to him that a god, when he was unhappy about the product, as it might be, maybe the plasterwork wasn't exactly as per spec, or perhaps a corner of the temple was a bit low on account of unexpected quicksand, a god didn't just come around demanding in a loud voice to see the manager. No. A god knew exactly where you were, and got to the point. Also, gods were notoriously bad payers. So were humans, of course, but they didn't actually expect you to die before they settled the account.

His gaze turned to his other son, a painted silhouette against the statue, his mouth a frozen O of astonishment, and Ptaclusp reached a decision.

"I've just about had it with pyramids," he said. "Remind me, lad. If we ever get out of here, no more pyramids. We've got set in our ways. Time to branch out, I reckon."

"That's what I've been telling you for *ages*, dad!" said IIb. "I've told you, a couple of decent aqueducts will make a tremendous — "

"Yes, yes, I remember," said Ptaclusp. "Yes. Aqueducts. All those arches and things. Fine. Only I can't remember where you said you have to put the coffin in."

"*Dad!*"

"Don't mind me, lad. I think I'm going mad."

I couldn't have seen a mummy and two men over there, carrying sledgehammers. . .

It was, indeed, Chidder.

And Chidder had a boat.

Teppic knew that further along the coast the Seriph of Al-Khali lived in the fabulous palace of the Rhoxie, which was said to have been built in one night by a genie and was famed in myth and legend for its splendour*. The *Unnamed* was the Rhoxie afloat, but more so. Its designer had a gilt complex, and had tried every trick with gold paint, curly pillars and expensive drapes to make it look less like a ship and more like a boudoir that had collided with a highly suspicious type of theatre.

In fact, you needed an assassin's eye for hidden detail to notice how innocently the gaudiness concealed the sleekness of the hull and the fact, even when you added the cabin space and the holds together, that there still seemed to be a lot of capacity unaccounted for. The water around what Ptraci called the pointed end was strangely rippled, but it would be totally ridiculous to suspect such an obvious merchantman of having a concealed ramming spike underwater, or that a mere five minutes' work with an axe would turn this wallowing alcazar into something that could run away from nearly everything else afloat and make the few that *could* catch up seriously regret it.

"Very impressive," said Teppic.

"It's all show, really," said Chidder.

"Yes. I can see that."

"I mean, we're poor traders."

Teppic nodded. "The usual phrase is 'poor *but honest* traders'," he said.

Chidder smiled a merchant's smile. "Oh, I think we'll stick on 'poor' at the moment. How the hell are you, anyway? Last we heard you were going off to be king of some place no-one's ever heard of. And who is this *lovely* young lady?"

"Her na — " Teppic began.

"Ptraci," said Ptraci.

"She's a han — " Teppic began.

"She must surely be a royal princess," said Chidder smoothly. "And it would give me the greatest pleasure if she, if indeed *both* of you, would dine with me tonight. Humble sailor's fare, I'm afraid, but we muddle along, we muddle along."

"Not Ephebian, is it?" said Teppic.

"Ship's biscuit, salt beef, that sort of thing," said Chidder,

---

*It was, therefore, colloquially known as the Djinn palace.

without taking his eyes off Ptraci. They hadn't left her since she came on board.

Then he laughed. It was the old familiar Chidder laugh, not exactly without humour, but clearly well under the control of its owner's higher brain centres.

"What an astonishing coincidence," he said. "And us due to sail at dawn, too. Can I offer you a change of clothing? You both look somewhat, er, travel-stained."

"Rough sailor clothing, I expect," said Teppic, "As befits a humble merchant, correct me if I'm wrong?"

In fact Teppic was shown to a small cabin as exquisitely and carefully furnished as a jewelled egg, where there was laid upon the bed as fine an assortment of clothing as could be found anywhere on the Circle Sea. True, it all appeared second-hand, but carefully laundered and expertly stitched so that the sword cuts hardly showed at all. He gazed thoughtfully at the hooks on the wall, and the faint patching on the wood which hinted that various things had once been hung there and hastily removed.

He stepped out into the narrow corridor, and met Ptraci. She'd chosen a red court dress such as had been the fashion in Ankh-Morpork ten years previously, with puffed sleeves and vast concealed underpinnings and ruffs the size of millstones.

Teppic learned something new, which was that attractive women dressed in a few strips of gauze and a few yards of silk *can* actually look far more desirable when fully clad from neck to ankle. She gave an experimental twirl.

"There are any amount of things like this in there," she said. "Is this how women dress in Ankh-Morpork? It's like wearing a house. It doesn't half make you sweaty."

"Look, about Chidder," said Teppic urgently. "I mean, he's a good fellow and everything, but — "

"He's very kind, isn't he," she agreed.

"Well. Yes. He is," Teppic admitted, hopelessly. "He's an old friend."

"That's nice."

One of the crew materialised at the end of the corridor and bowed them into the state cabin, his air of old retainership marred only by the criss-cross pattern of scars on his head and some tattoos that made the pictures in *The Shuttered Palace* look like illustrations in a DIY shelving manual. The things he could make them do by flexing his biceps could keep entire dockside taverns fascinated for hours, and he was not aware that the worst moment of his entire life was only a few minutes away.

"This is all very pleasant," said Chidder, pouring some wine. He nodded at the tattooed man. "You may serve the soup, Alfonz," he added.

"Look, Chiddy, you're not a pirate, are you?" said Teppic, desperately.

"Is that what's been worrying you?" Chidder grinned his lazy grin.

It wasn't everything that Teppic had been worrying about, but it had been jockeying for top position. He nodded.

"No, we're not. We just prefer to, er, avoid paperwork wherever possible. You know? We don't like people to have all the worry of having to know everything we do."

"Only there's all the clothes — "

"Ah. We get *attacked* by pirates a fair amount. That's why father had the *Unnamed* built. It always surprises them. And the whole thing is morally sound. We get their ship, their booty, and any prisoners they may have get rescued and given a ride home at competitive rates."

"What do you do with the pirates?"

Chidder glanced at Alfonz.

"That depends on future employment prospects," he said. "Father always says that a man down on his luck should be offered a helping hand. On terms, that is. How's the king business?"

Teppic told him. Chidder listened intently, swilling the wine around in his glass.

"So that's it," he said at last. "We heard there was going to be a war. That's why we're sailing tonight."

"I don't blame you," said Teppic.

"No, I mean to get the trade organised. With both sides, naturally, because we're strictly impartial. The weapons produced on this continent are really quite shocking. Downright dangerous. You should come with us, too. You're a very valuable person."

"Never felt more valueless than right now," said Teppic despondently.

Chidder looked at him in amazement.

"But you're a king!" he said.

"Well, yes, but — "

"Of a country which technically still exists, but isn't actually reachable by mortal man?"

"Sadly so."

"And you can pass laws about, well, currency and taxation, yes?"

"I suppose so, but — "

"And you don't think you're valuable? Good grief, Tep, our accountants can probably think up fifty different ways to . . . well, my hands go damp just to think about it. Father will probably ask to move our head office there, for a start."

"Chidder, I explained. You *know* it. No-one can get in," said Teppic.

"That doesn't matter."

"*Doesn't matter?*"

"No, because we'll just make Ankh our main branch office and pay our taxes in wherever the place is. All we need is an official address in, I don't know, the Avenue of the Pyramids or something. Take my tip and don't give in on anything until father gives you a seat on the board. You're royal, anyway, that's always impressive . . ."

Chidder chattered on. Teppic felt his clothes growing hotter.

So this was it. You lost your kingdom, and then it was worth more because it was a tax haven, and you took a seat on the board, whatever that was, and that made it all right.

Ptraci defused the situation by grabbing Alfonz's arm as he was serving the pheasant.

"The Congress of The Friendly Dog and the Two Small Biscuits!" she exclaimed, examining the intricate tattoo. "You hardly ever see that these days. Isn't it well done? You can even make out the yoghurt."

Alfonz froze, and then blushed. Watching the glow spread across the great scarred head was like watching sunrise over a mountain range.

"What's the one on your other arm?"

Alfonz, who looked as though his past jobs had included being a battering ram, murmured something and, very shyly, showed her his forearm.

"'S'not really suitable for ladies," he whispered.

Ptraci brushed aside the wiry hair like a keen explorer, while Chidder stared at her with his mouth hanging open.

"Oh, I know that one," she said dismissively. "That's out of *130 Days of Pseudopolis*. It's physically impossible." She let go of the arm, and turned back to her meal. After a moment she looked up at Teppic and Chidder.

"Don't mind me," she said brightly. "Do go on."

"Alfonz, please go and put a proper shirt on," said Chidder, hoarsely.

Alfonz backed away, staring at his arm.

"Er. What was I, er, saying?" said Chidder. "Sorry. Lost the thread. Er. Have some more wine, Tep?"

Ptraci didn't just derail the train of thought, she ripped up the rails, burned the stations and melted the bridges for scrap. And so the dinner trailed off into beef pie, fresh peaches, crystallised sea urchins and desultory small talk about the good old days at the Guild. They had been three months ago. It seemed like a lifetime. Three months in the Old Kingdom *was* a lifetime.

After some time Ptraci yawned and went to her cabin, leaving the two of them alone with a fresh bottle of wine. Chidder watched her go in awed silence.

"Are there many like her back at your place?" he said.

"I don't know," Teppic admitted. "There could be. Usually they lie around the place peeling grapes or waving fans."

"She's amazing. She'll take them by storm in Ankh, you know. With a figure like that and a mind like . . . " He hesitated. "Is she . . . ? I mean, are you two . . . ?"

"No," said Teppic.

"She's very attractive."

"Yes," said Teppic.

"A sort of cross between a temple dancer and a bandsaw."

They took their glasses and went up on deck, where a few lights from the city paled against the brilliance of the stars. The water was flat calm, almost oily.

Teppic's head was beginning to spin slowly. The desert, the

sun, two gloss coats of Ephebian retsina on his stomach lining and a bottle of wine were getting together to beat up his synapses.

"I mus' say," he managed, leaning on the rail, "you're doing all right for yourself."

"It's okay," said Chidder. "Commerce is quite interesting. Building up markets, you know. The cut and thrust of competition in the privateering sector. You ought to come in with us, boy. It's where the future lies, my father says. Not with wizards and kings, but with enterprising people who can afford to hire them. No offence intended, you understand."

"We're all that's left," said Teppic to his wine glass. "Out of the whole kingdom. Me, her, and a camel that smells like an old carpet. An ancient kingdom, lost."

"Good job it wasn't a new one," said Chidder. "At least people got some wear out of it."

"You don't know what it's like," said Teppic. "It's like a whole great pyramid. But upside down, you understand? All that history, all those ancestors, all the people, all funnelling down to me. Right at the bottom."

He slumped on to a coil of rope as Chidder passed the bottle back and said, "It makes you think, doesn't it? There's all these lost cities and kingdoms around. Like Ee, in the Great Nef. Whole countries, just gone. Just out there somewhere. Maybe people started mucking about with geometry, what do you say?"

Teppic snored.

After some moments Chidder swayed forward, dropped the empty bottle over the side — it went plunk, and for a few seconds a stream of bubbles disturbed the flat calm — and staggered off to bed.

Teppic dreamed.

And in his dream he was standing on a high place, but unsteadily, because he was balancing on the shoulders of his father and mother, and below them he could make out his grandparents, and below them his ancestors stretching away and out in a vast, all right, a vast *pyramid* of humanity whose base was lost in clouds.

He could hear the murmur of shouted orders and instructions floating up to him.

If you do nothing, we shall never have been.

"This is just a dream," he said, and stepped out of it into a palace where a small, dark man in a loincloth was sitting on a stone bench, eating figs.

"Of course it's a dream," he said. "The world is the dream of the Creator. It's all dreams, different kinds of dreams. They're supposed to tell you things. Like: don't eat lobster last thing at night. Stuff like that. Have you had the one about the seven cows?"

"Yes," said Teppic, looking around. He'd dreamed quite good architecture. "One of them was playing a trombone."

"It was smoking a cigar in my day. Well-known ancestral dream, that dream."

"What does it mean?"

The little man picked a seed from between his teeth.

"Search me," he said. "I'd give my right arm to find out. I don't think we've met, by the way. I'm Khuft. I founded this kingdom. You dream a good fig."

"I'm dreaming you, too?"

"Damn right. I had a vocabulary of eight hundred words, do you think I'd really be talking like this? If you're expecting a bit of helpful ancestral advice, forget it. This is a *dream*. I can't tell you anything you don't know yourself."

"You're the *founder*?"

"That's me."

"I. . .thought you'd be different," said Teppic.

"How d'you mean?"

"Well. . .on the statue. . ."

Khuft waved a hand impatiently.

"That's just public relations," he said. "I mean, look at me. Do I look patriarchal?"

Teppic gave him a critical appraisal. "Not in that loincloth," he admitted. "It's a bit, well, ragged."

"It's got years of wear left in it," said Khuft.

"Still, I expect it's all you could grab when you were fleeing from persecution," said Teppic, anxious to show an understanding nature.

Khuft took another fig and gave him a lopsided look. "How's that again?"

"You were being persecuted," said Teppic. "That's why you fled into the desert."

"Oh, yes. You're right. Damn right. I was being persecuted for my beliefs."

"That's terrible," said Teppic.

Khuft spat. "Damn right. I believed people wouldn't notice I'd sold them camels with plaster teeth until I was well out of town."

It took a little while for this to sink in, but it managed it with all the aplomb of a concrete block in a quicksand.

"You're a *criminal*?" said Teppic.

"Well, criminal's a dirty word, know what I mean?" said the little ancestor. "I'd prefer entrepreneur. I was ahead of my time, that's my trouble."

"And you were running away?" said Teppic weakly.

"It wouldn't," said Khuft, "have been a good idea to hang about."

"'And Khuft the camel herder became lost in the Desert, and there opened before him, as a Gift from the Gods, a Valley flowing with Milk and Honey'," quoted Teppic, in a hollow voice. He added, "I used to think it must have been awfully sticky."

"There I was, dying of thirst, all the camels kicking up a din, yelling for water, next minute — whoosh — a bloody great river valley, reed beds, hippos, the whole thing. Out of nowhere. I nearly got knocked down in the stampede."

"No!" said Teppic. "It wasn't like that! The gods of the valley took pity on you and showed you the way in, didn't they?" He shut up, surprised at the tones of pleading in his own voice.

Khuft sneered. "Oh, yes? And I just happened to stumble across a hundred miles of river in the middle of the desert that everyone else had missed. Easy thing to miss, a hundred miles of river valley in the middle of a desert, isn't it? Not that I was going to look a gift camel in the mouth, you understand, I went and brought my family and the rest of the lads in soon enough. Never looked back."

"One minute it wasn't there, the next minute it was?" said Teppic.

"Right enough. Hard to believe, isn't it."

"No," said Teppic. "No. Not really."

Khuft poked him with a wrinkled finger. "I always reckoned it was the camels that did it," he said. "I always thought they sort of called it into place, like it was sort of potentially there but not quite, and it needed just that little bit of effort to make it real. Funny things, camels."

"I know."

"Odder than gods. Something the matter?"

"Sorry," said Teppic, "it's just that this is all a bit of a shock. I mean, I thought we were really royal. I mean, we're more royal than *anyone*."

Khuft picked a fig seed from between two blackened stumps which, because they were in his mouth, probably had to be called his teeth. Then he spat.

"That's up to you," he said, and vanished.

Teppic walked through the necropolis, the pyramids a saw-edged skyline against the night. The sky was the arched body of a woman, and the gods stood around the horizon. They didn't look like the gods that had been painted on the walls for thousands of years. They looked worse. They looked older than Time. After all, the gods hardly ever meddled in the affairs of men. But other things were proverbial for it.

"What can I do? I'm only human," he said aloud.

Someone said, *Not all of you.*

Teppic awoke, to the screaming of seagulls.

Alfonz, who was wearing a long-sleeved shirt and the expression of one who never means to take it off again, ever, was helping several other men unfurl one of *Unnamed*'s sails. He looked down at Teppic in his bed of rope and gave him a nod.

They were moving. Teppic sat up, and saw the dockside of Ephebe slipping silently away in the grey morning light.

He stood up unsteadily, groaned, clutched at his head, took a run and dived over the rail.

*

Heme Krona, owner of the Camels-R-Us livery stable, walked slowly around You Bastard, humming. He examined the camel's knees. He gave one of its feet an experimental kick. In a swift movement that took You Bastard completely by surprise he jerked open the beast's mouth and examined his great yellow teeth, and then jumped away.

He took a plank of wood from a heap in the corner, dipped a brush in a pot of black paint, and after a moment's thought carefully wrote, ONE OWNER.

After some further consideration he added, LO! MILEAGE.

He was just brushing in GOOD RUNER when Teppic staggered in and leaned, panting, against the doorframe. Pools of water formed around his feet.

"I've come for my camel," he said.

Krona sighed.

"Last night you said you'd be back in an hour," he said. "I'm going to have to charge you for a whole day's livery, right? Plus I gave him a rub down and did his feet, the full service. That'll be five *cercs*, okay emir?"

"Ah." Teppic patted his pocket.

"Look," he said. "I left home in a bit of a hurry, you see. I don't seem to have any cash on me."

"Fair enough, emir." Krona turned back to his board. "How do you spell YEARS WARENTY?"

"I will definitely have the money sent to you," said Teppic.

Krona gave him the withering smile of one who has seen it all — asses with bodywork re-haired, elephants with plaster tusks, camels with false humps glued on — and knows the festering depths of the human soul when it gets down to business.

"Pull the other one, rajah," he said. "It has got bells on."

Teppic fumbled in his tunic.

"I could give you this valuable knife," he said.

Krona gave it a passing glance, and sniffed.

"Sorry, emir. No can do. No pay, no camel."

"I could give it to you point first," said Teppic desperately, knowing that the mere threat would get him expelled from the Guild. He was also aware that as a threat it wasn't very good. Threats weren't on the syllabus at the Guild school.

Whereas Krona had, sitting on straw bales at the back of the stables, a couple of large men who were just beginning to take an interest in the proceedings. They looked like Alfonz's older brothers.

Every vehicle depot of any description anywhere in the multiverse has them. They're never exactly grooms or mechanics or customers or staff. Their function is always unclear. They chew straws or smoke cigarettes in a surreptitious fashion. If there are such things as newspapers around, they read them, or at least look at the pictures.

They started to watch Teppic closely. One of them picked up a couple of bricks and began to toss them up and down.

"You're a young lad, I can see that," said Krona, kindly. "You're just starting out in life, emir. You don't want trouble." He stepped forward.

You Bastard's huge shaggy head turned to look at him. In the depths of his brain columns of little numbers whirred upwards again.

"Look, I'm sorry, but I've got to have my camel back," said Teppic. "It's life and death!"

Krona waved a hand at the two extraneous men.

You Bastard kicked him. You Bastard had very concise ideas about people putting their hands in his mouth. Besides, he'd seen the bricks, and every camel knew what two bricks added up to. It was a good kick, toes well spread, powerful and deceptively slow. It picked Krona up and delivered him neatly into a steaming heap of augean stable sweepings.

Teppic ran, kicked away from the wall, grabbed You Bastard's dusty coat and landed heavily on his neck.

"I'm very sorry," he said, to such of Krona as was visible. "I really will have some money sent to you."

You Bastard, at this point, was waltzing round and round in a circle. Krona's companions stayed well back as feet like plates whirred through the air.

Teppic leaned forward and hissed into one madly-waving ear.

"We're going home," he said.

*

They had chosen the first pyramid at random. The king peered at the cartouche on the door.

"'Blessed is Queen Far-re-ptah'," read Dil dutifully, "Ruler of the Skies, Lord of the Djel, Master of — "

"Grandma Pooney," said the king. "She'll do." He looked at their startled faces. "That's what I used to call her when I was a little boy. I couldn't pronounce Far-re-ptah, you see. Well, go on then. Stop gawking. Break the door down."

Gern hefted the hammer uncertainly.

"It's a pyramid, master," he said, appealing to Dil. "You're not supposed to open them."

"What do you suggest, lad? We stick a tableknife in the slot and wiggle it about?" said the king.

"Do it, Gern," said Dil. "It will be all right."

Gern shrugged, spat on his hands which were, in fact, quite damp enough with the sweat of terror, and swung.

"Again," said the king.

The great slab boomed as the hammer hit it, but it was granite, and held. A few flakes of mortar floated down, and then the echoes came back, shunting back and forth along the dead avenues of the necropolis.

"Again."

Gern's biceps moved like turtles in grease.

This time there was an answering boom, such as might be caused by a heavy lid crashing to the ground, far away.

They stood in silence, listening to a slow shuffling noise from inside the pyramid.

"Shall I hit it again, sire?" said Gern. They both waved him into silence.

The shuffling grew closer.

Then the stone moved. It stuck once or twice, but nevertheless it moved, slowly, pivoting on one side so that a crack of dark shadow appeared. Dil could just make out a darker shape in the blackness.

"Yes?" it said.

"It's me, Grandma," said the king.

The shadow stood motionless.

"What, young Pootle?" it said, suspiciously.

The king avoided Dil's face.

"That's right, Grandma. We've come to let you out."

"Who're these men?" said the shadow petulantly. "I've got nothing, young man," she said to Gern. "I don't keep any money in the pyramid and you can put that weapon away, it doesn't frighten me."

"They're servants, Grandma," said the king.

"Have they got any identification?" muttered the old lady.

"*I'm* identifying them, Grandma. We've come to let you out."

"I was hammering *hours*," said the late queen, emerging into the sunlight. She looked exactly like the king, except that the mummy wrappings were greyer and dusty. "I had to go and have a lie down, come the finish. No-one cares about you when you're dead. Where're we going?"

"To let the others out," said the king.

"Damn good idea." The old queen lurched into step behind him.

"So this is the netherworld, is it?" she said. "Not much of an improvement." She elbowed Gern sharply. "You dead too, young man?"

"No, ma'am," said Gern, in the shaky brave tones of someone on a tightrope over the chasms of madness.

"It's not worth it. Be told."

"Yes, ma'am."

The king shuffled across the ancient pavings to the next pyramid.

"I know this one," said the queen. "It was here in my day. King Ashk-ur-men-tep. Third Empire. What's the hammer for, young man?"

"Please, ma'am, I have to hammer on the door, ma'am," said Gern.

"You don't have to knock. He's always in."

"My assistant means to smash the seals, ma'am," said Dil, anxious to please.

"Who're you?" the queen demanded.

"My name is Dil, O queen. Master embalmer."

"Oh, you are, are you? I've got some stitching wants seeing to."

"It will be an honour and a privilege, O queen," said Dil.

"Yes. It will," she said, and turned creakily to Gern. "Hammer away, young man!" she said.

Spurred by this, Gern brought the hammer round in a long, fast arc. It passed in front of Dil's nose making a noise like a partridge and smashed the seal into pieces.

What emerged, when the dust had settled, was not dressed in the height of fashion. The bandages were brown and mouldering and, Dil noticed with professional concern, already beginning to go at the elbows. When it spoke, it was like the opening of ancient caskets.

"I woket up," it said. "And theyre was noe light. Is thys the netherworld?"

"It would appear not," said the queen.

"Thys is *all*?"

"Hardly worth the trouble of dying, was it?" said the queen.

The ancient king nodded, but gently, as though he was afraid his head would fall off.

"Somethyng," he said, "must be done."

He turned to look at the Great Pyramid, and pointed with what had once been an arm.

"Who slepes there?" he said.

"It's mine, actually," said Teppicymon, lurching forward. "I don't think we've met, I haven't been interred as yet, my son built it for me. It was against my better judgment, believe me."

"It ys a dretful thyng," said the ancient king. "I felt its building. Even in the sleep of deathe I felt it. It is big enough to interr the worlde."

"I wanted to be buried at sea," said Teppicymon. "I hate pyramids."

"You do not," said Ashk-ur-men-tep.

"Excuse me, but I do," said the king, politely.

"But you do not. What you feel nowe is myld dislike. When you have lain in one for a thousand yeares," said the ancient one, "*then* you will begin to know the meaning of hate."

Teppicymon shuddered.

"The sea," he said. "That's the place. You just dissolve away."

They set off towards the next pyramid. Gern led the way, his face a picture, possibly one painted late at night by an artist who got his inspiration on prescription. Dil followed. He held his chest high. He'd always hoped to make his way in the world and here he was now, walking with kings.

Well. *Lurching* with kings.

It was another nice day in the high desert. It was always a nice day, if by nice you meant an air temperature like an oven and sand you could roast chestnuts on.

You Bastard ran fast, mainly to keep his feet off the ground for as long as possible. For a moment, as they staggered up the hills outside the olive-tree'd, field-patchworked oasis around Ephebe, Teppic thought he saw the *Unnamed* as a tiny speck on the azure sea. But it might have been just a gleam on a wave.

Then he was over the crest, into a world of yellow and umber. For a while scrubby trees held on against the sand, but the sand won and marched triumphantly onwards, dune after dune.

The desert was not only hot, it was quiet. There were no birds, none of the susurration of organic creatures busily being alive. At night there might have been the whine of insects, but they were deep under the sand against the scorch of day, and the yellow sky and yellow sand became a anechoic chamber in which You Bastard's breath sounded like a steam-engine.

Teppic had learned many things since he first went forth from the Old Kingdom, and he was about to learn one more. All authorities agree that when crossing the scorching desert it is a good idea to wear a hat.

You Bastard settled into the shambling trot that a prime racing camel can keep up for hours.

After a couple of miles Teppic saw a column of dust behind the next dune. Eventually they came up behind the main body of the Ephebian army, swinging along around half-a-dozen battle elephants, their helmet plumes waving in the oven breeze. They cheered on general principles as Teppic went past.

Battle elephants! Teppic groaned. Tsort went in for battle elephants, too. Battle elephants were the fashion lately. They weren't much good for anything except trampling on their own troops when they inevitably panicked, so the military minds on both sides had responded by breeding bigger elephants. Elephants were impressive.

For some reason, many of these elephants were towing great carts full of timber.

He jogged onwards as the sun wound higher and, and this was unusual, blue and purple dots began to pinwheel gently across the horizon.

Another strange thing was happening. The camel seemed to be trotting across the sky. Perhaps this had something to do with the ringing noise in his ears.

Should he stop? But then the camel might fall off. . .

It was long past noon when You Bastard staggered into the baking shade of the limestone outcrop which had once marked the edge of the valley, and collapsed very slowly into the sand. Teppic rolled off.

A detachment of Ephebians were staring across the narrow space towards a very similar number of Tsorteans on the other side. Occasionally, for the look of the thing, one of them waved a spear.

When Teppic opened his eyes it was to see the fearsome bronze masks of several Ephebian soldiers peering down at him. Their metal mouths were locked in sneers of terrible disdain. Their shining eyebrows were twisted in mortal anger.

One of them said, "He's coming round, sarge."

A metal face like the anger of the elements came closer, filling Teppic's vision.

"We've been out without our hat, haven't we, sonny boy," it said, in a cheery voice that echoed oddly inside the metal. "In a hurry to get to grips with the enemy, were we?"

The sky wheeled around Teppic, but a thought bobbed into the frying pan of his mind, seized control of his vocal chords and croaked: "The camel!"

"You ought to be put away, treating it like that," said the sergeant, waggling a finger at him. "Never seen one in such a state."

"Don't let it have a drink!" Teppic sat bolt upright, great gongs clanging and hot, heavy fireworks going off inside his skull. The helmeted heads turned towards one another.

"Gods, he must have something really terrible against camels," said one of them. Teppic staggered upright and lurched across the sand to You Bastard, who was trying to work out the complex equation which would allow him to get to his feet. His tongue was hanging out, and he was not feeling well.

A camel in distress isn't a shy creature. It doesn't hang around in bars, nursing a solitary drink. It doesn't phone up old friends and sob at them. It doesn't mope, or write long soulful poems about Life and how dreadful it is when seen from a bedsitter. It doesn't know what angst *is*.

All a camel has got is a pair of industrial-strength lungs and a voice like a herd of donkeys being chainsawed.

Teppic advanced through the blaring. You Bastard reared his head and turned it this way and that, triangulating. His eyes rolled madly as he did the camel trick of apparently looking at Teppic with his nostrils.

He spat.

He *tried* to spit.

Teppic grabbed his halter and pulled on it.

"Come on, you bastard," he said. "There's water. You can *smell* it. All you have to do is work out how to get there!"

He turned to the assembled soldiers. They were staring at him with expressions of amazement, apart from those who hadn't removed their helmets and who were staring at him with expressions of metallic ferocity.

Teppic snatched a water skin from one of them, pulled out the stopper and tipped it on to the ground in front of the camel's twitching nose.

"There's a river here," he hissed. "You know where it is, all you've got to do is go there!"

The soldiers looked around nervously. So did several Tsorteans, who had wandered up to see what was going on.

You Bastard got to his feet, knees trembling, and started to spin around in a circle. Teppic clung on.

. . . let d equal 4, thought You Bastard desperately. Let a.d equal 90. Let not-d equal 45 . . .

"I need a stick!" shouted Teppic, as he was whirled past the sergeant. "They never understand anything unless you hit them with a stick, it's like punctuation to a camel!"

"Is a sword any good?"

"No!"

The sergeant hesitated, and then passed Teppic his spear.

He grabbed it point-end first, fought for balance, and then brought it smartly across the camel's flank, raising a cloud of dust and hair.

You Bastard stopped. His ears turned like radar aerials. He stared at the rock wall, rolling his eyes. Then, as Teppic grabbed a handful of hair and pulled himself up, the camel started to trot.

. . . Think *fractals* . . .

" 'Ere, you're going to run straight — " the sergeant began.

There was silence. It went on for a long time.

The sergeant shifted uneasily. Then he looked across the rocks to the Tsorteans, and caught the eye of their leader. With the unspoken understanding that is shared by centurions and sergeant-majors everywhere, they walked towards one another along the length of the rocks and stopped by the barely visible crack in the cliff.

The Tsortean sergeant ran his hand over it.

"You'd think there'd be some, you know, camel hairs or something," he said.

"Or blood," said the Ephebian.

"I reckon it's one of them unexplainable phenomena."

"Oh. That's all right, then."

The two men stared at the stone for a while.

"Like a mirage," said the Tsortean, helpfully.

"One of them things, yes."

"I thought I heard a seagull, too."

"Daft, isn't it. You don't get them out here."

The Tsortean coughed politely, and stared back at his men. Then he leaned closer.

"The rest of your people will be along directly, I expect," he said.

The Ephebian stepped a bit closer and, when he spoke, it was out of the corner of his mouth while his eyes apparently remained fully occupied by looking at the rocks.

"That's right," he said. "And yours too, may I ask?"

"Yes. I expect we'll have to massacre you if ours get here first."

"Likewise, I shouldn't wonder. Still, can't be helped."

"One of those things, really," agreed the Tsortean.

The other man nodded. "Funny old world, when you come to think about it."

"You've put your finger on it, all right." The sergeant loosened his breastplate a bit, glad to be out of the sun. "Rations okay on your side?" he said.

"Oh, you know. Mustn't grumble."

"Like us, really."

"'Cos if you *do* grumble, they get even worse."

"Just like ours. Here, you haven't got any figs on your side, have you? I could just do with a fig."

"Sorry."

"Just thought I'd ask."

"Got plenty of dates, if they're any good to you."

"We're okay on dates, thanks."

"Sorry."

The two men stood awhile, lost in their own thoughts. Then the Ephebian put on his helmet again, and the Tsortean adjusted his belt.

"Right, then."

"Right, then."

They squared their shoulders, stuck out their chins, and marched away. A moment later they turned about smartly and, exchanging the merest flicker of an embarrassed grin, headed back to their own sides.

BOOK IV

The Book of 101 Things A Boy Can Do

Teppic had expected —

   — what?

Possibly the splat of flesh hitting rock. Possibly, although this was on the very edge of expectation, the sight of the Old Kingdom spread out below him.

He hadn't expected chilly, damp mists.

It is now known to science that there are many more dimensions than the classical four. Scientists say that these don't normally impinge on the world because the extra dimensions are very small and curve in on themselves, and that since reality is fractal most of it is tucked inside itself. This means either that the universe is more full of wonders than we can hope to understand or, more probably, that scientists make things up as they go along.

But the multiverse is full of little dimensionettes, playstreets of creation where creatures of the imagination can romp without being knocked down by serious actuality. Sometimes, as they drift through the holes in reality, they impinge back on this universe, when they give rise to myths, legends and charges of being Drunk and Disorderly.

And it was into one of these that You Bastard, by a trivial miscalculation, had trotted.

Legend had got it nearly right. The Sphinx *did* lurk on the borders of the kingdom. The legend just hadn't been precise about what kind of borders it was talking about.

The Sphinx is an unreal creature. It exists solely because it has been imagined. It is well-known that in an infinite universe everything that can be imagined must exist somewhere, and since many of them are not things that ought to exist in a well-

ordered space-time frame they get shoved into a side dimension.
This may go some way to explaining the Sphinx's chronic bad
temper, although any creature created with the body of a lion,
bosom of a woman and wings of an eagle has a serious identity
crisis and doesn't need much to make it angry.

So it had devised the Riddle.

Across various dimensions it had provided the Sphinx with
considerable entertainment and innumerable meals.

This was not known to Teppic as he led You Bastard through
the swirling mists, but the bones he crunched underfoot gave
him enough essential detail.

A lot of people had died here. And it was reasonable to assume
that the more recent ones had seen the remains of the earlier
ones, and would therefore have proceeded stealthily. And that
hadn't worked.

No sense in creeping along, then. Besides, some of the rocks
that loomed out of the mists had a very distressing shape. This
one here, for example, looked exactly like —

"Halt," said the Sphinx.

There was no sound but the drip of the mist and the occasional
sucking noise of You Bastard trying to extract moisture from the
air.

"You're a sphinx," said Teppic.

"*The* Sphinx," corrected the Sphinx.

"Gosh. We've got any amount of statues to you at home."
Teppic looked up, and then further up. "I thought you'd be
smaller," he added.

"Cower, mortal," said the Sphinx. "For thou art in the
presence of the wise and the terrible." It blinked. "Any good,
these statues?"

"They don't do you justice," said Teppic, truthfully.

"Do you really think so? People often get the nose wrong," said
the Sphinx. "My right profile is best, I'm told, and — " It dawned
on the Sphinx that it was sidetracking itself. It coughed sternly.

"Before you can pass me, O mortal," it said, "you must answer
my riddle."

"Why?" said Teppic.

"What?" The Sphinx blinked at him. It hadn't been designed
for this sort of thing.

"Why? Why? Because. Er. Because, hang on, yes, because I will bite your head off if you don't. Yes, I think that's it."

"Right," said Teppic. "Let's hear it, then."

The Sphinx cleared its throat with a noise like an empty lorry reversing in a quarry.

"What goes on four legs in the morning, two legs at noon, and three legs in the evening?" said the Sphinx smugly.

Teppic considered this.

"That's a tough one," he said, eventually.

"The toughest," said the Sphinx.

"Um."

"You'll never get it."

"Ah," said Teppic.

"Could you take your clothes off while you're thinking? The threads play merry hell with my teeth."

"There isn't some kind of animal that regrows legs that have been — "

"Entirely the wrong track," said the Sphinx, stretching its claws.

"Oh."

"You haven't got the faintest idea, have you?"

"I'm still thinking," said Teppic.

"You'll never get it."

"You're right." Teppic stared at the claws. This isn't really a fighting animal, he told himself reassuringly, it's definitely over-endowed. Besides, its bosom will get in the way, even if its brain doesn't.

"The answer is: 'A Man'," said the Sphinx. "Now, don't put up a fight, please, it releases unpleasant chemicals into the bloodstream."

Teppic backed away from a slashing paw. "Hold on, hold on," he said. "What do you mean, a man?"

"It's easy," said the Sphinx. "A baby crawls in the morning, stands on both legs at noon, and at evening an old man walks with a stick. Good, isn't it?"

Teppic bit his lip. "We're talking about *one day* here?" he said doubtfully.

There was a long, embarrassing silence.

"It's a wossname, a figure of speech," said the Sphinx irritably, making another lunge.

"No, no, look, wait a minute," said Teppic. "I'd like us to be very clear about this, right? I mean, it's only fair, right?"

"Nothing wrong with the riddle," said the Sphinx. "Damn good riddle. Had that riddle for fifty years, sphinx and cub." It thought about this. "Chick," it corrected.

"It's a good riddle," Teppic said soothingly. "Very deep. Very moving. The whole human condition in a nutshell. But you've got to admit, this doesn't all happen to one individual in one day, does it?"

"Well. No," the Sphinx admitted. "But that is self-evident from the context. An element of dramatic analogy is present in all riddles," it added, with the air of one who had heard the phrase a long time ago and rather liked it, although not to the extent of failing to eat the originator.

"Yes, *but*," said Teppic crouching down and brushing a clear space on the damp sand, "is there internal consistency within the metaphor? Let's say for example that the average life expectancy is seventy years, okay?"

"Okay," said the Sphinx, in the uncertain tones of someone who has let the salesman in and is now regretfully contemplating a future in which they are undoubtedly going to buy life insurance.

"*Right*. Good. So noon would be age 35, am I right? Now considering that most children can toddle at a year or so, the four legs reference is really unsuitable, wouldn't you agree? I mean, most of the morning is spent on two legs. According to your analogy — " he paused and did a few calculations with a convenient thighbone — "only about twenty minutes immediately after 00.00 hours, half an hour tops, is spent on four legs. Am I right? Be fair."

"Well — " said the Sphinx.

"By the same token you wouldn't be using a stick by six p.m. because you'd be only, er, 52," said Teppic, scribbling furiously. "In fact you wouldn't really be looking at any kind of walking aid until at least half past nine, I think. That's on the assumption that the entire lifespan takes place over one day which is, I believe I have already pointed out, ridiculous. I'm sorry, it's basically okay, but it doesn't work."

"Well," said the Sphinx, but irritably this time, "I don't see what I can do about it. I haven't got any more. It's the only one I've ever needed."

"You just need to alter it a bit, that's all."

"How do you mean?"

"Just make it a bit more realistic."

"Hmm." The Sphinx scratched its mane with a claw.

"Okay," it said doubtfully. "I suppose I could ask: What is it that walks on four legs — "

"Metaphorically speaking," said Teppic.

"Four legs, metaphorically speaking," the Sphinx agreed, "for about — "

"Twenty minutes, I think we agreed."

" — okay, fine, twenty minutes in the morning, on two legs — "

"But I think calling it in 'the morning' is stretching it a bit," said Teppic. "It's just after midnight. I mean, technically it's the morning, but in a very real sense it's still last night, what do you think?"

A look of glazed panic crossed the Sphinx's face.

"What do *you* think?" it managed.

"Let's just see where we've got to, shall we? What, metaphorically speaking, walks on four legs just after midnight, on two legs for most of the day — "

" — barring accidents," said the Sphinx, pathetically eager to show that it was making a contribution.

"Fine, on two legs barring accidents, until least suppertime, when it walks with three legs — "

"I've known people use two walking sticks," said the Sphinx helpfully.

"Okay. How about: when it continues to walk on two legs or with any prosthetic aids of its choice?"

The Sphinx gave this some consideration.

"Ye — ess," it said gravely. "That seems to fit all eventualities."

"Well?" said Teppic.

"Well what?" said the Sphinx.

"Well, what's the answer?"

The Sphinx gave him a stony look, and then showed its fangs.

"Oh no," it said. "You don't catch me out like that. You think I'm stupid? *You've* got to tell *me* the answer."

"Oh, blow," said Teppic.

"Thought you had me there, didn't you?" said the Sphinx.

"Sorry."

"You thought you could get me all confused, did you?" The Sphinx grinned.

"It was worth a try," said Teppic.

"Can't blame you. So what's the answer, then?"

Teppic scratched his nose.

"Haven't a clue," he said. "Unless, and this is a shot in the dark, you understand, it's: A Man."

The Sphinx glared at him.

"You've been here before, haven't you?" it said accusingly.

"No."

"Then someone's been talking, right?"

"Who could have talked? Has anyone ever guessed the riddle?" said Teppic.

"No!"

"Well, then. They couldn't have talked, could they?"

The Sphinx's claws scrabbled irritably on its rock.

"I suppose you'd better move along, then," it grumbled.

"Thank you," said Teppic.

"I'd be grateful if you didn't tell anyone, please," added the Sphinx, coldly. "I wouldn't like to spoil it for other people."

Teppic scrambled up a rock and on to You Bastard.

"Don't you worry about that," he said, spurring the camel onwards. He couldn't help noticing the way the Sphinx was moving its lips silently, as though trying to work something out.

You Bastard had gone only twenty yards or so before an enraged bellow erupted behind him. For once he forgot the etiquette that says a camel must be hit with a stick before it does anything. All four feet hit the sand and pushed.

This time he got it right.

The priests were going irrational.

It wasn't that the gods were disobeying them. The gods were *ignoring* them.

The gods always had. It took great skill to persuade a

Djelibeybi god to obey you, and the priests had to be fast on their toes. For example, if you pushed a rock off a cliff, then a quick request to the gods that it should fall down was certain to be answered. In the same way, the gods ensured that the sun set and the stars came out. Any petition to the gods to see to it that palm trees grew with their roots in the ground and their leaves on top was certain to be graciously accepted. On the whole, any priest who cared about such things could ensure a high rate of success.

However, it was one thing for the gods to ignore you when they were far off and invisible, and quite another when they were strolling across the landscape. It made you feel such a fool.

"Why don't they listen?" said the high priest of Teg, the Horse-Headed god of agriculture. He was in tears. Teg had last been seen sitting in a field, pulling up corn and giggling.

The other high priests were faring no better. Rituals hallowed by time had filled the air in the palace with sweet blue smoke and cooked enough assorted livestock to feed a famine, but the gods were settling in the Old Kingdom as if they owned it, and the people therein were no more than insects.

And the crowds were still outside. Religion had ruled in the Old Kingdom for the best part of seven thousand years. Behind the eyes of every priest present was a graphic image of what would happen if the people ever thought, for one moment, that it ruled no more.

"And so, Dios," said Koomi, "we turn to you. What would you have us do now?"

Dios sat on the steps of the throne and stared gloomily at the floor. The gods didn't listen. He *knew* that. He knew that, of all people. But it had never mattered before. You just went through the motions and came up with an answer. It was the ritual that was important, not the gods. The gods were there to do the duties of a megaphone, because who else would people listen to?

While he fought to think clearly his hands went through the motions of the Ritual of the Seventh Hour, guided by neural instructions as rigid and unchangeable as crystals.

"You have tried everything?" he said.

"Everything that you advised, O Dios," said Koomi. He waited until most of the priests were watching them and then, in a rather louder voice, continued: "If the king was here, he would intercede for us."

He caught the eye of the priestess of Sarduk. He hadn't discussed things with her; indeed, what was there to discuss? But he had an inkling that there was some fellow, sorry, feeling there. She didn't like Dios very much, but was less in awe of him than were the others.

"I told you that the king is dead," said Dios.

"Yes, we heard you. Yet there seems to be no body, O Dios. Nevertheless, we believe what you tell us, for it is the great Dios that speaks, and we pay no heed to malicious gossip."

The priests were silent. Malicious gossip, too? And somebody had already mentioned rumours, hadn't they? Definitely something amiss here.

"It happened many times in the past," said the priestess, on cue. "When a kingdom was threatened or the river did not rise, the king went to intercede with the gods. Was *sent* to intercede with the gods."

The edge of satisfaction in her voice made it clear that it was a one-way trip.

Koomi shivered with delight and horror. Oh, yes. Those were the days. Some countries had experimented with the idea of the sacrificial king, long ago. A few years of feasting and ruling, then chop — and make way for a new administration.

"In a time of crisis, possibly any high-born minister of state would suffice," she went on.

Dios looked up, his face mirroring the agony of his tendons.

"I *see*," he said. "And who would be high priest then?"

"The gods would choose," said Koomi.

"I daresay they would," said Dios sourly. "I am in some doubt as to the wisdom of their choice."

"The dead can speak to the gods in the netherworld," said the priestess.

"But the gods are all *here*," said Dios, fighting against the throbbing in his legs, which were insisting that, at this time, they should be walking along the central corridor en route to supervise the Rite of the Under Sky. His body cried out for the solace over the river. And once over the river, never to return . . . but he'd always said that.

"In the absence of the king the high priest performs his duties. Isn't that right, Dios?" said Koomi.

It was. It was written. You couldn't rewrite it, once it was written. He'd written it. Long ago.

Dios hung his head. This was worse than plumbing, this was worse than anything. And yet, and yet . . . to go across the river . . .

"Very well, then," he said. "I have one final request."

"Yes?" Koomi's voice had timbre now, it was already a high priest's voice.

"I wish to be interred in the — " Dios began, and was cut off by a murmur from those priests who could look out across the river. All eyes turned to the distant, inky shore.

The legions of the kings of Djelibeybi were on the march.

They lurched, but they covered the ground quickly. There were platoons, battalions of them. They didn't need Gern's hammer any more.

"It's the pickle," said the king, as they watched half-a-dozen ancestors mummyhandle a seal out of its socket. "It toughens you up."

Some of the more ancient were getting overenthusiastic and attacking the pyramids themselves, actually managing to shift blocks higher than they were. The king didn't blame them. How terrible to be dead, and know you were dead, and locked away in the darkness.

They're never going to get me in one of those things, he vowed.

At last they came, like a tide, to yet another pyramid. It was small, low, dark, half-concealed in drifted sand, and the blocks were hardly even masonry; they were no more than roughly squared boulders. It had clearly been built long before the Kingdom got the hang of pyramids. It was barely more than a pile.

Hacked into the doorseal, angular and deep, were the hieroglyphs of the Ur Kingdom: KHUFT HAD ME MADE. THE FIRST.

Several ancestors clustered around it.

"Oh, dear," said the king. "This might be going too far."

"The First," whispered Dil. "The First into the Kingdom. No-one here before but hippos and crocodiles. From inside that pyramid seventy centuries look out at us. Older than anything — "

"Yes, yes, all right," said Teppicymon. "No need to get carried away. He was a man, just like all of us."

"'And Khuft the camel herder looked upon the valley . . .'" Dil began.

"After seven thousand yeares, he wyll be wantyng to look upon yt again," said Ashk-ur-men-tep bluntly.

"Even so," said the king. "It *does* seem a bit . . ."

"The dead are equal," said Ashk-ur-men-tep. "You, younge manne. Calle hym forth."

"Who, me?" said Gern. "But he was the Fir — "

"Yes, we've been through all that," said Teppicymon. "Do it. Everyone's getting impatient. So is he, I expect."

Gern rolled his eyes, and hefted the hammer. Just as it was about to hiss down on the seal Dil darted forward, causing Gern to dance wildly across the ground in a groin-straining effort to avoid interring the hammer in his master's head.

"It's open!" said Dil. "Look! The seal just swings aside!"

"Youe meane he iss *oute*?"

Teppicymon tottered forward and grabbed the door of the pyramid. It moved quite easily. Then he examined the stone beneath it. Derelict and half-covered though it was, someone had taken care to keep a pathway clear to the pyramid. And the stone was quite worn away, as by the passage of many feet.

This was not, by the nature of things, the normal state of affairs for a pyramid. The whole point was that once you were in, you were in.

The mummies examined the worn entrance and creaked at one another in surprise. One of the very ancient ones, who was barely holding himself together, made a noise like deathwatch beetle finally conquering a rotten tree.

"What'd he say?" said Teppicymon.

The mummy of Ashk-ur-men-tep translated. "He saide yt ys Spooky," he croaked.

The late king nodded. "I'm going in to have a look. You two live ones, you come with me."

Dil's face fell.

"Oh, come on, man," snapped Teppicymon, forcing the door back. "Look, *I'm* not frightened. Show a bit of backbone. Everyone else is."

"But we'll need some light," protested Dil.

The nearest mummies lurched back sharply as Gern timidly took a tinderbox out of his pocket.

"We'll need something to burn," said Dil. The mummies shuffled further back, muttering.

"There's torches in here," said Teppicymon, his voice slightly muffled. "And you can keep them away from me, lad."

It was a small pyramid, mazeless, without traps, just a stone passage leading upwards. Tremulously, expecting at any moment to see unnamed terrors leap out at them, the embalmers followed the king into a small, square chamber that smelled of sand. The roof was black with soot.

There was no sarcophagus within, no mummy case, no terror named or nameless. The centre of the floor was occupied by a raised block, with a blanket and a pillow on it.

Neither of them looked particularly old. It was almost disappointing.

Gern craned to look around.

"Quite nice, really," he said. "Comfy."

"No," said Dil.

"Hey, master king, look here," said Gern, trotting over to one of the walls. "Look. Someone's been scratching things. Look, all little lines all over the wall."

"And this wall," said the king, "and the floor. Someone's been counting. Every ten have been crossed through, you see. Someone's been counting things. Lots of things." He stood back.

"What things?" said Dil, looking behind him.

"Very strange," said the king. He leaned forward. "You can barely make out the inscriptions underneath."

"Can you read it, king?" said Gern, showing what Dil considered to be unnecessary enthusiasm.

"No. It's one of the really ancient dialects. Can't make out a blessed hieroglyph," said Teppicymon. "I shouldn't think there's a single person alive today who can read it."

"That's a shame," said Gern.

"True enough," said the king, and sighed. They stood in gloomy silence.

"So perhaps we could ask one of the dead ones?" said Gern.

"Er. Gern," said Dil, backing away.

The king slapped the apprentice on the back, pitching him forward.

"Damn clever idea!" he said. "We'll just go and get one of the real early ancestors. Oh." He sagged. "That's no good. No-one will be able to understand them — "

"Gern!" said Dil, his eyes growing wider.

"No, it's all right, king," said Gern, enjoying the new-found freedom of thought, "because, the reason being, everyone understands *someone*, all we have to do is sort them out."

"Bright lad. Bright lad," said the king.

"*Gern!*"

They both looked at him in astonishment.

"You all right, master?" said Gern. "You've gone all white."

"The t — " stuttered Dil, rigid with terror.

"The what, master?"

"The t — look at the t — "

"He ought to have a lie down," said the king. "I know his sort. The artistic type. Highly strung."

Dil took a deep breath.

"*Look at the sodding torch, Gern!*" he shouted.

They looked.

Without any fuss, turning its black ashes into dry straw, the torch was burning backwards.

The Old Kingdom lay stretched out before Teppic, and it was unreal.

He looked at You Bastard, who had stuck his muzzle in a wayside spring and was making a noise like the last drop in the milkshake glass.* You Bastard looked real enough. There's nothing like a camel for looking really solid. But the landscape had an uncertain quality, as if it hadn't quite made up its mind to be there or not.

---

*You know. The bit you can't reach with the straw.

Except for the Great Pyramid. It squatted in the middle distance as real as the pin that nails a butterfly to a board. It was contriving to look extremely solid, as though it was sucking all the solidity out of the landscape into itself.

Well, he was here. Wherever here was.

How did you kill a pyramid?

And what would happen if you did?

He was working on the hypothesis that everything would snap back into place. Into the Old Kingdom's pool of recirculated time.

He watched the gods for a while, wondering what the hell they were, and how it didn't seem to matter. They looked no more real than the land over which they strode, about incomprehensible errands of their own. The world was no more than a dream. Teppic felt incapable of surprise. If seven fat cows had wandered by, he wouldn't have given them a second glance.

He remounted You Bastard and rode him, sloshing gently, down the road. The fields on either side had a devastated look.

The sun was finally sinking; the gods of night and evening were prevailing over the daylight gods, but it had been a long struggle and, when you thought about all the things that would happen to it now — eaten by goddesses, carried on boats under the world, and so on — it was an odds-on chance that it wouldn't be seen again.

No-one was visible as he rode into the stable yard. You Bastard padded sedately to his stall and pulled delicately at a wisp of hay. He'd thought of something interesting about bivariant distributions.

Teppic patted him on the flank, raising another cloud, and walked up the wide steps that led to the palace proper. Still there were no guards, no servants. No living soul.

He slipped into his own palace like a thief in the day, and found his way to Dil's workshop. It was empty, and looked as though a robber with very peculiar tastes had recently been at work in there. The throne room smelled like a kitchen, and by the looks of it the cooks had fled in a hurry.

The gold mask of the kings of Djelibeybi, slightly buckled out of shape, had rolled into a corner. He picked it up and, on a suspicion, scratched it with one of his knives. The gold peeled away, exposing a silver-grey gleam.

He'd suspected that. There simply wasn't that much gold around. The mask felt as heavy as lead because, well, it *was* lead. He wondered if it had ever been all gold, and which ancestor had done it, and how many pyramids it had paid for. It was probably very symbolic of something or other. Perhaps not even symbolic *of* anything. Just symbolic, all by itself.

One of the sacred cats was hiding under the throne. It flattened its ears and spat at Teppic as he reached down to pat it. That much hadn't changed, at least.

Still no people. He padded across to the balcony.

And there the people were, a great silent mass, staring across the river in the fading, leaden light. As Teppic watched a flotilla of boats and ferries set out from the near bank.

We ought to have been building bridges, he thought. But we said that would be shackling the river.

He dropped lightly over the balustrade on to the packed earth and walked down to the crowd.

And the full force of its belief scythed into him.

The people of Djelibeybi might have had conflicting ideas about their gods, but their belief in their kings had been unswerving for thousands of years. To Teppic it was like walking into a vat of alcohol. He felt it pouring into him until his fingertips crackled, rising up through his body until it gushed into his brain, bringing not omnipotence but the *feeling* of omnipotence, the very strong sensation that while he didn't actually know everything, he would do soon and had done once.

It had been like this back in Ankh, when the divinity had hooked him. But that had been just a flicker. Now it had the solid power of real belief behind it.

He looked down at a rustling below him, and saw green shoots springing out of the dry sand around his feet.

Bloody hell, he thought. I really *am* a god.

This could be very embarrassing.

He shouldered his way through the press of people until he reached the riverbank and stood there in a thickening clump of corn. As the crowd caught on, those nearest fell to their knees, and a circle of reverentially collapsing people spread out from Teppic like ripples.

But I never wanted this! I just wanted to help people live more happily, with plumbing. I wanted something done about run-down inner-city areas. I just wanted to put them at their ease, and ask them how they enjoyed their lives. I thought schools might be a good idea, so they wouldn't fall down and worship someone just because he's got green feet.

And I wanted to do something about the architecture . . .

As the light drained from the sky like steel going cold the pyramid was somehow even bigger than before. If you had to design something to give the very distinct impression of mass, the pyramid was It. There was a crowd of figures around it, unidentifiable in the grey light.

Teppic looked around the prostrate crowd until he saw someone in the uniform of the palace guard.

"You, man, on your feet," he commanded.

The man gave him a look of dread, but did stagger sheepishly upright.

"What's going on here?"

"O king, who is the lord of — "

"I don't think we have time," said Teppic. "I know who I am, I want to know what's happening."

"O king, we saw the dead walking! The priests have gone to talk to them."

"The *dead* walking?"

"Yes, O king."

"We're talking about not-alive people here, are we?"

"Yes, O king."

"Oh. Well, thank you. That was very succinct. Not informative, but succinct. Are there any boats around?"

"The priests took them all, O king."

Teppic could see that this was true. The jetties near the palace were usually thronged with boats, and now they were all empty. As he stared at the water it grew two eyes and a long snout, to remind him that swimming the Djel was as feasible as nailing fog to the wall.

He stared at the crowd. Every person was watching him expectantly, convinced that he would know what to do next.

He turned back to the river, extended his hands in front of him, pressed them together, and then opened them gently.

There was a damp sucking noise, and the waters of the Djel

parted in front of him. There was a sigh from the crowd, but
their astonishment was nothing to the surprise of a dozen or so
crocodiles, who were left trying to swim in ten feet of air.

Teppic ran down the bank and over the heavy mud, dodging to
avoid the tails that slashed wildly at him as the reptiles dropped
heavily on to the riverbed.

The Djel loomed up as two khaki walls, so that he was
running along a damp and shadowy alley. Here and there were
fragments of bones, old shields, bits of spear, the ribs of boats.
He leapt and jinked around the debris of centuries.

Ahead of him a big bull crocodile propelled itself dreamily out
of the wall of water, flailed madly in mid-air, and flopped into
the ooze. Teppic trod heavily on its snout and plunged on.

Behind him a few of the quicker citizens, seeing the dazed
creatures below them, began to look for stones. The crocodiles
had been undisputed masters of the river since primordial
times, but if it was possible to do a little catching-up in the space
of a few minutes, it was certainly worth a try.

The sound of the monsters of the river beginning the long
journey to handbaghood broke out behind Teppic as he sloshed
up the far bank.

A line of ancestors stretched across the chamber, down the dark
passageway, and out into the sand. It was filled with whispers
going in both directions, a dry sound, like the wind blowing
through old paper.

Dil lay on the sand, with Gern flapping a cloth in his face.

"Wha' they doing?" he murmured.

"Reading the inscription," said Gern. "You ought to see it,
master! The one doing the reading, he's practically a — "

"Yes, yes, all right," said Dil, struggling up.

"He's more than six thousand years old! And his grandson's
listening to him, and telling *his* grandson, and he's telling *his*
gra — "

"Yes, yes, all — "

"'And-Khuft-too-said-Unto-the-First, What-may-We-Give-
Unto-You, Who-Has-Taught-Us-the-Right-Ways'," said

Teppicymon*, who was at the end of the line. "'And-the-First-
Spake, and-This-He-Spake, Build-for-Me-a-Pyramid, That-I-May-
Rest, and-Build-it-of-These-Dimensions, That-it-Be-Proper. And-
Thus-It-Was-Done, and-the-Name-of-the-First-was . . .'"

But there was no name. It was just a babble of raised voices,
arguments, ancient cursewords, spreading along the line of
desiccated ancestors like a spark along a powder trail. Until it
reached Teppicymon, who exploded.

The Ephebian sergeant, quietly perspiring in the shade, saw
what he had been half expecting and wholly dreading. There
was a column of dust on the opposite horizon.

The Tsorteans' main force was getting there first.

He stood up, nodded professionally to his counterpart across
the way, and looked at the double handful of men under his
command.

"I need a messenger to take, er, a message back to the city," he
said. A forest of hands shot up. The sergeant sighed, and selected
young Autocue, who he knew was missing his mum.

"Run like the wind," he said. "Although I expect you won't
need telling, will you? And then . . . and then . . . "

He stood with his lips moving silently, while the sun scoured
the rocks of the hot, narrow pass and a few insects buzzed in the
scrub bushes. His education hadn't included a course in Famous
Last Words.

He raised his eyes in the direction of home.

"Go, tell the Ephebians — " he began.

The soldiers waited.

"What?" said Autocue after a while. "Go and tell them what?"

The sergeant relaxed, like air being let out of a balloon.

"Go and tell them, what kept you?" he said. On the near
horizon another column of dust was advancing.

---

*But not immediately, of course, because messages change in the telling and some
ancestors were not capable of perfect enunciation and others were trying to be
helpful and supplying what they thought were lost words. The message received
by Teppicymon originally began, "Handcuffed to the bed, the aunt thirsted."

This was more like it. If there was going to be a massacre, then it ought to be shared by both sides.

The city of the dead lay before Teppic. After Ankh-Morpork, which was almost its direct opposite (in Ankh, even the bedding was alive) it was probably the biggest city on the Disc; its streets were the finest, its architecture the most majestic and awe-inspiring.

In population terms the necropolis outstripped the other cities of the Old Kingdom, but its people didn't get out much and there was nothing to do on Saturday nights.

Until now.

Now it thronged.

Teppic watched from the top of a wind-etched obelisk as the grey and brown, and here and there somewhat greenish, armies of the departed passed beneath him. The kings had been democratic. After the pyramids had been emptied gangs of them had turned their attention to the lesser tombs, and now the necropolis really did have its tradesmen, its nobles and even its artisans. Not that there was, by and large, any way of telling the difference.

They were, to a corpse, heading for the Great Pyramid. It loomed like a carbuncle over the lesser, older buildings. And they all seemed very angry about something.

Teppic dropped lightly on to the wide flat roof of a mastaba, jogged to its far end, cleared the gap on to an ornamental sphinx — not without a moment's worry, but this one seemed inert enough — and from there it was but the throw of a grapnel to one of the lower storeys of a step pyramid.

The long light of the contentious sun lanced across the silent landscape as he leapt from monument to monument, zig-zagging high above the shuffling army.

Behind him shoots appeared briefly in the ancient stone, cracking it a little, and then withered and died.

This, said his blood as it tingled around his body, is what you trained for. Even Mericet couldn't mark you down for this. Speeding in the shadows above a silent city, running like a cat, finding handholds that would have perplexed a gecko — and, at the destination, a victim.

True, it was a billion tons of pyramid, and hitherto the largest client of an inhumation had been Patricio, the 23-stone Despot of Quirm.

A monumental needle recording in bas-relief the achievements of a king four thousand years ago, and which would have been more pertinent if the wind-driven sand hadn't long ago eroded his name, provided a handy ladder which needed only an expertly thrown grapnel from its top, lodging in the outstretched fingers of a forgotten monarch, to allow him a long, gentle arc on to the roof of a tomb.

Running, climbing and swinging, hastily hammering crampons in the memorials of the dead, Teppic went forth.

Pinpoints of firelight among the limestone pricked out the lines of the opposing armies. Deep and stylised though the enmity was between the two empires, they both abided by the ancient tradition that warfare wasn't undertaken at night, during harvest or when wet. It was important enough to save up for special occasions. Going at it hammer and tongs just reduced the whole thing to a farce.

In the twilight on both sides of the line came the busy sound of advanced woodwork in progress.

It's said that generals are always ready to fight the last war over again. It had been thousands of years since the last war between Tsort and Ephebe, but generals have long memories and this time they were ready for it.

On both sides of the line, wooden horses were taking shape.

"It's gone," said Ptaclusp IIb, slithering back down the pile of rubble.

"About time, too," said his father. "Help me fold up your brother. You're sure it won't hurt him?"

"Well, if we do it carefully he can't move in Time, that is, width to us. So if no time can pass for him, nothing can hurt him."

Ptaclusp thought of the old days, when pyramid building had simply consisted of piling one block on another and all you needed to remember was that you put less on top as you went up. And now it meant trying to put a crease in one of your sons.

"Right," he said doubtfully. "Let's be off, then." He inched his way up the debris and poked his head over the top just as the vanguard of the dead came round the corner of the nearest minor pyramid.

His first thought was: this is it, they're coming to complain.

He'd done his best. It wasn't always easy to build to a budget. Maybe not every lintel was exactly as per drawings, perhaps the quality of the internal plasterwork wasn't always up to snuff, but . . .

They can't *all* be complaining. Not this many of them.

Ptaclusp IIb climbed up alongside him. His mouth dropped open.

"Where are they all coming from?" he said.

"You're the expert. You tell me."

"Are they *dead*?"

Ptaclusp scrutinised some of the approaching marchers.

"If they're not, some of them are awfully ill," he said.

"Let's make a run for it!"

"Where to? Up the pyramid?"

The Great Pyramid loomed up behind them, its throbbing filling the air. Ptaclusp stared at it.

"What's going to happen tonight?" he said.

"What?"

"Well, is it going to — do whatever it did — again?"

IIb stared at him. "Dunno."

"Can you find out?"

"Only by waiting. I'm not even sure what it's done *now*."

"Are we going to like it?"

"I shouldn't think so, dad. Oh, dear."

"What's up now?"

"Look over there."

Heading towards the marching dead, trailing behind Koomi like a tail behind a comet, were the priests.

*

It was hot and dark inside the horse. It was also very crowded.

They waited, sweating.

Young Autocue stuttered: "What'll happen now, sergeant?"

The sergeant moved a foot tentatively. The atmosphere would have induced claustrophobia in a sardine.

"Well, lad. They'll find us, see, and be so impressed they'll drag us all the way back to their city, and then when it's dark we'll leap out and put them to the sword. Or put the sword to them. One or the other. And then we'll sack the city, burn the walls and sow the ground with salt. You remember, lad, I showed you on Friday."

"Oh."

Moisture dripped from a score of brows. Several of the men were trying to compose a letter home, dragging styli across wax that was close to melting.

"And then what will happen, sergeant?"

"Why, lad, then we'll go home heroes."

"Oh."

The older soldiers sat stolidly looking at the wooden walls. Autocue shifted uneasily, still worried about something.

"My mum said to come back with my shield or on it, sergeant," he said.

"Jolly good, lad. That's the spirit."

"We will be all right, though. Won't we, sergeant?"

The sergeant stared into the fetid darkness.

After a while, someone started to play the harmonica.

Ptaclusp half-turned his head from the scene and a voice by his ear said, "You're the pyramid builder, aren't you?"

Another figure had joined them in their bolthole, one who was black-clad and moved in a way that made a cat's tread sound like a one-man band.

Ptaclusp nodded, unable to speak. He had had enough shocks for one day.

"Well, switch it off. Switch it off *now*."

IIb leaned over.

"Who're you?" he said.

"My name is Teppic."

"What, like the king?"

"Yes. Just like the king. Now turn it off."

"It's a pyramid! You can't turn off pyramids!" said IIb.

"Well, then, make it flare."

"We tried that last night." IIb pointed to the shattered capstone. "Unroll Two-Ay, dad."

Teppic regarded the flat brother.

"It's some sort of wall poster, is it?" he said eventually.

IIb looked down. Teppic saw the movement, and looked down also; he was ankle-deep in green sprouts.

"Sorry," he said. "I can't seem to shake it off."

"It can be dreadful," said IIb frantically. "I know how it is, I had this verruca once, nothing would shift it."

Teppic hunkered down by the cracked stone.

"This thing," he said. "What's the significance? I mean, it's coated with metal. Why?"

"There's got to be a sharp point for the flare," said IIb.

"Is that all? This is gold, isn't it?"

"It's electrum. Gold and silver alloy. The capstone has got to be made of electrum."

Teppic peeled back the foil.

"This isn't all metal," he said mildly.

"Yes. Well," said Ptaclusp. "We found, er, that foil works just as well."

"Couldn't you use something cheaper? Like steel?"

Ptaclusp sneered. It hadn't been a good day, sanity was a distant memory, but there were certain facts he knew for a fact.

"Wouldn't last for more than a year or two," he said. "What with the dew and so forth. You'd lose the point. Wouldn't last more than two or three hundred times."

Teppic leaned his head against the pyramid. It was cold, and it hummed. He thought he could hear, under the throbbing, a faint rising tone.

The pyramid towered over him. IIb could have told him that this was because the walls sloped in at precisely 56°, and an effect known as battering made the pyramid loom even higher than it really was. He probably would have used words like perspective and virtual height as well.

The black marble was glassy smooth. The masons had done well. The cracks between each silky panel were hardly wide enough to insert a knife. But wide enough, all the same.

"How about once?" he said.

Koomi chewed his fingernails distractedly.

"Fire," he said. "That'd stop them. They're very inflammable. Or water. They'd probably dissolve."

"Some of them were destroying *pyramids*," said the high priest of Juf, the Cobra-Headed God of Papyrus.

"People always come back from the dead in such a bad temper," said another priest.

Koomi watched the approaching army in mounting bewilderment.

"Where's Dios?" he said.

The old high priest was pushed to the front of the crowd.

"What shall I say to them?" Koomi demanded.

It would be wrong to say that Dios smiled. It wasn't an action he often felt called upon to perform. But his mouth creased at the edges and his eyes went half-hooded.

"You could tell them," he said, "that new times demand new men. You could tell them that it is time to make way for younger people with fresh ideas. You could tell them that they are outmoded. You could tell them all that."

"They'll kill me!"

"Would they be that anxious for your eternal company, I wonder?"

"You're still high priest!"

"Why don't you talk to them?" said Dios. "Don't forget to tell them that they are to be dragged kicking and screaming into the Century of the Cobra." He handed Koomi the staff. "Or whatever this century is called," he added.

Koomi felt the eyes of the assembled brethren and sistren upon him. He cleared his throat, adjusted his robe, and turned to face the mummies.

They were chanting something, one word, over and over again. He couldn't quite make it out, but it seemed to have worked them up into a rage.

He raised the staff, and the carved wooden snakes looked unusually alive in the flat light.

The gods of the Disc — and here is meant the great consensus gods, who really do exist in Dunmanifestin, their semi-detached Valhalla on the world's impossibly high central mountain, where they pass the time observing the petty antics of mortal men and organising petitions about how the influx of the Ice Giants has lowered property values in the celestial regions —the gods of the Disc have always been fascinated by humanity's incredible ability to say exactly the wrong thing at the wrong time.

They're not talking here of such easy errors as "It's perfectly safe", or "The ones that growl a lot don't bite", but of simple little sentences which are injected into difficult situations with the same general effect as a steel bar dropped into the bearings of a 3,000 rpm, 660 megawatt steam turbine.

And connoisseurs of mankind's tendency to put his pedal extremity where his tongue should be are agreed that when the judges' envelopes are opened then Hoot Koomi's fine performance in "Begone from this place, foul shades" will be a contender for all-time bloody stupid greeting.

The front row of ancestors halted, and were pushed forward a little by the press of those behind.

King Teppicymon XXVII, who by common consent among the other twenty-six Teppicymons was spokesman, lurched on alone and picked up the trembling Koomi by his arms.

"What did you say?" he said.

Koomi's eyes rolled. His mouth opened and shut, but his voice wisely decided not to come out.

Teppicymon pushed his bandaged face close to the priest's pointed nose.

"I remember you," he growled. "I've seen you oiling around the place. A bad hat, if ever I saw one. I remember thinking that."

He glared around at the others.

"You're all priests, aren't you? Come to say sorry, have you? *Where's Dios?*"

The ancestors pressed forward, muttering. When you've been dead for hundreds of years, you're not inclined to feel generous to those people who assured you that you were going to have a lovely time. There was a scuffle in the middle of the crowd as King Psam-nut-kha, who had spent five thousand years with nothing to look at but the inside of a lid, was restrained by younger colleagues.

Teppicymon switched his attention back to Koomi, who hadn't gone anywhere.

"Foul shades, was it?" he said.

"Er," said Koomi.

"Put him down." Dios gently took the staff from Koomi's unresisting fingers and said, "I am Dios, the high priest. Why are you here?"

It was a perfectly calm and reasonable voice, with overtones of concerned but indubitable authority. It was a tone of voice the pharaohs of Djelibeybi had heard for thousands of years, a voice which had regulated the days, prescribed the rituals, cut the time into carefully-turned segments, interpreted the ways of gods to men. It was the sound of authority, which stirred antique memories among the ancestors and caused them to look embarrassed and shuffle their feet.

One of the younger pharaohs lurched forward.

"You bastard," he croaked. "You laid us out and shut us away, one by one, and you went on. People thought the name was passed on but it was always *you*. How *old* are you, Dios?"

There was no sound. No-one moved. A breeze stirred the dust a little.

Dios sighed.

"I did not mean to," he said. "There was so much to do. There were never enough hours in the day. Truly, I did not realise what was happening. I thought it was refreshing, nothing more. I suspected nothing, I noted the passing of the rituals, not the years."

"Come from a long-lived family, do you?" said Teppicymon sarcastically.

Dios stared at him, his lips moving. "Family," he said at last, his voice softened from its normal bark. "Family. Yes. I must have had a family, mustn't I. But, you know, I can't remember. Memory is the first thing that goes. The pyramids don't seem to preserve it, strangely."

"This is Dios, the footnote-keeper of history?" said Teppicymon.

"Ah." The high priest smiled. "Memory goes from the head. But it is all around me. Every scroll and book."

"That's the history of the kingdom, man!"

"Yes. My memory."

The king relaxed a little. Sheer horrified fascination was unravelling the knot of fury.

"How old are you?" he said.

"I think...seven thousand years. But sometimes it seems much longer."

"*Really* seven thousand years?"

"Yes," said Dios.

"How could any man stand it?" said the king.

Dios shrugged.

"Seven thousand years is just one day at a time," he said.

Slowly, with the occasional wince, he got down on one knee and held up his staff in shaking hands.

"O kings," he said, "I have always existed only to serve."

There was a long, extremely embarrassed pause.

"We will destroy the pyramids," said Far-re-ptah, pushing forward.

"You will destroy the kingdom," said Dios. "I cannot allow it."

"*You cannot allow it?*"

"Yes. What will we be without the pyramids?" said Dios.

"Speaking for the dead," said Far-re-ptah, "we will be free."

"But the kingdom will be just another small country," said Dios, and to their horror the ancestors saw tears in his eyes. "All that we hold dear, you will cast adrift in time. Uncertain. Without guidance. *Changeable.*"

"Then it can take its chances," said Teppicymon. "Stand aside, Dios."

Dios held up his staff. The snakes around it uncoiled and hissed at the king.

"Be still," said Dios.

Dark lightning crackled between the ancestors. Dios stared at the staff in astonishment; it had never done this before. But seven thousand years of his priests had believed, in their hearts, that the staff of Dios could rule this world and the next.

In the sudden silence there was the faint chink, high up, of a knife being wedged between two black marble slabs.

The pyramid pulsed under Teppic, and the marble was as slippery as ice. The inward slope wasn't the help he had expected.

The thing, he told himself, is not to look up or down, but straight ahead, into the marble, parcelling the impossible height into manageable sections. Just like time. That's how we survive infinity — we kill it by breaking it up into small bits.

He was aware of shouts below him, and glanced briefly over his shoulder. He was barely a third of the way up, but he could see the crowds across the river, a grey mass speckled with the pale blobs of upturned faces. Closer to, the pale army of the dead, facing the small grey group of priests, with Dios in front of them. There was some sort of argument going on.

The sun was on the horizon.

He reached up, located the next crack, found a handhold . . .

Dios spotted Ptaclusp's head peering over the debris, and sent a couple of priests to bring him back. IIb followed, his carefully-folded brother under his arm.

"What is the boy doing?" Dios demanded.

"O Dios, he said he was going to flare off the pyramid," said Ptaclusp.

"How can he do that?"

"O lord, he says he is going to cap it off before the sun sets."

"Is it possible?" Dios demanded, turning to the architect. IIb hesitated.

"It may be," he said.

"And what will happen? Will we return to the world outside?"

"Well, it depends on whether the dimensional effect ratchets, as it were, and is stable in each state, or if, on the contrary, the pyramid is acting as a piece of rubber under tension — "

His voice stuttered to a halt under the intensity of Dios's stare.

"I don't know," he admitted.

"Back to the world outside," said Dios. "Not our world. Our world is the Valley. Ours is a world of order. Men need order."

He raised his staff.

"That's my son!" shouted Teppicymon. "Don't you dare try anything! That's the king!"

The ranks of ancestors swayed, but couldn't break the spell.

"Er, Dios," said Koomi.

Dios turned, his eyebrows raised.

"You spoke?" he said.

"Er, if it *is* the king, er, I — that is, we — think perhaps you should let him get on with it. Er, don't you think that would be a really good idea?"

Dios's staff kicked, and the priests felt the cold bands of restraint freeze their limbs.

"I gave my life for the kingdom," said the high priest. "I gave it over and over again. Everything it is, I created. I cannot fail it now."

And then he saw the gods.

Teppic eased himself up another couple of feet and then gently reached down to pull a knife out of the marble. It wasn't going to work, though. Knife climbing was for those short and awkward passages, and frowned on anyway because it suggested you'd chosen a wrong route. It wasn't for this sort of thing, unless you had unlimited knives.

He glanced over his shoulder again as strange barred shadows flickered across the face of the pyramid.

From out of the sunset, where they had been engaged in their eternal squabbling, the gods were returning.

They staggered and lurched across the fields and reed beds, heading for the pyramid. Near-brainless though they were, they understood what it was. Perhaps they even understood what Teppic was trying to do. Their assorted animal faces made it hard to be certain, but it looked as though they were very angry.

*

"Are you going to control them, Dios?" said the king. "Are you going to tell them that the world should be changeless?"

Dios stared up at the creatures jostling one another as they waded the river. There were too many teeth, too many lolling tongues. The bits of them that were human were sloughing away. A lion-headed god of justice — Put, Dios recalled the name — was using its scales as a flail to beat one of the river gods. Chefet, the Dog-Headed God of metalwork, was growling and attacking his fellows at random with his hammer; this was Chefet, Dios thought, the god that he had created to be an example to men in the art of wire and filigree and small beauty.

Yet it had worked. He'd taken a desert rabble and shown them all he could remember of the arts of civilisation and the secrets of the pyramids. He'd needed gods then.

The trouble with gods is that after enough people start believing in them, they begin to exist. And what begins to exist isn't what was originally intended.

Chefet, Chefet, thought Dios. Maker of rings, weaver of metal. Now he's out of our heads, and see how his nails grow into claws...

This is *not* how I imagined him.

"Stop," he instructed. "I order you to stop! You will obey me. I made you!"

They also lack gratitude.

King Teppicymon felt the power around him weaken as Dios turned all his attention to ecclesiastical matters. He saw the tiny shape halfway up the wall of the pyramid, saw it falter.

The rest of the ancestors saw it, too, and as one corpse they knew what to do. Dios could wait.

This was family.

Teppic heard the snap of the handle under his foot, slid a little, and hung by one hand. He'd got another knife in above him but...no, no good. He hadn't got the reach. For practical purposes his arms felt like short lengths of wet rope. Now, if he spreadeagled himself as he slid, he might be able to slow enough...

He looked down and saw the climbers coming towards him, in a tide that was tumbling *upwards*.

The ancestors rose up the face of the pyramid silently, like creepers, each new row settling into position on the shoulders of the generation beneath, while the younger ones climbed on over them. Bony hands grabbed Teppic as the wave of edificeers broke around him, and he was half-pushed, half-pulled up the sloping wall. Voices like the creak of sarcophagi filled his ears, moaning encouragement.

"Well done, boy," groaned a crumbling mummy, hauling him bodily on to its shoulder. "You remind me of me when I was alive. To you, son."

"Got him," said the corpse above, lifting Teppic easily on one outstretched arm. "That's a fine family spirit, lad. Best wishes from your great-great-great-great uncle, although I don't suppose you remember me. Coming *up*."

Other ancestors were climbing on past Teppic as he rose from hand to hand. Ancient fingers with a grip like steel clutched at him, hoisting him onwards.

The pyramid grew narrower.

Down below, Ptaclusp watched thoughtfully.

"What a workforce," he said. "I mean, the ones at the bottom are supporting the whole weight!"

"Dad," said IIb. "I think we'd better run. Those gods are getting closer."

"Do you think we could employ them?" said Ptaclusp, ignoring him. "They're dead, they probably won't want high wages, and — "

"Dad!"

" — sort of self-build — "

"You said no more pyramids, dad. Never again, you said. Now come on!"

Teppic scrambled to the top of the pyramid, supported by the last two ancestors. One of them was his father.

"I don't think you've met your great-grandma," he said, indicating the shorter bandaged figure, who nodded gently at Teppic. He opened his mouth.

"There's no time," she said. "You're doing fine."

He glanced at the sun which, old professional that it was, chose that moment to drop below the horizon. The gods had crossed the river, their progress slowed only by their tendency to push and shove among themselves, and were lurching through the buildings of the necropolis. Several were clustered around the spot where Dios had been.

The ancestors dropped away, sliding back down the pyramid as fast as they had climbed it, leaving Teppic alone on a few square feet of rock.

A couple of stars came out.

He saw white shapes below as the ancestors hurried away on some private errand of their own, lurching at a surprising speed towards the broad band of the river.

The gods abandoned their interest in Dios, this strange little human with the stick and the cracked voice. The nearest god, a crocodile-headed thing, jerked on to the plaza before the pyramid, squinted up at Teppic, and reached out towards him. Teppic fumbled for a knife, wondering what sort was appropriate for gods. . .

And, along the Djel, the pyramids began to flare their meagre store of hoarded time.

Priests and ancestors fled as the ground began to shake. Even the gods looked bewildered.

IIb snatched his father's arm and dragged him away.

"Come on!" he yelled into his ear. "We can't be around here when it goes off! Otherwise you'll be put to bed on a coathanger!"

Around them several other pyramids struck their flares, thin and reedy affairs that were barely visible in the afterglow.

"Dad! I said we've got to go!"

Ptaclusp was dragged backwards across the flagstones, still staring at the hulking outline of the Great Pyramid.

"There's someone still there, look," he said, and pointed to a figure alone on the plaza.

IIb peered into the gloom.

"It's only Dios, the high priest," he said. "I expect he's got some plan in mind, best not to meddle in the affairs of priests, now will you *come on*."

The crocodile-headed god turned its snout back and forth, trying to focus on Teppic without the advantage of binocular vision. This close, its body was slightly transparent, as though someone had sketched in all the lines and got bored before it was time to do the shading. It trod on a small tomb, crushing it to powder.

A hand like a cluster of canoes with claws on hovered over Teppic. The pyramid trembled and the stone under his feet felt warm, but it resolutely forbore from any signs of wanting to flare.

The hand descended. Teppic sank on one knee and, out of desperation, raised the knife over his head in both hands.

The light glinted for a moment off the tip of the blade and *then* the Great Pyramid flared.

It did it in absolute silence to begin with, sending up a spike of eye-torturing flame that turned the whole kingdom into a criss-cross of black shadow and white light, a flame that might have turned any watchers not just into a pillar of salt but into a complete condiment set of their choice. It exploded like an unwound dandelion, silent as starlight, searing as a supernova.

Only after it had been bathing the necropolis in its impossible brilliance for several seconds did the sound come, and it was sound that winds itself up through the bones, creeps into every cell of the body, and tries with some success to turn them inside out. It was too loud to be called noise. There is sound so loud that it prevents itself from being heard, and this was that kind of sound.

Eventually it condescended to drop out of the cosmic scale and became, simply, the loudest noise anyone hearing it had ever experienced.

The noise stopped, filling the air with the dark metallic clang of sudden silence. The light went out, lancing the night with blue and purple afterimages. It was not the silence and darkness of conclusion but of pause, like the moment of equilibrium when a thrown ball runs out of acceleration but has yet to have gravity drawn to its attention and, for a brief moment, thinks that the worst is over.

This time it was heralded by a shrill whistling out of the clear sky and a swirl in the air that became a glow, became a flame, became a flare that sizzled downwards, into the pyramid, punching into the mass of black marble. Fingers of lightning crackled out and grounded on the lesser tombs around it, so that serpents of white fire burned their way from pyramid to pyramid across the necropolis and the air filled with the stink of burning stone.

In the middle of the firestorm the Great Pyramid appeared to lift up a few inches, on a beam of incandescence, and turn through ninety degrees. This was almost certainly the special type of optical illusion which can take place *even though no-one is actually looking at it.*

And then, with deceptive slowness and considerable dignity, it exploded.

It was almost too crass a word. What it did was this: it came apart ponderously into building-sized chunks which drifted gently away from one another, flying serenely out and over the necropolis. Several of them struck other pyramids, badly damaging them in a lazy, unselfconscious way, and then bounded on in silence until they ploughed to a halt behind a small mountain of rubble.

Only then did the boom come. It went on for quite a long time.

Grey dust rolled over the kingdom.

Ptaclusp dragged himself upright and groped ahead, gingerly, until he walked into someone. He shuddered when he thought about the kind of people he'd seen walking around lately, but thought didn't come easily because something appeared to have hit him on the head recently . . .

"Is that you, lad?" he ventured.

"Is that you, dad?"

"Yes," said Ptaclusp.

"It's me, dad."

"I'm *glad* it's you, son."

"Can you see anything?"

"No. It's all mist and fog."

"Thank the gods for that, I thought it was me."

"It *is* you, isn't it? You said."

"Yes, dad."

"Is your brother all right?"

"I've got him safe in my pocket, dad."

"Good. So long as nothing's happened to him."

They inched forward, clambering over lumps of masonry they could barely see.

"Something exploded, dad," said IIb, slowly. "I think it was the pyramid."

Ptaclusp rubbed the top of his head, where two tons of flying rock had come within a sixteenth of an inch of fitting him for one of his own pyramids. "It was that dodgy cement we bought from Merco the Ephebian, I expect — "

"I think this was a bit worse than a moody lintel, dad," said IIb. "In fact, I think it was a lot worse."

"It looked a bit wossname, a bit on the sandy side — "

"I think you should find somewhere to sit down, dad," said IIb, as kindly as possible. "Here's Two-Ay. Hang on to him."

He crept on alone, climbing over a slab of what felt very suspiciously like black marble. What he wanted, he decided, was a priest. They had to be useful for something, and this seemed the sort of time one might need one. For solace, or possibly, he felt obscurely, to beat their head in with a rock.

What he found instead was someone on their hands and knees, coughing. IIb helped him — it was definitely a him, he'd been briefly afraid it might be an it — and sat him on another lump of, yes, almost certainly marble.

"Are you a priest?" he said, fumbling in the rubble.

"I'm Dil. Chief embalmer," the figure muttered.

"Ptaclusp IIb, paracosmic archi — " IIb began and then, suspecting that architects were not going to be too popular around here for a while, quickly corrected himself. "I'm an engineer," he said. "Are you all right?"

"Don't know. What happened?"

"I think the pyramid exploded," IIb volunteered.

"Are we dead?"

"I shouldn't think so. You're walking and talking, after all."

Dil shivered. "That's no guideline, take it from me. What's an engineer?"

"Oh, a builder of aqueducts," said IIb quickly. "They're the coming thing, you know."

Dil stood up, a little shakily.

"I," he said, "need a drink. Let's find the river."

They found Teppic first.

He was clinging to a small, truncated pyramid section that had made a moderate-sized crater when it landed.

"I know him," said IIb. "He's the lad who was on top of the pyramid. That's ridiculous, how could he survive *that*?"

"Why's there all corn sprouting out of it, too?" wondered Dil.

"I mean, perhaps there's some kind of effect if you're right in the centre of the flare, or something," said IIb, thinking aloud. "A sort of calm area or something, like in the middle of a whirlpool — " He reached instinctively for his wax tablet, and then stopped himself. Man was never intended to understand things he meddled with. "Is he dead?" he said.

"Don't look at me," said Dil, stepping back. He'd been running through his mind the alternative occupations now open to him. Upholstery sounded attractive. At least chairs didn't get up and walk after you'd stuffed them.

IIb bent over the body.

"Look what he's got in his hand," he said, gently bending back the fingers. "It's a piece of melted metal. What's he got that for?"

. . . Teppic dreamed.

He saw seven fat cows and seven thin cows, and one of them was riding a bicycle.

He saw some camels, singing, and the song straightened out the wrinkles in reality.

He saw a finger write on the wall of a pyramid: *Going forth is easy. Going back requires (cont. on next wall). . .*

He walked around the pyramid, where the finger continued: *An effort of will, because it is much harder. Thank you.*

Teppic considered this, and it occurred to him that there was one thing left to do which he had not done. He'd never known how to before, but now he could see that it was just numbers, arranged in a special way. Everything that was magical was just a way of describing the world in words it couldn't ignore.

He gave a grunt of effort.

There was a brief moment of speed.

Dil and IIb looked around as long shafts of light sparkled

through the mists and dust, turning the landscape into old gold.
 And the sun came up.

The sergeant cautiously opened the hatch in the horse's belly.
When the expected flurry of spears did not materialise he
ordered Autocue to let out the rope ladder, climbed down it, and
looked across the chill morning desert.

The new recruit followed him down and stood, hopping from
one sandal to another, on sand that was nearly freezing now and
would be frying by lunchtime.

"There," said the sergeant, pointing, "see the Tsortean lines,
lad?"

"Looks like a row of wooden horses to me, sergeant," said
Autocue. "The one on the end's on rockers."

"That'll be the officers. Huh. Those Tsorteans must think
we're simple." The sergeant stamped some life into his legs, took
a few breaths of fresh air, and walked back to the ladder.

"Come on, lad," he said.

"Why've we got to go back up there?"

The sergeant paused, his foot on a rope rung.

"Use some common, laddie. They're not going to come and take
our horses if they see us hanging around outside, are they?
Stands to reason."

"You sure they're going to come, then?" said Autocue. The
sergeant frowned at him.

"Look, soldier," he said, "anyone bloody stupid enough to
think we're going to drag a lot of horses full of soldiers back to
our city is certainly daft enough to drag *ours* all the way back to
theirs. QED."

"QED, sarge?"

"It means get back up the bloody ladder, lad."

Autocue saluted. "Permission to be excused first, sarge?"

"Excused what?"

"*Excused*, sarge," said Autocue, a shade desperately. "I mean,
it's a bit cramped in the horse, sarge, if you know what I mean."

"You're going to have to learn a bit of will power if you want to
stay in the horse soldiers, boy. You know that?"

"Yes, sarge," said Autocue miserably.

"You've got one minute."

"Thanks, sarge."

When the hatch closed above him Autocue sidled over to one of the horse's massive legs and put it to a use for which it wasn't originally intended.

And it was while he was staring vaguely ahead, lost in that Zen-like contemplation which occurs at moments like this, that there was a faint pop in the air and an entire river valley opened up in front of him.

It's not the sort of thing that ought to happen to a thoughtful lad. Especially one who has to wash his own uniform.

A breeze from the sea blew into the kingdom, hinting at, no, positively roaring suggestions of salt, shellfish and sun-soaked tidelines. A few rather puzzled seabirds wheeled over the necropolis, where the wind scurried among the fallen masonry and covered with sand the memorials to ancient kings, and the birds said more with a simple bowel movement than Ozymandias ever managed to say.

The wind had a cool, not unpleasant edge to it. The people out repairing the damage caused by the gods felt an urge to turn their faces towards it, as fish in a pond turn towards an influx of clear, fresh water.

No-one worked in the necropolis. Most of the pyramids had blown their upper levels clean off, and stood smoking gently like recently-extinct volcanoes. Here and there slabs of black marble littered the landscape. One of them had nearly decapitated a fine statue of Hat, the Vulture-Headed God.

The ancestors had vanished. No-one was volunteering to go and look for them.

Around midday a ship came up the Djel under full sail. It was a deceptive ship. It seemed to wallow like a fat and unprotected hippo, and it was only after watching it for some time that anyone would realise that it was also making remarkably fast progress. It dropped anchor outside the palace.

After a while, it let down a dinghy.

*

Teppic sat on the throne and watched the life of the kingdom reassemble itself, like a smashed mirror that is put together again and reflects the same old light in new and unexpected ways.

No-one was quite sure on what basis he *was* on the throne, but no-one else was at all keen on occupying it and it was a relief to hear instructions issued in a clear, confident voice. It is amazing what people will obey, if a clear and confident voice is used, and the kingdom was well used to a clear, confident voice.

Besides, giving orders stopped him thinking about things. Like, for example, what would happen next. But at least the gods had gone back to not existing again, which made it a whole lot easier to believe in them, and the grass didn't seem to be growing under his feet any more.

Maybe I can put the kingdom together again, he thought. But then what can I do with it? If only we could find Dios. He always knew what to do, that was the main thing about him.

A guard pushed his way through the milling throng of priests and nobles.

"Excuse me, your sire," he said. "There's a merchant to see you. He says it's urgent."

"Not now, man. There's representatives of the Tsortean and Ephebian armies coming to see me in an hour, and there's a great deal that's got to be done first. I can't go around seeing any salesmen who happen to be passing. What's he selling, anyway?"

"Carpets, your sire."

"*Carpets*?"

It was Chidder, grinning like half a watermelon, followed by several of the crew. He walked up the hall staring around at the frescoes and hangings. Because it was Chidder, he was probably costing them out. By the time he reached the throne he was drawing a double line under the total.

"Nice place," he said, wrapping up thousands of years of architectural accumulation in a mere two syllables. "You'll never guess what happened, we just happened to be sailing along the coast and suddenly there was this river. One minute cliffs, next minute river. There's a funny thing, I thought. I bet old Teppic's up there somewhere."

"Where's Ptraci?"

"I knew you were complaining about the lack of the old home comforts, so we brought you this carpet."

"I *said*, where's Ptraci?"

The crew moved aside, leaving a grinning Alfonz to cut the strings around the carpet and shake it out.

It uncurled swiftly across the floor in a flurry of dust balls and moths and, eventually, Ptraci, who continued rolling until her head hit Teppic's boot.

He helped her to her feet and tried to pick bits of fluff out of her hair as she swayed backwards and forwards. She ignored him and turned to Chidder, red with breathlessness and fury.

"I could have died in there!" she shouted. "Lots of other things have, by the smell! And the *heat!*"

"You said it worked for Queen wossname, Ram-Jam-Hurrah, or whoever," said Chidder. "Don't blame me, at home a necklace or something is usually the thing."

"I bet *she* had a decent carpet," snapped Ptraci. "Not something stuck in a bloody hold for six months."

"You're lucky we had one at all," said Chidder mildly. "It was your idea."

"Huh," said Ptraci. She turned to Teppic. "Hallo," she said. "This was meant to be a startling original surprise."

"It worked," said Teppic fervently. "It really worked."

Chidder lay on a daybed on the palace's wide veranda, while three handmaidens took turns to peel grapes for him. A pitcher of beer stood cooling in the shade. He was grinning amiably.

On a blanket nearby Alfonz lay on his stomach, feeling extremely awkward. The Mistress of the Women had found out that, in addition to the tattoos on his forearms, his back was a veritable illustrated history of exotic practices, and had brought the girls out to be educated. He winced occasionally as her pointer stabbed at items of particular interest, and stuffed his fingers firmly in his great, scarred ears to shut out the giggles.

At the far end of the veranda, given privacy by unspoken agreement, Teppic sat with Ptraci. Things were not going well.

"Everything changed," he said. "I'm not going to be king."

"You *are* the king," she said. "You can't change things."

"I can. I can abdicate. It's very simple. If I'm not really the king, then I can go whenever I please. If I *am* the king, then the king's word is final and I can abdicate. If we can change sex by decree, we can certainly change station. They can find a relative to do the job. I must have dozens."

"The *job*? Anyway, you said there was only your auntie."

Teppic frowned. Aunt Cleph-ptah-re was not, on reflection, the kind of monarch a kingdom needed if it was going to make a fresh start. She had a number of stoutly-held views on a variety of subjects, but most of them involved the flaying alive of people she disapproved of. This meant most people under the age of thirty-five, to start with.

"Well, someone else, then," he said. "It shouldn't be difficult, we've always seemed to have more nobles than really necessary. We'll just have to find one who has the dream about the cows."

"Oh, the one where there's fat cows and thin cows?" said Ptraci.

"Yes. It's sort of ancestral."

"It's a nuisance, I know that much. One of them's always grinning and playing a wimblehorn."

"It looks like a trombone to me," said Teppic.

"It's a ceremonial wimblehorn, if you look closely," she said.

"Well, I expect everyone sees it a bit differently. I don't think it matters." He sighed, and watched the *Unnamed* unloading. It seemed to have more than the expected number of feather mattresses, and several of the people wandering bemusedly down the gangplank were holding toolboxes and lengths of pipe.

"I think you're going to find it difficult," said Ptraci. "You can't say 'All those who dream about cows please step forward'. It'd give the game away."

"I can't just hang around until someone happens to mention it, can I? Be reasonable," he snapped. "How many people are likely to say, hey, I had this funny dream about cows last night? Apart from you, I mean."

They stared at one another.

*

"And she's my *sister*?" said Teppic.

The priests nodded. It was left to Koomi to put it into words. He'd just spent ten minutes going through the files with the Mistress of the Women.

"Her mother was, er, your late father's favourite," he said. "He took a great deal of interest in her upbringing, as you know, and, er, it would appear that . . . yes. She may be your aunt, of course. The concubines are never very good at paperwork. But most likely your sister."

She looked at him with tear-filled eyes.

"That doesn't make any difference, does it?" she whispered.

Teppic stared at his feet.

"Yes," he said. "I think it does, really." He looked up at her. "But you can be queen," he added. He glared at the priests. "Can't she," he stated firmly.

The high priests looked at one another. Then they looked at Ptraci, who stood alone, her shoulders shaking. Small, palace trained, used to taking orders . . . They looked at Koomi.

"She would be ideal," he said. There was a murmur of suddenly-confident agreement.

"There you are then," said Teppic, consolingly.

She glared at him. He backed away.

"So I'll be off," he said, "I don't need to pack anything, it's all right."

"Just like that?" she said. "Is that *all*? Isn't there anything you're going to *say*?"

He hesitated, halfway to the door. You could stay, he told himself. It wouldn't work, though. It'd end up a terrible mess; you'd probably end up splitting the kingdom between you. Just because fate throws you together doesn't mean fate's got it right. Anyway, you've been forth.

"Camels are more important than pyramids," he said slowly. "It's something we should always remember."

He ran for it while she was looking for something to throw.

The sun reached the peak of noon without beetles, and Koomi hovered by the throne like Hat, the Vulture-Headed God.

"It will please your majesty to confirm my succession as high priest," he said.

"What?" Ptraci was sitting with her chin cupped in one hand. She waved the other hand at him. "Oh. Yes. All right. Fine."

"No trace has, alas, been found of Dios. We believe he was very close to the Great Pyramid when it . . . flared."

Ptraci stared into space. "You carry on," she said. Koomi preened.

"The formal coronation will take some time to arrange," he said, taking the golden mask. "However, your graciousness will be pleased to wear the mask of authority now, for there is much formal business to be concluded."

She looked at the mask.

"I'm not wearing that," she said flatly.

Koomi smiled. "Your majesty will be pleased to wear the mask of authority," he said.

"No," said Ptraci.

Koomi's smile crazed a little around the edges as he attempted to get to grips with this new concept. He was sure Dios had never had this trouble.

He got over the problem by sidling round it. Sidling had stood him in good stead all his life; he wasn't going to desert it now. He put the mask down very carefully on a stool.

"It is the First Hour," he said. "Your majesty will wish to conduct the Ritual of the Ibis, and then graciously grant an audience to the military commanders of the Tsortean and Ephebian armies. Both are seeking permission to cross the kingdom. Your majesty will forbid this. At the Second Hour, there will — "

Ptraci sat drumming her fingers on the arms of the throne. Then she took a deep breath. "I'm going to have a bath," she said.

Koomi rocked back and forth a bit.

"It is the First Hour," he repeated, unable to think of anything else. "Your majesty will wish to conduct — "

"Koomi?"

"Yes, O noble queen?"

"Shut up."

" — the Ritual of the Ibis — " Koomi moaned.

"I'm sure you're capable of doing it yourself. You look like a man who does things himself, if ever I saw one," she added sourly.

" — the commanders of the Tsortean — "

"*Tell them*," Ptraci began, and then paused. "Tell them," she repeated, "that they may both cross. Not one or the other, you understand? Both."

"But — " Koomi's understanding managed at last to catch up with his ears — "that means they'll end up on opposite sides."

"Good. And after that you can order some camels. There's a merchant in Ephebe with a good stock. Check their teeth first. Oh, and then you can ask the captain of the *Unnamed* to come and see me. He was explaining to me what a 'free port' is."

"In your bath, O queen?" said Koomi weakly. He couldn't help noticing, now, how her voice was changing with each sentence as the veneer of upbringing burned away under the blowlamp of heredity.

"Nothing wrong with that," she snapped. "And see about plumbing. Apparently pipes are the thing."

"For the asses' milk?" said Koomi, who was now totally lost in the desert*.

"Shut up, Koomi."

"Yes, O queen," said Koomi, miserably.

He'd wanted changes. It was just that he'd wanted things to stay the same, as well.

The sun dropped to the horizon, entirely unaided. For some people, it was turning out to be quite a good day.

The reddened light lit up the three male members of the Ptaclusp dynasty, as they pored over plans for —

"It's called a bridge," said IIb.

"Is that like an aqueduct?" said Ptaclusp.

"In reverse, sort of thing," said IIb. "The water goes underneath, we go over the top."

"Oh. The k — the queen won't like that," said Ptaclusp. "The royal family's always been against chaining the holy river with dams and weirs and suchlike."

IIb gave a triumphant grin. "She *suggested* it," he said. "And

---

*A less desiccated culture would have used the phrase 'at sea'.

she graciously went on to say, could we see to it there's places for people to stand and drop rocks on the crocodiles."

"She said that?"

"Large pointy rocks, she said."

"My word," said Ptaclusp. He turned to his other son.

"You sure you're all right?" he said.

"Feeling fine, dad," said IIa.

"No — " Ptaclusp groped — "headaches or anything?"

"Never felt better," said IIa.

"Only you haven't asked about the cost," said Ptaclusp. "I thought perhaps you were still feeling fl — ill."

"The queen has been pleased to ask me to have a look at the royal finances," said IIa. "She said priests can't add up." His recent experiences had left him with no ill effects other than a profitable tendency to think at right angles to everyone else, and he sat wreathed in smiles while his mind constructed tariff rates, docking fees and a complex system of value added tax which would shortly give the merchant venturers of Ankh-Morpork a nasty shock.

Ptaclusp thought about all the miles of the virgin Djel, totally unbridged. And there was plenty of dressed stone around now, millions of tons of the stuff. And, you never knew, perhaps on some of those bridges there'd be room for a statue or two. He had the very thing.

He put his arms around his sons' shoulders.

"Lads," he said proudly. "It's looking really quantum."

The setting sun also shone on Dil and Gern, although in this case it was by a roundabout route though the lightwell of the palace kitchens. They'd ended up there for no very obvious reason. It was just that it was so depressing in the embalming room, all alone.

The kitchen staff worked around them, recognising the air of impenetrable gloom that surrounded the two embalmers. It was never a very sociable job at the best of times and embalmers didn't make friends easily. Anyway, there was a coronation feast to prepare.

They sat amid the bustle, observing the future over a jug of beer.

"I expect," said Gern, "that Gwlenda can have a word with her dad."

"That's it, boy," said Dil wearily. "There's a future there. People will always want garlic."

"Bloody boring stuff, garlic," said Gern, with unusual ferocity. "And you don't get to meet people. That's what I liked about our job. Always new faces."

"No more pyramids," said Dil, without rancour. "That's what she said. You've done a good job, Master Dil, she said, but I'm going to drag this country kicking and screaming into the Century of the Fruitbat."

"Cobra," said Gern.

"What?"

"It's the Century of the Cobra. Not the Fruitbat."

"Whatever," said Dil irritably. He stared miserably into his mug. That was the trouble now, he reflected. You had to start remembering what century it was.

He glared at a tray of canapes. That was the thing these days. Everyone fiddling about. . .

He picked up an olive and turned it over and over in his fingers.

"Can't say I'd feel the same about the old job, mind," said Gern, draining the jug, "but I bet you were proud, master — Dil, I mean. You know, when all your stitching held up like that."

Dil, his eyes not leaving the olive, reached dreamily down to his belt and grasped one of his smaller knives for intricate jobs.

"I said, you must have felt very sorry it was all over," said Gern.

Dil swivelled around to get more light, and breathed heavily as he concentrated.

"Still, you'll get over it," said Gern. "The important thing is not to let it prey on your mind — "

"Put this stone somewhere," said Dil.

"Sorry?"

"Put this stone somewhere," said Dil.

Gern shrugged, and took it out of his fingers.

"Right," said Dil, his voice suddenly vibrant with purpose. "Now pass me a piece of red pepper . . ."

*

And the sun shone on the delta, that little infinity of reed beds and mud banks where the Djel was laying down the silt of the continent. Wading birds bobbed for food in the green maze of stems, and billions of zig-zag midges danced over the brackish water. Here at least time had always passed, as the delta breathed twice daily the cold, fresh water of the tide.

It was coming in now, the foam-crested cusp of it trickling between the reeds.

Here and there soaked and ancient bandages unwound, wriggled for a while like incredibly old snakes and then, with the minimum of fuss, dissolved.

THIS IS MOST IRREGULAR.
We're sorry. It's not our fault.
HOW MANY OF YOU ARE THERE?
More than 1,300, I'm afraid.
VERY WELL, THEN. PLEASE FORM AN ORDERLY QUEUE.

You Bastard was regarding his empty hay rack.

It represented a sub-array in the general cluster 'hay', containing arbitrary values between zero and K.

It didn't have any hay in it. It might in fact have a negative value of hay in it, but to the hungry stomach the difference between no hay and minus-hay was not of particular interest.

It didn't matter how he worked it out, the answer was always the same. It was an equation of classical simplicity. It had a certain clean elegance which he was not, currently, in a position to admire.

You Bastard felt ill-used and hard done by. There was nothing particularly unusual about this, however, since that is the normal state of mind for a camel. He knelt patiently while Teppic packed the saddlebags.

"We'll avoid Ephebe," Teppic said, ostensibly to the camel. "We'll go up the end of the Circle Sea, perhaps to Quirm or over the Ramtops. There's all sorts of places. Maybe we'll even look for a few of those lost cities, eh? I expect you'd like that."

It's a mistake trying to cheer up camels. You may as well drop meringues into a black hole.

The door at the far end of the stable swung open. It was a priest. He looked rather flustered. The priests had been doing a lot of unaccustomed running around today.

"Er," he began. "Her majesty commands you not to leave the kingdom."

He coughed.

He said, "Is there a reply?"

Teppic considered. "No," he said, "I don't think so."

"So I shall tell her that you will be attending on her presently, shall I?" said the priest hopefully.

"No."

"It's all very well for *you* to say," said the priest sourly, and slunk off.

He was replaced a few minutes later by Koomi, very red in the face.

"Her majesty requests that you do not leave the kingdom," he said.

Teppic climbed on to You Bastard's back, and tapped the camel lightly with a prod.

"She really means it," said Koomi.

"I'm sure she does."

"She could have you thrown to the sacred crocodiles, you know."

"I haven't seen many of them around today. How are they?" said Teppic, and gave the camel another thump.

He rode out into the knife-edged daylight and along the packed-earth streets, which time had turned into a surface harder than stone. They were thronged with people. And every single person ignored him.

It was a marvellous feeling.

He rode gently along the road to the border and did not stop until he was up in the escarpment, the valley spreading out behind him. A hot wind off the desert rattled the syphacia bushes as he tethered You Bastard in the shade, climbed a little further up the rocks, and looked back.

The valley was old, so old that you could believe it had existed first and had watched the rest of the world form around it. Teppic lay with his head on his arms.

Of course, it had *made* itself old. It had been gently stripping itself of futures for thousands of years. Now change was hitting it like the ground hitting an egg.

Dimensions were probably more complicated than people thought. Probably so was time. Probably so were people, although people could be more predictable.

He watched the column of dust rise outside the palace and work its way through the city, across the narrow patchwork of fields, disappear for a minute in a group of palm trees near the escarpment, and reappear at the foot of the slope. Long before he could see it he knew there'd be a chariot somewhere in the cloud of sand.

He slid back down the rocks and squatted patiently by the roadside. The chariot rattled by eventually, halted some way on, turned awkwardly in the narrow space, and trundled back.

"What will you *do*?" shouted Ptraci, leaning over the rail.

Teppic bowed.

"And none of that," she snapped.

"Don't you like being king?"

She hesitated. "Yes," she said. "I do — "

"Of course you do," said Teppic. "It's in the blood. In the old days people would fight like tigers. Brothers against sisters, cousins against uncles. Dreadful."

"But you don't have to go! I *need* you!"

"You've got advisers," said Teppic mildly.

"I didn't mean that," she snapped. "Anyway, there's only Koomi, and he's no good."

"You're lucky. I had Dios, and he *was* good. Koomi will be much better, you can learn a lot by not listening to what he has to say. You can go a long way with incompetent advisers. Besides, Chidder will help, I'm sure. He's full of ideas."

She coloured. "He advanced a few when we were on the ship."

"There you are, then. I knew the two of you would get along like a house on fire." Screams, flames, people running for safety . . .

"And you're going back to be an Assassin, are you?" she sneered.

"I don't think so. I've inhumed a pyramid, a pantheon and the entire old kingdom. It may be worth trying something else. By the way, you haven't been finding little green shoots springing up wherever you walk, have you?"

"No. What a stupid idea."

Teppic relaxed. It really was all over, then. "Don't let the grass grow under your feet, that's the important thing," he said. "And you haven't seen any seagulls around?"

"There's lots of them today, or didn't you notice?"

"Yes. That's good, I think."

You Bastard watched them talk a little more, that peculiar trailing-off, desultory kind of conversation that two people of opposite sexes engage in when they have something else on their minds. It was much easier with camels, when the female merely had to check the male's methodology.

Then they kissed in a fairly chaste fashion, insofar as camels are any judge. A decision was reached.

You Bastard lost interest at this point, and decided to eat his lunch again.

IN THE BEGINNING . . .

It was peaceful in the valley. The river, its banks as yet untamed, wandered languidly through thickets of rush and papyrus. Ibises waded in the shallows; in the deeps, hippos rose and sank slowly, like pickled eggs.

The only sound in the damp silence was the occasional plop of a fish or hiss of a crocodile.

Dios lay in the mud for some time. He wasn't sure how he'd got there, or why half his robes were torn off and the other half scorched black. He dimly recalled a loud noise and a sensation of extreme speed while, at the same time, he'd been standing still. Right at this moment, he didn't want any answers. Answers implied questions, and questions never got anyone anywhere. Questions only spoiled things. The mud was cool and soothing, and he didn't need to know anything else for a while.

The sun went down. Various nocturnal prowlers wandered near to Dios, and by some animal instinct decided that he certainly wasn't going to be worth all the trouble that would accrue from biting his leg off.

The sun rose again. Herons honked. Mist unspooled between the pools, was burned up as the sky turned from blue to new bronze

And time unrolled in glorious uneventfulness for Dios until an alien noise took the silence and did the equivalent of cutting it into small pieces with a rusty breadknife.

It was a noise, in fact, like a donkey being chainsawed. As sounds went, it was to melody what a boxful of dates is to high performance motocross. Nevertheless, as other voices joined it, similar but different, in a variety of fractured keys and broken tones, the overall effect was curiously attractive. It had lure. It had pull. It had a strange suction.

The noise reached a plateau, one pure note made of a succession of discordances, and then, for just the fraction of a second, the voices split away, each along a vector . . .

There was a stirring of the air, a flickering of the sun.

And a dozen camels appeared over the distant hills, skinny and dusty, running towards the water. Birds erupted from the reeds. Leftover saurians slid smoothly off the sandbanks. Within a minute the shore was a mass of churned mud as the knobbly-kneed creatures jostled, nose deep in the water.

Dios sat up, and saw his staff lying in the mud. It was a little scorched, but still intact, and he noticed what somehow had never been apparent before. Before? Had there been a before? There had certainly been a dream, something like a dream . . .

Each snake had its tail in its mouth.

Down the slope after the camels, his ragged family trailing behind him, was a small brown figure waving a camel prod. He looked hot and very bewildered.

He looked, in fact, like someone in need of good advice and careful guidance.

Dios's eyes turned back to the staff. It meant something very important, he knew. He couldn't remember what, though. All he could remember was that it was very heavy, yet at the same time hard to put down. *Very* hard to put down. Better not to pick it up, he thought.

Perhaps just pick it up for a while, and go and explain about gods and why pyramids were so important. And then he could put it down afterwards, certainly.

Sighing, pulling the remnants of his robes around him to give himself dignity, using the staff to steady himself, Dios went forth.